THE BITTI

JANE GRAY

SilverWood

Published in paperback in 2011 by SilverWood Books
Bristol, BS1 4HJ
www.silverwoodbooks.co.uk

ISBN 978-1-906236-73-1

British Library Cataloguing in Publication Data
A CIP catalogue record for this book is available from the British Library

Set in Sabon by SilverWood Books
Printed in England on paper certified as being from responsible sources

This book is dedicated to...

Ambrose Gray
1892 – 1978

Edith Gray nee Atherton (*Gauja*)
1897 – 1980

Ambrose Gray
1851 – 1914

Reigneth Gray
1869 – 1928

Aaron Gray
1860 – 1916

Joseph Gray
1826 – 1905

Acknowledgements

First and foremost I must thank my wonderful editor Jo Field for all her help and support throughout the writing of the *Bitti Chai*.

The New Writers UK (newwriters.co.uk) for welcoming me and advising me on everything as I was only armed with the idea for a story. Also to Helen Hollick for her valued advice.

Thanks also to Cathy Helms, Avalon graphics for her fabulous cover design and to John and Diane Jordan for permission to use the image of their stallion Hisley Craftsman.

My story was inspired by my own family, by my Romany grandfather and *Gauja* grandmother who with care and devotion brought me up and treated me as their daughter, their *bitti chai*, the youngest child of a family of ten. My grandfather instilled in me a pride in our heritage and it was with him in mind that Joe was born, even down to his two gold teeth and cigarette in his mouth.

Many of the Romany characters are inspired either by family or friends.

Aaron was so named after my great uncle who, also small in stature holds a place in my heart. However this character soon became linked with a Romany young man, who step dances amazingly and with panache, and drives a sulky in much the same way. He very quickly became Aaron personified.

My thanks go to Ryalla Duffy and her daughters Queenie and Britannia for allowing me to use their names in my story. Ryalla, a Romany, who in the true sense is a Travelling woman, has for years campaigned for Romany rights.

My Aunt Betty whose love and devotion has never faltered. Her strength, bravery and sheer hard work have fortified and unified our family, a true matriarchal figure. She is Jessie.

Thanks also to Janet Keet-Black, the hard working editor of the *Romany Routes Journal* and fellow member of the Romany and Traveller Family History Association.

Although the place names of Throwleigh, Gidleigh and Chagford are real places the farms and homes referred to are all fictitious, as are the characters.

House Fear

ALWAYS – I tell you this they learned –
Always at night when they returned
To the lonely house from far away
To lamps unlighted and fire gone gray,
They learned to rattle the lock and key
To give whatever might chance to be
Warning and time to be off in flight:
And preferring the out- to the in-door night,
They learned to leave the house-door wide
Until they had lit the lamp inside.

Robert Frost (1874–1963)

Prologue

I begin Reigneth's story at a point in her life when everything changed one summer. You might ask how it is that I know so much about her, as though I am an all-seeing presence, even though I am not physically there. Well, I will tell you: I lived once, many years ago, and I myself was a great 'seer' in my homeland. I foresaw there would be another after me with far greater talents than my own. She would be born whilst Algol, the Demon Star, was eclipsing, and would have great power for good or evil. However, she would be vulnerable to both these influences until she was united with her soul mate. Then, and only then, would she have the power to control her gifts; until that time she must be protected at all costs.

For many years I have anticipated the coming of this shaman, longing for her presence. Reigneth Gray is that long-awaited child. She is the Prophet, and from my world I have watched her, knowing she is destined to be joined by three others: the Heart, the Guardian and the Chronicler. All are important; each of them vital to the other, though as yet only Reigneth is aware of it.

Now, at fifteen, Reigneth is at the beginning of her life's journey, but she does not feel young, she never has, for Reigneth 'sees' the past, present and much of the future with a clear and uncanny precision. Many of her other gifts she is, as yet, unaware of. This force – or whatever you want to call it – is growing within her, developing and becoming stronger as the years pass.

The fact is, Reigneth's world bears no resemblance to yours and never will. She is unlike any other teenager you have ever met. Yet despite her unique gifts, she is not infallible and is often afraid, especially when things happen that take her by surprise, for surprises are necessarily few and she does not like them. She will continue to feel afraid until she finds the one she has 'seen' who is to become her soul mate.

The events of the past few months have rocked Reigneth's world, for she did not foresee them. Her subsequent move from her homeland to live in Devon, is another of those rare, unforeseen occurrences, and it is here that I begin her story.

Chapter 1

The Journey

The van chugged noisily down the motorway doing far better than Reigneth had hoped. Jessie, her mother, had even joined the AA: she had seen one of their fella's selling membership at the supermarket door. A smile twitched at the corners of Reigneth's lips seeing the irony in a Romany having AA breakdown cover.

Despite feeling slightly happier with this added protection, Reigneth could sense her mother's nervousness, her posture stiff and rigid. She knew Jessie had never driven on the motorway before. The road, a metallic ribbon, stretched as far as they could see and the sunlight glinting on the stream of vehicles ahead strained their eyes.

They made one crucial toilet stop at the motorway services. Not bothering to lock the van – their possessions were few and it would be a brave man who touched it with the dog inside – they walked arm in arm, to the appreciative gaze of several passersby. With their jet black hair, dark skin and eyes, and an abundance of gold jewellery, it was evident what they were, yet on this day, the stares they attracted were not the prejudiced slights they were used to, but admiration for their outstanding beauty, which was all the more striking as both wore black, still in mourning for Joe.

It had been a few months since Joe's death, but Jessie Gray and her family were old-fashioned in that way. By choice the Gray's had rarely mixed with *Gaujas* – their word for people who are not Romany – and now, unlike Reigneth who had, of course, had contact with them at school, Jessie felt out of her depth. She had been used to leaving their village only once a week when she took the bus to the tiny and declining market town near to where they had settled in Lincolnshire. Their recreation time was always spent with their family. They had been happy and content, that is until Joe had passed away. Now Jessie was totally out of her comfort zone and it seemed to her that she had been plunged headlong into living someone else's life instead of her own.

Reigneth, too, felt bewildered. She could not believe how things had turned out; could not believe her dreams had revealed nothing until the morning of Joe's death. She was not permitted to say his name now he had passed away. Her people believed the *mulo*, the ghosts of the dead, haunted you if you spoke of them. She didn't care, she had said her father's name over and over; she wanted him with her. Her mother slept with his cap under her pillow. The shirt in which he died remained unwashed in Jessie's possession. Such things, like keeping his clothes instead of burning them, were frowned upon by their Romany family.

Her father's death was a mystery to Reigneth. She had tried to understand why she hadn't seen it coming. How was it possible when she saw so much of the future and had never been wrong? Yet Joe's death – not an inkling.

She had dreamt a couple of nights previously, but the dream had not made sense to her. Perhaps because her dad had not been old she had not been looking to lose him. A massive heart attack the post mortem had said. Her dad: a massive heart attack; fitting for a man with a heart as big as his. Unfortunately, as it turned out, weak heart too: one that had been filled with love for his wife, daughter and family, and anyone else who needed a hand. Joe Gray had been a good man.

But he was gone and Jessie and her daughter were on their way to the South West, eating up the miles that would undoubtedly be the death knell of their old transit van.

They had not needed to make the journey alone, but somehow Jessie had a compelling urge to take this step independently. The first thing she had ever done without Joe.

Jessie felt she would never become used to a life without him. For generations their families had intermarried and although Joe was much older than Jessie their parents had considered their marriage a good match.

Joe had no material wealth. His health and family were uppermost the things he treasured. He had a fear of loneliness and often felt insecure. When you had nothing, apart from each other, company of your own kind was paramount, but that brought with it a downside as privacy was rare. The Romany temperament – at least in Joe's family – was quick to anger, quick to forgive; always ready for a bit of fun and finding the joy in the simplest of things. They took care of their own. Some Romanies mixed with *Gaujas*; Joe's family did not.

He was a proud man, hardworking. His father had taught him to give *Gaujas* no cause for complaint as censure was always harder on the Gypsy. He took pride in whatever job he did and could turn his hand to most things. He had begun doing one or two jobs in the surrounding villages where they lived and soon had a regular round of customers. Joe was a realist, though: he knew that if there was ever anything missing or if the lead from the church roof was pinched, villagers would always blame the Gypsies.

The fact that Joe did not present the typical image of a Gypsy had always enabled him to get work. He was personable and charismatic, everyone liked Joe. He was a wiry sort of bloke, his lean looks belying his strength. Although his skin was fair he tanned easily as soon as the sun began to shine. His eyes were grey, unusual and piercing. He was a good looking chap with a cheeky disarming grin, emphasised by two gold teeth he sported in his upper jaw, the originals having been lost in a fight with his brother that had got a little heated. He was not ashamed of what he was but always felt it easier to pass for a *Gauja* rather than look for trouble. He was patient and kind until he was pushed, then he could be provoked to extreme rage. His family knew not to provoke Joe; they had seen him in a temper and never wanted to be on the receiving end of it.

The day Joe first saw Jessie he thought she was the most beautiful woman he had ever seen. At 33, he never thought he would fall in love. He had gone to Stow Fair intending to meet up with some pals whom he hadn't seen for a while. He had been feeling hemmed in at home so knew he needed to put a few miles on the road. Jessie bewitched him the first time he set his eyes on her: she was 18 and lovely. There was no mistaking what Jessie was. Her hair, which she wore pinned back and scraped away from her face, was pitch black and her huge eyes were dark, fringed with thick black lashes. Tall and extremely strong, Jessie was proud of her family but most of all she was proud to be a Romany. She had been attracted by the quietness of Joe and had known immediately that he liked her; in that moment, she knew that if he offered for her she would accept.

Once married, they had moved to Lincolnshire to live with Joe's parents. He had worried that Jess would not settle but he need not have done; she settled wherever he was because she adored him: something which constantly surprised Joe. He loved Jess passionately and considered that he was the lucky one since she had agreed to become his wife. He never got over his surprise that she had given him a second glance.

Their passion for one another did not fade over the years. Joe was a kind and considerate lover, but sometimes Jessie's need of him exceeded his energy. He had thought her physical needs would wane over the years, but if anything they had increased, or perhaps it was their age difference that at last was beginning to tell. Jess loved to be close to him and slept each night curled up – 'spooning' he called it – his arms around her, cradling her. He would nuzzle into her hair which always smelled of flowers.

Reigneth was born a year after Joe and Jessie were married; she was 'the little girl' – the *bitti chai* as she was affectionately known. As they looked down at their baby girl, Joe asked Jess if she would object to the child being named after his favourite aunt, and Reigneth she became.

The first Reigneth Gray had been born in a *vardo* on the roadside in Nottinghamshire, near a village of that name, pronounced Renath. The family had not known what to call the child; she was one of eight. Her parents had used many of their traditional family names as was their custom. Initially, the baby was called the Reigneth baby, soon to be just Reigneth. The family joked that it was a good thing she had not been born a few miles earlier or later as she'd have been Bilsthorpe or Farnsfield! They all thought this hilarious, with the exception of Reigneth Senior, with whom the joke eventually wore thin.

From the moment Joe's daughter was born he idolised her. She was loved and protected by them all, not only for the person she was, but because she was a very special child. Like her grandmother Mary, Reigneth had a very special gift: the gift of *dukkering*, which meant that she could predict the future. To her family she epitomised the Romany. She had been a bonny baby, a pretty child and had become a stunningly beautiful teenager. As she had grown so had her talent, but as beautiful and gifted as she was, she was also a perfect human being: she was kind and considerate and had the ability to bring out the very best in everyone. Reigneth made you feel a better person just for knowing her.

Although Reigneth was an only child she was never lonely, for the Grays had many children in their extended family and their family visited often. Among them were her cousins, James Boswell and Aaron Gray. By the time Reigneth was fourteen she had lost count of the number of times she had saved James's bacon. He was her favourite, a big scruffy lad who would defend Reigneth with his life, but Aaron came a close second. No one would have thought these two boys were even related, one so big and brawny the other slight and neat as a pin, but they had grown up together and were inseparable.

Reminiscing about her favourite cousin always brought a smile to Reigneth's face. She would cast her mind back to a time when they were small, sitting on the jetty near to the river. She had shouted at James to come off the end as he would end up in the drink. He had given her his big grin and she had thought, *Awh, I love you, my big daft cousin.*

"When I gets big, Reigneth, I'm going to marry you and you'll be my *monisha*," James had announced proudly, walking back to her.

"Don't be daft, James, I'm not to be your *monisha*. I love you like me heart's fit to bust, but I'm going to marry a lad with a face like a girl. It's his wife I'll be, not yours."

"Whatever would you want to do that for?" James was perplexed, a worried frown creasing his brow.

"It's not what I want; it's what's going to happen. I've seen it. He's right pretty an' all."

James scowled and kicked a pebble. "Well, I shan't let that happen, I'll knock his head in. He shan't marry you, Reigneth, so there."

"You shan't touch him, James Boswell. He's meant for me and I already love him, he's mine. I love you too though," she had added, not wanting to hurt his feelings. "You're just not meant to be my husband. We shall always be together. That's the way it's got to be."

"Well what's he like then, this girlie boy?" James had sniggered; he'd not want to be looking like a girl.

"Oh he's right pretty and clever and he loves me like me dad loves me mam."

James had hunched his shoulders and stormed off. Jumping up, Reigneth had run after him, hugging him as tightly as she could as though by increasing her pressure on him she would reassure him he was loved too.

"Well who'll love me then if not you," James had muttered, still angry.

"I'll always love you James, always, and he will too; he'll be your pal."

"I don't want a girlie boy as my pal." But James could not stay cross with her for long and soon they started laughing together as they made their way back arm in arm to the wagon that belonged to James's mam and dad.

"Well, tell me what he looks like then so's I'll know him," James had asked, but Reigneth, who knew him so well, heard his unspoken thought, *And then I'll smash his head in and tell 'im to scarper.*

"He's not big like you. He's got a right nice smile, the sort of smile that makes you warm inside and he's always messy and he never does as he's told." She smiled; she couldn't wait for her girlie boy to come into her life. She loved him already.

"I shall bash him," James had growled, pulling his arm away from hers and stomping ahead.

"James, stop being horrible or I'll go back home. I can't help what I see and I like my pretty lad. You're going to marry a *Gauja* lass anyway."

"I'll not! I'll not marry a *Gauja*, what's got into you Reigneth? You're a liar."

"You shouldn't say 'liar', it's 'fibber'. Mam said. And I'm not a fibber, so there."

An angry scowl had crossed James's face as he shouted, "I'll clip your ear for you if you don't shut up."

"Then I'll curse you, James Boswell!"

A look of horror had passed over James's face. "I'm telling Aunt Jessie; now you've done it," he had yelled, turning to run home.

"James, James, I'm sorry don't go, I didn't meant it." Reigneth had run after him, tugging at his jacket and crying, "I'm sorry James I didn't mean it, but I can't help what I see. You're my very best friend in the whole wide world."

He had stopped running and thrusting out his lower lip, spun round to look at her. "Well saying that was just dia, dia, d-i-a-b-o-l-i-c-a-l."

"What are you talking about?" Confused, Reigneth frowned. "What's that mean?"

"Granny Mary said it; it's summat bad, d-i-a-b-o-l-i-c-a-l." He pronounced the word out slowly.

They had looked at one another and started to giggle. "Is it Romany or *Gauja*?" Reigneth asked.

"I dunno." James, his anger evaporated, had put his arm around her and they made their way home.

This was their first conversation about Johnny; it was not to be their last.

For Reigneth, growing up was a happy time. As with all Romany children, she learned her people's traditions and history early by word of mouth. Practical skills, such as how to take advantage of nature's bountiful harvest, were taught later as the children grew. So it was that on Autumn weekends, Joe and Reigneth would rise at dawn and on Joe's bicycle, first with a child seat and then later with Reigneth on her own bike, they would take off together searching for mushrooms. Over time, Joe taught his daughter what to look for and how care for everything: the animals and the countryside, and Reigneth had a soft and natural way with her. He was clever, her dad, the things he knew: what mushrooms you could eat and which ones made you ill or could even kill you. Reigneth liked the big, dark field mushrooms best with their brown fleshy gills on the underside. Ma's favourite were blue buttons. Joe would take his penknife from his pocket, cutting through the stalks, leaving the roots and spores behind so that others would grow.

Reigneth could not remember ever going hungry. They never went short of food, Joe saw to that, but he only ever took what they needed to eat, his preference being to net a *shooshi* –rabbit – or two. Reigneth never went with him catching *shooshi*, she didn't like to think of her dad killing anything. He was always so soft and gentle: his hands were not made to harm things. Even so, with the aid of his ferrets and terrier, he was a proficient expedient of death. He had told her in the past their people had even eaten *hotchi witchi*, or hedgehogs. Well, she wouldn't be eating those no matter how hungry she got, dirty little critters, full of fleas. Reigneth liked the taste of *shooshi*, though, it was sweet. She was always given the best bit of meat and grew up healthy and strong.

Joe, Jess and Reigneth fell into a happy routine living with Joe's parents. Old habits died hard and even when he was settled, Joe had always kept a horse or two, Blue Boy being his favourite. Jessie grew lots of organically grown vegetables, Blue Boy providing the manure, and she was able to sell these around the village. The demand always outstripped supply and so Jessie had even begun to put a little money aside for Reigneth. There had never been any spare cash until then. They had never had any possessions and they lived very simply; you got used to making do.

In the autumn – 'the back end' as Jessie referred to it – they would gather up the sloe berries to make Granny Mary's favourite sloe gin. She liked it extra sweet. If James and Aaron were at the house a great adventure was made of it and they would set off, baskets in hand collecting the sloe berries. The hard black fruits were mixed with a good dosing of sugar and put in bottles, half and half with the gin. It made Mary's mouth water just thinking of the taste. Of course, if there was any gin left, maybe a tablespoon-full, well then, waste not, want not: cook's perks for Mary! Jessie didn't like the taste of neat gin. She was not a drinker.

They would turn the bottles periodically keeping them in the airing cupboard. The week before Christmas they would sieve out the berries and rebottle the dark red sloe gin. In the late afternoon they would scatter the used berries at the bottom of the paddock, later finding the intoxicated pheasants and partridges that had gorged on the spent fruit. Easy pickings for Joe: he would brace them up, male and female. A brace for themselves, the rest sold around the village. This generated their Christmas money for other essentials. Everything was made use of and everything had a use.

And so the years of Reigneth's growing up passed by. She could never really remember exactly when she first started having the dreams, they were so much a part of her life – of who she was – that it was difficult to put a time frame around it. She would wake up hot and bathed in sweat, her hair stuck to her neck; more often than not she would be very agitated.

The feelings she got when she touched certain people began to happen somewhat later. Sometimes the strength of the sensations was nearly enough to make her faint. She did not tell her parents at first as she was afraid there was something wrong with her, but eventually her constant crying and headaches prompted them to ask what the problem was. This one question resulted in floods of tears and everything came tumbling out. It was a relief to know her parents were not surprised and that her grandmother had those feelings too. They were able to reassure her and tell her what to expect and how they thought she and they should deal with it. The family knew that in order to protect Reigneth the secret had to be guarded.

Reigneth felt calmer as she always did when her parents took control of things. Strangely enough it was she they later looked to for guidance and the older she got the more their roles reversed. As she matured, Reigneth was able to channel the energy that came with the premonitions and it became a little easier to cope with the resulting sensations.

One of Reigneth's earliest, most vivid dreams – and the one which distressed her and her parents the most – occurred when she was just eight years old. She dreamed that she was on her own and could see her grandmother in the distance, yet as fast as she ran to catch her up, Granny Mary was getting further and further away. This dream continued for a few nights and seemed to get more vivid as each night passed. Every morning Reigneth went instinctively to cuddle her grandmother, flinging her arms around her, putting her hands on either side of her face and peering into her eyes. For some strange reason this seemed to upset her granny, as well as her mam and dad. She did not mean to upset them. She was just so pleased to see Granny Mary each morning that she started spending every day with her, not wishing to leave her side. So much so that Joe and Jessie had difficulty in getting her to go to school, until finally, Reigneth began being sick at just the thought of it. Her parents had seen other signs in their daughter and they understood that Reigneth's dreams were heralding the departure of Joe's mother.

Mary knew it too and she accepted it calmly, she was 85 and had been widowed for many years. She was weary and missed her man; her husband, Ambrose. When she and Joe's father had settled in Lincolnshire for the later part of their lives they had managed to buy a tiny wood and brick built bungalow in a small village. Even after many years of being settled, Mary had found the place too big, preferring to live in the back kitchen where she had the back door open constantly, regardless of the weather. The place was set on a fair-sized plot of land and her son Joe had parked his wagon there, until he too had eventually stopped travelling. It was his custom sometimes to take off and meet up with relatives or they would come and stay. Family was important to them. They could not go too long without seeing one another.

As much as Mary accepted the inevitability of her death, she dreaded the actual passing and her granddaughter's caresses emphasised that it would not be long now. She knew the child's actions were instinctive and that she had not yet learned to hide what she was seeing. She knew also that as Reigneth grew older she would gain the skill to hide her responses to the dreams. However, at eight, she was innocent and unskilled in protecting her loved ones from her gift.

Although Mary Gray possessed the same gift herself, it was not as strong, nor as intense as her granddaughter's. However, it was no surprise to her that her days on this earth were coming to an end. For her, the talent of *dukkering* had been a curse as well as a blessing. Everyone in the family knew about it, but there were others who had made Mary's life fraught at times with wanting readings doing. It was exhausting, but it had been her lot in life to live vicariously through other people, and there had been much sadness and pain as well as pleasurable things.

Mary knew her number was just about up and that was why Reigneth was so clingy and wouldn't go to school. She wanted to prepare her granddaughter for the life ahead of her. She had hoped she would have more time, but it looked as though that was not to be.

Joe and Jessie also knew what Reigneth's behaviour meant and Mary could see they were both distraught, especially her lovely lad Joe. He had been such a blessing to her. He had brought her joy from the moment he had entered the world and his only child was the same, she loved the very bones of them both. She had been a lucky woman.

Mary was determined that before she left them for good they would all be together one last time and so Joe and Jessie arranged for the family to come over for a meal. Too cold to be outside, the little prefabricated bungalow was full both in the kitchen and the small front room. Only Joe, Jessie and Reigneth were aware of the dreams the child was having and so the rest of the family were relaxed and happy to be together.

"Granny, tell us the story about how we came to England, you know Granny, I like that story," Aaron asked excitedly.

Aaron, the youngest son of Joe's brother, Elijah, was a weedy little thing and next to Reigneth he was Mary's favourite. Aaron cuddled up on Mary's knee, putting his thumb in his mouth, his eyes sparkling as he waited for her to begin. The rest of the family had all heard the story many times before, but made themselves comfortable; they were always ready to hear it again.

Mary gazed at her family, drinking each one of them in, greedy to see them all together. She had intended to tell the story anyway and they never tired of hearing it. "Story telling is a great part of our culture," she said, "mainly due to the fact that in the past most Romanies could neither read nor write, so our history has always been by word of mouth. It is why most of us have the knack of telling a good yarn."

"And none more so than you, Mary Gray," murmured Joe.

Over the children's heads, Mary smiled at him. "Many years ago," she began, "people known as Egyptians landed in Scotland. They were called this because they were thought to have travelled from a place known as 'Little Egypt'. They had journeyed many miles, originally coming from India and earning their living as they travelled. They slept in tents made from wooden rods covered with rugs; these were called 'bender tents' and they were transported on small carts.

"The Egyptians were talented in many ways, they could sing and dance and some of them could see into the future, telling fortunes like the Indian Seers. They were good at earning their living with their hands: making and repairing tinware; basket making; working on the land and with horses. The people's skin and hair were dark and both men and women had their ears pierced. They spoke their own language and looked very different from English people. As they didn't have houses or wealth, the ladies wore lots of gold jewellery so that if necessary they could sell it to buy food. Also, the wearing of gold signified that they were successful."

"Granny, Granny, did they look like James?" Aaron spouted, caressing his grandmother's cheek so that she would look at him.

"Yes Aaron, yes they did, just like James." It was important to Mary that none of them should forget who they were, she was sure that this little lad would not let that happen. "Right, young tike," she teased, "can I go on?"

"At first everyone liked the Egyptians. As I said, they looked very different and they dressed strangely, liking rich, bold colours, and they were very colourful and entertaining. The young ladies wore their hair in long plaits, weaving gold coins into them. The older ladies pinned their braids up. They went to posh houses to sing or dance for the grand families, but after a time they fell out of favour and the Egyptians, or as they were later known, Gypsies, became hated by just about everyone."

"Why, Granny?" Aaron knew the answer. Granny Mary had told him before, but he asked the question anyway.

"Because Gypsies were different from what everyone was used to, Aaron, and as people often do, they feared and hated what they did not understand. Life was much harder in those days than it is today and folk were more superstitious; they needed someone to blame for their bad luck and suffering and it was easy to blame a people whose lifestyle was so unfamiliar to them. Our people have always been a nomadic race; hunter-gatherers; independent and free-spirited."

Mary paused for breath, added with a rueful smile, "You wouldn't choose a Gypsy's life for comfort, that's for sure. Material possessions were few, they were not needed, especially when you were on the move, in fact they were an encumbrance. You began to value what was *really* important when stripped of all the artificial trappings of society. Our people's travelling had always been linked to where they could find work. Not aimless wandering, but regular routes governed by where the work was. For a long time, Gypsies were an itinerant workforce for farmers and were welcomed by the farming community, until things changed and they became hated by those who harboured preconceived, bigoted ideas. The hatred and fear of Gypsies grew so widespread that in the time of the first Queen Elizabeth, a law was passed banning them from living in England. They were hounded and if caught, they were beaten or even hanged. Yet they managed to survive and eventually the law was repealed, so at least they were not hanged anymore just for being what they were.

"When the roads improved our people took to wagons, which made their living a little better, but as time passed and mechanisation made work harder to find, it became more difficult to stop in different places and then many of our kind started to settle in houses and on permanent sites."

"Like you, Granny?" Aaron asked, his eyelids drooping.

"Yes, Aaron, like me and Grandpa Ambrose. And that is why we now see one another only on special occasions, like at Appleby and Stow Fair, and old 'uns like your granny find it hard to travel and so we miss our own kind. And so, young Aaron, we come to today and we Romanies still exist, living on the outside of communities, apart from, but part of the *Gauja's* world. Still earning our living at what we do best, working with our hands, good hard labour. All your kin were Romany Gypsies and you should all be proud of that."

Mary looked down at Aaron, his eyes now heavy with sleep, a smile hovering on his tiny lips, his small frame cuddled into her lap. She gently stroked his brow, sleep coming swiftly to him now. He looked like a little cherub on her knee. *These chavvies will be the ones to tell their familys' story,* she thought. *Future generations will know who they are because of these young ones; their heritage and culture will not be forgotten. Aaron, the Chronicler, James, the Guardian and Reigneth, the Prophet, and still yet to be joined by one who will become their Heart,* Mary smiled to herself. She did not know if Reigneth had seen him yet, but he would become her soul mate, her other half; the one with whom there would be no secrets and she could be her true self. Until those four were united, Mary knew there was danger to Reigneth from evil. She had prepared the children as best she could. Joe and Jessie were forewarned and she could do no more. Her family were grand; she was content.

Mary Gray passed away a fortnight after Reigneth's dreams about her had begun. Mary's children took turns to sit with their mother, watching over her until the day of the funeral, after which, other than one or two mementos, they burned her belongings as was their custom.

That Autumn, when the sloes came, Jessie could not bring herself to gather them. Joe understood. He missed his Mam even more than did Jessie. They never made sloe gin again while in Lincolnshire.

By the time Reigneth was fourteen her special gift was honed to perfection and she had learned to disguise her reactions to what she saw and felt. Sometimes it would still catch her unawares, but mostly she had things under control. She did not know when she first started dreaming about the pretty boy with dark hair. He had been coming to her in her dreams for as long as she could remember. She saw his face over and over so many times that she knew she would recognise him as soon as she saw him. She did not know when this would be or where. Each time the dream recurred some other detail was added to it. Reigneth was not afraid, she knew the life mapped out before her was to be a happy one, she was to be lucky. Now all she had to do was to wait for him to come along.

Meanwhile, she would experience everyone else's future, which was not always pleasant. Over time, the sensations she encountered when touching some people resulted in her becoming more reserved. She was naturally a warm and tactile person, but she began to shun contact afraid of what she would feel. Eventually, she became guarded in all her interactions with people who were not family.

The Grays' frugal ways extended also to their wardrobes and most of Jessie's and Reigneth's clothes were home made. They were made or altered from things that had been given to them by the people in their village. Reigneth had a style of her own in adapting things, she liked to look individual and had a flare for designing her own clothes. She was a good seamstress having been well taught by Jessie.

The family still practiced *mochadi*, part of Romany culture that imparted certain rules to do with cleanliness. Reigneth was not encouraged to bring friends home and when she began at the local senior school, many of the children assumed she had foreign relatives or some such background. At least this was easier than the 'dirty gypo' taunts she had heard her mother receive on occasion. Gypsies were still fair game and often received racist remarks. To be open about her heritage was difficult. When she was with her own kind Reigneth experienced such a sense of freedom and relief that she was able to be truly herself.

They still had relatives living at a local site at Drinsey and often visited, usually taking them a gift of something. Aaron and Ryalla lived there with their parents, Elijah, Joe's brother and his wife, Lydia. Joe and Jessie often looked after their nieces and nephews and it was on one of these occasions, on one cold November day, when they were returning from Hull with Ryalla in the van, that Jessie nestled a puppy in the crook of her arm. It was an early

Christmas gift for Reigneth who had long wanted a dog of her own.

Joe had always intended to get a pup for Reigneth when she was old enough to be master of it; at fourteen he thought the time was right. He did not want one of the long dogs, the Lurchers, his brothers kept. He wanted something to look after his *bitti chai*. A German Shepherd was his preferred choice: they were better with only one master or in this case mistress. Joe had always kept a terrier; there was nothing like these tenacious little dogs for rabbiting, but he had never participated in hare coursing. Joe did not hold with animals in the house and the pup would live outside with the others, but would have to stay indoors until Joe got a kennel made, so Jessie settled the pup in a makeshift bed in the back kitchen while they waited for Reigneth to get home from school.

"Hiya, I'm home," Reigneth called. "I've made a cake in Home Economics."

Jessie smiled; she knew Reigneth hated these lessons. Her daughter had eventually been allowed to take in her own prepared food and cooking bowls. Everything to do with food preparation had to be spotless in a Romany home. For instance, the pot washing bowl was never used for anything but pots, otherwise it became *mochadi*, unclean. *Gaujas* found this hard to understand.

"These girls couldn't bake a thing, Mam, they've never done aught like it before. Laughing and giggling they were. It was a nightmare." Reigneth's words came tumbling out as they always did, as if she had been storing everything up and had to get it out as soon as she could.

Just as she was about to rant on again, the pup whimpered and Reigneth spun round. Her face lit up, the flush spreading to her cheeks as she gazed down at the small bundle of fur. "Aw, Mam, he's so beautiful," she laughed, scooping the pup up in her arms where he was to remain indefinitely. "Is he for me?" She had wanted a pup for such a long time.

"Yes, he's for you. He can do two jobs when he's grown, look after you and the house." Joe's gruff voice concealed the emotion he felt. He loved to give Reigneth things although he could not afford much, but she never expected anything. "I'll start building a kennel after tea. He can sleep indoors tonight."

"What'll you call him, love?" Jessie asked.

Reigneth kissed the pup, feeling the fur soft against her lips,

"I don't know, I'll think on it."

After a week or two of calling him 'dog', nothing had sprung to mind. So 'dog' he became, only Reigneth used her Romany tongue so *Jukel* was his name and he followed Reigneth everywhere. By the time he was a year old he was huge, much bigger than a normal German Shepherd.

Reigneth loved the great brute of a thing. No one had ever taught Juk any commands, he had just seemed to know what she wanted right from being a pup; he was clever was Juk. They became inseparable and Reigneth never again looked so lonely and lost – and, of course, he never slept outside.

"You know, this child could wind us both round her little finger if she'd a mind," Joe sighed as he and Jessie walked hand in hand in the garden one evening.

"Good job she's not so inclined then, my man," Jessie said, edging a little closer to her husband.

Chapter 2

Changes and Lamentation

Even at her young age, Reigneth had known that nobody lived forever and although she missed Granny Mary more than she could express, her grandmother was old with a full life behind her and her death had come as no surprise. It was not so with Joe; she'd had no premonition about her father's passing until a day not long after Jukel had come into their lives. She got home from school with her head aching fit to bust. It was as if all the different thoughts were flooding around in her head, jumbled messages from the day all clamouring to be heard at once, making it so full that it felt as if it would explode. Reigneth knew from experience that the only way to clear it was to take some medication and go to bed. Perhaps she would be able to sleep and feel better in the morning, though she doubted it. Eventually, she drifted off into an uneasy sleep, her mind full of images.

> *Her grandmother was looking for her; they were all standing in the big meadow behind the house: Ma and her together; Dad and Gran over on the other side. Dad and Gran were waving...*

When Reigneth jolted awake next morning, she was red hot, her face, neck and upper body wet with sweat. She flipped back the duvet and drew her legs up placing her elbows on them and ducking her head between her legs, hoping to stop the nausea that was washing over her. "Oh no, God, no, not my Dad," she muttered, "anything but that, please no. I must be wrong, I have to be."

She had been dreaming a similar dream for over a week, but no one person was clear – apart from her gran – until last night. Even then it was not completely clear and Reigneth clung to the hope that she had been mistaken. She staggered out of bed, stumbling through to the kitchen to get a drink. Her mother was already up and making breakfast.

Reigneth took a glass from the kitchen cupboard and filled it with water glugging it down in one. She could see her dad from the kitchen window; he had just gone out to feed Blue Boy and the chickens. She could see the chicken run from the house and watched him bending through the doorway into the pen, stooping his head to pass through.

Reigneth heard him cry out with pain. He sank to his knees, the dish of chicken pellets spraying out around him as he lurched forward. She was already on her way, crossing the kitchen, darting through the back door, racing up the garden, the sharp gravel path cutting into her bare feet. She saw him sink to his knees among the frenzied, fluttering chickens, jostling and pecking at the pellets all over and around him.

Reaching her dad, Reigneth flung herself down and turned him over, cradling his head. He was smiling, his lips moving. She bent her head, felt his breath warm on her cheek, heard him whisper, "I love you both, Ma's here waiting for me. She's taking the pain away… " And then he was gone, the smile frozen on his face.

Jessie was not as quick as Reigneth, she did not hear the words, but she heard Joe's last breath and knew her man had gone.

Joe stayed at home the days before the funeral, family members keeping a vigil over him. Relatives visited; some putting small mementos into the coffin. This had been the hardest thing for Jessie, seeing her man with no life in him, touching him but no warmth in his flesh, she hardly ever left his side and was exhausted.

The day of the funeral dawned and the undertakers came to do the last minute things, putting the lid on Joe's coffin. Jessie gazed down at her man finding it hard to look away. This was the very last time she would see him, at least in this life. Joe was put into the hearse ready for his final journey on the road one last time.

It was cold in the church. Reigneth stood unmoving rooted to the spot, her breath coming out like gusts of steam. She was shivering, and yet she did not feel cold. Her whole body felt heavy, the weight of her torso unbearable and although she wanted to move she was quite unable to do so. She wanted to cry and scream and thrash about: anything but this heavy numb throbbing throughout her whole body. Jessie held on to her, or was it Reigneth holding Jessie. It did not matter, they were no longer two people, but hugging one another so closely they were as one.

There were nearly 200 people at Joe's funeral and they had come from miles around. Most followed the hearse on foot from Joe's house to the church. Everyone was dressed in unrelieved black and they moved almost as one body, locked in their grief. There was no shuffling or stumbling: they seemed to glide reverently, heads bowed, their hushed silence adding weight to the shock of their loss. Joe was respected, he was loved, but most of all he was one of their own. This was the last service they could offer him and his family. This was their tradition, their culture and their identity.

After Joe's death, Reigneth's dreams increased in intensity. Always it was of herself and her mam standing with Blue Boy in the paddock, her dad just watching them from the other side. She was sure he was not unhappy, just watching over them, but watching for what? Reigneth knew he was not coming for her as she had seen her future with the beautiful boy. It was such a solid image and so repetitive she knew it would come to fruition. She would be mad with Joe if he wanted to take Jessie. That just would not be fair. She did not want to lose her mam as well as her dad, even if he was unhappy, but Reigneth could not believe he would do that to her. He would not leave her unprotected. She felt sure he was trying to tell her something – but what?

In the last dream she'd had, only the night before, he had been smiling and waving. Reigneth woke up hot and considerably bothered. "Oh, just get to the point, Dad," she muttered under her breath, just as though they were having a real conversation. "What is it you want?"

Shaking her head, she smiled to herself, thinking, *It's a wonder any of the kids at school have anything to do with me, I'm seriously weird.* Shaking off the dream she jumped eagerly out of bed, the smell of toast luring her into the kitchen just as a letter was pushing through the letterbox. It fell with a whisper onto the doormat. Her mother was there before her, bending to retrieve it.

Why we do we always go through this with every item of post as though the handwriting is a precursor to doom – it's usually bills, thought Reigneth, watching Jessie holding up the envelope to examine it, looking relieved as she recognised the handwriting.

The letter was from Elizabeth Pritchard, Jessie's sister. Liz had married a *Gauja*, who fancied himself as an artist, and they had moved to Devon to live with his family in an old house with a dovecote of sorts attached to it. Liz was happy, the husband eccentric and the mother-in-law absolutely bonkers, but it worked. Everyone lived in harmony. Liz and Jessie had kept in touch over the years, but due to the distance, had seen one another only on special occasions. All the family had missed Liz; she had always written, often sending a few quid to help out and, of course, Reigneth had never been forgotten.

In an agony of anticipation, Reigneth sat at the breakfast table, barely aware of Juk's wet nose nuzzling her hand as she watched Jessie slide a knife under the envelope flap, pull out a sheet of paper and read the familiar writing, her eyebrows rising in surprise. After a time, she looked up at Reigneth and smiled.

"She wants us to go and live with her. She says there is plenty of room and we could live quite separately, but that it would be lovely to have us with her now that your dad has gone."

"Oh, Ma, can we?"

"I will have to think about it, love. Eat your breakfast, the toast's getting cold and you'll be late for school."

All through the day, Jessie kept picking up her sister's letter and reading it over. A part of her was excited by the thought of a fresh start, but she was loath to leave the place she had shared with Joe; he had been her only sweetheart. She had loved Joe so much and missed him more each day. Somehow leaving their home would be like losing him all over again. Besides, if she went to Devon who would tend to his grave? And yet...

The thoughts went round and round as she tried to think what was best to do. Since Joe's death, Jessie had been trying and failing to come to terms with it, wishing all the time that she could be with him, wherever he was. She knew Reigneth was anxious about her. Each night her daughter would come home from school and hug her, gently kissing her and stroking her brow. Jessie knew it was essential for Reigneth to touch her in order to read what was going on in her head, but though she did not want to worry her daughter, the caress was a comfort to her and she welcomed it.

The night after her aunt's letter arrived, Reigneth was agitated when she went to bed and knew she would probably dream again. It had been a month since her dad's death and she was more than a little irritated with him, scolding him for continuing to occupy her dreams and not coming to the point, and yet it made her smile to think that way, for it made her feel not quite so lost and lonely. She missed him so.

The dream was much the same, only this time her dad was further away. She saw herself and her mam, hand in hand, walking away from him. Reigneth woke in the early hours of the morning before it was quite light; something had disturbed her. Thinking about the dream, Reigneth knew with certainty that her dad wanted them to go to Liz's. She was convinced that was the point he had been trying to make. Determined to tell her ma in the morning, she got up to use the bathroom, wondering what had disturbed her. Out of the back window she could just make out Blue. He was running around the paddock like he was racing his own moon shadow, 'Barmy animal,' she thought, going back to bed.

The next morning, Jessie rose at first light, as was her habit. It wasn't a school day so they could take it easy. Once she had done Blue and the chickens they would have the day to themselves. She had been preoccupied, thinking about her sister's letter. Today she would talk about it with Reigneth.

She found Blue lying in the paddock; at least his body was, in spirit he was with Joe. Even though Jessie did not have her daughter's talent, she knew deep inside her that Joe had made the decision for her. Her man had cleared the way for them to leave, he wanted them to have a fresh start and Blue's place was with him.

Mother and daughter spent the day together; both saddened to lose Blue Boy, and yet comforted to know he was with Joe, where he belonged. There seemed to be no reason now to stay in Lincolnshire and they decided that at the end of the school term they would go to Devon to be with Liz.

Reigneth was excited to be moving from the area, overall she had not enjoyed her schooldays. She had been lucky in being able to share some of her classes with Aaron, but her heritage and culture had only served to emphasise the difference between the other children and herself. At her father's insistence, she had been removed from the sex education classes. She had coped well with her classmates' snide comments and had even succeeded in making one or two close friends whom she would miss. They had accepted her despite thinking her a little 'weird' at times.

Reigneth had tried to 'fit in' but always felt she failed miserably. Most of them had laughed and made fun of her old fashioned ways, so it was with a sense of relief and excitement that she counted off the days to their new life.

With the decision made to find pastures new; their clothes were packed – what few there were of them – and the van made ready. Jessie, secretly afraid of the long journey but practical as ever, just wanted to get on with it. Her main concern was whether or not the van would make it to their destination. Her nephews had offered to drive her, but she knew she had to get used to doing things for herself.

It had been arranged that James should live in the tiny bungalow and take care of things. If it did not work out for them in Devon they could always return. James had been a little uncertain about this as he had always lived in a wagon, but he loved his Aunt Jessie and would do anything for her and Reigneth. He had been distraught beyond measure at the thought of Reigneth moving to Devon with 300 miles separating them and did not know how he would cope without seeing her on a regular basis. Reigneth too was uneasy about their separation, but she knew that they would not be parted for long, James's destiny was so interwoven with hers.

Chapter 3

Chagford

The journey to Devon was further than either Reigneth or Jessie had realised and by the time they left the motorway network Jessie looked tired and strained. Reigneth revelled in what she could see of the countryside: the rounded hills, patchwork of fields and narrow twisting lanes bordered by high banks and hedges seemed to open up a secret world for her. The little town of Chagford was bustling and looked delightful with its ancient church and many side streets, where huddled whitewashed cottages seemed to cling to the pavement edge. Around the square was a wide variety of shops and businesses and Reigneth could not wait to explore.

Richard's and Liz's home was situated on the outskirts of the village and to Jessie's utmost frustration, her attempts to find it made them intimately acquainted with what seemed like every narrow and twisting lane in Devon. At last they saw someone to ask the way: an old man who, much to Jukel's excitement was out walking his dog. Even without the frenzied barking, the man's Devonshire dialect was unintelligible to Jessie, but Reigneth seemed to understand him and five minutes later they found the house, only to discover they had driven past it twice already. Relief overcame frustration and they both laughed as the van coughed, shuddered and came to a stop.

The house, which was set well back from the road, was lovely if somewhat dilapidated. It looked calm and tranquil with the evening sun cascading off its pale cream walls and lighting up a gnarled old wisteria that climbed over the front porch. Outbuildings on all sides formed a courtyard and set into the wall was a rickety gate with the name plaque 'Home Humber', leading through to an overgrown pathway.

Jessie emerged from the van, her muscles aching from the tension of the day. She was immediately and not too gently engulfed by her sister. She had not seen Liz for three long years. Time had been good to her: she looked exactly the same. Always a much bigger woman than Jessie, Liz was statuesque, with an open, smiling face. Both sisters pulled back from one another only to embrace again hugging and laughing.

"Come on, *chai*, give me a hug." Liz eyed Reigneth, a glint in her eye.

Reigneth loved her Aunt Liz, had always loved her: she was a clear and precise broadcaster and Reigneth had no problem picking up just how happy she was. Darting over to Liz, Reigneth hugged her first then her Uncle Richard, who was hovering on the periphery looking a little lost.

"Uncle Richard, you look exactly the same," Reigneth beamed.

"Well I cannot say the same for you, young lady; you're as pretty as a picture, speaking of which I shall have to sketch you, I'm sick of sketching your aunt, she always jiffles," he winked at Reigneth conspiratorially.

Liz took control. "Come on let's have you in, we'll get your stuff later. And you, Juk, out of the van now."

Juk gave her a disdainful look and remained exactly where he was until Reigneth clicked a command at him. Immediately he took his place beside her, as always.

"Well this is the famous Jukel is it," Liz laughed. "What are you feeding him on? He's enormous!"

Moments later they were all ensconced in the big kitchen, where Liz placed a cup of hot steaming tea, strongly laced with whiskey, in Jessie's hand. "I'm going to look after you, my love, like I did when we were growing up, it'll be like turning back the clock." Unshed tears filled her eyes as she looked into her sister's face, "Oh, love, you look so sad. You need a bit of nurturing that's for sure. I'm so glad you and Reigneth decided to come, this is where you both belong, here with me."

Just then, Emily, Richard's mother, came pottering into the kitchen quietly humming to herself. She smiled warmly at Reigneth, "I knew you would come; I've been waiting you," she gently stroked Reigneth's face.

"Don't mind Mother, she gets a little confused at times,"

Richard said absently. "I'll go and get your bags," and he pottered out to collect their few belongings.

"I'll help," Reigneth followed keen to look around this rambling place that was to be her home.

The building to the right of the house had been used as an annexe for Richard Pritchard's parents. Following his father's death and Emily's gradual decline into senility, she had moved into the main house with Richard and Liz so that they could keep a better eye on her and the annexe had fallen into disuse. It had seemed a waste that the building stood empty and Elizabeth, who so wanted to have her sister with her, had said that Jessie and Reigneth could live there independently or if they preferred, in the main house with the family, the decision was for Jessie to make.

Making up the left hand side of the courtyard was an old barn, which Richard had long ago converted as his studio and gallery. It had been made into one large room. The floors were wooden, with exposed beams straight up to the rafters. It was a huge space, light and airy and a spectacular display case for Richard's paintings. At one end of the barn, huge doors opened into an orchard, which led out onto open moorland. The light flooded into the room, ideal conditions for Richard to paint. As her uncle showed her around, Reigneth absorbed the atmosphere of the place. Richard and Liz were happy here and the very stones seemed to exude a welcome.

Liz had lived in a *Gauja's* world so long now that some things just seemed second nature to her. It brought her up short to realise that for Jessie and Reigneth it was all very strange and, as delighted as they were to see her, she could see they were both anxious about living here. Their first obstacle was that neither of them had ever lived in a house. They had gone from Joe's wagon to the tiny bungalow belonging to his mother. That in itself had been a huge step forward, and while they had been happy there, Liz knew they had always wedged themselves into the one back room, and more often than the back door was left wide open, whatever the weather. It was perhaps only natural that at first they would feel shut in at Home Humber, but Liz was optimistic that their claustrophobia would wear off once they got used to it. It had been the same for her when she first came into a house and now she thought nothing of it. Looking back on her life Liz began to realise just how much she had changed as a result of marrying Richard.

She led Jess and Reigneth to the stairs. "The bedrooms are up here. Come and see."

They both eyed the staircase with trepidation; to go upstairs was totally alien to them, but Liz chivvied them along. Jess, clinging white-knuckled to the banister, navigated the stairs. She could not be persuaded to look out of the landing window at the view, but stood with an anxious frown, her back against the wall. It was easier for Reigneth, she was younger, less set in her ways, but Liz observed that even she looked nervous as she reached out to take her mother's hand.

Hm, Liz thought, *this is going to be harder than I imagined; old habits die hard!*

Chapter 4

Antecedents

Chagford was the sort of town where everyone knew one another's business, so it was surprising that for the past twenty-one years, Grace Wilmott, who had lived there all her life, had kept a secret. To her knowledge, not one person suspected she even had a secret, never mind what it was. No one, that is, except the other person involved. His name was Matthew Holbrook.

Grace's stiff and austere personality had enabled her to keep people at a distance. Consequently, even had she been inclined to confide in someone, she had no close friend with whom to share her secret and at times the weight of it had felt as though it would crush her, but keep it she would, until her dying day.

Since Grace's marriage to Harry Wilmott, Matthew Holbrook had tried his utmost to stay away from the village and aside from dashing in for essentials, had succeeded for eight years. In all that time he had lived more like an animal than a man, until in the end he resembled something less than human. His social graces were non-existent, his appearance wild. A constant gnawing ache in his gut kept him as thin as a lat and he looked more than twice his age. Sometimes he felt that madness was encroaching and he would lose his sanity, but survival was his strongest instinct. He knew he would have to get a grip on himself. His sole reason for avoiding Chagford was to avoid Grace and the child; *his* child, for he was sure it was his.

On this particular day, Matthew parked up the Land Rover and darted into the village shop. Essential purchases in hand, he turned to leave. His foot had barely touched the footpath when a boy hurtled headlong into him and would have fallen had Matthew not caught hold of the child's school jacket. A scruffy kid, he noticed, not dirty, but untidy with his shirt tail hanging out, his school tie undone and his socks down around his ankles; the kind of child who would never be neat.

"I'm sorry. I'm late and I'll catch it," gasped the boy, then stopped and stared at the stranger holding onto him.

"Don't worry about it, lad, I just wish I could run as fast," Matthew said, releasing the boy. "What's your name?"

"Johnny – gotta dash."

Johnny's lop-sided grin as he scuttled off brought an answering grin from Matthew. He turned away and trudged back to his Land Rover, unsettled by the encounter. His own child would be about that age, he reckoned. For all he knew, Johnny could even be his son. He clenched his fists, feeling a welling emptiness as he thought about it. Matthew was lonely; his life had been one of constant loneliness tinged with disappointment and anger, mainly at himself but also at Grace for not being braver; for not being able to stand up to her parents and not being passionate enough about her feelings for him.

Matthew Holbrook had gone to school with Grace Gill, as she was then, and from the first day he saw her she had become his sweetheart. She was lovely, but her mother was a pretentious idiot; he had hated her. Grace's father, John Gill, was worse. Matthew hated him even more. The man was a bully. Each night he wedged his large frame into one of the seats in the Bullers Arms, his ruddy complexion the result of too much beer and whiskey. Matthew blamed Grace's parents for her cowardice far more than he blamed her. He had tried to hate her too, but failed miserably. Thinking about her did no more than make him love her more.

Grace's husband, Harry Wilmott, had moved to nearby Bovey Tracey when he was twenty. His parents had inherited a vast amount of money and used some of it to buy a large house. Harry's father had then proceeded to buy up every property with land that he could lay his hands on, reselling the houses and keeping the land. Always acquiring; always searching, always ferreting about for more. Money makes money and it had certainly been true in the Wilmotts' case. Within three years they owned a good chunk of the properties in and around the Dartmoor National Park, many of the cottages being sold off as holiday homes, locals being unable to afford to buy them. This had done nothing to improve the family's popularity with village folk, not that the Wilmotts noticed; their avarice made them blind.

Harry was a debonair, jovial sort of chap; blond and blue-eyed with an engaging smile; a bit of the buffoon if you believed the act, but Matthew wasn't fooled. Like his father, Harry set his sights on things and went all out to get them by fair means or foul. Grace was just another acquisition. Matthew felt sure she had been fooled by Harry; taken in hook line and sinker. Her parents certainly were, and they were flattered to boot – hadn't they always known their daughter was destined for better things than a poor, hard-working farmer like Matthew Holbrook?

Harry and Grace had become an item and Matthew had felt fit to burst, but he contained his anger, certain that his erstwhile sweetheart would eventually see her mistake and come back to him. And so he had waited. What a fool he had been. Why hadn't he taken action? His incredulity that Grace could be attracted to the big gormless lump had stopped him. He simply had not believed it until it was almost too late.

One frosty night – the night before Grace's and Harry's wedding in fact – Matthew had stood shivering beneath her bedroom window throwing pea gravel up at the glass and thinking, *If she doesn't pull up the bloody sash soon I'll freeze.*

The window had opened and Grace's head peeped out. Without more ado, Matthew had clambered up the trellising to her room. Grasping her in his arms was all too familiar; the scent of her was in his nose, in his head and he was lost. His mouth sought hers and she was kissing him back. Things were as they had always been, his need of her was urgent and desperate only matched by hers for him; the feel of her breasts and thighs a welcome resting place for his body. Strung out with tension and longing, Matthew lost control. All too soon the moments passed and all too soon he realised the risk they had taken. *What the hell does it matter?'* he'd thought, for he wouldn't lose her now and that was all he cared about: if there was a child then so much the better.

"Grace, you'll have to tell them first thing in the morning," he'd said urgently, his words hard to get out as he choked with emotion. "You can't get married to someone else, not now. You don't love him, it's me you love; you know you do."

"Matthew, they'll kill me," Grace had whispered, between

sobs, her eyes leaking tears.

He had kissed her tears away, "Better to kill you at home than make it as far as the church!" he had said, trying to make her smile. "It's all been a big mistake, my darling, but we'll sort it. Ring the vicar first, before they have the chance to persuade you to change your mind. Do you want me to come back first thing and talk to them with you?"

She had clung to him, weeping. "No, Matthew, it's something I have to do on my own."

Promising to return later that morning he had left by the window at dawn, running to where he had parked the Land Rover. He drove back far too quickly up the narrow winding road to Higher Wedicombe, the home he had always imagined he would share with Grace. His dream was not over, not yet. He had to see to the stock, but then he meant to return, for he wasn't going to leave Grace to deal with it all on her own. He had rushed around doing the essential chores and was just dashing to the bathroom to get washed and changed, when he heard the church bells begin to peal the way they did for a wedding. Matthew had stopped dead in his tracks, listening; the bells had sounded louder and louder, filling his head with their chimes until he thought he would go mad. He had begun to cry then, just like when Grace had pulled his hair in infant school. Why did she always have to hurt him? He had known there would be no recovery; not this time – at least, not for him.

After Matthew had climbed out through the window, Grace had eased herself out of bed, her whole body aching. She was unsure how to begin to tell her parents. She tried out the words: "Mum, Dad, I'm sorry, but I've changed my mind. I don't want to marry Harry Wilmott. The wedding's off." The thought of what they'd do to her had screwed Grace's stomach into a tight ball of tension. She had not been joking when she said they would kill her. At the very least, her father would take his belt to her as he had so often in the past. She decided to have a hot bath first and get a drink of tea while she psyched herself up to telling them; once that was done she would phone Harry and then the vicar.

Grace tried so many times to say the words, but each time they choked in her throat; she was such a coward. Perhaps she could just run out of the door? But no, her mother had watched her like a hawk, never giving Grace a minute to herself. And then it was too late and with the voice in her head screaming *No*' louder than the pealing church bells, she had been swept to the altar like a piece of flotsam on an ebbing tide.

The reception had been an ordeal; the wedding night worse. The night before she had made love with the man she truly loved, every action a delight, every sensation a revelation. The fumbling fool she had married had unknowingly attempted to follow in another man's place. Every action a poor imitation of what love should be like. It wasn't his fault. She should never have been taken in by him; never allowed her parents to browbeat her. She realised the only happiness she had known was at Matthew's moorland farm, in the days before the Wilmotts had moved to the area. Grace knew she had made a terrible mistake; one she would regret for the rest of her days.

Two months later, she had found herself standing in the cold downstairs cloakroom, waiting for the result of the pregnancy test, already knowing what it would be. The blue line showed clearly; she sat on the toilet and sobbed.

As time went on, Grace had felt worse and worse. She looked awful: worry, stress and aching unhappiness ever present. She had nothing to complain about. Harry was a kind and attentive husband, but compared to the man she loved, he was so boring. How could she leave him? It would be like kicking a puppy; besides, there was a chance that the child was his, though somehow she had known it was Matthew's. She could not have said how she knew; she just knew. She had expected that as soon as the news of her pregnancy got onto the village grapevine, Matthew would come to see her. He didn't. Time passed and she got bigger and bigger and more and more depressed. In the end, Harry, concerned, had called the doctor, who had reassured him that all would be well after the birth. It was because Grace had always been so active, he'd said, and pregnancy was hard for her.

Matthew had learned about the baby in the village Spar shop, overhearing the owner, Mrs Cooper, gossiping with a customer. "Did you hear about Grace Wilmott's honeymoon baby? They didn't waste much time did they? Bet she did it on purpose. Wouldn't want to let moneybags Wilmott get away! An heir and soon a spare, you'll see."

Matthew had paid and left, ducking down the passageway at the side of the shop, where he was violently sick. Most mornings when he woke he felt this way; sick to the pit of his stomach, but this was the first time he had been unable to hold onto his breakfast. At first he had been tempted to go and see Grace, find out more about the baby, knowing it could be his. But then, how would she be able to tell? And anyway, what was the point? It didn't change anything. Grace would still be married to Harry, who might equally be the father. The thought of it had twisted in Matthew's gut, huge racking sobs tearing at his throat as he had driven blindly away from Chagford, determined never to go near the place again.

Johnny Wilmott had bounced into the world on the fourth day of June, lungs screeching, red-faced, wriggling and complaining. He had continued in that way, or so it seemed, for at least ten months, at which point he decided that if he could walk he could make an even bigger nuisance of himself.

He was a horrendous child, such a handful, full of energy, mischievous and cheeky. And an absolute delight. Everyone loved him whilst being exhausted by him. He had inherited his mother's fine bone structure, high cheekbones and full lips in a perfect cupid's bow, but that was all anyone could see in relation to his parentage, much to the Wilmotts' disappointment. Grace, however, could see his father in him: Johnny was dark, just like Matthew, and every bit as untidy – everything about him was a mess. "You look like a bag of rags young man," Granny Gill would say, despairing of the young hooligan. Grace, who lived in constant fear that sooner or later, someone else would notice the resemblance, was grateful that Matthew stayed away from the village.

Soon after Johnny's birth, Harry and Grace decided they would like more children straight away, one after the other without a big age gap, but despite their best efforts, another child was not conceived. "Johnny was a one shot wonder," Harry would say jokingly, looking with pride at his son.

When, three years later, Grace suspected she was pregnant again, her only emotion was one of relief. Much to everyone's surprise, Grace landed twins: a boy and a girl. Somehow this seemed to divert everyone's attention from the fact that the babies, blue-eyed and fair, were so different from their dark little brother.

And still nobody suspected he was a cuckoo in the nest.

Johnny loved his siblings; Henry and Charlotte were perfect babies, both sleeping through at twelve weeks, model children, which only served to highlight how naughty Johnny could be. No one cared; he was their darling; he had only to smile and his misdemeanours were forgotten. Harry spoilt all the children shamefully, loving them all, but favouring Johnny without realising it. Everyone favoured Johnny, it was his role in life to be adored, but he was totally oblivious to it.

Grace was glad she had at least given Harry his family, it assuaged her guilt, but only a little, for though relatively content, she was ashamed for the deep longing she still harboured for Matthew. It ate away at her, unrelenting.

As the children grew, she introduced them to horseback riding and when they were proficient on their ponies, went with them up onto the moor, ambling along the bridle paths and enjoying the spectacular scenery all around. Places where she had been with Matthew. More often than not Grace struggled to hide her tears, blaming them on the cold moorland wind if any of the children noticed. Johnny, ever protective, usually did. His intuition with regard to the moor was amazing: he knew instinctively which places were dangerous and always kept a weather eye out. The moor could be treacherous, but he read it well. It was another similarity to his father and observing it, Grace was beset by memories that saddened her all the more.

By the age of eleven, Johnny was an accomplished horseman and rapidly outgrowing his Dartmoor pony. His parents were keeping an eye open for something bigger and Grace mentioned to one or two people what she was looking for. She knew exactly what she wanted for Johnny and could be patient until the right animal came along.

In the three years since Johnny had run into him outside the Spar shop, Matthew, driven by the need the incident had evoked in him to find out about Grace's firstborn child, had ventured more often into Chagford. He asked surreptitious questions in the shop, listened to gossip. Mrs Cooper was a fount of local knowledge and it did not take long for Matthew to discover that the untidy, dark-haired boy with the engaging grin was indeed Grace's son, Johnny Wilmott. He learned that the child was wild, rode like a cowboy and played the piano like an angel. It made Matthew's mouth lift in an involuntary smile; it sounded good enough to him. His own mother had been a gifted pianist and he wondered if things like this could be inherited. Filled with excitement, he nursed the knowledge that just as he had imagined, the boy, Johnny, was his son. With his looks he could not possibly be Harry's. Matthew no longer hurried when in the village in the hopes of seeing the boy again. Once he caught a glimpse of him out riding on the moor and was filled with pride at how well Johnny rode. Filled with bitter frustration too, for his son would never know his father.

In due course, Matthew heard that the Wilmotts were looking for a suitable horse for their son. Matthew, who longed to see the boy again, loaded up his favourite Highland mare onto the trailer, her foal following obediently. It was a corker; the best colt foal he had ever bred. He intended it as a gift to Johnny; somehow his son would have something precious from his father even if he did not know it.

Arriving at the Wilmotts' place, Matthew could not help but draw comparisons with his own farm, Higher Wedicombe. Having no focus; nothing to work towards, he had let things slide over the years and he felt ashamed at how run down it had become. As he drove into the yard, feeling unbearably nervous, he saw Grace and her son standing looking towards the sound made by his tyres on the gravel. At the sight of them, Matthew felt as though someone had punched him in the chest. He clung to the steering wheel, unable to get out of the Land Rover. The boy stood, hands on hips, a long dark curl dropping down over one eye, the scruffiest tyke Matthew had ever seen. Grace looked about to collapse, steadying herself on the gatepost. Her expression confirmed what they both knew as she gazed first at Matthew and then at their son.

Taking a deep breath to steady himself, Matthew eased his long body out of the Land Rover and said, "I cannot give colts away these days and heard you were looking for another pony. You'll have to wait until he's grown to ride him, of course, but I'll break him for you when he's three." Matthew, who had thought to keep the conversation casual, found the words spilling out of him all in a rush.

Grace nodded, but made no reply, her arm going protectively around Johnny's shoulders. The boy was like a young hound straining at the leash in his eagerness to see what was in the trailer.

Matthew proceeded to unload the mare and foal, saying over his shoulder, "Where do you want them, Grace?" Her name slipped off his tongue, the words uttered as if they had never been apart.

Johnny was beside himself with excitement. "Mum, do you know this man?" he whispered. "I've seen him once before. He's really nice."

"Yes, Johnny, his name is Matthew Holbrook," Grace said, her face ashen. "We were at school together."

"Is the colt really for me, what's his name Mr Holbrook?" Johnny called, as Matthew led the mare and her foal towards them.

"I thought we might call him Rannoch, if you like it."

"I do, I do, I really like it, can I really have him, Mum?"

Her eyes glistening with tears, Grace reached forward to slide her hand down the mare's nose. At last she found her voice. "You don't intend to sell Bess to me do you, Matthew?"

"No, Grace, she was intended for someone very special to me, but you can keep her here until the foal is weaned. Then she can come home – until her mistress comes home to her," he added pointedly. Handing the reins to Johnny, Matthew ruffled his hair and smiled down at him. "You take good care of them, now."

Johnny's face lit up, his winning, ingenuous smile directed at Matthew as he tried to express his delight. "I will, I will, I promise. Thank you. Oh, thank you, Mr Holbrook, he's the best."

"Yes, thank you, Matthew," Grace said. "That is really very kind of you. I... " her voice faltered as though she did not trust herself to say any more.

For a moment, Matthew lingered, then he nodded and with a gruff, "Goodbye then," he turned away and climbed back into the Land Rover.

Letting Johnny's excited chatter wash over her, Grace, her legs wobbling, watched Matthew driving away until the Land Rover and empty trailer were mere specks in the distance. All she could think was, *Thank God Harry's not here. How has no one else spotted the resemblance between these two?*' Matthew's words about the mare had not been lost on her: they hung in the air choking her until she felt she could not breathe. She had not seen Matthew for so long. She yearned for him each day, every day, the only thing that made the pain abate slightly was the boy now clutching the colt foal, blowing gently into its nose and whispering soft words into its flickering ears. Matthew's boy. Grace knew that Matthew knew it too; the similarity between them was unmistakeable. And although nothing had been said, she knew the colt was Matthew's gift to his son.

When he came back six months later to retrieve his mare, Grace was out and she did not see him. She did not know whether to be relieved or sorry.

By the time Johnny was fourteen and Rannoch was three, the colt was ready to be ridden. They had kept Rannoch whole; there had been no need to castrate him as he did not behave like other stallions. Even Grace's own Dartmoor stallion could be a handful at times and she had never got him out of the habit of nipping her hand when she was leading him. She was amazed that Rannoch had never once bitten or kicked her son.

Three years to the day that Rannoch had come into his life, Johnny got on the colt and rode him bareback with just a halter, up onto the moor. That was his breaking in: no bridle; no saddle. Johnny knew where he was going. He had seen Matthew Holbrook only once since the day he had delivered Rannoch, and then not to speak to. He was determined to thank him again. The colt had been his constant companion for the past three years and he wanted Matthew to know how much the gift had meant to him. He also wanted Matthew to be the first to see him riding Rannoch. Heading towards Higher Wedicombe Farm, Johnny spotted Matthew in the distance and waved to him like a long lost friend.

Matthew saw the boy and the stallion standing out against the horizon and watched them approach. The beauty of the pair of them took his breath away. His lad had come to visit – he could hardly believe it. Three years ago, the day after he had taken the colt foal to Johnny, Matthew had made an appointment with a solicitor in Exeter. A few days later he made a will leaving the farm to his sole heir, his son, Jonathan Wilmott. Using a city solicitor had seemed safer to Matthew. That done, he embarked on getting the farm into good order. Even though he knew that Grace was lost to him forever, she had given him a son. Things seemed a little better to him now that he had something to strive for.

There was a lot of work to be done: the farm buildings all needed repairing; the yard in winter was appalling, everywhere muddy and everything made twice as hard as the old machinery was constantly breaking down. Not just the farm, but the house too needed attention. Run down and untidy, but also inviting and homely, Higher Wedicombe had been home to the Holbrooks for years. Matthew's maternal grandparents and mother had lived there. He had not known his father, who died before Matthew was born, but in any event, his mother had not married him. Matthew did not know why; his mother had passed away when he was only twelve, before it occurred to him to ask. He could have asked his grandparents, who cared for him after she had gone, but somehow he found it hard to raise the subject. Old carers not making for a barrel of laughs, he had been buoyed up during those years by his childhood sweetheart, Grace Gill.

Eventually, his grandparents had passed away in their turn. By then, Matthew had taken over the running of the farm. He had always been a bit of a loner and when his hopes of marrying Grace had been dashed, he had not thought to find someone to take her place. Not that anyone could; and besides, he had always held onto the hope that she would eventually return to him.

While the farm might be run down, the land was good and fertile and Harry Wilmott had been trying to buy it for years, first anonymously through a solicitor, then openly, offering vastly inflated sums to try to tempt Matthew into selling.

"Just take my entire bloody life, why don't you?" Matthew had chuntered to himself when Harry had the cheek to approach him in person. It was all Matthew could do not to strike the big gormless lump. However, as much as he hated Harry Wilmott, he would not be the one to tell him about Johnny. Grace's secret was safe with him. Until his dying day he would not betray her. Until his dying day he would love her.

Had Matthew even considered selling the farm, Harry was the last person in the world he would sell it to; not that he ever would consider it. He had been born at Higher Wedicombe and as far as he was concerned, he would die there. He loved the house; he had thought Grace did too. For all that, taking care of it had never seemed a priority, it simply never occurred to Matthew to clean. It was not that he was a dirty person, but he had become so accustomed to the way things were that he failed to see the accumulation of grime. The ceilings were low and heavily beamed; the granite walls thick as a man's arm. There was a huge fireplace hewn out of granite, with a wood burner that chugged away for most of the winter months. The staircase was also made of granite: huge blocks of stone and no carpet to disguise the bare rawness of them. A few too many at the pub and it was curtains if you took a tumble down those stairs. Fortunately, Matthew was not a great one for the drink.

It was hard to be enthusiastic about looking after things when you had no incentive. Matthew blamed Grace for everything, but it occurred to him one day that perhaps he would have been like this even if she had married him. Maybe he was just a lazy slob. But no, he thought, it wasn't that; he wasn't afraid of hard work, he just lacked energy. What he needed was motivation. It came in the form of Johnny.

Watching his son coming towards him across the moor was like a dream come true for Matthew. Their first meeting in three years was only brief, but even in so short a time, man and boy struck up an immediate rapport.

"Hi, Mr Holbrook," Johnny called, bringing the stallion skidding to a halt in the yard. "I thought I'd come and show Rannoch off to you." He slid nimbly down from Rannoch's back and held his hand out to Matthew. "You may not remember me? I'm Johnny, Johnny Wilmott, I've grown a bit since we last met."

Almost overcome with emotion, Matthew grasped the proffered hand, "Well, you've certainly shot up a bit that's for sure." His voice sounded gruff in his effort to stop it from wobbling and there was a moment's awkward silence. Matthew was ill at ease. He had longed for this meeting, so wanted it to be perfect, but he wasn't used to speaking to young people. The tension was broken by Rannoch, softly whickering and shoving his nose in the boy's back.

They both laughed and Matthew released Johnny's hand. "Looks like I wasn't needed to break him in after all."

"No, he's took no breaking. He's as sweet as a nut. I've been able to swarm all over him ever since you left him. Fact is, I came to thank you again, Mr Holbrook. Rannoch is the best thing that's ever happened to me. I don't know what I'd do without him." Johnny laughed as he fondled Rannoch's mane.

"My friends call me 'Matt', why don't you?" Matthew said awkwardly, thinking: *What friends? I haven't got any!*

"I'd like that," Johnny grinned.

Feeling strangely shy, Matthew looked away, studied Rannoch with a critical eye. "There was no need to come all this way, lad, but I'm right glad you did. You don't need to thank me. He looks well; I can see how much you care for him." He looked back at his son and suddenly his shyness dropped away and he was grinning at Johnny as if they had known each other forever.

Laughing, Johnny said, "Yes, well my mum says if she turned her back I'd have him eating at the table with us, and his table manners would most likely be better than mine."

At the boy's casual mention of Grace, a nerve clenched in Matthew's stomach, but he ignored it. "Be careful up here on your own, Johnny; watch the weather. It can close in before you're even aware of it. Don't want you getting lost; your mother would never forgive me." He reached out and slapped Johnny on the back like they were old mates.

"I won't, Matt, don't worry. I like it up here, especially when it's a bit wild."

"I do too. Fact is, I wouldn't want to be anywhere else. Would you like to come in for a cup of tea or something? Might be able to rustle up a biscuit or two."

"Thanks, but I'd best be off. Mum'll be wondering where I've got to." Johnny rolled his eyes and grinned. "Given it's Rannoch's first outing, she'll be imagining us in a bog or something. But I'll pop by again if that's alright?"

"I'd like that." Matthew almost added, 'If that's alright with Grace', but thought better of it. "Off you go then."

He watched Johnny ride away, saw him stop, turn and wave. Matthew waved back and was still smiling when boy and horse disappeared over the horizon.

Over the next few months, the stallion with the boy perched on its back became familiar figures on the moorland scene. Rannoch's coat, mane and tail and Johnny's hair colour were the same dark brown. They could be seen constantly on the moor, hair and mane blowing in the wind, a law unto themselves. Johnny was naturally gifted; he excelled without apparent effort in everything he turned his hand to. He got top marks at school, was at one with nature and the moor, and his musical gift was outstanding.

"Well, Harry," remarked one of Harry's business partners when staying over one weekend, "that boy of yours plays like an angel. Who would have thought a great lug like you would have produced such a talented young 'un? Still, your talent is making money, eh?"

The statement was true enough: Harry's money making abilities seemed never to falter. By now he was a very rich man and his family reaped the benefits; Grace never had to worry where the next penny was coming from. The twins, now twelve, both pleasant children and amiable just like Harry, were at the local school, while Johnny had just finished GCSE's, with outstanding results. Not having had any more children, Grace, with time on her hands, had cast around for something to occupy her. She had started breeding from the children's outgrown Dartmoor ponies and finding some comfort in the project, was beginning to make a bit of a name for herself in showing circles.

Much to his parents' chagrin – though for different reasons – Johnny took a Saturday job at Matthew Holbrook's farm. He would ride to Higher Wedicombe every weekend and turn Rannoch out with the two new Highland mares Matthew had bought.

"We'll see what we get, eh, Jono?" said Matthew. No one else called Johnny that, but he rather liked it coming from Matt.

As the years drifted by, his relationship with Matthew developed into one of unshakeable friendship. Johnny, of course, had no notion of their true relationship, and as tempted as Matthew was at times to tell him, he could never quite bring himself to lay that burden of guilt on his son, and so he behaved towards him as he would to a younger brother. The boy's eagerness to please and his warm, open personality lifted Matthew's spirits. So much so that the years dropped off him and life took a turn for the better.

Chapter 5

Fleeing the Nest

By the time he was eighteen, with a string of academic achievements to his credit, Johnny had begun to focus on what he was to do next. Harry, always supportive, gave good, helpful advice – then just smiled when his son did exactly the opposite. Despite his doting father's urging, Johnny had no inclination whatever to go into business; the thought of it left him cold. Nor did he fancy estate management and so he found himself embarking on a music degree with no idea of what he would do after the three-year course.

Thanks to Harry's forbearance and understanding – and, of course, deep pockets – Johnny was able to follow his dream. He was in a very enviable position, with his fees paid for and a generous allowance enabling him to concentrate on his music, but Johnny never really thought about it. It was not that he was ungrateful, he was quite simply oblivious to the amount of money that came his way. In fact he rarely spent it. He was not interested in clothes and designer labels were foreign to him. If he saw something he liked and needed he would buy it, so long as the cost was not too outrageous. He tended to wear serviceable clothes that lasted, but almost anything looked good on him. He rarely wore trainers, preferring leather boots. He usually wore jeans with an assortment of tops and he had a liking for hats, the quirkier the better. His one extravagance was guitars and he suffered pangs of guilt if he spent too much money on one that he did not really need, especially when his mother moaned about the amount of room his instruments took up at home.

Freshers' week at university was something of a challenge to Johnny. Not having a particularly large build, he had never been able to drink huge quantities of alcohol, which seemed to be a prerequisite for undergraduates. Two pints of beer or lager were his limit, the third pint driving him to spend much of the evening in the gents. Spirits were even worse: he became very drunk very quickly. He was, however, an extremely amiable drunk and enormously entertaining. By the end of the week he was firmly established as a total lightweight in partying, but a great favourite, particularly with the opposite sex.

The first day of the course was nerve racking for everyone, all wondering whether their abilities would enable them to succeed. One or two, of course, never doubted their own brilliance, while others, like Johnny, were so nervous and their fingers shaking so much, that their talents were liable to remain hidden. It was to be a sharp learning curve.

Going without breakfast, having spent the first part of the morning ensconced in the shared bathroom, Johnny was not at his best. The tutor wanted to get some idea of the students' individual abilities, so the first lecture was very much a getting-to-know-you session. Each fresher was asked to perform two pieces, classical or contemporary, the choice was theirs.

As soon as the students began to play, Johnny became engrossed, his nervous tension dissipating. By the time his turn came he was feeling much better. For his first piece he had chosen a cover version of a contemporary song, accompanying himself on the piano. The second piece was one of his own; something he had written for the guitar. Johnny did not see himself as others did and had no idea just how talented he was. Having listened to his fellow students he decided that although he was not going to be the worst musician there, he was probably the weirdest. Certainly, the students in his group had eyed him with suspicion thinking he had perhaps entered the wrong room. Looking very relaxed, at least while the music was playing, he lounged casually, his feet propped on an empty chair. A shabby suede jacket hung loosely from his languid frame and he wore a black woollen hat pulled down almost to his eyes, his long hair escaping beneath it. Having had no time to shave, he knew he must look incredibly scruffy.

Only one student smiled across at him: a slight girl with short spiky hair. He barely noticed her. With little experience of the opposite sex – at least, none to write home about – Johnny, unaware of his sex appeal, was largely oblivious to the fact that most of the girls on the course had already checked him out and thought he was hot. Certainly, with his tanned skin, cupid bow mouth, and those dreamy green eyes fringed with long dark lashes, he was really handsome in a girlie sort of way – and yet there was nothing camp about him. His appeal extended to both genders and all ages: old ladies loved him because he had impeccable manners and his smile was heart-warming. Those in middle-age were often embarrassed at the direction in which their thoughts took them when they met him, while young adults, driven by their hormones rather than their thoughts, were not shy in coming forward. In a word, Johnny Wilmott had charisma; the fact that he was blissfully unaware of it only added to his charm.

Immersed in the various pieces being played, Johnny was a little startled when he heard his named being called. Feeling overawed, he made his way slowly to the stage. From habit, he began peeling off multiple layers of clothing until he was down to his jeans and a sleeveless T-shirt – performing always made him feel hot. Too nervous to register the appreciative titters of girls in the audience and with a pile of tops now heaped on the stage, he sat down at the keyboard. Musically, especially on the piano, Johnny was very gifted. He was a tenor, his voice rich and with a tremendous range, but for the first number he played it safe, singing a popular ballad. It was outstanding even so, and his fellow students were in awe of him – although the female half had been like that since he removed a good percentage of his clothing, unconsciously revealing his lean, muscular frame.

Johnny played his second piece in his own inimitable style of rock, this time letting rip with his vocal range, pitch perfect and never wavering, which had everyone amazed. At the end of this number every student in the auditorium stood to applaud, the tutor included. Coming to himself as the last chord died away, Johnny nodded his thanks, scrambled to gather up his clothes and hurried off the stage, his face burning.

Walking away from the auditorium he heard the quick light footsteps of someone running to catch up with him. Feeling a light touch on his arm, he half turned and registered a mass of spiky red-blonde hair framing a pert face and beaming smile.

"Hi, I just knew you'd be amazing. I'm Isobel; Isobel Pearson, but my friends call me 'Izzy' and I've decided to be your best friend," she purred. "Coffee? You look like you could use one."

At home in Chagford, Grace felt she would never get used to Johnny's absence. Each day she missed him more, it was almost like bereavement. She comforted herself with the thought that he would be back often. She knew he could not resist the moor for long.

Grace had grown accustomed to her life with Harry: he was an easy man to live with and not at all demanding. She was more or less content and these days rarely thought of Matthew. Johnny filled most of her waking thoughts. She did not mean to a have favourite, but he was so easy to love.

Despite having had three children, Grace had not changed much over the years. She had kept her figure, was slim and petite and her fair hair was always immaculately styled. It was from Grace that Johnny had inherited his fine bone structure: she had the kind of face that never seemed to age. Very pretty when she was young, now an attractive older woman, she was not at all given to displays of emotion and her rigid posture reinforced the impression that she was cold. In direct contrast to her oldest son, whom everyone loved, Grace did not endear herself to people.

Although Johnny came home at every available opportunity, Harry spent much of his time away on business so only rarely saw his son. When Johnny had been at university for a year and came down for the summer break, it was the first time Harry had seen him in months. He noticed the change straight away: gone was the boy and in his place stood a young man. As a teenager Johnny had been beautiful – far too beautiful for a boy – but now his face had matured and was more angular, though his lop-sided grin was as cheeky as ever.

Harry embraced him warmly. "Look at you! What have they been feeding you on at that university?"

Johnny's answering grin reminded Harry of someone. He could not quite place who: a celebrity perhaps? *Never mind, it'll come to me in a minute*, he thought, but it did not and the feeling persisted, niggling away at the back of his mind.

"It's great to have you home again, son," he said. "I've got a meeting in Exeter, but I'll be back in time for dinner and we can catch up on all the news then, OK? I shall look forward to it." Grabbing up his brief case and kissing Grace on the cheek, Harry dashed out to his car.

The meeting went well and he was in a good mood as he walked back to the car park in the gathering dusk, stopping on the way to buy some flowers for Grace. Not a day went by that he did not count his blessings. He loved his wife, he always had from the moment he first saw her. Placing the bouquet – red carnations, her favourite – on the back seat, he climbed into the Audi, still thinking about his family. They had probably been out riding today. It was the first time the kids had been together for a long time. Grace would be in her element to have Johnny home. Of their three children, Harry acknowledged to himself that Johnny was her favourite -his too. God knows he loved them all, but that boy did something to you. Thinking of Johnny brought the niggle back into Harry's mind to plague him. Dammit! Who was it the boy had reminded him of this morning? He just couldn't place it. Moving the Audi up through the gears he sighed. The journey back to Chagford was always tedious: the road a series of narrow double bends. Harry did not like the drive at the best of times. This evening it was dark and raining, his headlights lost on the wet road. He would be glad to get home.

Rod Jenkins worked for Simpsons Haulage. He had been to do a job just outside Moretonhampstead and was heading back on the Exeter road. The new lad working with him was a cocky little devil and had irritated the life out of him all day. Rod was keen to get home. They had tied down all the cables, catches and fasteners, but he was later than he expected to be and the crane was far bigger than he liked to drive down the small roads in the dark. It was difficult negotiating some of the bends and the lorry did not feel quite right. He had decided to stop over at the next lay-by to double check everything and if he was no happier he would ring the office and get someone to pick them up. They could collect the crane the following morning.

Harry's journey was monotonous, the sound of the windscreen wipers grating on his nerves. He kept thinking about Johnny: the tilt of his head; the slant of his smile. Then, like a bolt out of the blue, he had it. Why had he never seen it before? Now that the boy had matured, he was the spitting image of the man. Matthew Holbrook! As the realisation hit him, time ground to a stop for Harry. He cast his mind back twenty-one years or more, to when he had first taken up with Grace and as good as wrested her from Matthew Holbrook's arms.

Everything seemed to happen in slow motion as Harry grappled with the notion that Johnny was not his son; that his boy belonged to someone else and that someone else was Matthew. In shock, Harry's concentration wavered and he over-steered a bend, veering over the white line in the middle of the road.

Out of the darkness, closely hugging the same white line, Simpsons Haulage truck careered towards him. The road was very narrow on the bend; avoidance impossible. Harry jammed on the brakes. The Audi shrieked in protest, locked wheels skidded forward. In that instant, Harry knew he was going to die.

The impact was not huge, but the crane swung free. Acting like a large guillotine, it scraped along the car and in one easy motion transformed the Audi from a saloon to a convertible. Like a million fingernails scratching on a blackboard, the noise was a terrifying scream of metal on metal.

Rod Jenkins remained in the cab, rigid and unable to move, his hands and fingers clasped so tight to the steering wheel he felt they would have to be prised off with a crowbar. The lad next to him, for once silent, stared, eyes wide with horror. Caught in the headlights, the crushed stems of red carnations were strewn across the road like gouts of blood. Rod knew the poor bugger in the car had not stood a chance.

Grace was looking forward to dinner, it would be the first time they'd all been together in nearly a year; she had not been so happy for a long time. She knew most of the happiness sprang from the presence of her son, but even so, she thought kindly of Harry, and expected that, as usual, he would bring her a bunch of carnations – she had always loved the scent of them. There had never been any doubt that he loved her. She was just thinking how much she had to be thankful for, when the doorbell rang.

The horror of the accident stunned everyone in and around Chagford. Despite Harry's land-grabbing activities, no one would have wished him to meet such a dreadful end. Grace held up exceptionally well. Initially she thought this was because of the children, but as time went on and the tears still did not come, she just got on with things. She certainly missed Harry, but everything went along in its well-ordered fashion. He had often been away from home and to Grace it seemed like he was on an extended business trip and sooner or later would return.

Financially everything was sorted out. She was astounded at the lengths to which Harry had gone to assure his family's security. All three children were taken care of: enough money put aside for university fees and living allowances. When they reached the age of twenty-one, they would come into a large sum of money, more than enough to set each of them up in a small business or buy them a property should they wish.

Grace herself had been left a very rich woman; she would never have to worry about an income; never have to work. She could continue with her hobby of breeding and showing her ponies and there was plenty left over to employ an assistant. She was aghast at just how much money Harry had been able to amass, realising that she had hugely underrated his business acumen. Not that they had ever really discussed his work, Harry had always liked to play the game very close to his chest. Grace suffered occasional pangs of guilt when she thought about him, but as time passed these faded. She had kept her secret: Harry had died never knowing that his favourite son was not his – and while she had not been able to love him as he might have wanted, she had not been a bad wife. Thus consoled, she put her guilt behind her and got on with her life.

Chapter 6

Destiny

In the weeks since the Grays had moved to Home Humber, Jessie had discovered that she quite liked the house; it was so peaceful. She and Reigneth had managed to recreate their 'three-mile-an-hour-life', as Joe used to call it, everything done at a slower pace as if the world had passed them by. Accustomed to the flat, open landscape of Lincolnshire, Jessie did not like Devon's high hedges. She felt so enclosed by them that on some days she found it hard to breathe, but generally she was content – as much as she ever could be without her Joe. She gained comfort from the fact that she was with her sister whose ways were similar to her own, for although Liz had learned to accommodate her husband's *Gauja* lifestyle, at heart she was and always would be Romany.

Despite her increasing contentment, Jessie was worried about Reigneth. She knew Joe had wanted an education for their daughter and hoped that once the summer holidays were over, Reigneth would settle down and go to college. The girl was becoming as wild as a banshee living down here, always wandering out over the moor. Jessie understood that she found solace in this place, which robbed time of speed and laid bare the essentials. Nature felt close on the moor, whether on the hot balmy days or the rougher days, both so opposite, both equally addictive.

Jessie could see that the moorland climate and weather suited Reigneth and that she was flourishing here in the Devon air. Physically she had matured; all vestiges of her childhood figure gone. Jessie was continually startled by her daughter's developing physique. Shapely, with a tiny waist and full breasts, she had grown into a sinewy girl with long athletic legs, small-boned yet tall. Most stunning was her countenance: her features were flawless, her teeth perfect and when she smiled her whole face became animated. Her hair was black with no hues of any other colour. Extremely thick and wavy, it fell naturally away from her forehead and parted just off centre, shorter tendrils escaping onto her face.

Not only was Reigneth beautiful, but like her father she was very charismatic. Amazingly she remained unaware of it. No one seeing Reigneth would forget her and most were in awe of her, but she seemed not to notice when people stopped and stared. Her beauty was such that Jessie worried for her. Not for the first time she was glad they lived in a small town where admirers would be fewer than in a city. What astonished Jessie even more than her daughter's appearance was that Reigneth was perfect inside: her beauty was more than skin deep; she was a truly lovely person through and through. Her heart was huge and there was room in it for everyone. Jessie was aware that Reigneth's gift – the things she 'saw' – troubled her at times. Joe had been right in his decision to keep it a secret; Reigneth, in her willingness to please, would have been worn down with the worry of seeing things for everyone. It would have destroyed her. Her gift or talent, whatever people wished to call it, must be kept hidden lest it become her downfall. All Jessie could do was to encourage her daughter to lead as normal a life as possible while doing her best to ensure she came to no harm. Fortunately she had a large family, all of whom loved and protected her.

Jukel protected her too. He had grown huge and strangers were wary of him. He seemed to feed off Reigneth's every mood and movement. When she was observant and alert, so was he. If she relaxed so did he: it was almost as if there was some chemistry between them. So in tune was the dog to what his mistress wanted that commands were hardly necessary, but if they were given they were imperceptible. Jessie reflected thankfully that she and Joe had somehow selected the right dog for their daughter even though he had been just a scrap with no knowing what he would grow into. Thankful too that Reigneth seemed so happy with the changes in their lives. Yes, all in all, Jessie was glad they had made the decision to move to Devon.

Jessie was right: not only was Reigneth happy at Home Humber, she was happier than she had ever been before. Waking each morning, she felt strong, healthy and full of energy. At times she also felt guilty that she could feel this way, with her Dad not long passed away. But in her dreams she knew he was glad for her and this knowledge helped her to enjoy her life.

She took every opportunity to go out on the moor, often feeling the desire to run headlong into the open expanse that seemed to stretch away endlessly, but she knew that would be folly. Uncle Richard had warned her of the hidden dangers: the way the paths disappeared or led you round in circles until you were hopelessly lost; the way the tumbling streams could sweep you away, their currents so much stronger than they looked. The way the ground appeared to be solid and yet might conceal a bottomless bog, and the way a balmy, sunny day could suddenly give way to cold mist that enveloped the landscape in a thick, clammy white blanket, so you could hardly see your feet. She knew her uncle was afraid of the moor and rarely came up onto the rough terrain. His fears were not unfounded: many people, lured by Dartmoor's stunning magnificence and seemingly harmless landscape, got lost and ended up dead from exposure.

Reigneth, now turned fifteen and with a sensible head on her shoulders, always heeded Richard's warnings, taking careful note of the landmarks and carrying a map and compass, as well as a warm jacket tucked into her rucksack, even on the warmest days, but walking on the moor was her favourite pastime and she could never resist its pull.

Everything here in Devon was so different to Lincolnshire. Back home you could see for miles in any direction, breathing was easy. Here, with the high hedges, it was difficult to get a view of your surroundings. By now, Reigneth had grown accustomed to going upstairs to bed and never tired of the moorland views the house afforded, each bedroom window offering a different perspective. She liked the gently rolling landscape; it made her think of a huge, soft eiderdown, covering field after field. She loved how green the fields were, so lush and fertile. When she walked out with Jukel in the early mornings she could see the webs that tiny spiders had spun so carefully between the blades of grass, each one shimmering with droplets of dew. Even that seemed different here: the dew almost too excessive, too moist. Everything was in the extreme – a bit like her sensations were becoming. Her sense of smell seemed to be heightened; her taste buds too. *How odd,* she thought; it was as though she could almost *taste* the smells. Her perceptions of those around her were changing too: whereas before when she touched people she could see and feel things, now she could almost smell and taste their moods. It seemed crazy to Reigneth and she laughed to herself as she strode with Jukel along the bracken-strewn sheep trails up onto the moor. She had always thought she was a bit freaky, but it was really getting out of hand. "I am definitely in need of something to occupy my mind!" she said to Jukel, who wagged his tail at the sound of her voice.

Her dreams about the boy were increasing too, and now he was clearer than ever. She saw every detail of his face: his perfect teeth and wonderfully disarming smile. His nose small and straight, his cheekbones pronounced and his hair so dark, thick and untidy. His mouth was shapely and full, but she did not linger too much on thoughts of his lips as this brought other feelings that to her were as yet unfathomable and disturbing. She felt as if her bones turned to liquid when she thought of his body and on waking from dreams of him, the memory lingered, washing over her as though she were enveloped in a warm film.

On this particular day she had, as usual, escaped from the back of the house and with Jukel at her heels had run through the orchard and up onto the open expanse of the moor. The wind was blustery, the sky overcast and the landscape sharp with that clarity that often precedes rain. Breathless, she stopped and wrenched the constricting band from her hair, shaking out her plait and digging in her fingers, massaging the roots to disperse the pins and needles. She bent her head forward so that her hair cascaded around her like a black veil, reaching almost to the ground. It felt wonderful to have it loose; she had begun to resent the fact that her mother always wanted her to wear it braided. Laughing, Reigneth flung it back and raced on, Jukel leading the way. Ahead of her, smooth and grey like the body of a huge elephant, a large granite rock jutted out of the ground. Reaching it, she scrambled to the top and stood, breathing deeply, to gaze across the moor.

Just over a year since his father's death, Johnny was once again on his way home. For him, the months seemed to have passed very quickly. At first he had been worried sick about his mother, but she seemed to have coped with minimum fuss; seemed fine in fact, just the same as she always had. Johnny found this disturbing, for while he was used to his mother holding her emotions in check, he was sure her apparent lack of distress was not normal behaviour. It was almost as if she did not really care – and yet Johnny could not bring himself to believe that was true. For himself, he missed Harry keenly. They had not been particularly close, not like with his mother, but his father had always been there for him; always generous, both with his money and, more importantly, with his affection. After the funeral, Johnny had been relieved to get back to university; losing himself in his music made it easier to forget his father had gone forever. Now, on his way home, he felt the loss all over again.

His first priority when he got back was to ride Rannoch; the stallion was getting fat and lazy. It had been too long since they had ridden up onto the moor. Sometimes Johnny's homesickness for the Devon moorland was unbearable. None of his friends understood his need to get home to see Rannoch, the moor and his family – he acknowledged that his priorities were probably in that order, although Matthew had come to figure in there somewhere too.

Greetings accomplished; a quick change of clothes and with a sandwich in hand, he was off. It was a blustery raw day; threatening rain but with no mist, the sort of day he liked. Not many people would be out walking – or so he thought, so he was surprised when he saw the girl standing on top of a rock looking out over the moor. She seemed to be alone apart from a huge dog at her side. Curious, he rode slowly towards her. As he got nearer and took in her breathtaking beauty, he knew with absolute certainty that he would remember this moment for the rest of his life.

The dog itself was startling enough: an enormous German Shepherd. *Surely they don't grow that big?* thought Johnny, aghast. It was black with gold-coloured markings; its ears pricked, eyes alert and questioning, constantly looking from its mistress to their surroundings, scanning the moor. It was obvious to Johnny that the dog was guarding her and equally obvious that it adored her. He was hardly surprised. He had never seen the girl before and had no idea who she was, but on first sight, he adored her too.

As he approached she turned her head. She looked wild, her hair streaming out behind her, the wind whipping strands of it into her eyes. She seemed unperturbed, gently stroking the hair off her face while gazing at the view. Johnny reflected that anyone else out in this weather would by now have been making efforts to get inside, but she leaned against the wind, apparently happy and contented to be there.

Then she turned to face him and meeting her gaze, he could not look away. A look of recognition seemed to pass over her face and her lips lifted in a soft smile, the warmth of it reaching out to caress him. Johnny knew it was rude to stare, but he could not help himself. His heart lurched. He had never in his whole existence seen anyone so beautiful. She wore no makeup of any kind: hers was a natural beauty that nothing could enhance. And she was smiling at him as if she had known him all her life. From that moment, Johnny was lost. He knew that nothing would ever be quite the same again; knew that thoughts of her would fill his every waking moment – his dreams too – and that he would never be at ease unless he was with her. And to think he had always scoffed at the notion of 'love at first sight'!

Reigneth had known even at a distance that it was him; had she not seen him hundreds of times before? Her dreams had not done him justice though, he was beautiful. She was unable to control the rapid beating of her heart, felt her cheeks flush. As he came nearer and each one of his features became more clearly defined, she was amazed at just how accurate her dreams had been. She began to smile, the kind of smile that greets a long lost friend. He would think she was barmy, she thought, but still she could not stop smiling. She wanted to jump from the rock and fling her arms around him. He had taken his time showing himself, but here he was at last. Reigneth was not afraid or nervous, not even shy, just happy that she had found him. Now was the beginning of the better part of her life.

Johnny assumed the girl was on holiday. Locals would not come up here on a day like this unless they had to, and he knew most of them anyway. Tourists were always underestimating the weather conditions on the moor, many got lost; some stayed lost. Dartmoor was beautiful, but it was also treacherous, the weather could change so swiftly, you had to be able read the moor and know what you were doing. Much as Johnny loved it – more than that, it was his lifeblood – he knew not to take liberties with it. He glanced around at the lowering clouds: the wind had got up and at any moment the light drizzle would turn to heavy rain. His chest tight with inexplicable emotion, he felt a surge of protectiveness towards this stunning girl, who was looking at him as if he was a long lost friend. Johnny had never seen anyone more lovely. He was spellbound and knew he just had to speak to her. Nudging Rannoch to the foot of the rock, he looked up at her. The dog at her side growled a warning and she rested her hand on its head, the smile still lingering on her lips.

"Hi, are you lost?" Johnny had to shout to make himself heard over the noise of the wind.

"Not any more," she announced, holding his gaze.

To Johnny the moment seemed frozen in time, which was a strange feeling. There was something 'otherworldly' about her that made his spine tingle. He wondered fleetingly if his mind was playing him tricks. Nobody could be that beautiful for real. Maybe she was a figment of his imagination – a moorland sprite come to spirit him away. He chuckled at the preposterous thought, his face lighting up as he grinned at her. "The weather's closing in. Shall I show you the way back to where you are staying?"

"No thanks. We're fine, we know the way, but we'll walk a little of the way with you if you wish."

Johnny was at once intrigued by the girl. He noticed she said 'we' all the time, the dog was so much a part of her. Its gaze remained fixed on him, vigilantly following his every movement. He knew why the girl was not afraid; he doubted she was ever afraid. Warily, Johnny dismounted, sliding slowly off Rannoch's back. Even so, it was too fast for the dog. It rose to its feet, teeth bared, a low rumbling growl emerging from its lips. The stallion flinched away and Johnny went swiftly to his head to reassure him.

The girl put a restraining hand on the dog's collar, "Be quiet, Jukel, he's a friend."

Johnny liked her use of the word 'friend'; it made him feel warm inside. He watched as she climbed down from the rock, jumping the last bit to land both feet on the springy turf. He wondered how old she was and guessed about nineteen or twenty – not much younger than him – she seemed so self-assured.

"Jukel? That's an unusual name," Johnny remarked, holding out a cautious hand for the dog to sniff, relieved to find his fingers still intact.

"He's an unusual dog," the girl laughed, "and I am Reigneth."

"Reigneth?" He tried the name on his tongue, "So what does that mean?"

She giggled. "Nothing. It's the place where my great-aunt was born."

"Ah," he grinned, not sure if she was teasing him. "I live over there," he pointed in the vague direction of his home, "and this is Rannoch."

"He is beautiful." Reigneth reached out to stroke the stallion's soft nose. "Do you always ride him bareback?"

"Mostly; he's never needed breaking. It's like he always knows what I want him to do. Do you ride?"

"I used to. Not any more. Our horse died."

"Oh, I'm sorry." Johnny looked down, and fiddled with Rannoch's halter.

"No need. He's where he wanted to be."

Once again, Johnny was intrigued by the strangeness of her words. There was a moment's pause as he cast around for something else to say. "How long are you staying?"

"Quite possibly forever."

"Sorry?" he said, confused.

Snorting with laughter, Reigneth shook her head and set off down the hill. Entranced, Johnny fell in beside her, his heart beating double time. As he had predicted, it started to rain. They chatted for a while, but out of the sheltering lee of the rock it was hard to compete with the wind, so after a while they walked in silence, but it was an easy, natural silence. They made their way along the narrow path, Jukel wedged in between them. Johnny bent to pick up a stick and threw it for Jukel to fetch. The dog ignored it, looked up at him then at Reigneth.

"He's not much of a stick and ball kinda dog," Reigneth said.

"Surely all dogs like to play fetch."

"Not this one, certainly not when there's a stranger about," she smiled at him.

"What sort of dog is he then?"

"He's more of a guard and attack kinda fella," she laughed

out loud. "Don't worry I'll protect you." Serious now, she added, "Always."

Johnny gulped, looked at the dog then back at Reigneth. A teasing smile curved her lips as she idly fondled Jukel's ear and for a moment Johnny wished he could change places with the dog.

After they had gone about half a mile, the ground dipped down to a lane. Reigneth pointed, "I turn off here to go home."

Her face was wet with rain, her hair in rattails, her perfect lips lifted in an enchanting smile as she gazed at him. Johnny had never seen a smile so lovely; imagining kissing it made him feel dizzy and he put out a hand to Rannoch's neck to steady himself; tearing his gaze away to look to where she pointed. He knew the lane. There was nothing down there except the house where the Pritchards lived. Now he thought about it, he remembered hearing they had relatives living with them. All at once the pieces fitted into place. Johnny felt a huge surge of excitement: if this beautiful girl was here to stay he would surely see her again.

"Well, I'll leave you here then," he said. "My name's Jonathan, by the way. Jonathan Wilmot."

"Yes," she answered and smiled again. Turning away from him, she started walking down the lane.

He panicked. "Wait, wait. Will I see you again?"

She half turned; looked back over her shoulder, a slight frown creasing her brow as though he had asked a stupid question. "Of course you will," she said then walked on.

He stood watching her, thinking, *Look back at me; please look back at me.* Reaching the bend in the lane, almost as if she had heard his thoughts, Reigneth turned and waved. Overjoyed, Johnny raised his hand and beamed at her.

He slept badly that night, thoughts of Reigneth filling his head. His pillow was too soft, his bed too hard, duvet too thick, eventually he gave up trying, deciding it would be best just to get up early and make a drink. His head was throbbing and he could not stop thinking about her. Johnny felt as if the very point of his existence had been realised on the moor yesterday; the day he had met Reigneth. Nothing before that moment made any sense and he was unable to have any rational thought that did not include her.

His mother was already up and had one or two jobs in store for him. She was due at a show the following day and was busy;

the twins were staying with Granny Gill at the holiday house in Cornwall, so Johnny was the gopher. He was tired and irritable with his mother. He wanted to ride up onto the moor to see if he could see Reigneth again, but Grace had forgotten to collect her meat order from the butcher's in Chagford and wanted him to get it for her and she was insufferable when she did not get her own way. Johnny had not intended to stay at home for the whole summer break, but now he had seen the girl, he knew he would be unable to tear himself away, even if it meant putting up with his bad-tempered mother. Fuming, he jumped into the Land Rover, driving far too fast down the narrow lanes.

He abandoned rather than parked the Land Rover in a side street in Chagford and dashed to Price's, the butcher's, wondering what else his mother had forgotten and whether he should ring her before he went home to save being sent on another errand. Having collected the meat he rummaged for his mobile and rushed unseeing out of the door, cannoning straight into Reigneth.

Their heads collided knocking the girl off balance. As she lurched backwards Johnny shot out his left arm to catch her and Jukel bounded up to him, snarling, his lips turned back to reveal a wicked set of teeth.

"Down Jukel!" Reigneth shouted. The dog stopped in mid-stride and dropped instantly to the ground. Johnny was so amazed he let go of the girl's arm. She teetered, overbalanced and fell into the wall, crashing her head against the brickwork and sliding down it, coming to rest on the pavement.

Stunned by the rapid turn of events, Johnny looked down on the girl at his feet. She had gone a very peculiar colour; a thin film of sweat covered her face and upper lip, the dazed look in her eyes seeming to indicate that she had fallen with considerable force. "I am so sorry. I just didn't see you there," Johnny stuttered, overcome with remorse.

"So I should hope! I'd hate to think you would do this to someone on purpose." Reigneth sat up and bent her head between her legs.

"Let me help you up, you don't look at all well," Johnny spluttered, thinking, *Trust me to do such a good job! What an idiot.* He stretched his hand out towards her and immediately froze when he heard a low rumbling growl. The girl hissed at Jukel and the dog backed off, his head on one side, never taking his gaze off his mistress. Johnny was impressed. He had never seen a dog so obedient. "Let me help you up," he said again. "I could take you to get a cup of tea."

As he spoke, Reigneth leaned over and was sick. Mortified, Johnny threw down his mother's bag of meat and bent to help her. "You look awful. I'm not leaving you on your own," he stated, "I'll take you home." He put his arms around her and was momentarily stunned by her close proximity. She had just vomited all over the pavement; nothing could be less romantic, and yet she still looked beautiful. He could not look away from her.

Reigneth stared up at him, as though seeing him clearly for the first time, "What must you think of me," she grimaced, clearly stricken with remorse. "I'm sorry; I don't usually vomit over people."

"I'll try not to take it personally," Johnny grinned. "I think you might be a bit concussed. Come on, let's get you home. It's Home Humber isn't it?"

Not waiting for her reply, he lifted her to her feet and guided her to the Land Rover, thanking his lucky stars that he had an excuse to keep his arm around her. Only then did he notice that the dog had demolished Grace's prime cut of beef. Putting firmly out of his mind how he was going to explain it to his mother, he helped Reigneth into her seat, apologising for the bits of mud and straw littering the front of the vehicle. Jukel, not waiting for an invitation, jumped into the back.

Johnny drove very carefully to the Pritchard's place, helped Reigneth out of the Land Rover and around to the back door, where he was met by an extremely cross-looking woman. Johnny did not need to be told he was facing Reigneth's mother. She was dressed all in black and was almost as stunning as her daughter. She took in the state of Reigneth and turned on Johnny with a face like thunder.

"Who are you and what have you done to my daughter?"

Johnny gulped, the woman was formidable. "I'm so sorry, we just sort of collided, entirely my fault, but your daughter hit her head and it's made her sick and dizzy so I've brought her home," he said lamely, adding as an afterthought, "I'm Johnny Wilmott. I really am sorry."

He made to help Reigneth indoors, but her mother stopped

him. She was plainly angry, bristling with irritation that made it clear he was an unwanted addition to the scene, "I think it's time you made yourself scarce, young man. Thank you, I can take it from here."

"It's alright, Ma," Reigneth protested in a weak voice, her face the colour of dough.

At that moment Richard Pritchard entered the kitchen. An affable if somewhat absent-minded man, he strode forward with a smile, "Johnny Wilmott isn't it?" He held out his hand, "It's good to see you again... " Richard's voice trailed away as he caught sight of his very pale niece. "Good grief Reigneth you look a queer shade, what happened to you?"

After a brief explanation to Richard, Johnny bade a hasty retreat, saying he would call by tomorrow to make sure Reigneth was alright. Driving away he was, to say the least, in a confused and distracted state, aware that he now had to face his mother about the missing meat since he had no money on him to buy more. He did at least have a plausible excuse for visiting Home Humber tomorrow. With that thought, Johnny's natural humour reasserted itself. *The dog must've thought it was his birthday*, he thought with a grin. *Mine too!* It wasn't every day you concussed the girl of your dreams. She could shout and scream at him if she wished, she could set the dog on him, but he wanted – no, he *needed* – to see her again. He hoped she was OK; he'd done nothing but think about her since he first saw her on the moor. Somehow tomorrow seemed too long for him to wait to see her again.

Reigneth's head ached where it had thumped against the wall and she still felt nauseous. She had been eager to come to bed; not because she felt awful, though she did, but because she wanted to be alone to think about Johnny. When a man had blundered out of the shop and knocked her flying, her first emotion had been one of anger. When her vision cleared and she had seen who it was, she knew she could not be angry with someone who looked like he did, never mind that he was clumsy. Even viewing him through the misty, blurred vision of mild concussion, he was still the most beautiful person she had ever seen. She had been appalled when she had emptied the contents of her stomach all over the pavement; how gross was that – yuk! Yet he had seemed not to mind. Nor had he appeared to mind when Jukel ate his shopping. Despite how she was feeling, the memory made her smile. Having Johnny's arms around her had felt wonderful; he was not a large man, but he was strong and sinewy. There was something about him that made her feel safe – which was funny given what had happened. Thinking about it now, Reigneth hugged her arms around herself trying to recapture the feeling. Eventually, the painkillers her mother had given her began to take effect and she drifted off to sleep, Johnny's face filling her mind.

The following morning Johnny again stood at the kitchen door of Home Humber. He drew a deep breath and knocked loudly. In an instant Reigneth's mother answered the door. He had hoped it would be Richard, but was faced with the woman who yesterday had not been too impressed with him, and given the scowl with which she greeted him he doubted he would get past her today.

"I just wondered how Reigneth was," he tried to sound casual.

"She's well, no thanks to you."

With relief, Johnny heard Reigneth's voice on the other side of the door, "Oh, Ma, let him in, he didn't mean to knock me flying and Juk ended up scoffing his dinner."

"You had better come in then," Jessie said grudgingly.

Johnny eased himself through the door and was transfixed by the girl before him. She certainly looked a better colour than when he had last seen her. Her hair was scraped back from her face in a French plait and she wore a bright blue blouse and jeans. Johnny knew his mouth was hanging open. Even though he had expected it, her beauty still had the power to surprise him and he felt foolish.

Seeing his expression, Reigneth laughed. "Hi, I'm really sorry about your dinner. Juk doesn't normally do anything so disobedient."

"No worries; it was beef – irresistible to a dog. I wouldn't blame him." Johnny shot her his lop-sided grin and was amazed to see a faint flush of pink stealing into her cheeks.

"Well, you might as well stay for a cup of tea now you're here," said her mother, pointing at a chair by the kitchen table.

Feeling decidedly awkward, Johnny sat down where indicated. "Thank you, Mrs, err... "

"Gray," she said, handing him a cup of tea. Passing one to Reigneth, she looked at them both, frowned, shook her head slightly, then picking up a tray loaded with cups and saucers, a teapot and a jug of milk, she swept out of the room with a muttered, "I'll be back in a minute, I'm just taking the others some tea."

As soon as she had gone, Johnny relaxed. "I'm afraid your mother doesn't like me very much."

"She is shy of strangers. Don't worry, she'll come round. It was a bit of a shock seeing me like that yesterday."

"Yes, of course. I'm so sorry. Are you sure you're alright?"

"Yes, I think it was the knock on the head that made me feel so queasy, sorry about being sick, a bit revolting to say the least."

"Oh, I wouldn't say that." Johnny grinned, "Then again... " They both laughed.

Gazing into each other's eyes, they drank their tea, chatting as though they had known one another for years and arranging to meet the following day.

The intimate atmosphere was disturbed by Jessie's return to the room. She eyed them both suspiciously and Johnny decided it was time to go. It was clear to him she was very protective of her daughter, which seemed odd given Reigneth's age. But perhaps, he thought on reflection, not really surprising given the girl's extraordinary beauty. It must have caused trouble with admirers over the years – though he had the distinct impression that Reigneth could look after herself. He wondered if she had a boyfriend; dismissed the thought; it was too unbearable.

Once again, he had a very restless night. Excited about seeing Reigneth, he gradually dropped into a light sleep in the early hours of the morning. One thing about Johnny was that he needed a full eight hours to be anything like human. He looked dreadful when he woke, with dark circles round his eyes. He gulped down a scalding hot mug of tea, rammed a round of toast into his mouth and was quickly on his way out the back door. He wanted to be out of the house before his mother could find him a chore. Besides, he wasn't her favourite person at the moment after he had allowed her meat to be eaten by Reigneth's mutt. He had rehearsed all sorts of excuses and in the end had settled for the truth. His mother had failed to see the funny side of it.

Johnny had brought Rannoch in from the paddock the night before, so just had to groom him down quickly and he was ready for the off. As he leapt onto the stallion's back he could hear his mother shouting his name. *A lucky escape!* he thought, leaving the yard as quietly as he could.

Reaching the top road that dropped down to Gidleigh, he saw Reigneth was already there waiting for him, the dog alert and suspicious at her side. Johnny grinned ruefully; it seemed that even the gift of best beef had done nothing to endear him to Jukel. Seeing Reigneth, he could hardly contain his excitement: there could be no pretence or game playing where she was concerned. Johnny knew he was head over heels in love with her. He wondered how she felt about him; wanted so much for it to be the same, half afraid he was wishing for the moon. As he approached, she gave a casual wave and as usual he was stunned by her appearance: her hair was perhaps the most distinctive thing about her, pitch black and long, reaching almost to her waist. Each time he had seen her, apart from the first day on the moor when it had been loose and wild around her, she had worn it scraped back into a thick plait, emphasising her delicate bone structure. He had memorised each curve and contour of her face: her eyes were almost a violet colour, framed by thick, dark lashes. Today she wore jeans, a red jumper, stout boots and held a small black jacket over her arm.

Johnny leaned down and held out his hand to Reigneth to help her up onto Rannoch's back. She stared at his fingers momentarily then at his face. He sensed her hesitation and mistook it for shyness. He was struggling with his emotions: he wanted to leap off Rannoch, seize Reigneth and hold her in his arms. It was frustrating, tantalising that she was so near, yet he could not hold her. He wondered if she was embarrassed by his close proximity. After all, they barely knew each other. He gestured with his hand for her to come closer and gave her his most disarming grin.

Staring up at his beautiful face, Reigneth's head felt like it was full of cotton wool. *Well come on girl,* she chided herself, *you can't stand here gawping forever!* Preparing herself for her reaction to his touch, she grasped his hand and hoisted herself up behind him. The stallion shook his head and Johnny spoke softly to him, bending to stroke Rannoch's neck.

Wrapping her arms firmly around Johnny's torso, Reigneth leant her head against his back. Now close against him, she felt his body all the way through her, from her chest down to her legs. The

74

feeling was so powerful it made her dizzy and lightheaded and for one very real moment she thought she was going to faint. The surge of energy that passed through them was electrifying to her. Did he feel it as she did? How could he not? She inhaled deeply, partly to stop herself from fainting and partly to gain more of the wonderful smell of him. It was delicious: a mixture of his aftershave and a musky, sweet smell that was all his own. She remembered how her Mam used to say she could pick out Joe's clothes blindfolded, just by his smell. Reigneth now understood what she had meant: this boy's smell was glorious. She clung to him, warm, comforted, not wishing to speak, wanting to savour the moment, but becoming aware that she was perhaps clinging too tightly, she moved back to put a little distance between them.

"Are you OK?" he asked, turning to look at her. His face was closer to hers than ever before and she drank in every detail. His hair was explosive. She wondered if he ever combed it, it was sort of gloriously messy. Reigneth had never had a boyfriend before, but she imagined most girls would be attracted to him. She smiled at him, "Yes thanks, I'm fine."

They rode up onto the moor and dropped down by Higher Wedicombe, it was the most natural thing in the world to call in to say hello to Matthew. As he grasped Reigneth's hand in welcome she knew in an instant the secret he had carried for so many years. She read in his face the anguish he experienced daily in neither seeing nor being able to openly acknowledge this wonderful boy as his son, and she realised that Johnny had no idea that Matthew was his father – at least, not consciously.

"Hello, Reigneth," Matthew said, "Jono's mentioned you once or twice," he grinned, the same lop-sided grin she was beginning to know so well. She did not understand how anyone could fail to see the resemblance. As soon as she touched Matthew's hand, Reigneth knew he was unused to physical contact; that he was burdened by sadness and was lonely, and that he was a good man. She also knew she was destined to be his daughter-in-law and that they would become very close, which pleased her, but more than that she could not see, though she knew more would come.

Releasing her hand, Matthew scrutinised her face, his gaze on her intense. It was almost as if he could see what others could not and Reigneth felt a little ill at ease. Could he sense something about her, she wondered. Did he guess at the tumble of emotions raging through her right now? Despite his scrutiny, however, she felt comfortable, drinking tea and chatting with him as they sat next to the big warm range in his kitchen.

On reflection, Reigneth thought it strange that instead of taking her to meet his mother, Johnny had brought her here. In fact he had not once mentioned his mother and Reigneth was curious about her.

All too soon it was time to go. They said goodbye and rode back the way they had come, arranging to meet again the following day.

Afraid that her mother would insist they spent more time at Home Humber, Reigneth slipped out of the house without telling Jessie she was seeing Johnny today. She did not feel ready to share him yet. She was hungry for his company, eager to learn as much about him as she could and happy just to sit listening as he talked. She was aware that she stared at him all the time, unable to look away from his beautiful face, which embarrassed her until she realised Johnny was just as busy looking at her. He was animated when they discussed things, explaining everything in minute detail; she liked that. He was intuitive, in tune with the moor and observant about nature, wildlife and birds. Reigneth knew her dad would have liked him. It remained to be seen if her mother ever would.

She got to their meeting place somewhat later than arranged and saw Johnny walking to meet her, his step impatient as he hurried towards her.

The brief meetings with Reigneth were not nearly enough for Johnny; he wanted more. She was different, this girl, everything about her was different; special. He realised he hardly knew her, yet he knew he would never be able to stay away from her. He wanted to know everything about her and every moment away from her was a strain.

"I thought you weren't coming," he said, running to meet her. "Did you have a problem?"

"No, no, sorry, I got a little delayed," she said breathlessly as he reached her.

Unable to resist kissing her, Johnny leant forward, bringing his mouth close to hers, but she placed her fingers on his lips, gently pushing him away.

Too soon, too soon, Johnny thought, kicking himself. Taking her hand he turned it over to place butterfly kisses on her palm then hugged her, savouring the moment of tenderness. He so loved her; her closeness was as electrifying as a static charge.

They moved apart and walked in silence hand in hand up onto the moor. The weather was warm and dry, a light breeze soughing through the long grasses. A buzzard circled high above their heads and Jukel, nose to the ground, ran on ahead. After a time, Johnny broke the silence, the words tumbling out of him.

"Can you still ride? If so, I was wondering if you'd like to go for a ride with me? Matthew has a safe pony you could use and we could head out tomorrow, make a day of it – maybe take a picnic?" He waited anxiously for her reply, revelling in the thought of having her to himself for a whole day.

Reigneth laughed, "Of course I can still ride, it's not something you forget. All my family can ride. I can't imagine anything I'd like more. I'll bring the picnic if you like."

Wordless with delight, Johnny squeezed her hand. They walked on, up to a rock formation, clambering onto a large flat stone to sit side by side, chatting, lapsing occasionally into a companionable silence. Jukel, ever present, lay at the base of the rocks. He looked relaxed but his ears were as pricked and alert as ever. The time passed far too quickly for Johnny, and it seemed only minutes before they were wending their way back.

"See you tomorrow, then." He wanted to kiss her mouth, but he was not about to make that mistake again. Reluctantly letting go of her hand, he brushed his lips against her flawless cheek then watched her walk away from him, waiting until she turned to wave.

At Higher Wedicombe Farm the next day, Matthew was up before the sun rose in a cloudless sky. Johnny had delivered Rannoch over to Matt's the day before; now Matt brought both Rannoch and Belle into the stable and was grooming them, his head full of thoughts of Grace. He had once bought a mare like Belle for Grace, hoping that one day she would be mistress of his home. This pony was the offspring of that mare. Always when Matthew thought of Grace his thoughts were tinged with sadness. He finished grooming and was saddling and bridling the pony when he heard Johnny and Reigneth arriving. They were chattering constantly, their infectious laughter bringing a grin to his face as he led Belle out into the yard.

"Hello you two, it looks as if you've picked a good day for a picnic, keep a weather eye out though." He smiled at Johnny, no need to warn his lad about safety on the moor. Matthew knew Johnny loved the lass, he had never seen him like this before.

Reigneth mounted the mare swiftly and adeptly. It was obvious to Matthew that Johnny need not have worried about her riding ability. He exchanged glances with his son and they grinned at each other.

Johnny and Reigneth rode steadily up onto the moor and eventually found a grassy clearing amidst the bracken where Rannoch and Belle could graze and Johnny could keep an eye on them. From this viewpoint he could see much of the moor: sheep and ponies grazed in the distance and here and there were yellow spangled gorse bushes and the odd hawthorn – the only variety of tree brave enough at this particular place to push its roots into the hard moorland turf. Johnny loved the different textures of grasses interspersed with the granite throughout the moor. He cast his gaze over the place he loved so well, inhaling deeply. Smiling at Reigneth, he believed he had at last found someone who could compete with his love of the moor. Someone he could love completely.

Johnny laid down his jacket for Reigneth to sit on, his mouth watering as he watched her taking from her rucksack the packed lunch she had prepared. The ride had made him hungry. While they ate their sandwiches, he told Reigneth some of the old tales and superstitions of the moor, of ghosts and pixies and strange swirling mists that could spirit you away never to be seen again. Reigneth had mentioned that her family were very superstitious and Johnny laughed at her reaction when she gave a visible shudder at the old stories.

The sky was clear; hardly any cloud but as usual there was a breeze. After eating their sandwiches they lay back on the grass. There was not a sound to be heard other than the bees and insects and the steady munching noise as the horses grazed the close-cropped moorland grass. Johnny could not remember when he had felt so happy.

Reigneth had asked him all about his family, but when he asked about hers and she began to speak of her father, her voice faltered.

It was clear to Johnny that she found it hard, her emotions still raw and painful following her loss. Thinking to change the subject, he brought his hand up to her face and gently traced the outline of her nose and mouth. He half expected her to object to his touch, but instead she held his hand to her face and placed her lips softly against his fingers. He found the very touch of her electrifying. He wanted desperately to hold her close, to claim her as his own. She had eluded his kiss before and he knew he needed to take things slowly. His body told him otherwise: his heart was beating frantically. Unsure of his ability to hold himself in check he sat bolt upright edging away from her. Relaxing a little, he drew his knees up and placed his arms round them, his head bent as he stared unseeing at the ground trying to regain his composure.

Reigneth sat up, "Is anything wrong?" she murmured.

"Heavens no, far from it," he said, surprised by her puzzled frown. "It's just that I'm afraid of seeming overly familiar." He shrugged apologetically, "I find it hard to believe we only met a week ago. It's like I've known you always."

"I feel the same," she smiled shyly.

As the sun moved lower in the sky, much as he wanted to stay there with Reigneth forever, Johnny knew it was time to go. They collected the horses and started back, heading towards Higher Wedicombe. Coming to a broad stretch of grass he knew well, he grinned at Reigneth, "Do you think you dare go a little faster? It's safe to canter here."

Reigneth smiled and kicked her mare on, leaving Johnny behind. He laughed and urged Rannoch to catch up. She rode full tilt, her hair streaming behind her, the ribbon holding her plait in check blew away on the breeze leaving her hair billowing in the wind. Turning the mare abruptly, she watched as Rannoch skidded to a halt, leaving both Reigneth and Johnny out of breath and giggling. Their smiles faded as they stared into one another's eyes. Her hair without its constricting band hung down her back almost to her waist and with each gust of wind tendrils hovered around her face. They had come to a standstill overlooking Matthew's farm. Reigneth's colour had heightened with the speed of their ride, she looked wild and had a huge smile on her face. *Could anyone really be this beautiful?* Johnny thought distractedly. They walked the horses down to the farm, already discussing what they would do the following day.

Once back at Higher Wedicombe and with Rannoch and Belle turned out for the night, Johnny drove Reigneth to Home Humber in the Land Rover. It was hard to say goodbye; he lingered to watch as she disappeared indoors.

It had turned blustery now on the moor; they had most certainly had the best of the weather. He came alongside the place where they had cantered together, the picture of her face in his mind's eye bringing a smile to his lips. Parking up on the verge he walked the stretch of grass and there, caught on a gorse bush and blowing in the wind, was Reigneth's hair ribbon, still knotted as it had been when it slid from her plait. Disentangling it he held it to his face feeling its silkiness on his cheek then gently kissed it. Having no intention whatsoever of returning it to her, he slid the ribbon into his pocket where it was to remain.

Chapter 7

Wistman's Wood

Having been brought up on the moor, though he respected it, Johnny had never known any fear of it: he was not at all superstitious and tales of ghosts and witches were to him just silly stories. He had many times made up search parties looking for lost walkers, but he had never for one moment worried about being lost or alone himself. Like Matthew, he knew Dartmoor like the back of his hand.

He had again borrowed the Land Rover for the day and he and Reigneth – and of course Jukel – headed out towards Wistman's Wood. They left the vehicle at the nearest parking place and made their way on foot towards the ancient oak wood. Unlike other oaks, these had failed to make normal height, growing stunted and taking an almost miniature form, their gnarled branches reaching out like tentacles to grasp unsuspecting passers-by. The twisted, tortured shapes of these ancient trees was at the same time both fascinating and horrifying. Dense moss covered the trunks and branches, green and lush, almost too bright and colourful to the eye. The ground underneath and around the oaks was littered with large granite boulders and stones that were also covered in thick, luscious moss. Johnny thought it beautiful and was in a happy, jubilant mood as he led Reigneth towards the wood.

There was something about Wistman's Wood that worried Reigneth. Each step she took made her feel more uncomfortable and her mood began to change. She became increasingly quiet and withdrawn and Jukel pacing at her side emitted a low steady growl.

Letting go of Johnny's hand, Reigneth stopped walking and stared at the distorted trees. She could feel evil emanating from the place and knew Jukel felt it too: his hackles were raised and his slow steady growl continued unabated. She shivered; her skin crawled and she felt suddenly cold. Reacting to the atmosphere the hairs on her neck began to prickle and the cloying stench of rotting dead matter filled her nostrils until she felt she could not breathe. How could Johnny not smell it? It was overpowering. Reigneth knew she had to get away from here. She wanted to run as fast as her feet would carry her. She called out to Johnny, who had wandered on ahead, "Can we go back? I don't like this place."

Laughing, he turned to her, "So who's been saying what about it?" His smile was instantly erased as he looked at her more closely. "Whatever's the matter? You've gone as white as a sheet." Johnny frowned, his face a picture of concern.

"Get me away from here, Johnny, please help me," she pleaded, feeling as if her legs were about to give way.

Rushing to her side, Johnny half carried her back to the Land Rover. "Here," he grabbed the bottle of mineral water from his rucksack and held it out to her, "have some water, you'll feel better."

Reigneth shook her head, "Just drive; as quick as you can." Her whole body was shaking. She sensed the presence of evil and felt in real danger while she remained. *I will never return here,*' she thought, gripped by a terrible fear that something evil was going to seek her out and follow her.

Slamming the vehicle into gear, Johnny drove fast back to Home Humber. He kept looking at her and squeezing her hand. Reigneth was aware that he was both worried and perplexed by her behaviour, but she was too shaken and subdued to reassure him.

Arriving home, she rushed indoors and threw herself into her mother's arms, knowing she would understand.

Jessie was all concern. "What is it my love? You look as if you've seen a ghost. Calm down, you're safe now." She led Reigneth to a chair by the kitchen table. "Sit down there and I'll make you a cup of tea then you can tell me what's wrong."

Still shaking, Reigneth sank gratefully into the chair. She felt distanced as if she wasn't really there. Dimly she heard her mother asking Johnny what had happened and his reply that she'd had some kind of panic attack, but he had no idea why. Reigneth sensed he was thinking she was being theatrical: a real drama queen.

After a few moments her fear began to subside a little and she was able to speak. "Tell me about that place, Johnny. I have to know what it was I felt there. It wasn't just me. Juk felt it too."

Johnny shrugged, "It's nothing, Reigneth. I think it's quite beautiful in an eerie sort of way. The story goes that Wistman's Wood is where the Devil and his Whist hounds – the hounds of hell – start their hunt to the Dewerstone and back again to the wood... " Johnny broke off and grinned at her, "That's the Devil's stone; 'Dewer' is the local name for the Devil. They say human footprints have been seen there as well as horses' hooves – even cloven hooves and enormous paw prints – and there have been tales of people found dead, killed in mysterious circumstances, but it's all nonsense, of course."

Glancing at Jessie, Johnny walked hesitantly to the table and rested his hand lightly on the back of Reigneth's chair, looking down at her with his lop-sided grin. "It's just superstition, Reigneth. There are lots of legends about the moor, many places that are supposed to be haunted, but everyone knows it's rubbish. The worst thing that can hurt you up there is if the weather turns bad or you get stuck in one of the bogs." He laughed, "And if you don't get sucked under and manage to get out, you stink to high heaven."

Reigneth grabbed hold of his hand, grasping it tightly, "Don't ever go to that place alone, Johnny, promise me." She looked up into his face and could see that he was struggling to understand her fervour, the grin leaving his lips as he gazed down at her. "Promise me," she repeated, "please."

"Of course I promise, if that's what you want. I'd never do anything to upset or distress you, Reigneth."

Satisfied, she let go of his hand, a sudden rush of nausea making her feel dizzy.

"I think you should say goodbye to Johnny now and go and lie down, you look far from well," her mother said, placing the teapot on top of the Aga to keep warm. "I'll bring your tea up in a minute." She glared at Johnny with a look that said she took a dim view of him frightening her daughter with such tales, then she left the room.

When she had gone, Johnny stooped to kiss Reigneth, delicately taking her face in his hands and kissing her gently on the lips. She returned his kiss, their breath mingling as their lips held for all too brief a moment.

"I'm sorry, Reigneth. I would not hurt you for the world," he muttered softly.

She caressed his cheek, gently cupping his face and drinking in his beauty. She loved him more than she had felt was possible and never wanted to be parted from him. "I know," she whispered as he planted a kiss on the palm of her hand then, with a final look at her, turned away.

Feeling agitated and close to tears, Reigneth got up from the chair and went to the window, watching him walk down the path, almost overwhelmed by her sudden longing to run after him and beg him to stay. Wistman's Wood had disturbed her terribly, her head pounded and she felt unwell, but still she didn't want Johnny to leave her.

Reigneth knew she would dream that night and when it came it was terrifying. She was alone in the middle of the moor, a mist swirling around her feet. Then she saw the Dewar, or *Beng* as her people knew the Devil, mounted on a black horse. The pack of black Whist hounds ran slavering at its heels, their blood-red eyes hungry for her. She began to run, knew her very life depended on it, her chest heaving, her breath coming in deep, rasping gasps. On and on she ran, gulping in air until her lungs felt as though they would explode. She could see the gnarled trunks of the oak trees on the horizon, the branches waiting to grasp her. She screamed, but no sound came out.

Suddenly she was floating: someone was lifting her and enfolding her in his embrace. She recognised his smell and knew she was safe; safe in her father's arms. She felt a gentle kiss on her forehead and looked to see her dad right next to her, holding her tight. A warm, cosy sensation was spreading throughout her whole body. *Beng* would never get her now.

It was so good to see him, she smiled and he returned her smile, his lovely warm grin comforting her immediately and although his mouth did not move she heard his words. He told her he had not come for her, but only to reassure her. That he loved her and Mam and would never leave them. He was watching over them and she need never be afraid. *I'll only ever be one step away, my darling,* he soothed.

Jessie had got out of bed to use the bathroom and heard Reigneth mumbling in her sleep. Afraid her daughter was having a bad dream, she silently opened the bedroom door. The smell hit her like a wrecking ball as she entered the room. She would know that smell anywhere: her Joe was in here, the scent of him filled her nostrils. She froze on the spot. Her first thought was that Joe had come for Reigneth and she was afraid. Tears welled and her throat constricted with emotion. "No, Joe, take me, not our daughter. I want to go with you, I miss you so much," she whispered, looking frantically around the room.

Then she saw Reigneth's eyes were open and she was smiling. "Don't be afraid, Mam. He's not come for either of us. He just came to comfort me." As her daughter spoke, Jessie felt a tightening around her whole body and knew her husband was holding her. Reeling with shock and the agony of her loss, she felt a soft breath next to her ear. It reminded her sharply of the ecstasy she had known with Joe and for the first time in months she felt her body relax. This was where she belonged, in the arms of this man, this being whom she adored beyond reason. Jessie swayed forward, but as quickly as it had come the feeling was gone. For a moment she stood there, then regaining her senses, darted to Reigneth's side, enfolding her daughter frantically, her arms wrapping around her.

Easing back from her, Reigneth touched Jessie's cheek and smiled. "Don't be frightened, Mam, he will come to claim you back one day, but not for a long time yet."

They both heard the landing floorboards creak and Reigneth leaned across to the bedside table and switched on the lamp.

"Is everything alright?" Liz came cautiously into the bedroom and sniffed the air, "What's that strange smell? Not unpleasant, sort of sweet... and why does it feel so cold in here?" As if to emphasize the point, she shivered, "It's making my hair stand on end." As she spoke, she looked down at her sister and niece huddled together on the bed, a question in her eyes.

"Joe was here," Jessie said, knowing that Liz would accept it just as though she'd said the postman had been.

"Ah, so that's it," Liz smiled, visibly relaxing. "That's alright then."

Once again, Jessie thanked her lucky stars that she was living with one of her own and never had to explain the improbable.

Johnny woke the following morning just as it was getting light. He had been worrying about Reigneth all night and as a result hadn't slept well, yet again. Yawning, he lay for a while mulling over the events of the previous day. Reigneth's behaviour had freaked him out a little. He had tried to make light of it and be sympathetic, but seemed only to have succeeded in making things worse. Perhaps it was simply that she and her mother were very superstitious: they certainly seemed to have overreacted to what was just an old folktale.

As soon as he was up and breakfasted, he phoned Reigneth to check she was all right and they made arrangements to meet that afternoon. Assured that he would see Reigneth later, he decided to go for a ride. He did not go far, but he let the stallion have his head and the ride refreshed them both. Returning home, Johnny rubbed Rannoch down and turned him out into the paddock, then wandered indoors to make himself a drink. Just as he began to wonder where his mother was, she came into the kitchen. She was wearing a pair of trendy overalls, a sight that never failed to amuse him. She always looked so pristine. Even when he and the twins had been small and she had helped them muck out their ponies, she had always seemed so clean and tidy with never a hair out of place. He stooped over her to kiss her on the cheek. She smelt lovely: familiar.

She smiled up at him and ruffled his already messy hair. "Have you had a nice ride dear?" A slight note of reproach crept into her voice, "Rannoch could do with the exercise. You've been neglecting him of late."

Well here goes,' Johnny thought. He would tell her about Reigneth; it would be easier than having to keep sloping off. "I've been meeting up with the Richard Pritchard's niece and we've been going for walks on the moor."

"Oh, have you? I've not met them yet, but everyone says the girl is nice," his mother said absently as she began making a cup of tea.

Johnny was surprised. He had expected more of a reaction. "So where are the twins?" he asked. The house had seemed so quiet without them and he was glad when they had returned from Granny Gill's a couple of days ago, though he had hardly seen them since.

"They've just nipped down to Chagford, but they won't be long."

As if on cue he heard the front door bang. Henry and Charlotte, giggling about some private joke, dashed along the hall and tumbled into the kitchen, their cheeks flushed and their eyes sparkling with laughter.

"Hey you guys, what's so funny?" Johnny beamed, pleased to see them.

"Nothing, just Henry being stupid," Charlotte replied, flinging her arms around Johnny's neck. He grinned, he loved his little sister.

"Yuck! You stink like Rannoch!" She wrinkled her nose, "You've been riding."

"Yeah, and now I'm just off to meet up with Reigneth Gray."

"Who's she?"

"The Pritchards' niece."

"Oh yeah?" Henry butted in. "Wow! She's really something. Got an unusual name... yeah, Reigneth that's it."

"How do you know that, Henry?" Charlotte raised an eyebrow.

"Well, I've noticed, obviously, she's really pretty."

"Says you," Charlotte grinned.

Johnny found himself getting annoyed with Henry; it was not an emotion he was used to. "Get your eyes tested little brother, Reigneth is so much more than pretty, she's absolutely gorgeous."

"Yeah, well I've only seen her at a distance a couple of times," Henry said, "she doesn't seem to mix much. I'll get to see more of her soon though," he winked at Charlotte, who giggled. "She's starting at sixth form college same as us after the summer, so I heard."

"*What?*" Johnny's mouth dropped open and he stared at Henry in disbelief. "Are you saying she's the same age as you?"

"Yeah – well I think so, she'll either be doing AS's or A2's. She could be the same age as us or a year younger, why?"

"But that's only fifteen!"

"Well spotted, Bro, you are on form today!"

Johnny felt as if his world had suddenly collapsed. A short time ago he had been feeling elated and happy. Suddenly he felt miserable: Reigneth, his beautiful Reigneth, was a definite no go area. He was aware the twins were saying something to him, but he could not seem to focus. Nothing anyone said registered. Only *fifteen*! She was a *child*. Why had she not told him? Why had her mother not objected to him spending time alone with her daughter when it was obvious he was so much older than she? Why had Reigneth misled him?

He wondered if he should go down to Home Humber and have it out with her, he needed to get a grip on himself first though. At the moment he just felt like crying and that would never do. He needed to be alone to gather his thoughts. Quickly excusing himself, Johnny rushed out of the kitchen, dimly aware that his mother was staring after him over her cup of tea.

Pulling on his jacket he left by the front door, closing it quietly behind him. He decided to go for a walk: the cool air would help him get his thoughts in order, but his feet took him in the direction of Home Humber. By the time he reached the house he was running, out of breath and red in the face. He went round to the back as he had always done and Jessie answered the door.

"Good morning, Mrs Gray," he puffed, "I'm sorry to disturb you, but can I speak to Reigneth please?"

There was no hint of welcome in her expression as she looked him up and down. "You had better come in, I'll call her."

"Thank you."

By the time Reigneth entered the kitchen, Johnny's thoughts were a jumble and he felt close to tears. "Could we talk somewhere privately?" he asked.

Reigneth searched his face, her smile fading. "Of course, is something wrong?" She led the way through to a cosy sitting room at the back of the house. Johnny sat on the sofa and Reigneth perched beside him. Despite it being June a fire was burning in the grate and Jukel lay panting on the bare wooden floor near the door, trying to keep cool.

"I was in here reading," Reigneth said, gesturing to a book that was open face down on the small coffee table.

"Oh." Johnny knew he should say something more, but he was not into small talk just now.

"So what's the matter?" she asked. "You've obviously got something on your mind."

"My brother and sister have just returned home from holiday in Cornwall with our grandparents."

"That's nice, but what's it got to do with me?"

"I told them I'd been seeing you and they told me you'd be starting sixth form with them next term." Johnny spoke the words as quickly as he could, almost as if saying them would disprove their validity.

Reigneth looked taken aback. "I don't know who I'll be in class with, but yes, I will be starting at sixth form college next term," she replied a gentle smile hovering around her delicious mouth. "What about it?"

"How old are you Reigneth?" Johnny asked the question and braced himself for what he did not want to hear.

"I'm fifteen – why?"

It was the worst possible answer. Johnny looked down at the floor, covered his face with his hands. This was a disaster: he was rising twenty-two and she was a schoolgirl. Why could nothing be straightforward for him?

Reigneth pulled his hands down from his face, "What is it, Johnny, what's wrong?" Her innocence shone out of her eyes.

"I had no idea you were so young, you should have told me," he burst out, his voice breaking slightly.

"I'm sorry Johnny, but I don't see what difference my age makes to anything."

His mouth dropped open, "You don't see what *difference* it makes? And what if we had made love? What then? I had no idea you were so young. You are under age – we'd be breaking the law for God's sake!" Johnny spoke in a flurry of exasperated anger, barely registering Reigneth's expression of horrified shock at his words.

After a moment's stunned silence, Reigneth got up slowly and purposefully from the sofa. She looked down at him for a moment, her mouth twisted as though he was repugnant to her. "What an arrogant, presumptuous thing to say. I am afraid I shall have to ask you to leave," she said coldly.

Astonished, Johnny remained motionless gazing up at her. He opened his mouth, intent on justifying his anger, but she cut across him.

"No, Johnny, I don't want to listen to any more. I might lose my temper with you and say hurtful things. I really don't want that to happen. Please go." She turned away and walked to the door, clicking her fingers at the dog. Jukel moved immediately to stand at her side and she twisted her fingers into his thick coat and pulled him close – it was the only indication that she was less in control than she appeared.

Reigneth's actions made it clear to Johnny that he really was expected to leave. In silence he followed her as she walked steadily to the back door and held it open for him. Once out in the fresh air he turned to speak to her, but the door was already shut behind him. Feeling as though he had just been kicked in the pit of his stomach, Johnny turned away and walked blindly up onto the moor, his eyes filling with scalding tears.

Reigneth was not given to fits of emotion and had become used to disguising her feelings – it was so often necessary – but she stayed in the sitting room for much of the day not wanting to talk with her mother, who more than anyone was able to read her moods. Her book lay open on her lap, but she was quite unable to concentrate on reading. Johnny's words, so unexpected and so repugnant, went round and round in her head and she was still in a state of shock. Excusing herself on the grounds of a headache, Reigneth went early to bed and wept silently into her pillow. She knew she would not see Johnny for quite some time. He had a lot of growing up to do, she would miss him, but most of all she was disappointed in him.

The following day, Johnny was back at Home Humber and standing on the front doorstep. He hesitated to knock on the door, but after taking a deep breath he lifted the heavy brass knocker. The sound of it reverberated through the house. He did not know why he had gone to the *front* door – perhaps because it seemed more formal. He heard light, quick footsteps and Reigneth opened the door to him. He had never seen her looking more lovely. She did not smile, simply waited for him to speak, the dog as ever at her side.

"I wanted to talk to you about what happened yesterday," he said. She was so beautiful it took his breath away and he did not know if he would be able to get the words out that he wanted to say. At this moment he could easily forget she was just fifteen, she seemed so self-assured, so mature and it was he who felt like a callow schoolboy.

"Come this way," she showed him into a large sitting room at the front of the house. He had never been inside this room before and it was a revelation to him. The room was sumptuous and inviting, the colours rich and opulent. There were two sofas that looked old, but comfortable, the sort to curl up in and relax. It was a welcoming room – in stark contrast, Reigneth's expression was anything but.

"Please sit down. What was it you wanted to say?" She seemed detached from him, was that really how she felt?

"I'm really sorry if what I said yesterday upset you, you know I would never intentionally hurt you, but you should have told me you were only fifteen. It was a bit of a shock," he said, thinking *and that's the understatement of the year!*

"I'm sorry you felt it was relevant. I didn't know there was an age limit on friendship," she replied calmly.

"No, of course not, but is that what we are to be? Just friends? I had thought perhaps we were to be something more."

"Yes, you made that very obvious yesterday."

Johnny flushed. He could not understand why she was being so unreasonable. "Come on, Reigneth, be fair. I kissed you; you kissed me back. You cannot blame me for thinking there was more to it than mere friendship – and you cannot get away from the fact that if we had made love I would have been guilty of... well... you are under age."

"I'm sorry, Johnny, but I was under the impression that making love was a decision made by two people and it was never a possibility as far as I was concerned. I think perhaps you may have presumed too much."

Dropping his gaze, Johnny's flush deepened at her tone. Well that had put him firmly in his place. She obviously did not feel the same way about him as he did about her. "Clearly I've offended you and I'm sorry," he murmured, "it was unintentionally done. Perhaps I had better leave." He hoped against hope that she would ask him to stay, that they could put all this behind them, laugh about the misunderstanding and even though she was so much younger than he, start afresh.

"Yes, perhaps that would be for the best," she replied.

Johnny stared at her, unwilling to believe she was giving him the brush off, yet forced by her unbending expression to accept that it was over before it had hardly begun.

Reigneth's heart beat frantically in her chest. She did not want Johnny to go, but he had made assumptions about her that she found particularly offensive. One of her own kind would never have spoken to her as he had done. In fact, had any of her family got wind of what had taken place between them, it would not be the police he had to worry about! James, for one, would have used his fists to make Johnny pay. No Romany would ever treat a girl with the disrespect he had shown towards her.

With fresh eyes she looked at him now and saw a man instead of a boy. His boyish looks had deceived her. He was a man with very real needs. She had little knowledge of *Gauja* behaviour, but she remembered how the *Gauja* girls at her previous school used to tease each other about their boyfriends. They had not thought it unusual to have sex with boys they had known for only a short while, and many had been sexually active for quite some time. This was not Reigneth's way or that of her family. Romany girls were very definitely 'look but don't touch'. Most married young and were virgins when they married: sex before marriage was unthinkable.

Reigneth was confused: perhaps she had been wrong in what she saw of the future? She had been so sure Johnny was the love of her life, but now what she felt for him seemed to have been besmirched and it broke her heart. She became aware that she had drifted off into her own private world and that Johnny, still seated, was staring at her. She stood in order to show him out and he followed her lead, stepping out into the hot sun. He looked at her for a moment as though about to say something, then shook his head and turned away.

Johnny trudged back to the Land Rover, his legs seemed to weigh a ton and every movement was an effort. He felt like crying as he climbed onto the seat and turned the key in the ignition. He knew he did not want to return home in case his mother was there. He could not bear the thought of talking to her about Reigneth and she would be sure to ask. He would be too embarrassed, yet he needed to speak to someone. He found himself heading for Higher Wedicombe Farm, Reigneth's words echoing in his head. She was right, he had made assumptions and he had been arrogant. So used to everyone thinking he was wonderful he had just assumed this lovely girl would fall at his feet in adoration. What an idiot! He remembered how she had pushed him away when he had first tried to kiss her. He had thought her self-assured, but little things she had said or done came back to him now. If he had only had his eyes open instead of being so blinded by desire, he would have seen her naivety and recognised her innocence. He should have known.

Kicking himself, Johnny swung the Land Rover into the farmyard and got out just as Matthew came walking round the side of the barn towards him.

"What's up lad – you look dejected. Want to come in for a chat?" Matthew led the way to the house.

"I'm just an idiot, Matt," Johnny burst out, slumping onto the rickety wooden chair in front of the range.

"Lass trouble, eh? I thought that bonnie girl was keen on you."

Johnny groaned. "Did you really, Matt? So did I, but it's not as simple as that."

"Well I didn't really think it would be, couldn't be really, knowing what she is."

"What do you mean, *what she is*?" Johnny bristled.

"Easy there, I didn't mean any harm, but you're different; things to work out... " he shrugged, "it was never going to be easy."

"I have not the faintest idea what you're talking about."

"Well, her sort don't often mix with our kind, they are different," Matthew said, filling the kettle and reaching in the cupboard for two mugs.

"Matt, can you please just explain what you mean because at the moment I have no idea. I've had a fall out with Reigneth because she's only fifteen."

His eyes widening in surprise, Matthew ran his fingers through his hair. "Well, I can see that's a shocker, but that's only one of your problems."

"For God's sake will you stop talking in riddles and tell me what you're getting at, my temper is on a short fuse."

"You're really suffering aren't you? Don't misunderstand me, Jono. It was obvious to me the first time I saw you together that you were made for each other. She's a great girl, plenty of spirit and proud of what she is, I like that."

Johnny gritted his teeth, "What is she, Matt? What do you mean? I'm running out of patience. Tell me!"

"Well, patience is something you may have to learn to cultivate young man," Matthew grinned, handing Johnny a mug of tea. "Jono, you must know she's a Gypsy – and proud of it I'd guess. Romany, you can't miss it. Did you not notice she looks a bit foreign like?"

"Yes, of course I noticed that, but I never thought she was a Gypsy. Besides, it doesn't make any difference to me, Matt, I couldn't care less. It's just her age that's the problem."

"That's as may be, but it will make a difference to her I'm guessing. The age thing doesn't matter, Jono. When she reaches eighteen you'll be rising twenty-five; when she's twenty-two you'll be twenty-eight, do you see what I'm getting at? It's nothing; the problem is only of this minute. The age gap will shrink. Time will change it; you will just have to be patient. I should think, though, that it will not be the only problem you'll face. Whether we like it or not, you are both from different backgrounds, the Romany culture is a lot different from ours. And then there's the prejudice you'll face: your mother for one will not like it one bit."

"I still don't see what difference it makes," Johnny looked down at his feet, brow furrowed in concentration, would his mother not like it? He did not think she was prejudiced at all. His thoughts busy, he became aware that Matthew was prattling on, saying something about Gypsies. "Sorry, Matt. What did you say?"

"I was telling you there was a Romany family used to come by here every year when my mother was young. I remember her talking about them. They used to stop by in late June, help my grandfather with haymaking and any other jobs we had. Good workers. There were quite a few of them, from what my mother said. She liked them. Said they looked after their own and kept themselves to themselves, especially the lasses – didn't let them run around getting into trouble, if you know what I mean. And they tend to marry young, as I remember."

As he listened, Johnny began to realise why Reigneth had been so offended and the more he thought about it, the more reasonable her attitude seemed. He was the unreasonable one. Coming from her background it was only natural she would be upset by his crass behaviour. What an idiot he was.

"Matt, tell me what else you know about Romany culture, I need to know so I don't go making any more gaffs."

"Sorry, I've told you all I know. The best person to talk to is Richard Pritchard; after all, he's lived with a Romany for twenty years or more."

"Elizabeth? I didn't know she was a Gypsy."

"Well, I suppose it's not obvious, she's lived amongst us for a long time, but she doesn't mix in much. She's pleasant enough, but she doesn't get involved with anything, keeps herself to herself like.

And your lass's mother is her sister."

"Yes, of course. Mrs Pritchard is Reigneth's aunt – I'm not thinking straight." Johnny glugged down his tea, now lukewarm, and stood up to go. He was determined to have a private word with Richard Pritchard as soon as he could. He found himself questioning his motives, though: if the age thing was an insurmountable problem for him, what was the point of speaking to Richard? It did not add up.

Back at Home Humber Reigneth sat in the kitchen quietly reflecting on her conversation with Johnny. He obviously had a problem with her age, but it was strange to her. She did not feel young; in truth she never had. It was ironic to her that Johnny thought she was too young for him. The obstacle was of his own making and all in his mind. Her people did not view this sort of thing as a problem. If two people where right for one another their respective ages were immaterial. And whatever her age, how dare he assume she would let him make love to her before marriage.

Not only was Reigneth irritated with Johnny, but she had inadvertently overheard Richard talking about Emily, his mother, and that had made her bad mood even worse.

"We will have to put her somewhere," he had said casually to Elizabeth, referring to the old lady as if she were a book he had misplaced. Reigneth repeated the words in her mind, this was his mother he was talking about: 'put her somewhere'. It seemed as if Emily was an inanimate object to him, devoid of thought and feeling now that she was old. The thought upset Reigneth, who sometimes, when she looked at Emily, saw her as she had been: a young wife and mother; the loved one.

These Gaujas are so different to my family, she thought. Gypsies took care of their old folk; respected them. She could not envisage a Romany dispensing with elderly parents so easily, discarding them like worn out shoes. In the old lady's brief moments of lucidity she said some witty things that made Reigneth smile and she knew the old lady loved her.

Emily Pritchard was very small and stooped, she wore an assortment of cardigans, which Reigneth knew she removed when she went to bed, as some days they were on correctly and some days they were inside out. Reigneth suspected it was the way in which she took them off that dictated the way in which they would go back on next day. Emily had a faint whiff of 'old lady' about her, but never any evidence that she was incontinent. She mostly pottered around Home Humber humming tunelessly and was not a nuisance to anyone or a danger to herself. So why had Uncle Richard said that?

Reigneth had begun dreaming about the old lady recently. In her dreams Emily was young and was searching for someone and Reigneth knew she would not be with them for much longer. The thought of Emily's passing made her feel sad and she was determined to do all she could to ensure Richard's mother passed away in the comfort of her own home and did not have to know the terror of being somewhere unfamiliar. Like a child, the old lady became easily disorientated and then frantic until she got her bearings. She was adept with door catches and locks and Reigneth dreaded the thought of her wandering off somewhere and getting lost, so always made a point of ensuring the doors were locked each night and the keys placed out of reach, to reassure herself that Emily was secure.

Chapter 8

Melancholia

Grace Wilmott was irritated with her son. He was morose and moody of late and reminded her more and more of Matthew as time went on. He was just like Matt in one of his moods. It was strange how she could remember this from so long ago.

It had been over a year since Harry's accident and she knew Matthew would have expected to hear from her by now and would be angry that she had not called. In truth, she liked being Harry's widow. Did she like it more than being his wife? Perhaps! Once she was over the initial horrifying shock of his death, she had coped very well. Everyone had waited for the tears and anguish, but they never came. Grace was content to remain a widow. She knew Matthew would never mould to her ways as Harry had done. Was having a husband important to her? She thought not. Not anymore.

It took a lot to shake Grace, not many things or many people had the ability to do that, Johnny was the exception. She did not know what his problem was, but whatever it was, it seemed he was not about to share it with her. She loved him so much, yet sometimes she wondered if he even liked her. He spent more and more time on the moor and she suspected that more often than not he was with his father. Could he know? Had Matthew told him? Probably not. Johnny would have faced her with it had he known. So what was he not telling her?

His thoughts a million miles away from his mother, Johnny was out walking. He wandered in a daze down to Chagford and through the churchyard. He did not know what to do next. He had known Reigneth for only a short while, yet without her he was lost. It was ridiculous. He passed beneath the large yew tree and was walking towards the bench when he noticed it was already occupied by, of all people, Richard Pritchard. Johnny smiled when he saw him, he liked Richard. A typical artist: absent minded and eccentric, but harmless. The day was sunny and warm and Richard wore an old-fashioned panama hat and a cream short-sleeved shirt. His face was turned up to the sun and he was clearly enjoying the spate of good weather. Johnny was delighted to see that he was on his own, it was an ideal opportunity to ask about Reigneth.

"Hello there, Jonathan, we've not seen you lately, are you well?" Richard said, watching him approach. "What a lovely day."

"Yes, isn't it – I'm OK, thank you. And you? Is Reigneth well?"

"Yes, yes, she always is – strong as an ox that girl."

Johnny smiled, "Do you mind if I join you?"

"Of course not," Richard moved to make room on the bench and Johnny sat down beside him.

For a moment they sat in silence. Richard seemed to have gone off into his own little world and Johnny needed to bring him back to the moment. He cleared his throat wondering how to begin. "About Reigneth… " he said hesitantly.

"Yes? What about her?"

"Well, we've had a bit of a tiff, a misunderstanding really, I didn't realise she was so young, I'm probably too old for her," Johnny explained.

"You think so? Shouldn't let it worry you myself, she's wiser than the lot of us put together."

Johnny was astounded; was Richard not at all worried about his niece? "Don't you think I'm a little too old for her, sir? Surely her mother wouldn't approve?"

Richard turned to look at Johnny, a big smile on his face. "Rubbish! Reigneth's father was fifteen years older than Jessie. Lovely man, Joe Gray. Reigneth is much like him. I shouldn't worry if I were you. It'll sort itself out. Besides, if that's what's worrying you, she'll be sixteen soon, we're planning a bit of a do for her, perhaps you'd care to come? Just a few close friends – and family, of course. Some will be coming from quite a distance away – Lincolnshire most of them."

Didn't he hear a word I said? thought Johnny, beginning to wonder if Richard was going as batty as old Mrs Pritchard. "Thanks, but I'm sure Reigneth wouldn't want me there, she's angry with me at present."

Richard just smiled absently, as though he was enjoying a private joke. Feeling slightly embarrassed, Johnny got up to go, "Well, I'll be on my way." He turned to leave and bumped straight into Reigneth. He had been so busy looking at Richard he had not seen her approach. His heart started racing and he just could not look away from her. They gazed at each other in silence as though spellbound.

Still smiling, Richard muttered, "Well, don't mind me – I'll be off home now." He eased himself up from the bench, stretched and strolled away.

"Wait for me, Uncle!" Reigneth dropped her gaze and walking past Johnny without even a smile, set off up the path after Richard.

Johnny stood rooted to the spot, the scent of her filling his nostrils. Bereft, he stared at her until she disappeared from view. She did not look back.

Chapter 9

Bereft

Jessie let herself out of the back door and walked up the lane away from Home Humber. It was so infrequently used that earth had been blown into the centre and weeds grew in it. A wide car had trouble passing down the lane and if by chance they met someone coming in the opposite direction, it meant a long reverse for one of them. On each side of the lane, trees grew so closely out of the banks that they formed a green archway, making the lane almost like a tunnel. It was very gloomy in wet weather, but on sunny days, like today, it was brighter, with shafts of light penetrating the leafy canopy. Even so, Jessie felt hemmed in and while she could appreciate the beauty of her surroundings, she missed the flat landscape of Lincolnshire and the softly undulating Wolds.

She carried on walking until she was out of the lane and onto the open moorland. It was only up here that her claustrophobia subsided and she felt she could breathe. Seeing a large flat stone, she stumbled over to it and sat down. Folding her arms tightly around her chest she began rocking back and forth, her tears coming in loud hacking sobs as if she had never cried before. The ache of missing Joe was almost a physical pain it hurt so much. She missed his warm arms around her every night; his tender kisses and gentle caresses. She felt as if her life was over and knew that were it not for Reigneth, she would no longer be here.

Eventually, all cried out, she wiped her face with her handkerchief, feeling foolish for letting go like that, but she had needed to cry. It seemed to Jessie that she was living someone else's life and she was keen to get back to her own: her life with Joe where she had been happy, where he had loved her. Everything seemed misplaced. Looking back on things she realised her way of coping had been to block it all out. Now, however, reality had slapped her in the face and she felt stunned by it and filled with self-doubt. Perhaps she had been wrong to leave the house they had shared together. Maybe if she had stayed, the visions of his handsome face would have been clearer instead of fading in her memory as they seemed to be now. This distressed her even more. Sometimes she felt it was a good thing as it would enable her to move on, but at other times it made her feel utterly panic stricken. She did not want to forget a single thing about his face; his body. Ignoring what the rest of her family thought about it, she had kept some of his clothes, wrapping them in an airtight bag so that when she was feeling very low she could remove them, inhaling deeply and drinking in Joe's smell. If her mother had known she would have said it was why she was getting no respite or lessening of her grief: that she was trapping Joe's spirit, his *mulo*, with her and should have burned the clothes with the rest of his things.

Despite her heritage, Jessie had been unable to do this and had kept one or two mementos: she slept with his cap under her pillow, along with his wallet – not that there had ever been much in it – and his watch. Oh God, how she missed her man. She felt she would never recover. Sometimes she would wake in the night and feel he was with her, his body lying next to hers, fitting into her shape. Was it because she wished for it so much? Was her mind playing tricks on her?

Lost in her thoughts, Jessie did not hear the horn blaring as she stood and turned abruptly, stepping into the road. The Land Rover screeched to a stop almost on top of her, the horn still blaring. Startled she jumped back, began to cry all over again. What on earth was the matter with her?

Swearing under his breath, Matthew kept his hand on the horn, angry with the stupid woman, whoever she was, until he caught sight of her shocked, distressed face. Filled with remorse, he jumped out of the vehicle, "I'm so sorry, I didn't mean to startle you, but I didn't want you to be hurt."

"No, no, I'm sorry, it's my fault; you just frightened me. Please excuse me, I was miles away." She turned and hurried away as though embarrassed that he should see her tears.

Matthew stared after her wondering who she was and what the hell she had been blubbing about. She was an attractive woman, despite her red-rimmed eyes and grief-ravaged face. In the next instant he placed her. With her pitch black hair, dark skin and distinctive jewellery, it could only be Reigneth's mother. Poor woman; he knew she had been recently widowed and was clearly still grieving.

He got back in the Land Rover and drove on down to Chagford, putting the incident out of his mind, but later that evening his thoughts kept returning to the woman, whose name he did not know. He could not help but compare the desolation he had seen in her face with the composure he had seen in Grace after Harry Wilmott had passed away. Matthew wanted nothing more than to be loved like Reigneth's mother had loved her husband. He knew Grace would never be capable of that depth of feeling. As the days went by, his thoughts of Reigneth's mother kept returning and thoughts of Grace, after a lifetime of longing, began to recede.

Chapter 10

Merriment

The phone calls to Home Humber were increasing and it was becoming evident to Richard that the house would not be big enough for Reigneth's birthday party. Many family members were determined to journey down to stay for a few days, so he booked the private room in the village pub. He reflected that for someone who shunned attention, Reigneth was surprisingly enthusiastic about the forthcoming celebration, though he knew she relished the opportunity of having all her family around her. He had not been overly surprised when she had asked if she could invite both Johnny Wilmott and Matthew Holbrook to join them.

A few days before the party, Reigneth woke from what had been a wonderful night's sleep and although she had dreamt, for a change it had been lovely; comforting. She had seen her dad and he was happy and smiling. Strangely, Matthew was also in the dream and Joe had been smiling at him too: not in a sinister way, but warm and friendly. Reigneth could make neither head nor tail of it, except that she felt sure it did not mean anything bad. She wondered if, as she matured, she would be able to understand the meaning of her strange dreams. Warm and cosy, she stretched out her legs and felt rested and strong. She had promised to write out the birthday invitations today. Ma had been on at her about it and she needed to crack on to get some peace. She got up, washed and dressed and set about getting herself breakfast, humming as she sliced some bread and put it in the toaster and surprising herself that she felt so happy. Her anger with Johnny seemed to be a thing of the past.

The blank invitations were on the kitchen table with a pen, a not so subtle hint from Jessie. There were only a few to be written as Reigneth had spoken to most of her family on the phone, but she wanted to send Johnny one personally. She would send one to Matthew too so that Johnny would have some company. She never doubted they would accept. Uncle Richard wanted her to invite one or two of his friends too, which meant her family would be a bit subdued: by choice they were not used to mixing with *Gaujas*.

Reigneth had never had a party before and sixteen was no great milestone, but for once she was enthusiastic, though if she was honest, her pleasure was as much about seeing Johnny again as it was about seeing her cousins. Staying away from him had been hard, the hardest thing she had ever had to do and in her opinion quite unnecessary. Each day that she was without him was agony to her and she constantly pictured his face. Invitations completed, she decided to post them rather than deliver them by hand. *Reigneth Gray, you are a coward,* she thought.

The dream came again the following night, but with subtle differences. This time her mother was there with her and Matthew. Her Dad was watching them and seemed at ease, smiling in a friendly way as before. Reigneth could see that he liked Matthew, but still could not work out what it was the dream was telling her or why Johnny's father should be there. She woke early, the images still vivid in her mind. She felt warm and comforted after seeing her dad, as if he was hugging her. She still missed him terribly, but knew her Mam missed him more; heard her weeping most nights. Sometimes, when it was really bad, Reigneth would sneak into her room to hug and comfort her.

Still moping about Reigneth and the way she had so coldly brushed past him in the graveyard, Johnny was of the view that his summer was turning out to be the worst in living memory. It was made even worse when he received a text from Izzy to say she was coming down the following week. *Oh damn it – that's all I need!* he thought. Knowing Izzy, she would quickly suss that he fancied himself in love with a local girl and would want to know all the details, and then would make it her mission to put things right. Izzy with a mission was a formidable force. Until a month ago she had been his inspiration, his muse, but not his partner. They had been firm friends for two years at university, ever since Izzy had commandeered him on that first day. He grinned at the memory – she was good fun; might cheer him up.

Johnny was surprised to receive an invitation to Reigneth's party and wondered if Richard had sent it without her knowledge. He noted it was to be held in the private room at the *Three Crowns* in Chagford and that the date coincided with Izzy's visit, which made things awkward; he could hardly go out and leave Izzy on her own. There was nothing for it, he would have to phone Home Humber and decline the invitation. Relieved when Richard answered the phone, Johnny explained the problem, but Richard would have none of it, insisting that he bring his friend Isobel with him. He also said that Reigneth, not wanting him to be completely swamped by strangers, had invited Matthew.

Touched by her thoughtfulness, Johnny rang off, but while he was happy to learn the invitation had come from Reigneth and longed to see her, he felt a bit anxious about how it would be between them and wondered how she would feel about Izzy.

As Izzy alighted from the train she scoured the platform for her friend. She smiled when she saw him. Johnny sat with his legs propped on the arm of the bench, a black woollen hat pulled down over his head, nearly covering his eyebrows. His clothes were as freaky as ever and yet looked good on him. *How can someone look so attractive in such a collection of crap,* she wondered. Other guys on their course tried to emulate Johnny's style and failed miserably. He was quirky, the thing that Izzy liked the most. You could not guarantee what Johnny's reaction to things might be, the same as you could never tell what he would turn up in. She absolutely adored him: he was her best friend and companion for the majority of the time at university. Izzy knew that for a while he had imagined himself in love with her and she had gently put him right. If she had been straight – well who knows? But as it was they inspired one another musically and were enjoying the journey together.

As far as Izzy was concerned, Johnny could have had any girl on the course. They all fancied him rotten. She sometimes wondered if he was the sort of guy who only wanted what he could not have. Was it because she was unattainable and presented a challenge that he had made such a play for her? It had been difficult at first: she had soon discovered that Johnny was not used to rejection. But they had got over it and stayed friends, and he had tried to sink himself into university life; certainly he found the parties and booze to his liking. Taking pity on him, Izzy had pushed him in the direction of a talented oboe player and he'd had a brief fling with her, but it transpired that her personal hygiene was somewhat lacking and that had put an end to that! The trouble with Johnny was that he was way too picky.

His music, however, well that was something else. He sang with real emotion, played with feeling and there was a depth and intensity to his voice that sent shivers down Izzy's spine. *Fact is*, she thought, *he almost makes me wish I was straight!*

As she got nearer, Izzy could see that Johnny looked tired. He had dark circles round his eyes as if he had not been sleeping and there was a tormented look about him. In their brief phone conversations she had managed to get out of him that he had hooked up with someone from home during the summer break, but things had not worked out. He had confided that he was in a bit of a state about it and had been hitting the bottle. Izzy was worried about him. From the look of him 'a bit of a state' was something of an understatement. She hated to see her friend so unhappy and was determined to get to the bottom of things. It was the main reason she had invited herself to Devon, aside from the fact that she needed a holiday, and besides, she was desperate to know what this girl with the unusual name was like who had so captivated her best friend.

She did not have long to wait. After they had hugged and said all the usual 'How was your journey' type things, they drove into Chagford to get some shopping for Johnny's mother. Izzy loved the town: so much old world charm. She could not resist window shopping and had stopped at the window of a leather goods shop when Johnny gave her a nudge.

"That's Reigneth, Izzy, over there," Johnny nodded to the young woman walking in their direction.

"Blimey, Johnny, you didn't tell me you were in love with Snow White!" Izzy was every bit as transfixed as Johnny by the sight of Reigneth, her movements so graceful she seemed almost to glide towards them. A slight smile hovered on her lips and tendrils of hair floated free, softly framing her perfect face. "God, she's *beautiful*," Izzy gasped, aware that her mouth was hanging open in a very unattractive way as, she noticed, was Johnny's. "Stop gawping," she hissed, digging him in the ribs.

"Hello Johnny, nice to see you," Reigneth smiled.

"Reigneth, Izzy – Izzy, Reigneth," Johnny sounded strained as he made the introductions.

"Hi, Reigneth," Izzy grinned, stunned as she took in the girl's flawless complexion and the deep violet colour of her eyes. Her eyelashes were disgustingly long too. As far as Izzy could see, not one thing was less than perfect. Reigneth wore jeans and a red blouse, which looked amazing set against her jet black hair. Scraped around to one side of her head, it hung in pony tail to her left shoulder and was tied by a red ribbon.

Reigneth flashed Izzy a smile. It was hypnotic and Izzy was dazed, never had she seen anyone so lovely. No wonder Johnny was having problems. She could tell that this girl had an overpowering effect on him – he was speechless. Izzy recalled herself enough to seize the moment. She had a mission after all.

"We're going to do a little sightseeing whilst I'm here, perhaps you'd like to join us, Reigneth? Johnny tells me you like walking on the moor. I can't wait to see it for myself."

Not looking at all surprised by the invitation, Reigneth directed her gaze first at Izzy and then at Johnny, smiled and said, "I'd love to. But please excuse me. I'm in a bit of a dash getting ready for the party. See you later." And with that she glided off down the street, leaving the pair of them looking after her.

Johnny said very little on the way home and for once neither did Izzy. As soon as they had arrived and Izzy, having been introduced to Grace – whom she thought seemed nice enough: refined but a bit distracted – had unpacked, she showered and got ready for the party. What to wear? In the end she decided to go for smart casual and pulled on a pair of black trousers with a clingy, blue strappy top.

Once ready, she wandered down the corridor to Johnny's room and looked round the door. He was half dressed: a bundle of clothes lay discarded on the bed and he was pulling yet another pair of trousers out of a wardrobe, his face creased with anxiety. She burst into laughter at the sight of him.

"Shut up Izzy, I can't decide what to wear," he said, adding, "you look great."

"Need some help?" she asked, still giggling. "How about

these?" She pulled a pair of dark-coloured trousers from the bottom of the pile on the bed and held them up. "And what about this?" she selected a cream shirt and matching waistcoat, "Mm, trendy, especially if you wear it unbuttoned," she grinned, pleased when Johnny agreed with her choice. She eyed him critically, "Just need to tame your hair a bit and you'll do fine," she said, thinking: *You gorgeous creature. If Reigneth can't see it she's either blind or daft.*

Wanting to have his wits about him and savour every moment of being with Reigneth, Johnny had arranged to borrow his mother's Range Rover and transport Matt to the party. That way, he knew he would have to stay sober and Matt could have a drink or two.

Matt must have been waiting for them to arrive, as they had only just pulled up at Higher Wedicombe when he came out of the door. He looked impressive in a dark grey suit and tie. Johnny had never seen him looking so smart and it made him anxious. "Do you think I should have worn a suit, Matt? You make me feel a bit underdressed."

"Don't ask me; it's the first do I've been to in years, my suit is probably older than you." Matthew laughed, "Can't you smell the mothballs?"

In the front seat, Izzy giggled.

"You must be Izzy?" Matthew smiled, settling into the back.

"Oh, sorry, yes," said Johnny, hastily making the introductions as he drove away from the farm.

The room at the *Three Crowns* was already crowded and to Johnny's surprise was set up for live music. He exchanged a glance with Izzy, both excited as always by the prospect of a live performance.

Johnny had purchased a Victorian necklace for Reigneth, a gold chain made of fine links with a pendant attached: a delicate scrolled setting around a single amethyst. He had chosen it because the colour of the stone reminded him of Reigneth's eyes. He scanned the room for her and found she was looking right at him. As they exchanged glances, she smiled and gave a little wave. He realised he had never seen her wear a dress before: it was a shade of purple with shoestring straps and hugged her figure in a way that made Johnny's pulses race. The fabric flared out from her hips with godet pleats and swayed with her every movement. For once her hair was loose, the top part scraped back from her forehead and fastened with an antique comb, the rest hanging in gentle curls nearly to her waist. Gold hoops dangled from her ears and she wore a single gold chain and a gold bracelet.

Words failed Johnny; she had never looked lovelier. He noticed her mother standing at her side. She too looked outstanding: her skin was a few shades darker than Reigneth's and she wore a black dress which, although not revealing, showed her figure to its best advantage. Many of Reigneth's relatives were there and much to Johnny's chagrin, all were very smartly dressed. Embarrassed, he wished he had made more of an effort. It had simply not occurred to him that the occasion would be so formal or he would have worn a suit.

Leaving Izzy and Matt chatting, and without taking his gaze from Reigneth, Johnny crossed the room towards her as though drawn by a magnet.

"Happy birthday, Reigneth," he handed her the gift and card. He was rewarded with a dazzling smile. Leaning forward she kissed him on the cheek, thanking him very sweetly. The place where her lips had caressed him felt on fire and his heart beat double-time as he watched her rip open the wrapping paper, exchanging a glance with him while struggling with the packaging. Holding up the necklace she gave a small gasp of delight and her eyes glistened with tears. *God, how I've missed you*, Johnny thought, feeling himself welling up too. *Get a grip Wilmott!*

She held the necklace out to him, "Will you fasten it for me please?"

He took it with some difficulty, his hands shaking. Reigneth turned her back to him, whisking her hair away so he could fasten the clasp. He had a strong urge to kiss her neck, the desire almost overwhelming. Fortunately, she turned back to face him before he was able to act on the impulse.

"Thank you, it's beautiful," she said, kissing his cheek again and whispering, "I wish I could give you a big hug, but... well, you know."

Johnny held her gaze for a moment longer and they exchanged a smile of understanding, but a woman was standing hesitantly beside him, holding out a card and obviously waiting to speak to Reigneth, so Johnny was forced to move aside.

"I'll see you in a little while, Johnny," Reigneth said, her eyes gleaming.

It was obvious from the woman's appearance that she was family, but whoever she was, she had spoiled the moment and Johnny felt an irrational surge of anger as he watched Reigneth accept the card. She smiled hesitatingly, but did not hug the woman, who extended her right hand to Reigneth as if waiting for permission to touch her. Reigneth grasped her hand lightly and in return the woman cupped her other hand around Reigneth's. Only then did Reigneth put her arm around her, completely enfolding her, closing her eyes as her face touched the other woman's cheek. Opening them after a moment to give the woman a warm smile, she said, "Come and sit with me a while Susan."

Taken aback by this hesitant display of affection between the two women, Johnny wondered if perhaps this Susan was some long lost relative. He was unaware that Richard had moved up behind him until he heard a quiet voice in his ear.

"I expect you are wondering who all these people are? That is Susan Elliot, related by marriage to the Grays. It's a big family – as you will have gathered," Richard said with a grin, "and they are all very close."

Johnny felt that he should move away, but he found it hard to leave Reigneth. He then took in several things simultaneously: Jessie Gray and Elizabeth Pritchard were hovering nearby and both seemed anxious, and a big, muscular guy was walking quickly to Reigneth's side. As he approached her, she seemed to sway towards him and Johnny heard her gasp, "James!"

Not jealous by nature, Johnny knew he was overreacting, but he could not help feeling a hurtful pang of envy as the big man threw him a cold glance and led Reigneth away. She went without looking back, clearly affected by this James, whoever he was. She seemed a little unsteady on her feet as they crossed to the other side of the room to sit side by side. Susan joined them and Reigneth held her hand, both women smiling at each other through their tears.

Following slowly in Reigneth's wake, Johnny rejoined Matthew and Izzy. He felt excluded. Why had she invited him and Matthew just to ignore them? As if she had read his thoughts, he saw her speak briefly to James, who left her side and came forward to welcome them and offer them a drink. Johnny could not fail to

110

notice that Reigneth had instructed James to do this and that he had immediately complied, although it was obvious to anyone but an idiot that the big man did so under sufferance.

"Blimey," Izzy whispered after he had gone, "what's his problem?"

"They're not used to mixing with us *Gaujas*," Matthew whispered back.

"Eh? What are we?"

"*Gaujas*, Matthew repeated. "It's what they call people who are not Romany."

"Well it makes me feel like I've got an infectious disease or something."

"It doesn't mean anything, Izzy, it's just their way. Chin up, Jono. I told you they were different, but you'll get used to it," Matthew grinned.

As they stood awkwardly by the door and sipped their drinks – Johnny regretting he was confined to fruit juice when as never before he fancied something stronger – he watched various members of Reigneth's family greet her in much the same way as Susan had done. He could not pinpoint what troubled him about their interaction and could not quantify it, other than to note that they treated her with the utmost respect, or rather, reverence. The question followed, why she should be treated in this way? She was beautiful, undoubtedly, but beauty did not deserve what he could only describe as a kind of 'homage'. With that thought he had hit on the very word he was searching for. This family paid *homage* to Reigneth. She did not seek it or manipulate it, yet somehow she earned it.

Despite himself, Johnny found he kept looking at James, increasingly jealous of this man who seemed to be constantly at Reigneth's side. He must be closely related: his skin was dark, much like Jessie Gray's, his hair almost as black. He was tall and muscular, extremely handsome and seemed attentive to Reigneth's every need. Determined not to get any more upset than he already was, Johnny turned his back on them and engaged Izzy and Matt in conversation – anything to take his mind off Reigneth.

James Boswell had experienced feelings of intense jealousy when he first laid eyes on Johnny Wilmott. His fury knew no bounds. He was astounded at how right Reigneth had been in her description of this 'girlie boy' – as he had himself christened him all those years ago. He did look like a girl too, with his long hair and eyelashes fit for a lass and his delicate little face and hands. Only about 5' 9" tall James reckoned, but not weak. No, definitely not weak: a tough little cookie, in fact. Johnny's eyes were huge and filled with resentment and fury. There was no doubting what he was feeling or that he would fight for Reigneth. Yes, he would fight for her: even if it took his life, the girlie boy would fight for her. The lines were drawn, but James knew he was the loser, for Reigneth would never be his *monisha*. Just as she had told him all those years ago, she would be his friend and companion, but never his wife. The girlie boy had made his appearance and James was filled with desolation.

The evening sped by quickly; the food was good as it always was at the *Three Crowns*. Background music was provided by CD, but once everyone was fed and having had a few drinks, the musicians – all Reigneth's relatives by the look of them – came on stage. Johnny identified the various instruments: violins and guitars, dulcimer's and melodeons, zithers, accordions and squeeze boxes, bodhram drums and penny whistles.

"They are a very musical people," Matthew remarked. "In days past these instruments would have gone with them on their travels, all small instruments you'll notice; portable. When they were on the move space was at a premium."

A great sense of anticipation filled the room and Johnny nodded, eager to hear them play. The band struck up and within the first few chords everyone cheered. It was obviously a song they all knew and enjoyed and Reigneth looked delighted, beaming with pleasure. It was clear she was in her element, surrounded by her family.

Johnny and Izzy were surprised at the choice of music. They had anticipated something traditional and folksy, but it was a modern, familiar song though played in a way they had never heard it played before – and played fabulously.

James stood up to the microphone to sing, *Wouldn't you just know it*, Johnny thought, *is there nothing this guy can't do?* His voice had a wonderful resonance to it, and as the music started to build and swell the family clapped their hands and stamped their feet along to the beat. The atmosphere was electrifying. Reigneth, her eyes sparkling, was more relaxed than Johnny had ever seen her, she had never looked so animated or enchanting. He knew that with her own people there were no boundaries for her, she was completely free and uninhibited. He looked across to James and saw that as he sang, he never took his gaze from Reigneth's face. Watching him, stomach churning, Johnny felt sick with jealousy. He balled his fist and thumped his thigh, imagining it was James's face.

"Steady on, Jono," Matthew said in his ear. "Don't let the green-eyed monster take root. If there was anything between them other than friendship, she would have told you before now."

Matthew had arrived at the party feeling ill at ease. It was years since he'd been to any kind of do and having lived like a recluse since Grace rejected him, the noise was almost more than he could bear. He was glad to be there, though, if only to keep an eye on Johnny, who was clearly upset. One of the first things Matthew had realised on arrival was that the woman he had seen crying on the moor was at the party. This evening there were no tears: she looked both happy and extremely beautiful. Matthew was drawn to her in a way he would not have believed possible. The only woman he had ever found attractive was Grace – until now. He was sure she recognised him and placed where she had seen him, for she had looked a little embarrassed when she glanced in his direction. He nodded towards her, "That must be Reigneth's mother," he said to Johnny.

"Yes, her name is Jessie Gray," Johnny replied.

As the evening progressed people began to dance and much to Johnny's amazement Matthew went purposefully across the room to Reigneth's mother and asked her to dance. Every member of Reigneth's family looked dumbfounded and slightly ill at ease. Jessie too, her face bright pink, was clearly embarrassed, but in moments she was gliding around the floor with Matthew, who must have said something to make her smile.

Johnny could not conceal a grin and when he glanced across at Reigneth and saw the disbelief on her face, he grinned even more. She looked transfixed by the sight of Matthew and her mother dancing.

Not to be outdone, Izzy winked at Johnny, "Well here goes.

Send out a search party if I don't come back!" With that, she made her way to where James was standing, having relinquished his place on stage to another cousin. Johnny watched as the big man bent his head to Izzy, nodded, grinned and swept her into a waltz.

Reigneth was still staring open-mouthed at her mother and Matthew. Johnny decided the time had come to bite the bullet. He walked around the edge of the room to where she stood, summoned a contrite expression and asked, "Please would you dance with me, Reigneth?"

"Yes, of course, I'd love to."

Holding Reigneth in his arms, Johnny at last felt complete, surely this was what was meant to be? His head filled with tumultuous thoughts: he would wait for her if she would have him. Was she too young to think of committing herself to someone like him? He did not know what he would do after university, but his father had left him enough money for it not to be a problem. He wondered what her relations would think of having a *Gauja* in their family. How had it been for the Pritchards? Was Reigneth even interested in him? At the moment she looked preoccupied, still watching Matthew and her mother. One thing he did know: he had to make his feelings known; he had to ask her if she cared for him. Everything hinged on that.

It was a slow number. With his hand resting on Reigneth's waist, Johnny felt her fingers touch the back of his neck, twining into his hair. His skin prickled into goose-bumps at her touch. Lost in the moment, he smiled at her and held her other hand in his, closely enfolding it into his body as they swayed gently to the music. He wanted the dance to go on forever, but all too soon the music changed and James was at Reigneth's elbow, whisking her away.

Cold with fury, Johnny sloped back to the side of the room and watched them. James and Reigneth were perfectly synchronised, displaying an easy familiarity as they danced. It was easy to see they were used to being together. They twisted and turned, keeping perfect time with the pulsating beat of the music. For a big man, James was agile and light on his feet. Johnny wondered now how he had never realised that Reigneth was so different. Until Matthew had pointed it out to him, he'd had no idea she was a Gypsy, but now her heritage was so obvious. She was magnificent. He had to concede that James looked spectacular too. As a couple they were an exact match – in fact they looked as if they were meant for one another. Johnny was distressed, but as if hypnotised, he could not look away as James twirled Reigneth around, her dress clinging to her and exposing her upper thigh. The music went faster and faster, the steps so intricate Johnny wondered how she managed in her strappy high-heeled sandals.

"Aren't they just *fantastic?*" Izzy said, having moved to stand beside Johnny, "I gather it's their party piece. They've done it often before, you can tell."

Johnny nodded, not trusting himself to answer. The look he had just received from James was like a challenge. *This is what we are. Can you hope to capture her? Do you really think you can be one of us?*

Johnny looked away; the only answer he could come up with was, 'No'.

Izzy never missed a trick and she was observant. *Two could play at that game,* was her main thought as she saw the wordless exchange between James and Johnny. Quick as thought, she clambered up to the musicians, took the mike and announced Johnny. She had heard a couple of new songs he had been working on at the end of term and although raw, she thought they could wing it. Everyone in the room went silent, expressions of surprise and curiosity directed at the stage. Izzy watched Johnny stumble over. He looked on the point of collapse, his face bright red. Deliberately she avoided his gaze and with a muttered apology to one of the musicians, she filched a violin and stood waiting.

"I thought we could perform your two newest songs," she said, her lips twisting in an apologetic grin.

Looking daggers at her, Johnny nodded, flung off his waistcoat, undid the top two buttons of his shirt and sat at the piano. She knew he would lose himself in the music as soon as he started to play. Any thoughts of James would be erased from his mind and he would focus on the girl he appeared to love beyond reason. At least, that is what Izzy was counting on.

And she was right. Any music that had been played earlier was forgotten, James's recent performance fading into insignificance beside Johnny's. He excelled himself, the look on his face was heavenly, *Surely an angel never looked so beautiful?* Izzy thought.

His voice was wonderful and the lyrics pure poetry. It told of a love so desperate, so passionate that the man would rather die than be without the object of his love. The depth of feeling could not be mistaken, the emotion of its delivery earth-shattering.

Glancing around the room over her violin, Izzy saw the audience was rapt, everyone visibly moved: Reigneth's mother held her hand to her throat, tears flooding down her face. Matthew was reaching for her hand, looking as if at any moment he too was going to weep. James Boswell's face was rigid, like he knew when he was beaten, while Reigneth was watching this boy with the angel's face and voice, her love shining out like a beacon. Izzy was well satisfied; her mission was off to a good start. Johnny would very likely kill her later, but it was worth it.

She was a little frustrated when they left the party to note that Johnny's mood had not lifted. In fact he looked even more dejected than before. He had to be possibly the most unobservant bloke on the planet. Izzy wanted to shake him. Could he not *see* how much Reigneth loved him? As far as she could see, it was all-consuming. As an outsider, she had been able to discern much that was going on: the obvious chemistry between Matthew and Jessie Gray and the provocative, challenging behaviour of James. She had observed Reigneth throughout the evening, seen the way her eyes sought Johnny at every opportunity, aware of him at all times in spite of having to be busy playing the perfect hostess. Izzy had been impressed by Reigneth's maturity, it was easy to see why Johnny had not realised she was so young. Her family did not treat her as though she were young, she was obviously much loved and cared for, but something more than this; they protected her – but from what? She puzzled about that, determined to find out more.

Izzy was quietly confident that things would work out for her best friend. Perhaps she could be a bridesmaid – or best man, more like – she smiled at this thought.

Chapter 11

Mixed Feelings

Consumed by jealousy, Johnny had spent the night after the party tossing and turning, plagued by images of James's darkly handsome face and the way Reigneth had looked when she danced with him. Unable to sleep he had fiddled around with his guitar trying to write a new song, but unable to concentrate, had given up and taken Rannoch out early for a gallop. The gunmetal skies on the moorland horizon seemed to mirror Johnny's mood and even following his brisk ride, his spirits did not lift. He rode up past Higher Wedicombe and in the distance saw Matt in the yard doing his rounds.

Matthew, still suffering from the after effects of too much booze and a sleepless night, was barely awake when he saw Johnny riding down towards the farm. The real problem, which he was not yet ready to admit, was not that he was tired, but that he could not get thoughts of Jessie Gray out of his head. He inevitably found himself comparing her dark, warm beauty with Grace's fair frigidity: Jessie was the sun and Grace the moon. But it wasn't all about looks. There was something about Jessie that had struck a chord with Matthew: he felt he had always known her, found her easy to talk to and even though he respected her grief, had managed to make her laugh a time or two. She made him feel more alive than he had felt in years. He wanted to ask her out on a date, but knowing she was newly widowed he wondered if it was too soon for her to consider spending an evening in his company. Or even many. Or all...

He was getting ahead of himself. He would be happy just to be Jessie's friend; she looked as though she needed one and he knew how to be a good friend; fact is, he did not know how to be anything more, he'd had very little practice. It was astounding to Matthew that after all these years of agonising over unrequited love, his longing for Grace had completely disappeared. Gone as if it had never been. In some ways it made him feel that his whole life had been a sham. Had he been fooling himself? Was it just because Grace was unattainable that he had wanted her so badly; not love at all, but a fantasy of love? He was only forty-three and old before his time. Until now it had not once occurred to him that there was life after Grace. He had imagined that he would never be anything but a lonely old codger, living out a life of solitude at Higher Wedicombe, with occasional visits from the son he loved but could never acknowledge. Well, things had changed. And how!

Wandering out to the barn to check the stock, Matthew dared to consider that his life might not be over after all. Maybe, just maybe he was not doomed to spend the rest of his days alone. Thoughts of spending them with someone like Jessie filled him with pleasure.

Reigneth too had slept badly worried that Johnny had seemed unhappy and ill at ease. Deciding it was pointless lounging around in bed, she eased herself up, and stuffing her feet into her slippers made her way downstairs, stomping into the kitchen in a thoroughly bad mood. She made herself a cup of tea and had just sat down when James came into the kitchen.

She could tell from her cousin's expression that he wanted to have a heart to heart. Unable to cope with a confrontation she stalked out of the kitchen and went back her bedroom. It was the only place she could get some peace – and then only when she was awake. Sleeping was often not as peaceful for her as for some people.

Reigneth replayed the party in her mind thinking of Johnny. Perhaps she had been a bit off hand. Trying to be the perfect hostess had left no time to dote on him. Perhaps she should go and see him, talk candidly to him. Then again, perhaps not – arrogant little devil, but oh, how she missed him. Her thoughts moved on to the image of her mother dancing with Matthew. That was so unexpected – and yet should it be? Did that explain what Dad had been trying to tell her in her dreams? Reigneth pondered the question for a while, recognising that part of her hurt to think about it. How could her mother possibly find another man attractive after Joe? At least not yet – it was too soon. And yet the signs had all been there. Certainly Matthew seemed smitten and he was such a good man. Was it really such a bad thing? Having finished her tea Reigneth snuggled down into her duvet and eventually drifted back to sleep, reassured by the image of her dad's smiling face.

Chapter 12

Emily's Passing

Waking from her dream, her hair wet in the nape of her neck, her pyjamas soaked and clinging to her body like a second skin, Reigneth threw back her quilt. Jumping out of bed she sprinted down the hallway to Emily's room, shivering as her wet nightclothes chilled her body.

Emily's bed was empty.

Reigneth spun round and ran to rouse her ma, aunt and uncle and tell them Emily was missing, then back to her room to pull on a track suit and some trainers before rushing down the stairs. She had been feeling uneasy about Emily all week and had made doubly sure that the house was securely locked at night with the door chains on, hoping it would contain her. Reigneth had seen in her dreams that Emily would pass away soon, but it was the manner of her passing that concerned her. She kept seeing the old lady alone, afraid and still wandering about on the moor searching for her husband, Tom.

Halfway down the stairs Reigneth felt the draught and knew what she would find: the back door was wide open. Gazing at it, she burst into tears. She heard a noise behind her and turned to see her mother staring at her.

"We're too late, Ma, she's gone. We're too late!"

Richard came thumping down the stairs still buttoning up his jacket. He shouted up to Liz, "Ring Jack Tomlinson. You'll find the number in the book under Dartmoor Search and Rescue. Tell him Emily's gone missing and can he assemble a search party."

"Where did you see her, Reigneth?" her mother asked quietly.

"I don't know," Reigneth was inconsolable, "it was marshy ground. There was nothing distinctive to identify the exact spot."

"We need some help," said Richard. "I don't know the moor well enough – marshy ground could be anywhere. We could go round in circles and walk right by her. Liz, ring Johnny Wilmott too, he knows the moor like the back of his hand. Tell him we're on our way over. Reigneth, you come with me."

"Put this on, Darling," said her mother, pushing a jacket into Reigneth's hands. As she rushed out of the door Richard had already started the car.

Grace Wilmott was both annoyed and panic stricken when she heard the phone ringing so late at night. The voice, which she did not recognise, asked for Johnny. "Do you know what time it is?" she said, flustered. "Is it an emergency? He's in bed asleep."

"It's Elizabeth Pritchard here. I'm really sorry to disturb you, but Emily is lost on the moor and we need Johnny's help. My husband is on his way over to you now. I hope you don't mind, but your son knows the moor so well. Will he help us?"

"Oh goodness, I am sorry. Of course he will. I'll get him up at once."

She slammed down the phone, ran upstairs and shook Johnny awake, "Get up, love, Mrs Pritchard just called. Someone's lost on the moor, she's asked for your help. Her husband is already on his way over here."

"Mrs Pritchard?" Half asleep, Johnny stumbled out of bed. "Who? Who is lost? Oh my God, it's not Reigneth is it?"

Grace could hear the panic rising in her son's voice. "No, it's the old lady, Emily. Get dressed; be quick." Leaving Johnny scrambling for his clothes, she went downstairs to put the kettle on. *Make tea; everyone always wants a cup of tea in an emergency,* she thought.

Still feeling groggy, Johnny dressed in cord trousers, a fleece top and thick socks then stumbled across the landing, almost colliding with Izzy, who looked very disoriented in her pyjamas, her hair sticking out in tufts. Henry and Charlotte were already on their way down the stairs. The Wilmotts had all been through this procedure before: their brother was often asked to help find people lost on the moor.

Feeling ashamed of his initial feeling of relief that it was Emily and not Reigneth who was lost, Johnny was in the boot room lacing on his walking boots when he heard the sound of Richard's car. His mother had gone into the kitchen, he could hear her clattering about with cups, guessed she was making tea; her answer to everything. Sure enough, he heard her call out, "Tea for everyone then or would you prefer hot chocolate?" His mother could always be relied upon to keep her cool in a crisis.

There was a knock on the door. Johnny rushed to answer it, taken aback to see Reigneth and Jukel standing beside Richard on the step. Reigneth looked terrible, her face pale and strained, eyes wide and staring.

"Hello, come in." Johnny held the door wide to let them into the hall. "Have you any idea where she might have headed?"

"She went out of the back door so she must have headed up through the orchard," Reigneth said. "I think she's-" she broke off, looked up at her uncle.

It was clear to Johnny that they were both panicking. The old lady was probably only a few yards from Home Humber. He saw that Reigneth was shaking. "Calm down, she couldn't have got that far, she's old," Johnny reassured her. "Do you have any idea how long she's been missing?"

Reigneth shook her head, "No, I don't know, but she's quite agile really, she may be senile but physically she's fit for her age. The wall at the top of the orchard has a lot of stones missing; she'd easily get over them." Reigneth was clearly at her wits end and close to tears.

Johnny turned to Richard, "I'll take Rannoch. Why don't you call Jack Tomlinson and ask him to get Search and Rescue out?"

"I've already done that, or at least, Liz has by now."

"Good. It will be getting light soon, which will make their job easier." Remembering Reigneth telling him her uncle was frightened of the moor, he added, "Mum's in the kitchen making tea, if you'd like to go through. Maybe it would be best if you and Reigneth stayed here and co-ordinated everyone?"

"You may be right," Richard said. "I'm as likely to get lost myself as find Emily, but take Reigneth with you, Johnny; she'll be able to help. I'll call to see how far they've got assembling a search party and tell them you are setting out now. Call me on your mobile if you see anything."

"OK; and I'll take some flares; can't always get a signal on the moor." Johnny could not imagine what help Reigneth would

122

be since she did not know the moor that well, but he would like nothing better than to take her with him and the ever-present Jukel might be of some help. Grabbing up a torch and some flares from the adjacent boot room, Johnny loaded up a rucksack then led Reigneth out to the stables. He bridled Rannoch, leapt onto the stallion's back and hoisted Reigneth up behind him. She clung to him tightly as he walked Rannoch out of the yard. Johnny could feel her shuddering against his back. Concerned for her he asked, "Are you cold?"

"No, I'm OK."

"Afraid I'll have to take it fairly slowly, at least until it's light enough to see."

"There's no need to rush, Johnny. We're not searching for a living person, she has already passed away."

Johnny assumed she was being pessimistic. She was probably right to be: hypothermia was a very real possibility, especially for someone of Emily Pritchard's age. But it was odd that Reigneth sounded so sure, almost as if she knew.

With Jukel running at Rannoch's heels, they made for the lane at the top of Home Humber, which would bring them out above the orchard. Johnny rode on a loose rein allowing the stallion to pick his own way up the track onto the open moorland. Very conscious of Reigneth's arms about his waist, he began shouting Emily's name, the sound all but lost on the wind that whipped their hair into their faces.

Reigneth remained silent. There was little point in shouting. The howling wind sounded like some sort of wild animal and made her think of the Whist hounds. The moor at night was a terrifying place to be on your own. She had felt Emily's fear as keenly as if the old lady's feelings were her own: knew she had wandered away from Home Humber searching for her lost love, she had been talking constantly of Tom over the past few days, for though he had been gone for years, in Emily's mind he was still alive. Well, she had found him now. Whatever terror she had experienced at the end, Emily was now at peace.

Reigneth's thoughts strayed to the man she was holding: he was not afraid to be up here alone. *How like the moor he is, untamed and wild.* With the feel of his body under her hands, she knew that true contentment had evaded Johnny all his life except for when he

123

was on the moor. Her nature and his were alike in many ways, they had more in common than perhaps he realised.

The going was difficult on the open moorland, the ground soft and wet. The risk of straying into a bog lessened only slightly by the moonlight, the moon often obscured by thick, racing clouds. Uncle Richard had told Reigneth that the bedrock of Dartmoor was granite, which made the drainage poor in places. Water collects in huge basins of rock, he had said, and combines with the soil to become a bog; a mire just waiting for unsuspecting walkers. Reigneth could tell by the sucking noises made by Rannoch's hooves that they were now on marshy ground like that in her dream.

Johnny had stopped shouting and was concentrating on keeping Rannoch to the narrow path while peering all around into the darkness. Jukel ran on ahead, his nose to the ground. Suddenly the dog veered over to their left. Reigneth leaned forward and said in Johnny's ear, "Juk will find her. Let Rannoch have his head, he will follow." He did as she bade, letting the reins go slack. They had gone only a short distance further when they heard Jukel bark.

"He's found her; she's over there," Reigneth pointed to a distant blur of white: Emily's nightdress, becoming increasingly visible with the now lightening sky. Reigneth slid down from Rannoch and started to run. She could see Emily clearly now; her body was lying half-submerged in the mud. Jukel, not prepared to venture into the mire, was standing a few feet away from her and whining plaintively. Reigneth heard Johnny come rushing up behind her, stopping to peer where she pointed.

"Oh, Reigneth, I'm so sorry, she must be dead." He caught hold of her arm as she stepped forward. "No, don't go any further you'll get stuck in there, we'll have to call for help."

Reigneth nodded, soothing Jukel and pulling him away from the soft mud, while Johnny sent up a flare to signal the search party.

The only way to retrieve Emily's body was by air ambulance and it was an intricate process to negotiate the bogs to get her out. Eventually, accompanied by an insistent Reigneth, she was winched on a stretcher into the helicopter.

Johnny was left with Rannoch and the dog, *What the hell am I supposed to do with the dog?* he wondered. Jukel eyed him and emitted a low growl, hackles raised. Had the dog sensed he and

Reigneth were no longer friends? Was that really true? Clearly the dog must think so: it looked as if it hated him and would bite at the first opportunity. Surprisingly, though, it did not, and merely followed as he rode home. He arrived to find that Reigneth had phoned her uncle on her mobile. Richard had already left to drive to the hospital and fetch her home.

Once Johnny had stabled Rannoch, he collected the Land Rover keys and took Jukel back to Home Humber, the dog sticking as close to him as it normally did to its mistress. Jessie Gray ushered him into the kitchen and in between mouthfuls of scalding tea, he told her what had happened. Richard had already spoken to Liz on the phone, so they knew Emily had passed away. To Johnny's amazement, while he was talking, the dog padded over and rested its head on his knee. He had found the whole experience surreal: Jukel had found Emily, but Rannoch had known to follow the dog, and Reigneth had seemed to sense where Emily was. How had she known the old lady was dead before they had even set off to search? It was all very strange.

"You know, Mrs Gray," he said, suddenly aware that for the first time he felt comfortable in her presence, "I've never been frightened on the moor before, but tonight it was a bit scary. It was as if the dog, my horse and Reigneth all knew where to find Emily and Reigneth already knew she was dead. It was really weird." Johnny could not quite put his finger on what he meant, but he could begin to believe all the superstitious tales about the moor on nights such as he had just experienced.

Reigneth's mother made no comment, nor did she look surprised, but merely nodded sadly.

He stood up, "I'd better be off home, Mrs Gray. My mother may have waited up. Thanks for the tea."

"Good night, Johnny – you may call me 'Jessie'," she smiled.

Johnny's jaw dropped. "Thanks. I'll call by tomorrow then... er... Jessie, if that's OK?"

"Yes. I'll tell Reigneth to expect you."

After he had gone, Jessie cleared away the tea things, thinking about Emily and what Johnny had said. It seemed he was only just beginning to sense what Reigneth's capabilities were and she wondered if he would cope. She had decided that she liked the boy after all. He seemed quite a sensitive lad and anyway, if her girl liked him he must be all right.

"What do you think of him, Joe?" She still talked to her man, it brought her comfort.

Chapter 13

Last Rites

Reigneth missed Emily's quirky ways and was saddened by her passing. The house seemed so silent without her persistent humming. Richard had long treated his mother as a sort of non-person, but her total absence now had hit him very hard. He did not seem to know what to do about the funeral and gave Elizabeth free rein to make what arrangements she wished. She decided that for someone as loved and respected as Emily had been, it would be a Romany burial and all the family, as well as the many local people who had known her, would be invited. Richard, who had lived so long with his wife's traditions, was happy to go along with this. There was more than enough room at Home Humber to accommodate those who wanted to come and pay their respects. With Jessie and Reigneth's help, everything was set in motion.

Perhaps not surprisingly, the church was full. Johnny sat in the pew next to his mother; his sister and brother sitting on the other side. He reflected that Emily Pritchard had been around a long time: she had taught both Grace and Matt at junior school and she had been a little eccentric even then. Johnny had always liked her even when he was a small child. He glanced around looking for Matthew, but could not see him, though he recognised a good many of the mourners.

Matthew was in fact sitting to one side, right at the back of the church and partially concealed by a pillar. He had been torn about attending, wanting to pay his respects but, as always, reluctant to be at a public function where he might be seen alongside Johnny.

The resemblance between himself and his son had become even more pronounced as the boy had reached maturity and Matthew worried that someone would notice. Not because he cared what people thought, on the contrary, at times he could hardly contain his pride, but he dreaded Johnny finding out in that way. He did not feel it was his place to tell him, always hoping that Grace would find the courage. He wished she would; he could not understand why she had not now Harry was no longer alive to be hurt by the truth. He wondered if she realised that sooner or later, Johnny would see it for himself. It would go much worse for the boy if that happened.

Keeping his head down, Matthew decided he would leave at the end of the service and not attend the interment. Again, he was torn. More than anything he wanted to greet Jessie, but if he left he would not be able to. From behind his hymn sheet he had watched her come into the church and had felt a huge surge of protectiveness towards her. Her distress was plain to see and he knew she must be sharply reminded of her husband's recent funeral. From where he sat he could see the back of her head and once again found himself comparing her understated elegance to Grace, whose airs and graces had begun to set his teeth on edge.

When the congregation all stood for the coffin, Johnny looked once more for Matt and was forced to conclude that he was not there, which was strange. He thought no more about it, however, for just then he caught sight of Reigneth's handsome cousin. James Boswell was one of the six well-built pallbearers, none of whom – apart from James – Johnny recognised. They were all dark in colouring and wore black suits and ties. In fact everyone in Mrs Pritchard's family wore unrelieved black, including Reigneth. Johnny had seen her sitting next to her mother a few rows in front of him. Her short jacket and dress were of a style that was too old for her and her hair was scraped back from her face and held in a tight pleat on the back of her head. No tendrils or wisps of hair escaped today, emphasising the severity and solemnity of the occasion. Her gold earrings were more noticeable with her hair back; perhaps she had always worn them, Johnny could not remember. It was obvious she had been crying, her face was pale and her eyes looked enormous, too large for her face.

The coffin was placed before the altar and the pallbearers took their seats with the family. Johnny could not stop himself from staring at the back of Reigneth's neck. She sat erect and very still, as did they all.

The vicar spoke eloquently about Emily, giving snippets of information the family wished to share about her life, much of which Johnny had not known and some that made him smile. He was glad no one mentioned her senility or the circumstances of her death.

After they had sung a couple of hymns, Reigneth left her seat and walked to stand before the congregation. Looking tense, yet not unduly nervous, she began to sing without accompaniment of any kind. Her voice was wonderful: strong, pitch-perfect and effortless. She sang a melody Johnny did not recognise, but it was haunting and beautiful. More than ever he yearned to be with her. He could not stop staring, but neither could anyone else. She was perfection.

Everyone followed the coffin out to the graveside, which was completely surrounded by flowers. After the interment, mourners were invited back to Home Humber. Johnny's mother did not want to go, but his sister, eager and nosey, persuaded her and so as a family they attended. Johnny went along in an almost trance-like state unable to forget the image of the girl he loved singing so beautifully.

Thinking about the funeral, he realised that what had struck him as odd was not that each and every one of Reigneth's family had worn unrelieved black – they were obviously traditionalists and everything had been done in a somewhat old fashioned way – nor was it that they had all looked visibly saddened, which of course was only natural. Something else had prevailed and it came to him that it was the sense of respect and dignity offered to Emily Pritchard by all the family that was somehow different from other funerals he had attended.

Back at Home Humber, Johnny fumbled idly with a sandwich and drink while his gaze constantly sought out Reigneth as she circulated, busily handing out drinks and chatting to the pallbearers, whom she clearly knew well. Some of the conversation Johnny could hear, but some he did not even understand, the Romany language sounding strange to his ears. He found the whole business very frustrating and began to realise that this girl, whom he thought about constantly, was a complete stranger to him. He was obsessed by her and try as he might he could not forget her. Johnny felt he just had to get away from the house, away from the desperation he felt at the sight of her.

Opening the French windows he let himself out into the garden and wandered over to sit under an old apple tree, where he pondered on how useless it all was. He could hear two men chatting behind the hedge: they had come out for a smoke, he could smell it. He recognised James's voice. He did not mean to eavesdrop, but they were obviously unaware of his presence and if he moved now he would only draw attention to himself, so he stayed where he was, wishing he had a cigarette too.

"Reigneth and Jessie are looking well, it suits them down here," said one.

"I didn't think they'd stay – may not yet, Jessie doesn't like it as much as Reigneth, says she can't breathe down here with all these high hedges; not like Lincolnshire." That was James.

"Still hoping Reigneth will give you the nod are you?"

"And why shouldn't I? I've got to keep hoping. I know I can provide for her. When we were both little she told me she would never be my *monisha,* but she might have changed her mind now she's older."

"Maybe, though from what I know of Reigneth, once her mind is made up that's it. Anyway, James, I think Jessie wants her to stay at school, it's what Joe wanted. Above all, her ma wants her to be settled, doesn't want everyone to know about her – or so me mam says, anyway."

"That's as may be, but before I set off back home I shall be asking her if she'll have me, she'll not keep me dangling; she's not like that."

Johnny could not believe his ears. They were talking about marriage and Reigneth was only just sixteen! He was so angry he felt he was going to explode – how dared they? And what were people not to know? A secret obviously; why did everything to do with this family have to be so mysterious? The insane jealousy and rage that consumed him was quite alien to Johnny. He was not used to being in a situation where he was not in control, unable to get what he wanted. He did not think of himself as manipulative and he tried to be a good person, but where Reigneth was concerned he felt helpless and it was not a feeling he liked.

As the two men's voices receded, Johnny leant back against the tree and allowed his thoughts to drift. He had not slept well over the past few weeks and felt quite drowsy sitting here in the afternoon sunshine, enjoying the smell of the honeysuckle in the garden. He closed his eyes and tried to conjure the image of Reigneth the first time he had seen her on the moor.

He woke with a start some time later to find Richard Pritchard was lightly touching his sleeve. The man looked exhausted. "Johnny your family are leaving now, but we wondered if you would like to stay on with us for a while. We have a small ceremony to go through in memory of my mother; it would be nice if you could stay."

Johnny appreciated Richard's kindness in trying to include him. "Yes, thank you, I'd like that very much as long as I'm not intruding," he said, thinking, *Of course I'd like that, I'd like nothing better.* The thought uppermost in his mind was that he needed to watch James, who was obviously keen to get Reigneth alone so he could propose. Well not if Johnny Wilmott could help it!

He followed Richard back to the house conscious that his head was throbbing and that he felt both tense and tired. His mother and the twins had already gone, which meant he would have to walk home, but he'd worry about that later. He made his way to the downstairs cloakroom and splashed cold water on his face, which seemed to refresh him somewhat. Sinking his face into the soft hand towel he stood for a moment, wishing his headache would go away. Emerging from the comfort of the thick cotton pile, Johnny heard raised voices.

It seemed it was his day for being in the wrong place at the wrong time; this time captive in the cloakroom. On the other side of the door James and Reigneth were clearly having a heated discussion. Johnny certainly wasn't about to leave while they were there – it would be just too embarrassing if they knew he had overheard. He did not want to listen, but short of sticking his fingers in his ears there was nothing he could do.

"James, this isn't you," Reigneth was saying, her tone pleading.

"Yes it is, Reigneth, this is me hurting. You're hurting me yet again. I can't see why we have to change our ways just because of *Gaujas.*"

"Emily was a *Gauja* and so is Richard, do you hate them too, or is your prejudice just selective?" Her tone was scathing.

"There's no *rokkering* with you, you've got blinkers on, your eyes don't see right these days, Reigneth."

"You're talking with me now aren't you – and I see everything just as much as I always have, James. Nevertheless, the eulogy is not to be in Romany. In English please, so everyone can understand."

"By everyone you mean your girlie boy," James huffed and clattered noisily down the corridor, his voice receding. "Then perhaps you'd like to do it yourself," came his parting shot.

"Oh *dordi* James, what shall I do with you?" Reigneth sounded exasperated.

Johnny hardly dared to breathe; he could hear her muttering and knew she was still there on the other side of the door and was upset. He ached to comfort her. A moment later he heard her light footsteps walking quickly away.

Waiting a few more moments until he was sure the coast was clear, Johnny let himself out of the cloakroom and made his way to where the family was gathered. He immediately spotted James, who looked shamefaced and was casting apologetic glances at Reigneth. She smiled wistfully back at him and it was obvious to Johnny that these two could not remain angry with one another for long.

People began to make their way outside and Johnny, feeling like a gatecrasher, tagged along. Reigneth was carrying what looked like a bunch of old letters held together with blue ribbon. The family walked sedately up the garden through to the field beyond, where someone had built a bonfire. As Johnny got closer he saw that it was heaped with what looked like personal effects: he could see clothes and various artefacts, including a couple of walking sticks. It dawned on him that these things had belonged to old Mrs Pritchard. He watched, fascinated, as Reigneth placed the letters on top of the heap. James then stepped forward and lit the fire, which must have had some sort of accelerant added to it as it went up in a surge of flame.

Standing around the fire, people turned their faces expectantly to James as though waiting for him to speak. He cleared his throat and casting a quick glance at Reigneth began to deliver the eulogy, not in Romany but in English. As the flames licked up through Emily's belongings, James's voice rang out clear and true. He spoke of her achievements, her love for her husband and family, her kindness and the way she had always gone out of her way to help others; how everyone who knew her respected and loved her. As the eulogy continued, Johnny looked around at people's faces. Most were looking at James, but Richard was staring at the fire, his face awash with tears.

As he finished speaking, James smiled at Reigneth with such a look of love that Johnny could not help but be moved. In different circumstances he could have liked the man; perhaps they could have been friends, but as things were – he and James both loving the same girl with such intensity – he knew without doubt that he could easily become James's worst enemy. He sighed, thought, *Yes; if only circumstances were different.*

After the fire had burnt down to embers everyone filed back to the house. Richard organised the men to carry chairs outside so they could sit out in the garden and the women disappeared into the kitchen to make tea.

The male members of the family all sat around chatting, at ease with one another, except for James who kept scowling over at Johnny. It made him feel even more uncomfortable. He wished Izzy was there so he had someone to talk to, but she had elected to give the funeral a miss on the grounds that she had never known Emily Pritchard and would be in the way. Johnny was just thinking he would make his excuses and leave, when Richard wandered over. He looked at Johnny and then at James and frowned.

"Listen everyone," Richard said loudly. They all fell silent and looked at him expectantly. He placed his hand on Johnny's shoulder, "I'd like to introduce you all to Johnny Wilmott, a neighbour of ours. We have known him a long time – my mother taught him as a boy. He was the one who helped us find her on the night she passed, and I want to take this opportunity to thank him publicly." Richard shot a pointed look at James and added, "He will always be a welcome guest in our house."

Flushing to the roots of his hair, Johnny allowed himself to be led around the circle as Richard introduced him individually to members of the family. He knew he would never be able to remember all their names, but he noted that most of them were called either Gray or Boswell. As they shook his hand, smiled and thanked him, he began to feel less like an outsider and by the time the women emerged with the refreshments he had started to enjoy himself. Most of the men drank whiskey; Johnny chose to drink tea and discovered it was laced heavily with brandy.

As the light began to fade, some of the men produced accordions and squeeze boxes. Then began what Johnny could only think of as a magical evening. The music was like nothing he had ever heard: melancholy and haunting, hinting at a past life and full of nostalgia for times that were long gone. He saw in every one of the family's faces a pride in what they were and he recalled what Matthew had told him about the Romany culture. He knew in a sudden flash of understanding why Richard had taken such pains to include him in the proceedings. If he had not done so, Johnny knew he would have felt like an alien being among these people. They were different; a race apart. Though they lived alongside ordinary folk, they were certainly not ordinary in the way Johnny understood. One thing he noticed again and again was the respect – almost reverence – they showed towards Reigneth and her mother. Each time Johnny looked at Reigneth he caught sight of James Boswell glaring at him; James was not a happy man. Pondering on reasons for this Johnny began to feel a shred of hope.

The music shifted from melancholy to lighter-hearted tunes and James got up and started to sing. His voice was quite beautiful and so full of emotion it brought many people to tears. The mood lifted slightly and as James swung round he caught hold of Reigneth's arm twirling her up close to him. As he did so, Reigneth seemed to stumble then fell heavily against him.

The music ground to a halt and there was a low anxious murmuring as people saw what was happening. Reigneth seemed to be having some sort of dizzy spell and was clinging frantically to James as though her life depended on it.

Johnny started towards them, heard James say, "What is it, Reigneth? Can you hear me my *bitti chai*? What do you see?" Reigneth made no reply, her head lolled back and Johnny could see she was unconscious. He stopped in his tracks as James scooped her up like a rag doll and carried her into the house.

Following behind with everyone else, Johnny surveyed the sea of stricken faces. Nobody spoke as James carried Reigneth into the sitting room and laid her gently on the couch. Jessie Gray was immediately at her daughter's side. James remained at her head. Moments later Elizabeth Pritchard came rushing from the downstairs cloakroom carrying a bowl of water, flannel and towel.

Slowly Reigneth came round, reached frantically for James's hand and clutched it tightly, muttering something under her breath. He leaned over her to hear what she was saying. She went chalk white and looked as if she was about to pass out again, but her mother murmured something to her, soothing her and bathing her face. Still no one spoke, all watching the scene unfold, their expressions anxious and strained.

All this was too much for Johnny. He could neither understand nor cope with it. Clearly Reigneth had fainted and he was worried sick, but equally clearly, there was nothing he could do about it. There was no room for him beside her even had she wanted him. There had been times at the funeral when she had glanced in his direction and he had felt she was no longer angry with him, but now she seemed oblivious to him and all he could see was this girl he loved beyond reason, clutching at James's hand as though she never wanted to let him go.

It was obvious with this turn of events that the evening was over for anyone who was not family. Richard apologised and thanked them all for coming, and people began to leave. Johnny lingered almost to the last, reluctant to go until he knew Reigneth was going to be all right, but he was not encouraged to stay and so, with a last look at her, he left.

Stepping outside Home Humber, Johnny was beginning to wish he had not come. He felt dejected and alone and was almost glad he had to walk home; it would give him time to clear his head. Racked with anxiety about Reigneth and cut to the quick by her apparent devotion for James, he wondered if there was anything he could do to resolve the situation. Thrusting his hands deep inside his pockets he began the long trudge home.

Chapter 14

Sojourn

James Boswell had been persuaded to stay on at Home Humber until Reigneth thought it safe for him to leave. He was not hard to persuade: it suited him fine except for the fact that wherever he went, he kept bumping into this namby-pamby runt, Johnny Wilmott, and it was getting on his nerves. He could not believe this guy was special to Reigneth, but he very obviously was. *He looks like a girl and he's half my size*, James thought, when they met in the main street in Chagford a few days after the funeral.

"Hi Reigneth," said Johnny. "You still here, James? Thought most of your family had gone home."

"Yeah, thought I'd hang around for a while and keep my cuz here company," James smirked, conscious of Reigneth standing close by his side. Taking pleasure from Johnny's dejected expression he wanted nothing more than to pick a fight. That was out of the question; Reigneth would kill him. He would never understand how she could reject him in favour of this girlie boy, but she had and he was heartbroken. James had loved and worshipped Reigneth since they were both small children. It was infinitely better to be in her life as a friend than not be in it at all, so he held on to his temper.

James knew he must stay close to Reigneth just now, at least until she could read something different for him. She touched him frequently and James noted with some satisfaction that this fact had not escaped Johnny Wilmott's attention. The girlie boy would not realise, of course, that it was unusual.

The day after the funeral, James's parents had driven the car home leaving their son to return home by train; he was taking no chances. Reigneth's collapse when he had twirled her round had been caused by a vision so clear it had made her faint. She had seen him in a road accident. When she had come to her senses the following day, she had insisted that he stayed. James had no complaints about that: he would not be going anywhere without Reigneth for a while.

Although she occasionally saw what was about to happen to someone, Reigneth knew from experience that the view could be changed, depending on what that person did. She did not try to understand how this could be. She just accepted it. She loved James and did not want anything to happen to him and so was keeping him close, constantly touching him to 'see' when the picture changed.

It was not hard to tell that Johnny was unhappy or that he looked on James as a rival and she could see from his expression that he was confused and annoyed. His jealousy was driving a wedge between them, but for the time being there was nothing she could do about that. She also knew how hard it was for James: he had always thought they would be married, despite her insistence that it was not going to happen. She had long known she was intended for someone else: her soul mate; her other half. That person stood before her now and she smiled at him, delighting in the beauty of his face. She adored him, but he had a journey to travel before he was ready to come to her. She could be patient and wait, although the waiting was hard. She wanted to be close to him and her physical need of his presence was demanding. She had found sleep even more difficult of late, not because of visions of the future, but because of thoughts of Johnny. She was often a little embarrassed by the intensity of her dreams.

She allowed James to lead her away and fought with herself not to look back. Johnny's dejection cut her to the quick. The funeral had given him an insight into her lifestyle, but it was clear he was still unaware of her gift and how this placed her within her family.

Johnny watched her go thinking that the main street in Chagford was suddenly fraught with disaster. It seemed he could go nowhere without bumping into James; James and Reigneth, Reigneth and James. Round and round in his head, his thoughts about them being always in each other's company were driving him crazy. Here they were again, laughing and joking together, not arm in arm but as good as. He could not help noticing how often Reigneth touched James as though seeking reassurance that he was still there. Johnny was miserable; he had never felt this way before. He hated the person he was becoming, he was not usually a morose sort of bloke, but James had really got under his skin.

Chapter 15

Fundraising

Each summer, Chagford put on a village fete to raise money for charity and this year a local hospice was to benefit from the proceeds. It had been organised for some considerable time. Johnny always helped to set it up, but this year he had been so preoccupied with Reigneth that it caught him unawares when his mother asked if he had thought about the marquee. No he had not; in fact it had completely escaped his mind. Grace, of course, was a leading light on the organising committee and her head was full of things to do. The twins were roped in too and this – thankfully – deflected his mother's constant requests and gave Johnny some respite. Let off the hook he allowed himself a wry smile when she had the twins running backwards and forwards doing errands. He could hear them whingeing constantly.

Johnny had made a couple of visits to Home Humber since the day of the funeral and had been made welcome, but had not plucked up the courage to ask Reigneth out on a date. The age difference was still an issue for him. Somehow it did not seem right, though her family did not object to his visits and while Jessie was less than welcoming, he had come to realise it was just her way. She seemed to have accepted him and he no longer felt so uncomfortable.

He and Reigneth were not as relaxed in each other's company as they had been at first, but at least they were now speaking. James, of course, was still hovering in the background, which Johnny found difficult, unable to overlook the closeness between Reigneth and her cousin. It seemed to Johnny that many things had changed lately and since Izzy had removed her cheerful presence and gone home, he had no one to confide in. At least for the time being she had given up on her mission to get his love life back on track; he did not know whether to be relieved or sorry. Johnny knew her relationship with her parents was not any easy one, but she tried to be a dutiful daughter and not deprive them of her company for too long. However, she had promised to return for the fete weekend. Izzy was a member of the band that Johnny had got together at university and they had promised to do a gig. She was not going to let them play without her.

Matthew was acting oddly too: every time Johnny visited Higher Wedicombe, Matt could not wait to ask if he had been to Home Humber and if so, had he seen Reigneth's mother. It seemed to Johnny that Jessie Gray was all Matt wanted to talk about these days and he found it mildly irritating.

Johnny's mood was often low. He felt as if the only time he truly existed was when he was with Reigneth. Those times were all too few. Perhaps it would be better just to tell her how he felt, but he was reluctant to do this with James in the background. Consequently, when they did meet, their conversation was stilted and awkward and he came away seething with frustration and even more depressed.

Musically at least he was motivated: thoughts of Reigneth were inspirational when he was composing. The other musicians were due to come down a few days before the fete and would stay on for a week or so, there was plenty of room to put them all up at the Wilmotts' palatial home. Depending on what musical interests prevailed at university, the size of the band fluctuated. Currently it consisted of five members. They were all very different, but equally talented musically and they worked well together. It would be fun to see them and Johnny looked forward to a week of trying to hammer out the songs that were floating around in his head. It would give him some respite.

Grace was happy when Johnny's friends arrived, perhaps their stay would change his moods, which had begun to cause her concern. She did not know why he was so unhappy, though suspected it was something to do with the Pritchards' niece. Richard had introduced her to Reigneth Gray and her mother after the funeral, but there had been no opportunity on that sombre occasion to do more than express her sympathy for their loss. Johnny had been extremely reticent about them and she knew better than to push him, he was so like Matt in that respect. She had tried to find out more, but other than the fact that the niece was a beauty – which she had seen for herself – no one seemed to know anything about the Grays, not even Mrs Cooper at the shop. Either that or they were not telling.

When the day of the fete arrived Grace was in a flat spin. Johnny's friends had helped to put up the marquee, so at least she no longer had that to worry about, but she still had the ponies to see to before she could leave home and she felt as if she needed to be in half a dozen places at once. Johnny, of course, could be relied upon to help with the ponies; it was a labour of love to him.

Fortunately, the day had dawned dry and sunny and by midday the fete was in full swing and running like clockwork. Watching a group of children running by laughing and getting under the feet of the judges, who were busy tasting the homemade chutneys on the WI stall, Grace listened to the cacophony of happy voices and wondered why she had expected anything less. She had always had a flair for organising. She was silently congratulating herself on how well things were going, when she caught sight of her darling boy walking towards her. He was laughing out loud and he looked so beautiful it quite took her breath away. How had she ever given birth to anyone so handsome? She took in the wider picture and saw the girl walking beside him. There was no denying that Reigneth Gray was equally stunning and watching them laughing together, deep in conversation, Grace thought what an amazing couple they made. It brought a lump of nostalgia to her throat and made her think of herself and Matthew at the same age.

Grace gave an involuntary gasp: *talk of the Devil… what's he doing here?* Matt never usually came to these things, but there he was, large as life, walking over to Johnny. Seeing them together was startling; you'd have to be an idiot not to realise they were father and son. Anxiously she glanced around to see if anyone else was staring at them. Only then did she notice the woman approaching the group. Matthew seemed suddenly to stiffen and even from a distance, Grace could see his gaze was fixed on the elegant figure walking towards him. With a pang she recognised the look: he used to look at her like that once, as if he wanted to devour her. As the woman drew closer, Grace saw it was Jessie Gray and observed her lock onto Matt's gaze then look away as though embarrassed. She was almost as breathtaking as her daughter, thought Grace, a sour taste in her mouth. No wonder Matt was gaping like a landed fish. Even had she not already known the woman was a Gypsy, it was obvious now, with her olive colouring, her jet black hair fastened at the nape of her neck and the customary gold earrings and jewellery. Jessie wore a black skirt and blouse and sensible shoes, and moved with undeniable grace and elegance.

As Grace watched, Reigneth said something to Johnny then put her arm around her mother and kissed her tenderly on the cheek. Johnny looked all around, caught sight of Grace and hailed her, causing Matt to glance in her direction. Grace felt her lips tightening into a hard line, the muscles in her jaw and neck constricting. She was consumed with jealousy. Who did this woman think she was, stealing Matt away from under her nose? Well Jessie Gray was no match for her, she'd put a stop to this and no mistake. Purposefully fixing her mouth into her most engaging smile she walked forward, holding out her hand as Johnny stepped forward to effect the introductions. He must have forgotten they had all met at the funeral, but she did not remind him.

Reigneth assessed Johnny's mother immediately, she did not need to touch her. Grace had been pretty when younger and was still an attractive woman, her perfect bone structure giving her face an ageless appearance. Immaculately turned out as always, she approached them with a mask of civility; a facade she adopted with everyone except her children. Reigneth could not imagine Grace ever giving way to her emotions, she was a woman used to hiding things. After exchanging pleasantries, the party said their 'goodbyes' and strolled away.

Looking back, Matthew saw Grace was staring after them and knew from the venom in her eyes that he had not heard the last of this encounter. Strange how he could read her, he had always thought she was so lovely, so delicate. Now his thoughts were all for the beautiful woman walking beside him, who needed to be loved and protected – especially from Grace.

The only physical contact he'd had with Jessie was when they had danced at Reigneth's birthday party, but the chemistry between them was electrifying. Matthew was a patient man, especially when he knew what he wanted. Before too long he would make his feelings known to her. Jessie was kind, she would not keep him waiting longer than was necessary – she was not that sort of woman. He hoped she would have him.

The four of them wandered over to the marquee where Johnny and his band were to play to the assembling crowd. Izzy was there, larking about with the others on the makeshift stage as they set about unpacking and tuning their instruments. Matthew laughed to see them, feeling suddenly more light-hearted than he had in a very long time.

Two days after the fete, Grace, who had thought Matthew would be sure to ring her, was still waiting for his call. *If that's the way he wants to play it,* she thought, getting into the Land Rover, *the mountain will just have to go to Mohammed!* She was angry enough to do just that. All the way to Higher Wedicombe she was thinking about the look Matt had bestowed on that woman and winding herself up to such a pitch that when she turned into the yard and saw him standing there, she leapt out of the vehicle and waded straight in.

"What the hell do you think you are playing at making sheep's eyes at that woman?" Grace hurled the words at Matthew.

"Whatever do you mean?"

"Have you taken leave of your senses, Matt? She's a Gypsy!" Grace knew she was losing her customary control, but could not help it: she was incensed by Matthew's calm, slightly contemptuous expression.

"Yes she is and I'm appalled that you should think it matters, Grace – it's not a side of you I've ever seen before. I should tell you that I count myself privileged even to keep company with her. Jessie is a very special person. She is brave and beautiful and would do anything for her family. And in any case, I cannot imagine what you think it has got to do with you. You don't own me, Grace. You gave up that option a very long time ago. What was I supposed to do, wait for you forever? I think twenty odd years is enough don't you? It's been over a year since Harry died and not one single call have I had from you. Well I'm done waiting. I have a chance of happiness and I'm grabbing it for all it's worth."

Grace was so taken aback by this unaccustomed outburst from the normally reticent Matthew that for a moment she was rendered speechless – only a moment, however. "You are stark raving mad, Matthew!" Grace sneered, added, "Is it you she's after or the farm, do you think?" She almost spat out the words.

A look of utter disgust passed over Matt's face. "The farm is for our son, Grace, always has been."

Horrified, Grace stared at him, "You can't be serious; you cannot leave Johnny the farm. Everyone will know... Johnny will know."

Matthew shrugged, "We'll just have to face that hurdle when we come to it. I don't intend to pop my clogs just yet, Grace, I've got a lot of lost time to catch up on. But you mark my words, that boy is going to find out for himself soon enough and it'll be worse for him if he doesn't hear it from you. But that's all I am going to say on the matter – and now, if you'll excuse me, I'm expected elsewhere."

Dumbfounded, Grace stared at Matthew's rigid back as he walked back down the yard. She had never heard him say so much. And what he had said both enraged and worried her. Rather than stand there with her mouth open, she concluded this was not a battle to be won today and got back into the Land Rover. But she was not done; not by any means.

Chapter 16

Jalling the Drom (Travelling the Road)

Since the day of the fete, Reigneth had felt much less stressed about Johnny. They had managed on that fun day to regain something of the rapport they had lost over the previous weeks. She was sorry James was having such a hard time, though, and while she would miss him, for his sake she would be relieved to see him go. A friend of his, who did horse transport up and down the country, was passing through Exeter at the end of the week and since Reigneth had foreseen that it would now be safe for James to travel home by road – and much cheaper than by train – he was thinking of catching a lift with him. Reigneth knew her cousin was hoping she would ask him to stay permanently, but as much as she wanted to, she resisted the temptation. She was not so selfish as to inflict such a huge move on James if it was not what he really wanted – at least not yet – he needed to make his own decision. She knew he would get around to it eventually because she had seen that was the way it would be in the future. She also knew that one day, he and Johnny would be friends – but try telling either of them that!

Today they had gone into Chagford for some shopping and Reigneth found herself casting around hoping to see Johnny's battered old Land Rover, James trudging morosely at her side.

Fuelled by James's constant attendance on Reigneth, Johnny's feelings towards the man had not abated. *Will this guy never go home,* he thought, catching sight of them across the street. He saw Reigneth disappear into the butcher's and James kicking his heels as he waited with Jukel outside the shop. Schooling himself to appear nonchalant, Johnny sauntered over and bent down to pat the dog, which, he was pleased to see, wagged its tail.

"I expect you'll be leaving us soon, James, or have you decided to settle down here?" Johnny asked in a bored tone as if he could not have cared less, when in fact he needed desperately to know.

"I'll be leaving at the end of the week you'll be pleased to hear. Don't worry, I'll not *chor* aught of yours and she's been yours all along even before you knew her. I'll say this though, you don't deserve her and if you hurt her I'll break your neck."

Johnny did not understand half of it, but knew he was being warned in a threatening way. What did *chor'* mean? And what was he saying about Reigneth? Johnny did not doubt James meant what he said about killing him. It had been clear all along that he loved Reigneth, but now it dawned on Johnny that perhaps the love was not reciprocated – at least, not in the same way. For an instant he almost felt a shred of sympathy for the man: he looked utterly dejected. Johnny recalled the conversation he had overheard that day in the garden. Had James asked Reigneth to marry him and been turned down? From his demeanour it seemed likely. Before Johnny could respond, Reigneth came out of the shop.

"Hello, Johnny," she flashed him a smile just as her cousin turned away. "James, where are you going? I've just got to pick up Mam's prescription."

"Give it here, I'll collect it." Frowning, James snatched the prescription from Reigneth's hand and trudged across to the chemist's, head down, shoulders slumped.

Reigneth raised one eyebrow in query, "What have you said to upset him?" Before Johnny could protest his innocence, she said with a smile, "Nothing I daresay. Don't be angry with him, Johnny, it's not easy for him and he won't be here much longer."

"I know, he told me," Johnny muttered, feeling immediately ashamed of the way he felt. "What does *chor'* mean?"

She laughed, "It means 'steal'. Look, I'll have more time to myself when he's gone. Perhaps we could ride out one day like before? If you'd like to, that is."

Johnny felt overwhelmed. She had forgiven him for being such an arrogant, foolish idiot. She cared for him after all. He felt like bursting into song, but instead said, "I'd like nothing better. Reigneth, I've been such a fool, I'm so sorry, can you forgive me?"

The sweetness of her smile melted him. "There is nothing to

forgive. I'd better go and catch up with James. Ring me, and we'll arrange a day." With that she turned and hurried across the road.

Feeling the first trickle of happiness he had experienced in a long time, Johnny stood in the middle of the pavement where she had left him. He had completely forgotten why he had come into Chagford. Making his way slowly back to where he had parked, he could not help feeling that it was somehow a hollow victory. James was leaving, but so was he, going back to university to complete the last year of his degree. They had only a few days left before the summer break came to an end. She must know that he loved her. He dare not assume his feelings were returned... and yet, the way she had looked at him and the things James had said, which now began to make some sort of sense, gave him cause to hope. How stupid to have wasted the whole summer over petty differences when they might have spent more time together.

Climbing into the Land Rover, Johnny slammed his hands on the steering wheel in frustration. A few short days. The next time he would be home would be in November for Matt's birthday. He knew he would never last that long.

Chapter 17

Education

Naturally, Jessie was glad her daughter had settled so well at Home Humber, but thought it strange that Reigneth should like it so much when she herself was having such difficulty in settling. She missed Lincolnshire; it was all she had known since she had married Joe. With no busy motorway network, it was a place that time forgot and its rural nature added to that feeling. Jessie had always felt free there. She supposed many of her family felt the same; it was probably why they had stayed there. In Lincoln itself were two large areas of common land, and those of her family who had settled in houses had gravitated to those wide open spaces. All living within a stone's throw of one another, their extended family structure had remained strong and supportive. Each April and September the South Common hosted a fair and some of her Gray cousins arrived with the fair each year. They would be gathering there now, Jessie thought with a pang of sadness. When she had mentioned this to her sister a few days ago, Liz had confided that after she had married Richard she had been terribly homesick, missed her kin for ages, but eventually she had got used to it and Jessie would too. "Give it time, Jess," Liz had said. But Jessie could not imagine she ever would. She continued to miss her family and the area – but most of all Joe. The pain never went away.

Reigneth was in her element. She loved it here: the narrow roads and enclosing high hedges that her mother so disliked made it such a private place. *A good place to keep a secret*, Reigneth thought. Beyond the tiny streets and shaded lanes of Chagford, the moor rose bleak and beckoning, wild and mysterious. She could hide here in Devon, or at least hide her gift of *dukkering*. She felt free and uninhibited for the first time in her life. Her rapidly approaching first day at sixth-form college, however, made her anxious. Reigneth's experiences of both primary and secondary school had at times been difficult. At least she did not have to wear uniform at college and would be allowed to wear her jewellery. Her gold hoops were an intrinsic part of her personality. She had lost count of the times she had been stripped of bracelets, necklaces and earrings in front of her classmates, but that humiliation would not happen again. College was a new start for her and she was not about to hide who or what she was. At least not if she could help it, but, as well she knew, sometimes things are easier said than done.

A school bus left Chagford every weekday morning at eight o'clock to make the twenty-mile journey to Exeter. Waking early with butterflies in her stomach and no appetite, Reigneth forced down some breakfast – she did not want to feel faint during the morning. She had dressed very simply in a blue shirt, black jeans and black jacket, her hair scraped back from her face in a long plait.

As she queued at the bus stop, four other teenagers lined up behind her. They smiled and Reigneth, feeling suddenly shy, smiled back. When she recognised Charlotte bounding up to her, followed at a more leisurely pace by Henry, she relaxed a little. The twins were kind; perhaps she would be alright after all. Charlotte insisted on sitting next to her leaving Henry to sit by himself. He sat across the aisle and kept stealing glances at her. Reigneth was used to the way boys looked at her and had long ago given up worrying about it. Henry, however, was Johnny's brother and she felt it safe to tease him a little, so she met his gaze. He blushed and looked away.

"Don't worry about Henry," Charlotte said. "He's been looking forward to this morning. He thinks you're fit and Johnny's lucky."

It was Reigneth's turn to blush, liking the sense of togetherness with Johnny that this implied.

The bus ride took ages, stopping and starting in all the villages until finally it arrived in Exeter with a full load. The students came from several schools round about so many were strangers to one another and all those in Reigneth's year were new to college, which made her feel a little less uncomfortable. She was to study English Literature, Art and Psychology. She had no idea what she wanted to do after that, but still, she had two years to make up her mind. Her

Dad had wanted her to get an education and she intended to do her best in his memory.

The first day went by faster than Reigneth had thought possible, but as she stepped aboard the bus to go home she was exhausted. She had not realised, until she sank back into the seat, that she had been holding herself stiff and tense all day, rigid with the stress of anticipating someone would taunt her or grasp hold of her, afraid she would not be able to control her reactions if they did. Vaguely aware that Henry was once again eyeing her up, she found herself nodding off and within ten minutes of the bus setting off she was asleep.

The week passed uneventfully without any nasty remarks, which was in itself amazing. Reigneth had endured her fair share of these in the past, often experiencing prickling sensations in her eyes, her throat constricting as she frantically held back tears when the 'dirty gypo' or 'pikey' taunts came her way. Her dad had mistakenly believed that by not letting on what he was, he was protecting her. He had not realised it was the worst kept secret ever. Reigneth reflected that when you constantly denied what you were, as though you were ashamed of it, you devalued yourself and eventually you became less of a person. No one was going to make her feel like that ever again.

Lately, she had been able to talk with her mother about how she felt. Jessie was as proud as she was beautiful. It was why she had never mixed with *Gaujas*, only with her own kind. She had never wished to deny what she was, but for Joe's sake she had often done so. He had a quick temper and Jessie had not wanted him constantly fighting. But those days were gone. Reigneth had been thankful to hear her mam say she was not keeping quiet any longer. "If that's what you want, my *bitti chai*, I will support you," she had said with a smile. There had been ample evidence that she meant what she said on the day of the fete when, for the first time, Jessie had accompanied her to a *Gauja* function and had not attempted to hide that she was Romany. It had gladdened Reigneth's heart.

Chapter 18

Exposure

Matthew had not had a birthday party since he was a child. Having lived like a recluse for so many years he had few friends, but he intended to change that. If he was honest, the main incentive for having a party now was that he could get to see Jessie without compromising her, since it would be only natural to invite her and her daughter along with the Pritchards, whom he thought of as friends. Having made the decision, Matthew looked around at his living room and for the first time saw it as others would see it: there was no denying it was a mess. Also, he hadn't the first idea of how to cook – beyond his staple diet of anything that came out of a can – but these were not insurmountable obstacles; he could clean the place up and Johnny could give him a few pointers about what food to buy in.

"Blimey, Matt," said Johnny, when Matthew asked his advice. "I don't mean to be rude, but have you had a personality transplant lately?" Grinning, he ducked as Matthew threw a mock punch at him. "I mean, for as long as I've known you, you've never done anything remotely sociable."

Conceding the point, Matthew laughed. *You don't know the half of it, my boy*, he thought, glad the reason for the intended party had not dawned on Johnny. It seemed he was not the most perceptive of people when it came to affairs of the heart; his own relationships included, and clearly he had no idea of Matthew's growing affection for Jessie.

"Look, Matt, don't take offense, but your place is not exactly... err, well, I mean... " Johnny hesitated, eyeing the cobweb-festooned ceiling and the stained, threadbare carpet.

"Habitable?" Matthew finished for him.

"You said it," Johnny grinned. "How many people were you thinking of inviting?"

"Well, the Pritchards and the Grays – and you, of course."

"Well if that's all, why don't you invite everyone out for a meal instead?"

With an answering grin, Matthew clapped his son on the back, "Great idea!"

As excited as they were to receive Matthew's invitation, Reigneth and Jessie had a problem: they had nothing decent to wear. Neither one had ever really been interested in clothes: Reigneth, because there had never been any money to buy them; Jessie, because even had she been able to afford them, she hated shopping. New clothes had always seemed an unnecessary extravagance to them both. Mostly they wore hand-me-downs, altered in some way to give a good fit. Reigneth was an excellent seamstress having been well taught by both her mother and grandmother, but although she had a flair for re-making garments, this time she had nothing to work with.

Seeing their predicament, Liz came to the rescue. With a wide smile at Jessie, she said to Reigneth, "I've just thought of something. Come with me." Mystified, Reigneth did so, wondering why her aunt was leading her up to the top of the house. She soon had the answer: for most of his adult life, Uncle Richard had in a quiet sort of way been able to make enough from his paintings to get by, but there had rarely been much left over for new clothes. One or two of his wealthier female clients, who had come to know the Pritchards quite well over the years, had taken pity on her and from time to time had passed on their hardly worn cast-offs. Not one to take offense, Liz had accepted them gratefully and then, hating waste of any kind, had layered them with lavender and rosemary to deter the moths, stowed the bags of clothes in the box room and forgotten all about them. Like her sister, Liz wasn't particularly bothered about clothes unless they were practical and these were not the sort she would normally wear, so she'd had no use for them. Until now.

Rummaging through the box room, Reigneth felt a thrill of excitement. Incredibly there were clothes in there from years ago. She was amazed to find retro evening gowns and prom dresses as well as ordinary everyday clothes, although, she noticed with a

152

wry grin, not with ordinary everyday labels! All of this unexpected bounty she could set to and re-make. There were even a few black items that could be altered for her mother, who had said she was tired of her same old black dress. Problem solved. In no time at all, the kitchen was heaped with material and she and Jessie were industriously cutting and sewing. It was the first time Reigneth had heard her mother laugh in a long time.

Matthew had booked a table at a restaurant in North Bovey. He had even invested in a new suit and shoes for the occasion and looked very smart when Johnny, having insisted that Matt should relax and enjoy some wine with his meal, picked him up in the Wilmotts' Land Rover. He was relieved to see that Johnny had made an attempt to clean the vehicle: he did not want his new clothes getting stuck up with mud and straw. It was not that Matthew was particularly fastidious, but the clothes had been expensive and he liked to hang on to his money.

Seated at the head of the table, he could not have been happier. He had managed to manoeuvre the two people he cared for most to sit on either side of him: Jessie on his right and Johnny on his left. Matthew was touched that both Jessie and Reigneth seemed to have taken the trouble to dress up for the occasion; they had never looked lovelier. The conversation flowed easily and what with Richard's dry wit and Matt and Johnny teasingly outdoing each other with ever more unbelievable stories, there was much laughter round the table.

Having finished their starter and main course they were just deciding what to have for dessert when Johnny received a call on his mobile. He frowned, looked up at Matt, "Sorry everyone, I'll have to take this. Please excuse me."

"Problem?" Matthew queried when Johnny ended the call and turned back to the table.

"Afraid so. That was Dave Hancock from the National Park Rescue Team. A couple of lads staying at the *Three Crowns* went out walking this morning and haven't returned. Their parents are frantic." He shrugged, "I'm sorry, but Dave's asked for my help. I'll have to go."

"No problem, lad, I'll come too," Matthew volunteered immediately, pushing back his chair and getting to his feet. He paused, grimaced, "Look, I'm really sorry to break up the party... "

"Don't worry about it," said Richard. "There's only one person knows the moor better than Johnny and that's you, Matthew. You go. It's been lovely, thank you. I'm too full for a dessert anyway."

"That goes for me too," said Elizabeth, patting her stomach in a way that made them all laugh and relieved the sudden tension.

Matthew nodded gratefully and smiled at her, gestured to the waiter for the bill and explained what had happened. Behind him he could hear Reigneth and Jessie talking in hushed voices. Glancing round he saw that Jessie was distressed and her daughter was trying to calm her. Catching the end of the conversation he heard Reigneth say, "Ma, you wouldn't let me leave them to come to harm would you?" She looked up at Matthew and said firmly, "We'll go with you."

Taken aback, he raised an eyebrow and exchanged a doubtful glance with Johnny, who gave a quick nod and said, "That's fine. The Team is assembling in the *Three Crowns*. We should go. I keep a change of clothes in the Land Rover for just this eventuality. I can change when we get to the pub," he said in an aside to Matthew.

"Well then," announced Liz, "you're not leaving us behind. Come on Richard, we'll take Jess and Reigneth in the car. You surely can't expect them to go in the back of the Land Rover in all their finery," she smiled at Johnny.

They collected their coats and left the restaurant, hurrying out to Richard's battered old Volvo estate, Jessie looking so agitated that Matthew wished he could give her a hug.

"Great party, Matt," Johnny grinned climbing into the Land Rover. He reached over and dug Matthew in the ribs, "Couldn't help noticing the way you were looking at Jessie."

"Not sure how, since as far as I could see you spent the entire evening with your eyes glued to Reigneth," Matthew retorted, his voice gruff.

Chuckling, Johnny put his foot down and they drove the rest of the way in companionable silence.

Two of the Search and Rescue Team's big 4x4s were parked outside the *Three Crowns* and the pub was crowded and noisy, the search party already assembled and kitted out with gear. The parents of the missing boys, very obviously distressed, were explaining that their sons were well equipped, had told everyone where they were going and had mobile phones with them.

"I just don't know what can have happened," sobbed the mother. "They should have been back hours ago or at least made contact."

"Now then, love," said the boys' father, "don't take on so. They'll be fine, don't you worry. They've just got lost is all. These kind people will find them."

"The phones won't do much good on the moor; poor reception," Matthew commented in an undertone to Dave, who had come across the room to greet him and Johnny.

Reigneth, who had been standing just inside the door with her arm around her mother and watching the distressed couple, went forward to speak to them.

"Do you have something belonging to the boys, something they have worn – anything at all?"

"Not on us," the mother responded with a startled look at Reigneth. "But we are staying here. I can go upstairs and get something, but what's it for?"

"I might be able help," Reigneth said gently, adding, "and paper and pencil if you can." Looking mystified, yet hopeful, the woman rushed away.

Conscious of Johnny frowning at her from across the room, a look of disbelief stamped on his face, Reigneth shook her head at him and mouthed, 'I'll explain later.'

At her elbow, Jessie, increasingly agitated, whispered urgently, "Think what you are doing girl!"

"Would you rather I let them die Ma? It's November and cold." Reigneth grasped her mother's hand and reassured her, "Hush, it's OK. Stop worrying."

She waited until the boys' mother rushed back with two sweaters, a sheet of paper and a pencil. "Thank you," said Reigneth, taking them over to a dark corner of the pub. Sitting at the most tucked away table, Reigneth took a deep breath and allowed her surroundings to fade from her consciousness, bringing all her concentration to bear on the two sweaters. Putting first one and then the other to her face, she inhaled deeply. Then pulling the paper towards her, she quickly began to sketch. A detailed drawing of a rocky outcrop, distinctive in shape and instantly recognisable, appeared on the page.

Johnny, having changed out of his suit, had come forward and was leaning over her shoulder to see what she was drawing. She looked up at him and heard his gasp, saw reflected in his anxious eyes the startling pallor of her face. It always happened when she was *dukkering*; as if all the blood rushed away from her head, leaving her exhausted and faint.

Again she buried her face in the two garments then placed them back on the table. "You'll find them where these rocks are, Johnny," she pointed to her drawing. "One of the lads is injured but not seriously, his leg is broken. He has fallen off the rocks. The other boy is trying to find his way down to him."

Johnny looked stunned; Jessie, as though she could hardly contain her anxiety, stood beside him. Reigneth knew what her mother was thinking. Never in her life had she allowed her gift to be witnessed by any but close family, but in the circumstances, what else could she do? The moor was a vast area, it could take hours to find the boys and both would die from exposure unless they got help soon. Neither was as well equipped as their parents had thought them. Incomers never really understood the moor; so often underestimated the dangers. Unable to speak, she handed Johnny the drawing and gazed up at Matthew, who had come up behind him, Liz on one side and Richard on the other, all of them protecting her from the gaze of people in the pub.

Matthew smiled down at her, said, "Well done, Reigneth. You are a remarkable girl." Struggling not to pass out, Reigneth heard his words as from a great distance.

This girl is extraordinary,' thought Matthew. He now knew what Jessie and her family had been at such pains to hide. Reigneth had a spectacular gift, but her amazing feat had clearly taken its toll. Her face was chalk white and she looked as if she was about to faint. He reached out to hold her, hesitated, murmured, "May I help you?" She nodded and Matthew, placing his arm about her waist to support her, helped her out of her chair.

"Johnny, go find the boys, you know where they are, I'll get Reigneth home," Matthew urged, keen to get the girl away before anyone in the pub realised what had transpired. Over Reigneth's head he exchanged glances with Jessie and smiled reassuringly, seeing the relief in her eyes when she understood he was aware of the need to get her daughter home quickly.

Without hesitation, Johnny stepped forward to kiss Reigneth's cheek.

"Johnny, take Juk," she whispered. "He'll go with you. He's in the back of Richard's car."

"OK, my love, don't worry. You are amazing. I'll see you later." He whisked the drawing out of sight of prying eyes and was gone. Seconds later came the sounds of the 4x4s starting up and driving away.

Still supporting Reigneth, Matthew waited a moment while she found her feet, then steered her out to the Volvo, Jessie, Richard and Liz following close behind. Johnny must have gone with Jukel in one of the Search and Rescue vehicles because his Land Rover was still there. Matthew thought about taking it and catching up with the search, but Reigneth was still clinging to him and both she and Jessie seemed to need him. He helped them into the back of the Volvo and squeezed in beside them. Soon, Richard was speeding to Home Humber, all of them anxious to get Reigneth home safe and out of harm's way.

Once back in the big farm kitchen, Liz made tea for everyone. No one spoke and Matthew wondered who would be first to break the silence. It was Jessie. Seated next to Reigneth with her arm around her, she asked, "Are you alright my *bitti chai?*"

"Yes Ma, I just feel a bit tired, the boys will be OK. I think I'd like to go up to bed now, if you don't mind. Matthew, we have a gift for your birthday, Ma will sort it." Reigneth smiled and clutching her tea, supported by her aunt, she went up to bed.

Alone – Richard, diplomatic as ever having made himself scarce – Jessie and Matthew quietly sipped their tea. Hesitantly, Jessie said, "Matt, I feel I ought to explain, but first I'd like to thank you for getting Reigneth out of the pub so quickly."

"There's no need to thank me, Jessie, it was obvious she wasn't feeling well and I figured if I got her away quickly no one would cotton on to what they had just seen. In fact, I'm still trying to figure it out myself," Matthew grinned.

"It takes you by surprise when you first witness it, doesn't it," Jessie remarked.

"Well, I'd just like you to explain exactly what it was I saw because I'm none too sure that... " Matthew paused, "well, err, that is to say, what Reigneth said, will it be right?"

"Yes, it will be exactly as Reigneth told it. She has been able to foresee things ever since she was a little girl, it's an uncanny gift. We call it *dukkering*. It is not something we wish to be common knowledge, you understand. Her life would become quite intolerable if everyone knew of it and as a family we have always hidden it in an effort to protect her."

Matthew nodded. He could quite see how difficult it would become for Reigneth if people knew, and for the first time he appreciated the risk she had taken for the sake of those two unknown boys. "Tell me more about it, Jessie. I've never seen anything like it and yet I knew there was something different about her the very first time we met," he smiled, relieved to know at last what he had sensed in Reigneth on the day they had been introduced.

"She dreams things usually, and they all come true. She sees things when she touches someone; sometimes she doesn't even have to touch them. Perhaps you've noticed how she avoids physical contact? It's not because she's unemotional or unfeeling, it's that some of the things she sees are disturbing." Giving a huge sigh, Jessie slumped in her chair. "I haven't ever spoken about this to anyone, Matt. Fact is, I haven't spoken much at all since my Joe passed."

With a sympathetic grimace, Matthew nodded, "I know how much you still grieve for him, Jessie. I'm sorry if this is difficult for you. Would you like me to go?"

"Oh no, at least, not till you've drunk your tea."

She smiled at him and he felt his heart skip a beat. Gazing at her intently, he was aware that somehow their relationship had strengthened during the evening. He knew Jessie had appreciated the care and consideration he had shown towards Reigneth and he was torn: he wanted to linger over his tea and stay and talk to her, but he also wanted to get out onto the moor to his lad.

Looking into Matthew's face, Jessie felt she was seeing him for the first time. She saw how kind and considerate he was and that he cared for her, even that he loved her, and she could see that his feelings were intense and passionate. She felt a little light-headed and her pulse quickened. From the way he had behaved in the pub she knew this man would protect Reigneth as if she were his own, he was a good man. She was surprised that she found Matthew so attractive and also how easily she could talk to him. Sharing the secret with him felt like lifting a weight from her shoulders.

To her consternation and embarrassment, Jessie found herself comparing Matthew to Joe. She began to notice other things about him: his clothes were ill-fitting and old-fashioned; he was a man who didn't go out often and didn't care much for his appearance when he did. Very different to her Joe, who had always been tidy and well-dressed even if only out working, his clothes always presentable. Like Joe's, Matthew's hair had obviously been dark when he was young, though now it was streaked through with grey and, unlike Joe's, extremely untidy. He had quite large eyes and a full mouth with nice teeth. Jessie found herself smiling and when Matthew finished his tea and put his empty mug down on the table, she felt a tinge of disappointment that the brief interlude had come to an end.

"Well, if you're sure you're all OK," he said, "I'll take my leave and go and find the others, check to see if Johnny needs me." Matthew stood, "I'll call by in the morning, if that's all right?"

"Yes, of course. Does that mean you are going up onto the moor, Matt?" Jessie frowned; the thought of it worried her. She could hear rain splattering on the kitchen window; it sounded as though it was blowing up a storm.

He gave her a reassuring grin, "I'll not leave Johnny up there alone, Jess, but don't worry. We were both raised on the moor, we'll be OK," Matthew said, walking towards the door.

"He's a good boy. You're very fond of him aren't you?" Jessie observed. Matthew just smiled and was about to let himself out when Jessie remembered his birthday gift. "Hang on, Matt, I must give you your present."

"Shall we open it together tomorrow, Jessie, only... " he hesitated.

"Yes of course, you want to get off," she smiled hesitantly, not wanting to detain him and worried about both of them being in danger. "There'll be time tomorrow."

Just then, Richard came back into the kitchen. He had changed his clothes and looked as if he was ready to explore Antarctica. He carried walking boots and clothes for Matthew to change into.

"Just a minute, Matt," he said, holding them out. "I thought it would be a shame to ruin that suit; it must have cost a bob or two. I'll take you up to the moor in the Volvo. You can't walk all that way and I might be able to help."

"Not wishing to sound ungrateful, Richard, and I really appreciate the clothes, but the moor is no place for you, especially tonight. Truth be told, even as old as I am and used to it, I take no chances with it. I could do with a lift into Chagford though, to pick up Johnny's Land Rover."

Jessie listened to their footsteps crunching down the path and for a few moments she stayed sitting at the table trying to work out what it was she was feeling. "Oh, Joe, my love, what do you think about it all?" she sighed.

They took only a few minutes to get back to the *Three Crowns*. Matthew reached inside the Land Rover and felt for the spare key always taped under the dash. With a quick wave to Richard, he was soon driving through Gidleigh and Throwleigh and up onto the moor. The rain battered relentlessly against the windscreen and visibility was poor. He could see the lights from the search and rescue vehicles in the distance and pulled to a hasty stop, skidding on the carpet of leaves and slush on the road.

As he trudged towards the rescue team, his thoughts drifted as he tried to make headway, the wind buffeting against his face. Thinking of Reigneth, he wondered just how far this talent of hers extended. He knew the landmark she had drawn, and sure enough, that's where the rescue team were.

Once again, Matthew cast his mind back to the first day he had met her, recalling the strange expression that came over her face when she touched his hand. He had thought her a funny little thing then. Now he wondered if her talent extended not only to the future but also to the past. Then he thought about Jessie's comment about his fondness for Johnny. Had there been a hidden message there? Was his secret still safe? He wondered how much she knew, more importantly, did Reigneth know, and if she did, had she already told his son – or if not, would she? *Will I be able to tell? Will he change – hate me?'* The thought made Matthew feel physically ill.

As he came up to the top side of Throwleigh, he heard an approaching ambulance siren, the sound almost blown away on the wind. So they had found the boys then. The girl had been right. Somehow he had never doubted that she would be.

Up on the open moorland the wind howled mercilessly, the rain lashing at Johnny's face. It had been hard for him to make progress towards the outcrop he knew so well and he had been relieved to have Jukel up there with him. The dog had gone with him willingly, much to his surprise – but surprises had been the order of the night. Now he wanted answers.

Jukel had needed no torch or light to find his way, he had sniffed out where the boys lay and led Johnny straight to them. The uninjured lad, exhausted and cold, had been trying to reach his brother, who, just as Reigneth had said, had broken his leg in a fall. The paramedics had been swift to respond and Johnny's part was over. He had been amazed at the accuracy of Reigneth's prediction. It was something so beyond reason he could hardly believe it. Somehow he knew tonight's events were pivotal to his relationship with her. He had uncovered the reason why her family paid homage to the girl he was in love with. That at least he could now understand. She had looked so pale and shaken, exactly like when she had been dancing with James after the funeral. It occurred to him to wonder if she had been predicting something then too – but how was this possible? His thoughts going round in circles, Johnny was relieved to see Matthew walking towards him, could not wait to ask the question, "Hi Matt, is Reigneth all right?"

Matthew held up the torch and peered at him, intently searching his face. "She was exhausted and went straight to bed. She'll be OK though."

Blinking, Johnny pushed the torch away. "Hey, you're blinding me! What're you looking at me like that for?"

"Like what?"

"Like you're not sure if it's me!"

"Just wanting to make sure you're OK. Why else would I be looking at you?"

"I can't imagine," Johnny grinned. "Yeah, I'm OK, bit tired is all. Those lads were exactly where she said they would be, even the older one on the rock side trying to get to his injured brother. It's so weird. If I hadn't seen it with my own eyes I wouldn't have believed it. Has Jessie said anything?"

"Not a lot, I think she'll leave it to Reigneth to explain. I told her we'd call by and see them tomorrow. I've brought up your Land Rover," Matthew gestured to the road below them. "Could you give me a lift home?"

Johnny heard the anxiety in the question and could tell Matt was keen to get back to the farm. He looked unusually tired; he supposed they all did. It had been quite a night. "No problem. I'll drop you off and then take Juk home."

They stumbled back to the Land Rover, not bothering to make further conversation. There was little point since the wind whipped away their words as soon as they were spoken.

Driving somewhat recklessly for the conditions, Johnny soon had Matt home.

"See you in the morning then. Oh, and happy birthday, Matt!"

They parted company, both laughing.

At Home Humber Jessie pottered about in the kitchen while she waited for Johnny and Jukel to return. She liked Johnny more and more, but however nice he was, he was still a *Gauja* and she was worried about Reigneth's obvious affection for him, fearing the girl had heartache ahead of her. Jessie had been increasingly aware of changes in her daughter and was concerned that she no longer confided in her as she used to do when Joe was alive.

A light knock at the door heralded Johnny's arrival. Jessie already had the kettle boiling; he would need a hot drink to warm him, he must be bitterly cold. The weather was filthy, the worst she had known it since she and Reigneth had moved here.

The door opened and Jukel slid past Johnny, making straight for his usual place by the Aga, stretching out his long wet body on the rug. Johnny followed his example, moving to lean against the warm range. He was visibly shivering and Jessie guessed his muscles ached from the effort of trying to stave off the cold. He dragged his sopping hat from his head, his hair a tangled mess beneath it. Jessie noted it was almost as dark and thick as Reigneth's. His face was beautiful, his cheekbones pronounced like his mother's. *Far too pretty for a boy*, she thought.

He looked down at the mud from his boots and the water dripping off his clothes onto the floor, "Sorry, Jessie, I should've taken my boots off – the moor is treacherous tonight, gale force wind and torrential rain. But we found the boys, just like Reigneth said."

"Take your wet coat off, Johnny," Jessie said. "Don't worry about the mess, we're used to that. It'll soon wipe up." She took his coat and hung it over the Aga rail. "Why don't you sit down? You look done in."

"I am a bit weary, thanks." He huddled on the chair closest to the range. "Err... where's Reigneth – is she OK?"

"She'll be fine after a good night's sleep. She went straight to bed. I don't want to disturb her."

"No, of course not," he said, disappointment etched on his face.

He had been hoping to see Reigneth; that much was obvious. Of course, he would have many questions after what happened this evening. "You look like you could use something stronger than a cuppa," she said.

Johnny shook his head, "Just tea would be great, Jessie, thanks. Look, I don't want to badger you, but I need to know what happened tonight. I just need to understand. Can you explain?"

Ignoring the question, she passed a mug of steaming tea to him, which he cupped in both hands, his face hovering just above the rim as though he was taking comfort from the warmth on his face. He glugged it down greedily, said, "That's the best cuppa I've ever tasted, even if it has scalded my throat!"

"Top up?"

"Thanks," he held out his mug.

He took a little longer over the second cup and Jessie stood watching him in silence. She had never really *looked* at him before: his fingers were long and slender, not like Joe and Matt, whose hands were used to hard manual work and calloused and worn. This boy's were soft and delicate, yet she knew he was strong and never shirked hard work. He was a complex lad; sensitive. It occurred to her that he was quite like Matthew, and despite her misgivings she felt herself warming towards him.

He began to talk and she drew up a chair beside the Aga, listening as he described the moor to her, all its different moods and how he felt when he was out there, riding Rannoch, free and wild. He talked about his music and about the songs he was writing. And he talked about Reigneth.

It was the first time Jessie had been alone with Johnny and most certainly the first time he had talked with her at length. When

163

he spoke he focused on her totally, she was aware of his intense gaze and just how beautiful he was. She began to understand the attraction and devotion Reigneth felt for him. Jessie was surprised she felt so relaxed. A feeling of calm seemed to emanate from this boy sitting beside her. He was without guile and was obviously turning over the events of the evening in his mind. "Please tell me about Reigneth, about what happened tonight," he asked again, echoing her thoughts.

Jessie considered him a moment then shook her head, "It's up to Reigneth to tell you, Johnny, and we won't see her until late morning, she'll sleep heavily now, she always does when something like this happens." Jessie felt she had already said too much.

"How long has she had this... this... " he hesitated, "I mean, how long has she been able to do this thing that she did?" He was clearly desperate for answers.

"Don't talk about it like it's an affliction, Johnny, this is Reigneth. It's what she is. Always has been, she was born like it, she has been able to 'see' things, sense things since she was in the cradle." Suddenly afraid, Jessie clamped her lips. She gazed at Johnny, said urgently, "You cannot tell anyone, Johnny. You *must* not."

"I'm not about to. I just need to know – to understand." Quite unexpectedly he focused intently on Jessie's eyes, his own alert and intense. She could not doubt his sincerity. "I love her, Jessie. I'd protect her with my life. I'll never let her down, no matter what."

Jessie knew he meant every word. He spoke almost as though he was paying homage, his face flushed and glowing with the intensity of his devotion. Then he grinned, looked away and said, as though to himself, "I bet she saw me coming even before we met."

"We've always known you would come," Jessie smiled, "it was just a question of when. Look, come back tomorrow with Matt. Reigneth will tell you everything then. I know she would prefer to tell you herself."

"OK," he stood. "Good night then, and thanks for the tea. I'll see you tomorrow," and shrugging into his steaming coat, he strode across to the door and was gone.

Jessie stayed where she was, enjoying the warmth of the Aga and lost in her thoughts. She had always hoped that one day James and Reigneth would be married, despite Reigneth always declaring to the contrary. In Jessie's eyes it was a good thing to marry within your own kind, they knew your ways and the family were always supportive. She knew Reigneth had predicted she would marry a beautiful boy. She and Joe had laughed at that when their daughter was small. They had not suspected at that time just how precise Reigneth's gift could be. Jessie now realised that Johnny was the one her daughter had been waiting for. It dawned on her that this *Gauja* was to be her son; Reigneth's partner for all time.

Her thoughts strayed to Mary Gray. Jessie had long ago realised she had greatly underestimated Mary's gift. Joe's mother had warned them to protect her granddaughter, for until the prophecy was complete and she was united with her soul mate, Reigneth was vulnerable.

When the old lady was dying she had mumbled about stars and destiny, and Jessie had been unable to understand much of what she said, but only hours before she passed away, Mary had become quite lucid. She had always been watchful of her beloved granddaughter, she said, not just because of Reigneth's gift, but because the girl had been born under the light of Algol, the Demon Star.

It was considered a bad omen: in medieval times Reigneth would have remained a spinster, for no man would marry a woman born at so inauspicious a time. Almost certainly she would have met an untimely death and had she the gift of sight, been hanged as a witch.

Superstition had demonised Algol for centuries, but Jessie knew, because Reigneth had been determined to discover more about it, that it was merely a beautiful star that seemed to come and go, its light vanishing in a frequent eclipse as it revolved around its neighbouring star in a rhythmic, gravitational dance. But Mary had insisted that the superstitions were not without foundation and Reigneth was in danger.

Alone, she had not the strength to resist the evil forces that would seek to possess and use her, a threat not just to her but to others close to her. Only when she and her soul mate were united under Algol, would she become invincible. It had been prophesied that her powers would then grow and magnify; a reflection of the heavenly body that would strengthen her with its variable light.

Jessie, remembering Mary's words, intended to make sure that if Johnny and Reigneth were to be married then their union would be consummated under the light of Algol.

Only then would the prophesy be complete.

Chapter 19

Declaration

Reigneth woke late after a long, dreamless sleep to see the sun streaming through her bedroom window, it promised to be a beautiful day. She rolled over, hunching the duvet around her curled up form. She loved this drowsy warm feeling first thing in the morning and the realisation that she did not have to hurry to get up. She had only a hazy memory of the events of yesterday and was just trying to piece them together in her mind when the door creaked slightly and her mother came in with a cup of tea. She was smiling, an enquiry in her expression.

"I'm alright Ma. Did you hear how the boys are? Did Matt or Johnny ring or call?"

Jessie sat on the side of the bed and leant over to give her a hug. "Matthew rang to say the boys were shipped to the hospital last night, they're both alright, but one has a nasty compound fracture of his leg. I've invited both Matt and Johnny over for lunch. I had to tell them about you, Reigneth. I'm sorry, but there was no way I could *not* tell them after they'd seen your gift for themselves." Jessie looked almost ashamed: the secret she had kept for so long had been told to two *Gaujas*. "I have left it for you to fill in the details," she added.

"Of course you had to tell them, I had expected that you would."

Smiling, her mother ruffled Reigneth's hair. "Look at you, curled up there like a young child, and yet sometimes you seem so grown up I feel as if you are older than I am, my 'ancient child', old beyond your years."

Reigneth giggled, "I certainly feel a bit ancient today."

There was a tap on the door, "Are you decent?" called Richard. "Yes," they chorused.

He emerged round the door and beamed at Reigneth, "Better get up sleepy head. You've got visitors who seem extremely anxious to see you."

"Sounds like the brothers Grimm have arrived," Jessie said. "I'll leave you to get dressed."

Reigneth gave a nervous laugh, wondering if her mother was aware how close she had come to the family connection. The similarity between Johnny and Matt was so marked it was amazing nobody seemed to know. She smiled to herself; her mam was naive in some respects. It would never occur to her that anyone would have a child by someone other than her husband.

Scalding her throat in her haste, Reigneth drank her tea then reached for her clothes. Home Humber was always a bit chilly in the mornings and today was no exception. She pulled on her jeans, T-shirt and jumper then quickly dragged a comb through her tangled hair, but couldn't wait to braid it so left it loose and started down the stairs, back tracking to the bathroom to at least brush her teeth. She was vain enough not to want to breathe over Johnny without having first made sure she did not reek of last night's garlic.

Quietly making her entrance into the kitchen, Reigneth was greeted by smiles from everyone and for some stupid reason she felt embarrassed. She never did with her family, but *Gaujas* knowing about her was somehow different, although she knew her secret was safe with Matt and Johnny. Immediately she homed in to the fact that Matt was worried and she knew why. Knowing of her gift, he was wondering if his secret was safe. Smiling at him she passed behind his chair, put her hand on his shoulder and gave an almost imperceptible squeeze. She saw the relief in his answering smile and knew he was reassured.

Aware of Johnny's gaze following her every movement Reigneth knew it was plain for everyone to see that he adored her and she him. It seemed almost as if, with the revelation of her second sight, the blinkers were off in regard to many things, not just her and Johnny's love for one another, but the stirrings of another new relationship; that of Matt and Jessie. She had never seen her mother so relaxed in another man's company, not since Joe. Matt was not troubling to hide his feelings. It did not need second sight to see he was mad about her.

Johnny followed Reigneth and Jukel into the snug. With a sigh, the dog plonked himself down in front of the fire and Johnny, after a moment's hesitation, sat with Reigneth on the small sofa. It seemed so natural to hug that in no time they were entwined within each other's arms, and so they remained. Now he knew about her she felt she could be at ease: he was still there next to her despite things about her being a bit odd, and he no longer seemed bothered about the difference in their ages. She wondered if he would kiss her and whether she would be able to resist if he did, but he seemed content to let her dictate the pace. Things that before she had been unable to share with him she shared with him now. He had to know all about her in order to make his decision on whether to remain with her or not.

The hours passed by as she talked, describing everything in minute detail, until eventually the sun dimmed in the sky.

Listening to her soft voice, Johnny knew this was the beginning of the rest of his life. Reigneth's age no longer mattered to him and he wondered why it ever had. She had never seemed immature in any way. He now realised it was because all her life she had carried the responsibility of her family and loved ones on her own. She was no longer alone. His life without her would be meaningless and thankfully –amazingly – she felt the same; had always felt the same. He was astounded that she had been only a small child when she had first seen him in her dreams and had recognised him immediately the day she first saw him on the moor. She explained that it seemed to her the moor was acting as a sort of catalyst, for her gift since she moved here was heightened and more sensitive than it had ever been.

He marvelled that she was meant for him and only him; there had never been any possibility of her marrying James. Johnny had guessed rightly that the angry exchanges they'd had stemmed from jealousy: James had always loved and wanted her and found it hard to accept that it was not to be.

As the day wore on Reigneth unburdened herself to Johnny, describing all the things she had foreseen throughout her life: of how her father had tried to protect her from being teased and taunted; of her love for her paternal grandmother, from whom she had inherited her gift. While she was speaking, Johnny watched her lips and was mesmerised by the way they moved, full and inviting. He so loved her, his heart was hers and just at that present moment it was hammering fast against his chest, as if it wanted to break out and be with its new owner.

Finally, she warned him that if he chose to remain with her and be her soul mate then he would change – become different – but she did not know how. That much had not yet been shown to her. Johnny chose to ignore the warning, too overcome with elation and relief that she was his. Looking into her lovely face, he could see that she was exhausted. He held her tenderly in his arms, feeling a great surge of protectiveness. "I love you so very much, Reigneth," he murmured.

"And I you." She twiddled idly with a lock of his hair, seemingly unaware of the effect this was having on him. He wanted so much to kiss her, but too afraid she would reject him as she had done before, he held back. She reached up and gently stroked his face and his lips with her finger tips. His skin was on fire, tingling sensations rippled throughout his body. No longer able to resist, he held her in his arms and bent to kiss her, moving slowly closer to her, inching his way so that she could stop him if she wished. He need not have feared. He felt her breath on his lips and then her lips were on his. So gently, his hands held her face, could anything be more wonderful? His head was swimming. His lips parted, grew insistent, matched by hers. He did not realise one kiss could be so wonderful. He traced the outline of her face with his finger delicately touching her brow, her nose, her mouth as if trying to memorise every contour of her face. He did not want this day to end.

Chapter 20

Decisions

It had been almost three months since James Boswell had returned to Lincolnshire from Devon, moaning constantly about Reigneth's 'girlie boy' and confiding in his cousin, Aaron Gray, that he did not know where he belonged anymore. Secretly, Aaron was looking forward to meeting this Johnny, whom Reigneth talked about at length when they spoke on the phone. He would soon have the opportunity, as the family had been invited down to Home Humber for Christmas.

As the end of term approached, Aaron looked forward with increasing excitement to the holiday in Devon, as did his mother, Lydia, and sister, Ryalla. True to form, their father, Eli, had refused the invitation, but the Boswells would be going: James, his parents and sister, Britannia, and as a surprise for Jessie, they were to tow her wagon down, James having checked it over to make sure it was roadworthy.

The school year had been long and arduous for Aaron, even more so since Reigneth had left for Devon and he no longer saw her every day. Although he had not realised it at the time, when Reigneth was there school had been easy. They had shared English classes and had usually managed to have their lunch together. Life had been good; good for Gypsy kids especially. By and large the other kids had left them alone, giving Reigneth a wide berth, perhaps because they sensed something different about her. It had made Aaron feel special to be her cousin. Then Reigneth had left and everything changed. It seemed that the lads he was now having so much trouble with had always planned to nail him once she was no longer there to protect him.

Aaron's nickname in the family had often been 'the runt' – only in jest, but at 5' 6" he was definitely on the short side. Being small, however, had made him tenacious, he knew his way in life had to be by brain rather than brawn and he wanted to stay at school; he wasn't a quitter. His parents would happily have let him leave, there was no pressure there, but he was determined to tough it out. Little by little things changed until every day was hard, so hard it did cross his mind to give up after all. He'd had more than one set-to with the lads in his year. When it was one lad or even two he could hold his own, despite his small stature, for like most Romany boys, he could scrap.

Aaron knew his father took no pride in him, disappointed that his son was weedy compared to James and often voicing his incredulity that two cousins could be so different. Maybe that was why Eli had been so determined to ensure Aaron would be able to look after himself, insisting to the point of ruthlessness that he toughen up. As with everything to do with Eli, he took it too far and bullied his son unmercifully – until Joe and Jessie got involved. In fact, all the family had eventually warned him to lay off the lad. Despite everything, Aaron loved his dad. He loved his mam too, though he wished she would stick up for him sometimes.

The week before the Christmas holidays, Aaron felt elated: only four more days and he would be with Reigneth. He was making his way towards the bus stop for the journey home when the *Gauja* lads, four of them, sauntered up to him. They had been waiting for him and he had not stood a chance. This time it was really bad; they knew no matter how much they leathered him he would not 'grass 'em up'.

Back at the wagon, with a great shiner and ribs too sore to touch, Aaron swallowed some painkillers and sloped off to bed, relieved to find his parents were out. His dad would certainly have sent him back, along with three of his cousins, with instructions to find the *Gauja* lads and beat the hell out of them. Aaron knew his cousins would take it too far, they always did. He was not like that; not at all aggressive, but it was his dad's way of looking at things: "Teach them a lesson," he would say, for Eli was a hard nut. Only one person had ever bested him in a fight: his brother Joe, who had floored him and lost two teeth in the process. So it would not matter to Eli that Aaron was hurting, he would make him go anyway and while his mam may try to stop it, his dad ruled the roost.

Aaron heard the wagon door open and steeled himself for the tirade, relief spreading through him when he saw it was his cousin. "What're you doing here, James? Weren't expecting you," he mumbled between swollen lips, trying not to grimace.

Looking down at him, James smiled grimly, "Reigneth rang me, she saw you'd been hurt, told me to take care of you. Where's your dad?"

"Don't know." Traitor tears began coursing down Aaron's cheeks. He held back a sob, "There was just too many of 'em."

"Aye, well – why don't we go back to mine so your dad don't know? Then we'll fathom what to do about them buggers."

Not used to sympathy, Aaron had to fight back more tears. He could see the anger in his cousin's eyes and knew James wanted nothing better than to beat the cowards to a pulp, but even Eli would not hold with that. His dad would send lads, not full-grown men like James. Lads the same age as Aaron, who would beat the crap out of the *Gaujas* so they would never risk messing with a Gypsy lad again, but not half kill them as James might do in the heat of the moment. And what could that lead to? Things like that could escalate; get out of control. It was not Aaron's way.

"Don't want your mam to worry," said James, his fists bunched, visibly holding down his temper. "I'll give her a call on her mobile and tell her you're stopping over at mine for the night, OK?"

Aaron nodded and allowed his cousin to help him into the truck.

Back at Joe and Jessie's bungalow, where James had been living since Reigneth and Jessie had moved, James ran a bath for Aaron and helped him into the bathroom.

"I don't want a bloody bath, are you trying to polish me off?" Aaron was unimpressed by his cousin's attentiveness.

"Well I've got quite used to 'em and it don't 'arf soothe your muscles when you're achin'," James coaxed Aaron into the bath.

He was right of course and Aaron, not used to lying in so much hot water, felt his aches and pains beginning to ease. He heard James's mobile and knew without being told that it would be Reigneth. He strained to listen.

"I'm sorting it, I tell you," James sounded irritated. "The runt's OK; had a beating though. Yes, I've got him in the bath. Yes, I know you've been trying to get me all day, I've twenty missed calls and nearly as many texts, but there was no signal where I was working so I couldn't pick them up. Calm down, Reigneth, I know it would have stopped him getting hurt, but what's done is done. Yes, I know. I'll tell him to charge his mobile and keep it charged, OK?"

James had moved out of earshot and Aaron missed whatever else he was saying to placate their cousin. He knew Reigneth would be distressed. Lying in the steaming water, he kicked himself; he had forgotten to charge his phone and had paid dearly for his mistake. Had she been able to, Reigneth would have warned him to avoid the lads that day. Easing himself into a more comfortable position, he began to relax. He was pleased to be here with James, who was so different to his father. His dad wasn't a bad bloke, but he'd had to fight all his life; most of the family's fellas were like that. James, however, was calmer, did not normally resort to violence and was never the first to pull a punch. He was a big bloke; could handle himself like no one else Aaron had ever seen. If pushed, James would usually give fair warning then down them in one. If he lost his temper, mind, then watch out!

Aaron looked up as his cousin came back into the bathroom.

"You OK?" James eyed him.

"Yeah, much better. You were right, it helps."

"That was Reigneth. She's cross and says you gotta keep your mobile charged."

"I forgot," Aaron sighed, thinking about Reigneth. "You know, all the time before... you know, before she left, there was never any trouble, I thought they didn't know we were Gypsies. But ever since she's been gone it's like they've just found out. It's been getting worse and worse."

James nodded, "I think Reigneth may have prevented it. People sense she's different and are frightened of her – with reason; she could be dangerous if she wanted."

"Do you really think she could?" Wincing, Aaron sat up, his curiosity aroused.

"Yes, of course I do, especially when she's protecting her own. You should have heard her on the phone, she was hopping mad. I wouldn't give much for those *Gauja* lads' chances if she ever comes back here." James shook his head as if trying to disperse the memory of Reigneth's anger from his mind. "C'mon lad, get out and dried and I'll find you some salve for that shiner."

Later, tucked up snug in the bed that had been Joe and Jessie's – James slept in Reigneth's old room – Aaron could not get her out of his mind. He missed her so badly. If she could see what had happened to him she must also know he wanted to be in Devon, not just on a visit, but to live with them permanently. He'd had enough. Strangely, it was not just the beating or his missing Reigneth. He missed Jessie too, so much that he wanted to cry just thinking of her. He loved Jessie, she was brave; she would stand up for Reigneth against anyone. His own mam, well, she was always wary of his dad; never lifted a finger to stop Eli when he took his belt to their son. It wasn't her fault and he loved her anyways, but even when he was little he had envied Reigneth her parents and had wanted to live here with them. He had always felt a little ashamed of feeling like that, but there had been so much love and laughter in this house. Reigneth's mum was lovely, warm and gentle, and Uncle Joe had taught him how to do loads of things, not like his dad who only ever barked orders.

Thinking about it now, Aaron knew that if he asked, Jessie would not turn him away. He could start college afresh next year and he could work to pay for his board. As soon as his mobile was charged up, he would call Jessie about moving to Devon. His mam and dad would not stand in his way – might even be relieved – it was one less mouth to feed. Perhaps things were not so bad after all. His mind made up, Aaron rolled over, wincing as James's much too big pyjamas bunched up around his bruised ribs. He could hear his cousin talking on the phone again. He wondered what James would say when he told him what he had decided. Aaron knew it was a life-changing decision. He had a mind to persuade James to come too. Maybe he would. With that thought, he drifted off to sleep.

Chapter 21

Warrior

The Christmas holidays were looming large on the horizon and Johnny was quietly getting himself in a state about it. He was excited about going home, his need for Reigneth was physical, wanting to hold her, see her, telephone calls were not nearly enough. He found it almost painful to be away from her. He knew his mother had yet to make a decision about where they would spend Christmas this year and sure as hell he did not want to go to Granny Gill's as so often in the past. He would not even consider being separated from Reigneth. Whatever his mother decided, she would want them all to be together, but he could not see Reigneth leaving her family, especially Jessie, added to which, James and his family had already arrived at Home Humber for the Christmas holidays. The thought of him there with Reigneth still made Johnny irrational and possessive.

He knew he would have to discuss arrangements in detail as soon as he arrived home. His mother had never spoken against Reigneth, but neither had she invited her to their home. Matt's words echoed back to him saying Grace would not approve of his marrying a Gypsy – strange how he was thinking so soon of marriage. He had yet to broach the subject with Reigneth, but he knew that she would expect nothing less, any more than would her family, and he respected her values. It was what he wanted too: he needed to know she was his for all time.

Alighting from the train at Exeter he was surprised that no one was there to meet him. Had he given them the wrong time? He tried ringing the house phone and then his mother's mobile; no reply on either, so he left a voice message to say the next bus was due and he'd hop on it, no need to pick him up.

Johnny and his first pony, Warrior, had been born in the same year and the animal had become Grace's foundation stallion. For two days she had been worried about his absence at the gate. Warrior usually came every afternoon to see her and she was uneasy, it was not like him; he was a creature of habit. On the morning of the third day, forgetting in her anxiety that she was supposed to be meeting Johnny's train, Grace rode up onto the moor and eventually found a group of Warrior's mares huddled in an exposed position. This was uncharacteristic; they normally sought shelter when the weather was really bad as it was now. Dismounting, Grace walked slowly towards them. In the midst of them she spotted the stallion and realised the mares had encircled him to protect him from the elements. What was wrong?

Wary of her, the mares tossed their heads and cantered off a little way, leaving Warrior still standing there. On closer inspection she saw that his foot was wedged between two sharp pieces of granite. His coat was matted and he looked hollow and exhausted. He eyed her nervously, his eyes showing the whites as he struggled and she saw fresh blood rimming his fetlock. Soothing him with her voice and hands, she tried to pull the rocks away from his foot, but it was hopeless; Warrior was stuck fast. In despair, Grace looked around the deserted moor then, with only a moment's hesitation, she dialled Matthew on her mobile.

At Higher Wedicombe, Matthew was looking forward to seeing his son. He was also worrying about Christmas and what he imagined would be a period of inevitable separation from Jessie, with whom he increasingly wanted to spend more time. She would be busy with all her family around her, while for him there was always the farm to see to, the stock to be tended. For the first time he could remember, Matthew felt bone weary. His joints ached and as soon as he sat in his armchair he dropped off to sleep. Was this what getting old was like? It was a depressing thought.

He had heard that a farmhand, Jed Cummings, was looking for work and it set him to thinking: if he employed someone to help with the stock it would ease his load a little. Having asked around and learned that Jed was considered reliable, if not very bright, Matthew had invited him over for a chat and was now trying to get the measure of the man. So long as he showed up and was trustworthy, he did not need to be bright and Matthew, always ready to give anyone the benefit of the doubt, was prepared to give him a trial. He was just about to ask when Jed could start, when the phone rang.

"Hello?" Matt snapped into the phone, irritated by the interruption.

"Matt, is that you Matt?" Grace shrieked between tears.

"Calm down, Grace, who the hell else would it be? Take deep breaths and tell me what's wrong." Matt knew from experience to be calm with Grace and that it must be a real emergency for her to ring him. The realisation hit him that now Harry was gone she had no one else she could she rely on when Johnny was away.

"It's my old stallion, Matt. His foot's trapped in some rocks on the moor. He must have been like it for days and I don't know what to do." Grace well and truly lost it at this point: Matthew could hear her weeping down the phone and knew he would get precious little sense from her.

"Grace, listen, you must listen. Where are you? Focus, Grace," he kept his voice calm and reassuring. "Tell me where you are."

"Over the top side of Throwleigh up near Shilstone," she said between sobs.

"OK, I'll be there as soon as I can." Hanging up the phone, Matt directed his attention back to Jed, "If you want the job, it's yours and the first task has just come up – there's a pony needs rescuing. Are you up for it?"

Jed, who seemed not at all perturbed by the turn of events, simply nodded.

"Good. I'll just ring Mike Jarvis and see if he can meet us," said Matthew, "we're gonna need some muscle."

Within half an hour of her call, Grace heard the sound of an engine and voices, one she recognised as Matthew's. He had brought a trailer, but could not get nearer than fifty metres from where Warrior was trapped. Her tears flowing readily now, Grace saw he had a couple of men with him. They scrambled up to where she stood, Matthew carrying a crow bar and pick axe. Grace shuddered, hysteria close to the surface.

Matthew quickly assessed the situation. The pony's foot was

firmly wedged and it was obvious from the droppings and upturned earth around him that he had been there for quite some time. It was tricky: the problem was not to catch the stallion's hoof with the tools, and damage his pastern any more than it already was, while releasing him.

"Don't worry, Grace," he gave her a reassuring smile. "We'll get him out. You go and wait in the Land Rover; best call the Vet." He passed her a none-too-clean handkerchief, which she took with a wan smile and wiped her tearstained face.

It took them almost an hour to free the stallion, but getting him to the trailer presented the next problem, Warrior was clearly dehydrated and exhausted. After much coaxing, pushing and pulling and eventually manhandling, they managed to load him. Assigning Mike Jarvis to walk Grace's horse back for her and Jed to ride in the trailer, Matt towed it to her home.

By the time the Vet arrived at the Wilmotts', Warrior was unloaded and in his stable. As soon as the stallion got as far as the thick straw bed he had collapsed and stayed there, trembling. The Vet was not hopeful; anti-inflammatories and antibiotics were administered and the wound cleaned and dressed. All the while Warrior lay still, his breathing laboured.

After everyone had gone, Matt to drive his two helpers home and the Vet to another urgent call, Grace sank into the straw beside the stallion. Only then, as she gave way to a storm of weeping, did she remember Johnny was coming home today and she had forgotten to send someone to pick him up.

Arriving home, having walked from the bus stop in Chagford, Johnny was surprised to find the house so quiet. One look at Henry's face told him something was very wrong. Henry had barely got the words out before Johnny was out of the door and dashing across to the stable to be with his old friend; his first pony.

Hearing Johnny's voice the stricken stallion lifted his head almost imperceptibly. Grace, her eyes red with weeping, whispered, "Oh, Johnny, you're here. I'm so sorry. I'm afraid we're going to lose him." Haltingly, she described what the Vet had done and said, then stumbled out of the stable and left him alone with Warrior.

Johnny dropped to his knees in the straw, trying to hold back his tears. He could not remember a time when the stallion had not been part of his life. They had grown up together. He ran his fingers along Warrior's neck, all the while talking to him, telling him how much he loved him. In the midst of this Johnny's mobile rang; it was Reigneth. He quickly explained what had happened and abruptly she rang off. Obviously she was too distracted to talk to him, Johnny thought, hurt.

Some fifteen minutes later a car screeched to a stop in the yard, he heard Reigneth's voice and realised he should not have been so judgemental. He was so distressed about Warrior and so overcome with emotion to see Reigneth standing there, he hardly noticed that James had brought her.

Reigneth knelt in the straw beside him and frowning in concentration, began to stroke the stallion, running her hands all over his body. "What has the vet put on underneath the dressing, Johnny?"

"Mum said he just cleaned it with some salve and gave him a couple of jabs. He hasn't got up since they brought him in," Johnny murmured. "I don't know when he last had anything to eat or drink. Matt reckoned he had been trapped for at least two days – and in all that rough weather too." Johnny could feel a sob rising in his throat and swallowed it down.

"James, nip to Mam and tell her what's happened, ask her to make up a poultice," Reigneth said urgently.

When James had gone, she took hold of Johnny's hand and squeezed it. "He knows you are here. For all he is an old boy, he has a lot of courage and he will fight this, but he is completely exhausted and becoming dehydrated. We *must* get some fluids into him, Johnny. Be strong for him, my love."

"That's what the Vet said. He left some electrolytes for him," he mumbled.

"All in good time, Sweetheart; stay calm."

Within half an hour James returned. Reigneth removed the dressing from the stallion's leg and James applied the poultice. The two of them worked together quickly and efficiently and Johnny could see both were entirely used to handling horses. He did not ask what was in the poultice; he trusted Reigneth completely.

"Can I get you anything?" Grace said from the doorway. She looked as though she was in a stupor.

"Tea would be good, hot and strong, we're in for a long night,"

James commented softly.

Warrior had begun to sweat: with each wave of heat that passed through his body, Reigneth and James wiped him down, covering him carefully with one of Grace's expensive horse blankets, which wicked away the moisture. This went on throughout the night, as soon as one rug was wet replacing it with another. The stallion made no effort to stand, remaining where he had collapsed.

By the early hours of the morning Johnny thought he saw a glimmer of recognition in Warrior's eyes instead of the glazed look that was so upsetting. Reigneth prepared a warm and sloppy bran mash and with James's help, the stallion lurched to his feet and managed to eat a couple of mouthfuls. Reigneth tried to encourage him to drink a little of the water, to which she had added the electrolytes, but the effort exhausted Warrior and after taking a sip or two, he collapsed back down on the straw. The fact that he had tried at all was a hopeful sign.

Grace, arriving with yet more tea, looked down at him sadly, "His system seems to have shut down, he hasn't passed anything, nor has he urinated."

"Don't worry," Reigneth smiled up at her, "I should think he hasn't eaten for a couple of days so there is nothing to come through. We just need to try to get him to eat and drink a little; thankfully he hasn't colicked. He's had the stuffing knocked out of him though, nothing worse for a stallion than to be trapped and helpless."

Reigneth talked as though she could understand the pony's thoughts; perhaps she could, Johnny thought. He had long since given up trying to put logical reasons to anything Reigneth said or did. He just accepted at face value that she was right. With the exception of the night of his father's accident, this had been the worst night of his life. And yet, he found to his surprise that he had begun to view James in a new light. The man had tirelessly tended the stallion to Reigneth's direction, his big hands extraordinarily gentle, and once or twice he had smiled encouragingly at Johnny. It was as though the three of them had bonded in a common cause, past jealousy forgotten.

Johnny took the tray of steaming mugs from his mother and gave her a weary smile of thanks, noting that she looked dreadful, almost skeletal.

"Do you think he is going to make it, Reigneth?" she whispered.

"Yes, of course he's going to make it... I know he will make it," Reigneth answered confidently.

For some reason, Grace found she believed the Gypsy girl implicitly. Grace was exhausted. She had been up all night, as had they all. Each time she had carried mugs of tea to the stables, she had stayed a while to watch the girl and her cousin working on Warrior. There was no doubt in her mind that but for them he would have died. The injuries to his foot did not seem that extensive, but his spirit had seemed broken. When he crashed to the stable floor it was as if he was defeated and had made it home to die.

There was no denying what these people were and Grace had ever nursed a poor opinion of Gypsies. She did not for one moment think of herself as prejudiced; it was a commonly held view after all. But that night her long held opinion began to change. She witnessed the devotion and love these strangers had given to the old stallion and it made her feel strangely humble and ashamed. Not only that, but she felt she had also witnessed something more. She could not say exactly what, but it was the way in which the girl behaved: something in her eyes and the way she spoke. Almost as if she had the power of healing. Was it possible? Looking at Johnny, Grace was suddenly aware that the girl's actions had been no surprise to her son. Observing the way they looked at each other, almost as if they communicated without the need for words, it came to her in a flash of apprehension that all their lives were about to change forever.

By eight o'clock next morning, not long after James had once again replaced the pony's dressing with a fresh poultice, Warrior was once again making attempts to get to his feet. The injured limb was unable to take any weight and as soon as he was standing, Reigneth bandaged his three good legs to give them support.

An hour later, the first glimpse of a relieved smile crossed James's face and the three of them stood back to watch the stallion blowing into his freshly made warm bran mash and munching with obvious enjoyment.

Reigneth laughed, "He'll be all right now."

"I don't suppose we could follow his example?" asked James.

"What?" Johnny grinned, "You want me to make you some bran mash?"

They all laughed and leaving Warrior to himself, trooped into the house. By nine-thirty James was tucking into the biggest breakfast Johnny had ever seen, lovingly prepared for him by Charlotte. Afterwards, James drove Reigneth home, promising to return that afternoon.

The vet arrived mid-morning. Leading the way into Warrior's stable, Johnny enjoyed the look of amazement on the Vet's face as he viewed the stallion.

"Well, lad," he said to Johnny, "I don't mind telling you I did not expect this old fella to make it through the night. I came prepared to put him out of his misery in case he was still lingering, but I can see there'll be no need for euthanasia today." He examined Warrior minutely then turned back to Johnny, "How did you do it? You must give me some tips."

"It wasn't down to me," Johnny grinned. "I'll get my two friends to tell you if you like. They were the ones responsible." As soon as he said it, Johnny realised that he now thought of James as a friend. Gone were any shreds of anxiety or jealousy; it was like a weight had lifted from his shoulders and he could not wait to see him again to thank him properly.

As it happened, he did not see much of him, for as soon as James drove into the yard, Charlotte dragged him off to see the mares. Johnny went with Reigneth into the stable and watched as she deftly folded back Warrior's rug revealing the front of his body. She stripped off her jacket and jumper and nimbly and adeptly began to massage the stallion's chest and shoulders, the muscles in her arms rippling with the pressure she exerted. Once the front of his body was done she folded the rug back, thereby ensuring he was never exposed to the cold, and repeated the procedure on his back and hindquarters until she had manipulated and massaged all his muscles. Warrior had visibly relaxed and towards the end of the procedure was nodding off. Johnny watched in awe, Reigneth just smiled.

At first he wondered why Reigneth was massaging the pony when James was obviously more muscular for the job. Instantly he realised it was because Reigneth's hands could do what James's could not. "Why do you massage the whole body when it's just the leg that's injured?" He thought perhaps he already knew the answer, but wanted some sort of logical explanation for what he had seen.

Reigneth smiled, "He's been flailing about for a couple of days at least and every muscle in his body is taut and pulled. Massaging relaxes him and helps him to mend, so he doesn't feel so helpless and defeated."

It was a logical answer for once. Johnny had seen Reigneth do things before that could not be so logically explained. Was that all she had done or did her hands have a power to heal too? He would not be surprised. Reigneth's talents increasingly delighted him. In fact he was delighted in more ways than one as he watched her work. Over her jeans she wore only a skimpy vest having removed her outer garments. Her body was slender yet muscular in an athletic way, her breasts full. He longed to take her in his arms. He flushed as she turned to look at him, aware that he had been focussing on her body.

Catching his gaze, she grinned at him, "Are you blushing, my girlie boy?"

She had never called him that to his face before, but somehow it sounded not like an insult but an endearment and he was forced to smile. "Whatever gives you that idea?" They both laughed as he took her in his arms.

Each day Reigneth came with James to massage the pony and Grace was always pleased to see them. Charlotte usually found some pretext on which to claim James's attention while Reigneth tended Warrior. The old stallion whickered now whenever he saw them and was scoffing hay as if he had never been fed before. His coat had begun to regain its bloom and he was gradually putting more weight on his foot, though Reigneth kept it bandaged. By the end of the week, the Vet declared Warrior sound enough to be turned out on the grass.

That day, Grace announced that Warrior would never go back up onto the moor and instead, put him in the small homestead paddock with a mare for company, she was not taking any chances. The stallion was now officially retired.

She still thought there was something odd about Reigneth, but thanked her lucky stars that there was. If it were not for the girl's skill and devotion they would have lost Warrior and for that she would be eternally grateful. The fact that she and James were

Romany Gypsies no longer seemed of any consequence. Grace had begun to think that if the girl would have Johnny he was fortunate indeed. Above all else, she loved her son and every inch of him declared his love for Reigneth. Grace had known for some time that she had two choices: she could battle against their relationship and lose her son or she could accept it and gain a daughter. After what she had witnessed, Grace knew what her choice would be and she soon came to believe not only that Johnny was a lucky man, but that she too would be lucky to have such a daughter. When Reigneth looked at her and smiled it was almost as if the girl could read her thoughts. She was extraordinary, not just in what she could do, but in what she was. Love oozed out of her and Grace knew it would encompass her too, simply because she was Johnny's mother. For the first time in her life, Grace acknowledged that she did not deserve it; that she was mean-spirited and selfish. It was as though Reigneth had touched something deep inside her and she felt liberated: *I will become a better person for knowing this girl,* she thought.

Grace also knew that she had found the help she had been seeking for a long time. She was not getting any younger and needed someone she could rely on to help with the ponies. Reigneth, with her abilities, was more than she could have imagined or hoped for. Also, by employing the girl it would give her a chance to get to know her better. However, there was more to it than this: having made the decision to accept Reigneth's and Johnny's burgeoning relationship, Grace thought it would be a good way to forge links between the two families. She was still harbouring jealous feelings towards Jessie Gray, even though she knew she had no right. Her own feelings for Matthew had subsided years ago and when she thought about him now she was awash with guilt. She blushed to think of her reaction at the fete and the things she had said to him afterwards, but when he had come instantly to help free Warrior and behaved as though no ill words had been spoken between them, she had begun to put it behind her, even to hope that he would indeed find happiness with Jessie Gray. *God knows, he deserves it,'* she thought. And so, after a great deal of soul searching, she drove over to Home Humber resolved to do the decent thing, atone for her past behaviour and heal any rift between their families.

Arriving at the Pritchards' lovely if somewhat dilapidated home

Grace felt ill at ease wondering how Jessie would receive her. She had never been outwardly rude to her and felt sure that Matthew would not have repeated their heated argument. Even so, knocking lightly at the back door her nerve almost failed her. It seemed all her teenagers had decamped to Home Humber, she could hear their laughter: Charlotte's giggling, Henry's distinctive guffaw and Johnny's honeyed tones.

Richard Pritchard answered the door. "Grace, how lovely to see you, you've come at exactly the right time: Jessie is just serving up lunch, come through," he smiled in welcome and Grace, her tension easing slightly, followed him into the big kitchen.

Jessie was dishing out bowls of stew and hunks of homemade bread and seemed unaware that her face and hair were smeared with flour. She looked up from the crowded table, "Come in, Grace, have a seat if you can find one! You'll stay for lunch won't you? There's enough for everyone. That is if your son doesn't eat the lot," she added with a smile wielding the bread knife.

Johnny laughed and tucked into a large plate of stew and dumplings, "Hi, Mum, you just have to taste Jessie's dumplings, they're fabulous."

The sight of her son's beautiful face melted Grace in an instant.

Chapter 22

Festivities

Reigneth, of course, was not surprised by Grace's offer of a weekend job. She was happy to accept it, although it was understood that her studies would take priority until she left college, but since she did not have the first idea what she wanted to do thereafter, the possibility of eventually working full time at the Wilmotts' and becoming increasingly involved in breeding and showing ponies appealed to her greatly. Not only was a love of horses in her blood, but it meant she would have an excuse to be with Johnny at every opportunity. She knew, as only she could, that their working lives were not destined to fit into a normal 9 to 5 pattern. This suited Reigneth: like all the members of her family she felt at ease only when not confined and constricted. Grace's offer of employment meant she would at least have money to buy gifts. This first Christmas without Joe would be hard, for Jessie especially, but it would help that some of the family would be there; James had already arrived. Reigneth knew about the surprise lined up for her mother and couldn't wait to see Jessie's face when her wagon turned up.

Not long before Christmas, Reigneth organised a shopping trip into Exeter and would allow only Uncle Richard to accompany her. Johnny's dejection at being left out made her laugh. "We can't do absolutely everything together!" she teased.

"Can't I just tag along? I've got shopping to do too," he grumbled.

"No you can't, you'll have no surprises on Christmas Day," she coaxed him playfully. "You'll just have to stay at home for once. Besides, Juk needs dog sitting."

Noticing James's amused expression she turned her attention

on him. "And what's so funny, Mr Boswell?" she asked, hands on hips, fixing him with a glare.

"I've heard these stories about controlling and obsessive boyfriends," James chuckled, enjoying Johnny's obvious discomfort. "Perhaps one day he'll realise that you do have a mind of your own!"

For Johnny, the Christmas arrangements had worked out better than he had hoped. For once, Grace had invited the grandparents to come to them and the Wilmott family would all be at home, which meant he could go to Home Humber and be with Reigneth in the afternoon. The only disadvantage as far as Johnny could see was that he would have to eat two Christmas dinners, as at Home Humber they planned to eat in the evening. Somehow he felt that to be no sacrifice at all!

His Christmas Day really only began when he bounded through the Home Humber kitchen at four o'clock, dashed into the front sitting room and without stopping to think, scooped Reigneth into his arms and kissed her so passionately that the rest of the family watched, mouths agape. Reigneth managed to prise herself away from him, laughing at his bashful smile when he became aware that everyone had fallen silent.

"Well, I see you've managed to look a little tidier today," she teased to cover his embarrassment, her fingers twiddling with a lock of his hair. "I think you've actually combed your hair."

Johnny grinned and looked around at the people watching this exchange, some smiling in approval, others looking surprised. He had dropped presents off at Home Humber on Christmas Eve, but everyone had been waiting for him to arrive before they opened anything. Johnny had met some of the family at Emily's funeral, although he could not at first put names to faces. Seeing his dilemma, Reigneth performed brief reintroductions to James's parents, James Senior and Constance, and his sister, Britannia, whom everyone called BB. A small, sharp-featured boy came forward, hand outstretched. Johnny noted he had a firm handshake and his smile looked sincere and welcoming.

"This is Aaron Gray, Johnny," Reigneth hugged the boy tightly.

"Pleased to meet you, Johnny, Reigneth has told me so much about you."

"Good to meet you too. She's been looking forward to your

arrival. I hear you're going to be staying permanently?"

Aaron nodded and Johnny smiled, but as he turned away, he caught a glance from James across the room and noted his troubled frown. He also noted that Matthew, who had been at Home Humber for much of the day, was looking like the cat that got the cream. His face was split in a broad grin and he was clearly very much at home. James was draped over a large armchair, disgruntled as ever, while BB sat on the floor with Jukel beside the fire, which smelled deliciously of apple wood.

Reigneth grasped Johnny by the hand and led him over to the sofa. He smiled at Jess, surprised to see that on top of her now standard black garments she wore an embroidered waistcoat. It was richly coloured in differing shades of purple and was so out of the ordinary that Johnny could not help but comment. "Jessie you look lovely; that waistcoat's grand."

"She looks like a set of loose covers," James scoffed.

Jessie quickly cuffed him round the ear. "Don't you be so cheeky, *mush*, you's not too big to have your ears boxed." She looked very contented as she beamed round at her family, "Nothing and no one will upset me today, James Boswell. My day's just perfect," she retorted.

Reigneth laughed and hugged her, "Mam's had the best Christmas present in the world, Johnny. Our wagon's here. We had breakfast in her this morning."

Looking at their happy faces, Johnny had to smile. "Wow, that's great. I can't wait to see her."

"If we get fed up here in Devon, we can always up sticks now," Jessie joked.

"Don't fool yourselves," said James, "that van of yours is knackered. It'll never tow aught again." His chuntering only made Jessie and Reigneth laugh the more.

Sitting down in the space beside Matthew, Johnny was tempted to say something about the way Matt's eyes seemed to be turned permanently in Jessie's direction, but decided it would not be fair to embarrass him in front of her family. Besides, Johnny knew his own eyes were similarly attuned to Reigneth, wherever she was in the room. As always, she looked exquisite: today in a purple dress, her hair loose and flowing.

"What about the stock, Matt," he asked, when the family had

resumed talking. "Want a hand? Are we going up together to feed them?"

"Nope; all sorted. I've got a fella working for me now."

"Never! Well would you believe it? After all the times you ignored me when I said you'd need help after I went to uni," he grinned. "So what changed your mind?"

Glaring at Johnny, Matt muttered, "Other things take priority these days."

"Who is it – anyone I know?"

"I shouldn't think so. He's not from these parts, a fella called Jed Cummings?"

"Never heard of him – is he as good as your last bloke?" Johnny teased.

"Wouldn't take much, he was useless that one, always off courting some lass," Matt smiled first at Johnny then at Reigneth. "Anyway, the job's yours again if you want it, just as soon as you finish this university lark."

Soon afterwards, Jessie announced that Christmas dinner was ready and they all filed through to the big dining room where Richard took his place at the head of the table and proceeded to carve. The food was fabulous and Johnny had no problem in fitting in another meal.

"Tell me, where does a scrap of a lad like you fit in all that food?" Liz asked, as he helped himself to another roast potato.

"It's your sister's cooking, I can't resist it." Johnny gave Jessie a lingering smile then turning to look at Reigneth, he saw her shake her head in mock disbelief.

"What now?" he asked, raising his eyebrows.

"You'd charm the birds out of the trees you would," she placed a kiss on his cheek.

"Is it time to open the presents yet?" he queried as everyone was about to leave the table. By nature Johnny was generous and he loved giving presents. This evening was no exception. He had even enjoyed choosing a gift for James. For Reigneth he had once again visited his favourite jewellers and purchased a beautiful rose-gold Edwardian bracelet. It had cost a small fortune: the links were particularly intricate, adorned at the fastener with a small tassel made up entirely of gold links. It was fabulous and extremely unusual, he felt sure Reigneth would like it.

Money had never been a consideration for Johnny and he delighted in buying things for Reigneth, but it was difficult. He knew it only made her feel the disparity between them more keenly as she could not afford to buy things for him. Regardless of this Johnny had got a little carried away with present buying for Reigneth. With his reasoned but biased logic he had managed to go through a list of essentials for her comfort. He was happy; he was hopelessly and completely in love.

Knowing that Jessie's family had never been able to buy expensive gifts and that for them, Christmas was not about presents so much as being together with their loved ones, Johnny showed great enthusiasm for the gifts he received. He noticed that Reigneth was hanging back and deduced that she was shy about giving him her gift in front of everyone. He was about to reassure her when she wandered out of the room.

Carrying a pile of dirty dishes through to the kitchen for Jessie, Johnny heard Reigneth calling to him from the small sitting room.

She stood with her back to the fire waiting for him. "Hold out your hand," she said, placing a small box in his palm. He opened the lid to reveal a gold signet ring. Before he could speak, she said, blushing, "I've had it engraved inside," and directed her gaze to the floor.

Looking on the inside Johnny examined the inscription and read: 'For my beloved'.

"Oh, Reigneth!" Welling up, he murmured, "I don't know what to say... "

"Then don't say anything," she whispered, taking the ring out of the box. She went to put it on Johnny's right hand, but he swiftly changed hands, extending his left one to her. Holding it out he gestured to the third finger.

"I'll have it on this one until it's replaced with my wedding ring," he smiled intently at her. "It's absolutely lovely, thank you *my* beloved." Gently, he put one hand on either side of her face, raining tiny kisses on her lips. "I love you so much," he murmured, his eyes wet with unshed tears.

After a while, they wandered back into the sitting room and there followed an impromptu recital: Johnny played the piano and Reigneth produced Joe's accordion, which James and Reigneth took turns to play. Johnny knew Reigneth could sing beautifully as he had heard her at Emily's funeral, but he was completely unaware she had any musical ability. Surprises were obviously the order of the day and not to be outdone, Aaron joined them in song. His voice had a wonderful gravelly tone, unusual and haunting.

God, what I couldn't do with that voice! Johnny thought, ideas for melodies springing into his mind.

At eight o'clock there was a loud pounding on the back door and before anyone could get to answer it, Henry and Charlotte came rushing through. Charlotte's beaming smile made it evident she was thrilled to be at Home Humber, her gaze immediately searching out James.

"*Sar shin*, James," she beamed at him.

"*Kushti* Lotti," he beckoned for her to join him. She squashed herself into the large armchair alongside James, who happily hunched over to make room for her.

Johnny was dumbfounded at this interchange: *When did they become so friendly with one another?* he wondered, gazing askance at his little sister. He had not the faintest idea what they had said to each other, and James's shortened name for Charlotte amazed him.

Clearly it had amazed Jessie too, "Well, whose been teaching you how to speak Romany, LOTTI?"

Charlotte laughed, "James has been teaching me and I quite like 'Lotti'."

Shaking her head in disbelief, Reigneth stared across at James.

"What? What have I done now?" James had a bewildered expression on his face as he held out his hands in innocence, presenting the face of a saint to his cousin and aunt.

"Well I'd like to know what they said. Is it repeatable?" Johnny asked Reigneth.

"Of course – it's just a greeting, that's all. And are these lessons to continue?" she enquired of James, tongue in cheek.

"Well yes, maybe they will," James's eyes twinkled as he looked at Charlotte. He gave her an exaggerated wink and everyone burst out laughing. Johnny could not help noticing that his sister had transformed James's mood. Gone were the glowering glances; he was positively sparkling. *So that's the way the wind is blowing,* Johnny thought with a wry grin at Reigneth, who raised her eyebrows and grinned back.

Their teasing didn't bother James. Over the last few weeks, he had become increasingly aware of Charlotte. She was kind and quite pretty: small-boned and with high cheekbones like Johnny's – obviously both had inherited this feature from Grace. The similarity to her brother ended there, however. Her eyes were large and bright blue; her skin and hair were fair. The things James most liked about her were her sunny disposition and generous nature. Charlotte had a big heart.

He looked over at Reigneth: he knew he could never love anyone as he loved her, but he felt protective towards Charlotte and had begun to feel that more would come in time. The resentment he felt towards Johnny had been diminishing ever since they had rescued the old stallion together. It brought relief to James not to be eaten up with jealousy as he had been before. Today, until Lotti had arrived, he had been worrying about Aaron and his intention to live in Devon, but now his mood lightened and he found to his surprise that he was content – at least for now – something he had not felt for a long time.

The room was full to overflowing. James gazed over to Reigneth. "Hey cousin, give us one of Uncle Joe's stories," he piped up, winking at Aaron.

"No, James, I can't tell them like my dad," Reigneth pleaded.

Aaron grinned, "You're not getting out of it that easy."

"You're ganging up on me, you wretches," said Reigneth, but she smiled at her cousins. "Oh, alright then, but it won't be nearly as good as Dad used to tell."

Everyone settled themselves down, Jessie making sure they each had a drink before Reigneth began.

"It was Christmas time and our great, great grandfather, Ambrose Gray, had bought in two new horses from Ireland to sell at a profit. They were lovely animals and in order to show them off to their best advantage he had asked his sons, Ambrose and Joe, to ride with the local hunt.

The hunt was in full flow and the Gray brothers were up with the Master and his hounds. The pack started baying as they got scent of their quarry. Suddenly, a huge hare bounded up and ran headlong across an open ploughed field. The hounds gave chase. On and on they went and the Master and one or two stragglers kept pace, including the Gray brothers.

The Master tried to call the hounds to heel, but they took no notice and one especially, a young dog, gave chase and would not come back. It caught up with the hare and clamped its jaws onto the creature's leg and shook it violently. Somehow the hare struggled free and took refuge by jumping clean through the window of a rundown hovel at the far side of the field. The hound followed.

The Master dismounted and pushed open the door to the untidy, dirty building. The hound was crouched down in the corner whining. Of the hare there was no sign, but a tiny old lady stood in the middle of the room in grubby, torn and tattered clothes. At the Master's entrance she peered at him. He made no apology for bursting into her home, merely calling the hound to heel. The dog did not move and he chided the animal for its disobedience, still it did not move. The old lady hissed at the animal and it went cringing on its belly to the Master. He turned to leave the building and as he did so, he noticed the woman wore no shoes and that her leg was bleeding profusely. Unnerved, the Master beat a hasty retreat from the hovel. The dog never hunted again nor did the man."

An eerie silence spread over the room when Reigneth finished.

Johnny shivered; his skin prickling. He had noted that the old lady in the story 'hissed' at the hound by way of command, the same as Reigneth did to Jukel. He was about to remark on it when Aaron broke the silence with a laugh.

"Ha, well done, Reigneth, nearly as good as my Uncle Joe," he beamed.

Everyone was laughing and smiling now, except Charlotte, who said, wide-eyed, "That was a true story, wasn't it, Reigneth?"

James grinned at her, "What? You believe in witches do you, Honey?" He hugged her playfully.

"OK, well not to be outdone, Reigneth, my darling, I have a story too," Johnny smiled at his sweetheart, not worried that everyone must see how much he adored her.

Once again, everyone settled down, all eyes turned to Johnny.

"There was once a young moor-man, devilish handsome he was too, like many of his kind." Johnny paused here for the expected hisses from his audience; he was not disappointed.

"This moor-man was making his way across the moor when he

saw a fabulous hat lying on top of a bog. Now it was a lovely hat and he wanted it for himself, but he was not foolish enough to step into the bog, so he armed himself with a stick and tried to retrieve the hat. Knocking it to one side, he was astonished to see a head underneath it. Much to his amazement, the gentleman beneath the hat smiled and asked him very politely if he could extricate him from the mire. The young moor-man said he would, but only on condition that the hat would be his. The gentleman agreed, but asked for one other consideration before the deal was finally struck.

"And what might that be?" the young moor-man enquired.

"Why," the gentleman replied, "to remove my horse on which I am sitting."

Johnny looked around the room, a cheeky grin on his face. There was a short silence followed by peals of laughter.

Chapter 23

Separation

Christmas soon passed and Johnny was in deep depression at the thought of going back to university. It was his last evening with Reigneth and he was distraught. With only Jukel for company, they sat in the snug nestled in one another's arms. Johnny could hardly bear the thought of leaving her. His lips found hers, his need of her urgent to the point of desperation. They would have to be together soon; he could not cope for much longer. Her hands caressed his neck, her fingers entwined in his hair. His breathing became ragged, his mouth more demanding. She did nothing to stop the kisses. He could feel her mounting desire and knew that her need for him was as great as his own for her. Something checked him: he was supposed to be an adult while Reigneth, however mature she might appear, was only just sixteen. With great reluctance he drew away from her, knowing that he must exercise control for both of them. Much as he wanted to make love to her, it was going to have to wait.

Six months more and he would be home for good but then what? How would he support them? His father had left him enough money to start his own business – but in what? Johnny had not the first idea. The future was so unclear, which was ironic given Reigneth's gift of foresight, but she never mentioned the future and he was too afraid to ask.

Johnny checked his watch; he had an early train and would soon have to go. He was catching a lift home with Matt, who would be back soon. He had taken Jessie out on their first 'real' date. Johnny smiled at the thought.

"What are you smiling at?" Reigneth asked, flushed from his kisses, her breathing still uneven.

He chuckled, "I was just thinking of Matt and Jessie on a date. Who would have thought it? I wonder what they'll talk about."

"I wonder," she grinned.

Jessie and Matt had gone to a pub in a nearby village for a meal. The evening had been wonderful for both of them, with no prying eyes to speculate on their being together. For the first time, Jessie was out of black and wearing a blue dress and high heels. Matt had never seen her in heels before. Her hair was caught up in a French pleat rather than her usual braided style, which he had always thought endearingly old-fashioned. It did not really matter what she wore. To him she always looked lovely and never more so than tonight. Matt had put on a new suit and even he thought that for once he looked very smart, but when he had set off to collect Jessie he had been so nervous he could hardly start the Land Rover, which he had spent the entire day cleaning until it looked like new both inside and out.

"Shall we go home for a coffee, Jessie?" Matthew asked, wanting to prolong the evening for as long as possible.

"I think that would be a grand idea, but let's drive the long way back."

Matthew smiled, hardly daring to believe that she felt the same as he.

The evening was cold but clear and as he drove he told Jessie of the things he had done as a child on the moor, neglecting to mention that most of those adventures had been with Grace.

Once back at Home Humber, Jessie put the kettle to boil as she had done for him a hundred times before, yet somehow things were different now. He stood smiling beside her, his hand lifted gently to her face and slowly he brought his lips to hers.

Neither of them was prepared for each other's reactions as their lips met. A kiss that had begun with such gentleness was soon so passionate as to take Matthew completely by surprise. He enfolded Jessie tightly his arms, feeling her body responding to his, pressing against him; her mouth urgently seeking his.

A moment later they heard voices and sprang away from each other. Jessie returned to the Aga to inspect the kettle and Matthew suddenly found the kitchen curtains extremely interesting.

"Hi, you two, had a nice evening?" Johnny smiled as he passed through the kitchen to let Jukel into the garden.

Matt cleared his throat, "Yes, smashing thanks," he said, with a sidelong glance at Jessie, noticing her hands were shaking.

"You ready to drop me home, Matt?" Johnny whistled for Jukel, who came bounding in.

"Almost; Jessie was just making me a cup of tea. Give me five minutes."

Later, back at Higher Wedicombe, Matthew sat by his fire long into the night. There was no point in going to bed; he knew he would never be able to sleep. He was in a state of shock; completely stunned. Never had he thought Jessie capable of such passion, his body burned just thinking about that kiss. There was a lot more to this woman than even he had realised. Matt knew his patience was at an end. He looked down at the ring in his hand. It was a solitaire diamond and had belonged to his grandmother. He thanked the good Lord that for whatever reason he had never given it to Grace. Tomorrow he would go to Home Humber and ask Jessie to marry him. He hoped to find her alone. He hoped she would say yes. He hoped the ring would fit her. He hoped and prayed the wedding could be soon. So much to hope for!

Bright and early the next morning, Matt was at Home Humber and after knocking briefly, he let himself in as was now his custom. Reigneth was sitting at the table a cup of tea in hand, half poised to take a bite out of a slice of toast.

"Morning, Matt," she smiled with a knowing twinkle in her eye. "Would you like a drink? Ma will be through in a minute."

He felt the engagement ring in his pocket and he knew Reigneth knew: it was like the ring was shouting out to her, 'Yes I'm here. He's finally plucked up enough courage to ask!'

"I'll make myself scarce," she mumbled, mouth half full.

Matt had always resisted asking her questions, he had thought it unfair before. Now he asked, "Will it be alright, Reigneth?" As soon as the words were out of his mouth, he wished them back. He had not really intended to ask.

She spun around smiling widely, "Of course it will, you ninny, there are so many good things in store for you both, for us all, don't worry."

A slightly clouded expression crossed her face. It worried

Matthew. "What is it, there is something else you can see isn't there?"

"Yes... I think... " she paused, took a deep breath. "I think Johnny will soon discover who he really is and it's going to be distressing, but I cannot as yet see how. I just know we will need to be supportive to him."

It was the first time Reigneth had openly alluded to the fact that Johnny was his son and though Matt had guessed she knew, it still took him by surprise. "Who else knows?" he asked, perturbed.

"Just you and me – and presumably Grace, but I don't like keeping secrets from Johnny, Matt, it distresses me so I'll be glad when he knows. At the same time I am worried how he'll take it. I'm sorry, I can't see any more – I can't see how it comes about, only that it will be painful."

They were both silent for a moment, then Reigneth smiled, "Hey, what's with the long face? I'll leave you to it, don't worry." She gave him a swift kiss on the cheek, murmured, "Congratulations," and walked out of the kitchen, clicking her fingers to Jukel.

Jessie passed her in the doorway. A blush came to her cheeks as she saw Matthew. In two strides he was at her side, scooping her into his arms.

Chapter 24

Commitment and Grief

Jessie and Matt's wedding was set for the first week in May, she had avoided the beginning of June, Appleby Fair Week, as she knew her relatives looked forward to that. It was the highlight of the year, a chance for all Romanies and Travellers to get together. This was the week when the town of Appleby was virtually taken over and filled to capacity with Gypsies. She had loved it when Joe was alive; had loved to watch the horses being washed in the River Eden and the *chavvies* riding them through the water.

Every Romany girl looked forward to fair week; it was one of their few chances to meet their own kind. They would dress in their best finery hoping to attract the eye of Romany lads. However, it was definitely 'look but don't touch'. Many teenagers met their future partners there. Jessie smiled thinking of this: she herself had met Joe at Stow Fair.

Now she was making wedding plans again. Wedding plans to marry a *Gauja*. She had wanted a small and quiet affair but she knew that would never do for the rest of the family. With Romany weddings less was never more: her smile widened at the thought. The phrase 'over the top' could have been coined to describe them: weddings were one of the few times when family members all got together, so the bigger the bash the better. Jessie knew that when it came to Reigneth getting married, there would be no concessions made. She knew too that it would be soon and was concerned about the amount of money it was all going to cost.

Jessie and Matt had decided to live at Higher Wedicombe, and of course, Reigneth and Aaron would live with them, but the place would not do as it was and needed a makeover.

Liz and Jessie went over there to clean – as only they could – but came away in desperation, completely overwhelmed by years and years of accumulated clutter and dirt. Arriving back at Home Humber they sat without speaking, cups of tea in hand, each preoccupied with her own thoughts.

Eventually, Liz broke the silence, exclaiming in disbelief, "I've never seen anything like it! The man has been living like that for years. I couldn't even have had a drink there!"

"Any tea left in that pot, Ma?" Reigneth came bounding into the kitchen, Jukel at her heels.

"No, I'll make you fresh, Darling," Jessie made to stand but Reigneth placed her hand on her Mam's shoulder. "No, don't get up, I'll do it. How did you get on at Matt's?"

"Not so good; it's… it's… " Jessie struggled for the words not wanting to decry Matt by saying the house was truly awful and everything in the kitchen gross.

"That bad, eh?" Reigneth grinned, "Actually I know, I've had drinks there before," she added.

"You never have, child, what were you thinking!" Liz curled her lip in disgust.

"You two are so old-fashioned and Matt can't help it, he's so busy," Reigneth jumped to Matt's defence. "Anyway, Johnny and I will help."

Jessie, who knew when she was beat, snorted, "I think the best we can do is to box everything up and leave it to the decorators; I wouldn't know where to start." She caught her sister's glance and giggled. Soon the two of them were helpless with laughter, tears running down their cheeks.

"Are you sure you're doing the right thing?" Liz gasped.

Sober now, Jessie said, "Yes, absolutely sure – he's a good man."

Liz wiped her eyes, "We'll fettle him. You could say he's a blank canvas," she said, trying to keep a straight face.

"Well, perhaps a slightly smudgy one… " and their laughter erupted again.

"He's got some nice china anyway… " and the giggling continued.

Jessie saw Reigneth staring at them in disbelief and started to laugh all over again. "It really is bad isn't it!" she hiccuped to Liz. Nodding together, they shrieked with laughter and it came home to

Jessie, as so often before, just how much she had missed her sister all the years they had been apart.

"What has got into you both? I'm amazed you're being so silly," Reigneth retorted.

"I think it's hysteria, love." Afraid to look at Liz, Jessie tried to behave, "If you and your sweetheart could help us that would be great."

Reigneth, her face pink, nodded, "Yes, of course we will."

Reigneth and Johnny had been keen to help render the house at Higher Wedicombe habitable, the main focus being to clear some of the clutter in order for the decorators to move in. They had arranged to go on the Saturday afternoon to begin boxing things up and were to start in the spare room, which would be Reigneth's bedroom.

Reigneth had not wanted to go to Higher Wedicombe that morning, she was moody and out of sorts. As preparations went ahead for Jessie and Matt's wedding, she had become more and more concerned, sure that Johnny's parentage was about to be revealed. She wanted to protect him from all that was hurtful and was wary of any situation that might give rise to his finding out in a less than sensitive way that Matt was his father. She had hoped his mother would find the courage to be honest with him, but knew Grace was afraid; could read the fear behind her eyes. As Reigneth's gift was increasing, so it was becoming easier to read people's moods, and Grace's demeanour was one of constant worry: the woman was scared witless of losing her son.

Reluctant as she was, Reigneth agreed to help and soon she and Johnny were packing things away in boxes for Matt to sort through later.

"Your turn to make the tea, Reigneth, this is thirsty work," Johnny's nose had a large smudge of dirt on it from the boxes.

"Oh no, I hate those old stairs, I'm always afraid of tripping," she grumbled, trudging off, Jukel loping after her.

While she was gone, Johnny started opening the drawers of the old dresser. Each one would need to be emptied, too heavy to lift full. The drawers held a bundle of old school photos and Johnny's curiosity was aroused: he felt sure Matt would not mind him looking. He had never seen any school photos of his mother and he knew she had gone to school with Matt. He flicked through the bundle until he came to one of the whole class. His mother was easy to pick out; she was sitting in the front row, her hand clasped by the child sitting next to her.

Johnny's mouth gaped open: he was looking at a photo of himself! How could that be? He wasn't even born yet; his mother was a child! And yet, there he was, clasping her hand, plain as a pikestaff! It was not possible.

Johnny remained staring, his brain working overtime. And then it came to him: of course, the photo was of Grace and *Matthew*! Matthew, who looked identical to himself – the way he looked in his own school photo taken at a similar age. Just to be sure, Johnny riffled through the bundle again and found a snap of himself aged about nine – taken before he had even known Matthew existed. Placing the two photographs side by side, the similarity was unmistakeable; peas in a pod. There was nothing to choose between them.

Johnny did not want to believe it, but the evidence in his hands was undeniable. He knew in that moment that Harry had not been his father, and clearly his mother knew it too. He looked at the other photos, obviously taken annually, Grace and Matt always sitting together through infant and junior school, Matt looking more and more like his son as he got older. *His son*: he was Matt's son. It explained so much: the instant rapport; the affection; the trouble Matt had taken always to be there for him and the way he evaded certain questions about the past.

With tears coursing down his cheeks, Johnny sifted through the entire bundle of photographs: Grace and Matt as teenagers, arms locked around one another, riding on the moor, laughing, joking and his mother looking happy and relaxed as he had never seen her before. The photos were dog-eared and had obviously been looked at again and again. With that thought he felt a spike of anger so severe it almost made him retch. Why had they never told him? Not even after his father, or rather, Harry, had died? Did Harry know? What had happened to stop Matt and his mother being together? So many questions – and he wanted answers. Fists clenched, he could hear Reigneth making her way carefully up the granite staircase. Trying to marshal his thoughts and failing as soon as she entered the room, he knew she would realise straight away that something was wrong.

So many things were swirling through Johnny's head, everything making more and more sense: the reason why Matt had given him Rannoch; why the twins looked so different to him, and why his mother had been so obviously anxious last year when Matt had accompanied him to the summer fair. Johnny's head began to throb, his palms to sweat, his emotions reeling, from anger and shock to distress and back again to anger, at the sheer deceitfulness of his parents – both of them – for all those years.

He spun round from the dresser and gazed at Reigneth; knew immediately from her expression that she had known about it and yet had chosen not to tell him.

Abruptly the implications came home to him: the pathos of his situation reflected in the pity he could see in Reigneth's eyes; his sudden loss of identity – he was no longer 'Johnny Wilmott', he was a nobody.

"Who else knows, Reigneth, does Jessie know?"

"No one – just me."

"Since when?"

"Since the first day I met Matt, but it was not my secret to tell, Johnny," she pleaded.

"Did you not think it would be better coming from you than for me to find out like this?" He thrust the photos towards Reigneth, his face twisted with anger. "How could you not tell me? I... I thought we had no secrets," he choked on his words and could not continue.

Reigneth's heart sank as she glanced down at the tattered, tear-stained photographs. She had known this was coming, just not when or how. It explained her reluctance to come here today. She stepped towards him, "I so wanted to tell you, I just didn't know how, or where to start – and it wasn't my secret to tell," she repeated, holding her hand out to him.

There was no point in saying anything to him; he would not be prepared to listen. She could see that much in his traumatised face; could see also that he was directing all his anger at her simply because she was there. Perhaps she should have told him, perhaps she should have told her mother. How come suddenly she was responsible for everything and everyone. At times things were so unfair.

Reigneth placed the drinks down carefully and went to put her arms around Johnny. As soon as she touched him she felt his tension. He was taut with fury and choked with emotion. Reigneth felt as if an electric shock passed through her system; she actually *felt* Johnny's distress as if it was her own and she cried out with the pain of it.

He pushed her away and was down the stairs and out of the house quicker than she would have thought possible. She could not follow; the shock to her system had been too great. Heat pulsated through her body where he had touched her. She felt faint and lowered herself quickly onto the floor feeling waves of nausea washing over her. She wanted to chase after him, but knew this to be impossible. The day seemed to grow dark then everything went black.

When Reigneth came to, Jukel was whining and licking her face. "Yuck, Juk, don't do that," she grumbled affectionately, pushing him away. She was unaware how long she had lain there, but she knew she needed to find Johnny and that only Matt could help her with this.

Sitting up, a flood of dizziness threatening to engulf her, Reigneth stood and leaned against the furniture. Gazing down at the scattered photographs, she knew she had to find Matt and tell him what had happened. Hearing a noise in the room below, she thought briefly that Johnny had returned. She began to make her way slowly downstairs, one hand holding tightly to the handrail, the other clutching Jukel's collar for support. Reigneth hated this feeling of frailty, always the aftermath of any strong sensation she experienced.

Coming into the living room, Reigneth saw Jed Cummings. He was walking out of Matthew's office, tucking something hastily into the breast pocket of his overalls. Reigneth did not have to touch Jed to know he was a bad lot; she had disliked him from the first moment she had met him and could not bring herself to trust him. Jukel clearly felt the same: his hackles were raised and he was growling deep in his throat.

"What were you doing in Matthew's office?" she asked, knowing full well and not attempting to hide her dislike.

"Looking for Matt, do you know where he is?" Jed replied, his eyes shifty.

"Not far away," she stared at him. "Perhaps you would like to put down the money you have stolen. Put it on the table over there as you leave," she gestured at the table beside the door.

"I've no idea what you're talking about," he said, clearly trying to bluff his way out of the situation.

Reigneth shrugged, "Then perhaps we'll just ring Matthew." She reached for her mobile, not prepared to argue with Jed when she felt so vulnerable. At least the dizziness was beginning to abate.

Jed took one menacing step towards her. At her side, Jukel snarled.

"I wouldn't take another step closer if I were you," Reigneth eyed Jed levelly. "In fact, if I were you I would just put the money down and leave."

"Oh, you would, would you, stinking Gypsy bitch," he spat. "Do you think I'll take any notice of the likes of you?" He took another step towards Reigneth, his fat lips glistening with saliva, his large hands balling into fists at his side.

"If you move one more step I'll set the dog on you."

Jed stared down at Jukel. "Huh, what'll he do, lick me to death? Looks placid enough, he wouldn't hurt a fly darlin'."

Reigneth hissed a command. Already alert to the situation, Jukel moved in front of her, his body rigid. She put a restraining hand on his head, "If I tell him to, he will rip out your throat or any other area I specify. Don't doubt he will do it," she warned.

Jed looked from Reigneth to the dog and hesitated.

She whispered another command. With a rumbling growl, teeth bared, Jukel lowered his haunches, ready to spring.

For the first time alarm showed in Jed's eyes. He backed off, "Alright, I'll do as you say, but you won't always have that damned animal with you and I have a very long memory, bitch."

Reigneth eyed him coldly, "You may not always be in a position to carry out your threats, Mr Cummings. If I were you I'd just put the money down slowly and get out of here, *now*."

Swearing crudely, the stockman did as he was bid. Plonking a rolled wad of notes on the table, he barged out of the door and headlong into James. Brushing past him, Jed almost ran across the yard.

"Hey! Watch where you're going, Jed," James shouted after him. "What is the matter with everyone today?" he added, turning to Reigneth.

Jed paused at the gate to fling a parting shot over his shoulder, "I'll be glad to get out of here. Place is overrun with you stinking gypos."

James spun round about to go after him, but Reigneth's grasped his arm. "Leave it, James, just leave it," she placated, "let him go."

"What's been going on here?" James looked closely at her face, panic making his voice rise. "I've just passed Johnny in the Land Rover. He nearly took the side out of my truck!"

"We need to find Matt quickly. I'll tell you then." Reigneth had no intention of repeating her story twice.

As if on cue, at that moment Matthew's drove into the yard on his quad. "What's going on, summat up?" he queried, leaping off the vehicle and striding to the door.

Reigneth swayed and James thrust his arm out to support her, a nervous tick starting in the side of his face, always a sure sign that he was agitated.

"What's happened here, Reigneth?" Matt said in alarm, looking at the two of them.

"I caught Jed coming out of your office, Matt, he'd been stealing. I threatened him with Juk and he left the money on the table – but that's not my main concern, we have to find Johnny. Matt, he knows."

"Knows what?" asked James.

"How?" said Matt.

Speaking simultaneously, the two men eyed Reigneth intently. She shook her head, not sure how to answer.

"Will someone please tell me what's going on?" James looked from one to the other, his irritation obvious.

Reigneth gazed beseechingly at Matthew, who gave her a searching look then nodded and turned to James, "Johnny is my son, he never knew it, but it seems he does now. How did he find out, Reigneth?"

"He was looking over some old school photos of you and Grace, and saw his resemblance to you." Unable to help herself, Reigneth started to cry, aware that James was staring at her in disbelief. She was not normally a cry baby, but with everything that had happed, first with Johnny and then with Jed, it was all too much for her. "He's so angry with me because I never told him and he realised I knew," she sobbed, looking helplessly at Matt, her tears spilling onto her cheeks.

"But how could he *not* have known?" James retorted, looking at Matthew's features as though for the first time. "It's pretty obvious you're at least related."

"People don't always recognise what they don't expect to see," Matt said shortly. "Where's he gone, Reigneth?"

"I have no idea; my head is so fuzzy I'm not seeing anything."

"I think we need to get down to Grace's place and tell her what's happened. Perhaps by then you'll have calmed down a bit and things may become clearer to you," Matt said.

Climbing into James's truck, they proceeded to Johnny's home. As James drove, Matthew tried Johnny's mobile. It was switched off. Where had he gone? Matt's head was filled with tumultuous thoughts: anxiety about Johnny; anger at Grace; anger at himself for not remembering the photographs. By the time they drove into the Wilmotts' yard, he was in no better a state than Reigneth.

He strode across to the back door and rapped loudly, entering the kitchen without waiting to be invited in, Reigneth, James and Jukel at his heels.

Grace was mid-way across the kitchen and at the sight of Matthew, her face paled. She moved to sit down at the kitchen table as if her legs would not hold her up. "What is it? What's happened, is it Johnny?" she asked, her hand clutching at her throat.

"He knows, Grace, he knows about us... he knows he is my... " Matt choked on the words.

"How," was all she said, as if she found even that small word difficult to say.

"He saw old photos of us," Matt replied.

Grace stared down at the floor. "It's my fault, I should have told him before now. I'm so sorry." She shook her head, tears starting to her eyes, "Forgive me, Matt," she whispered.

He sat down at the table beside her, "It's him has got to do the forgiving, Grace, not me. I don't want him to hate us; I love him."

James looked from one to the other, a puzzled expression on his face. "Did none of you think to be honest? The poor sod! Just wait till Jessie finds out."

"It's not been as easy as that, James, the time was never right," Grace tried to explain.

"Well sure as hell the time ain't right now," James sighed deeply. "I just don't understand you people. Why did you never tell him, especially once your husband passed away? I imagine he's the other injured party – or didn't he know?"

207

Grace's lips tightened into a thin line. "I know you are only trying to help, James, and I'm grateful, but I hardly think this is any business of yours."

Before James could reply, Matthew cut across him. "Where do you think he might have gone? What's important right now is to find him and try to sort this out. Recriminations can come later."

Reigneth had been sitting quietly at the kitchen table. Bringing her gaze up to Grace, she said, "He's angry with me too. I knew, you see; he's angry I kept the secret from him. Now he is hurting: in the space of an hour, his whole world has come tumbling down around him."

"What a bloody mess," James muttered. He wandered over to the sink and filled the kettle then turned back to the table, "Anyone fancy a cuppa?"

Grace nodded, looked up into James's face, "Why did you say that about Jessie? What will she think? Will she be very upset?"

"I have not the faintest idea. She's a bit straight-laced, though, is our Jessie, and even if she wasn't, she would never understand why you guys have been so deceitful. Lying is not in her nature."

Hearing these words, Matthew felt utterly devastated. He stood up, "Johnny may have gone to Home Humber. I'll go and see – and it's for me to tell Jessie. God knows what she will think of me." He turned away, "Keep ringing Johnny's mobile, I'll be back later."

"Take the truck, Matt," said James. "I'll stay here with Reigneth."

Watching Matthew go, Grace attempted to pull herself together. *What's done is done,* she thought, gratefully accepting a cup of tea from James. She dared not think about the thing she most dreaded – had always dreaded – that her son would reject her. The merest hint of it brought fresh tears to her eyes.

The three of them sat quietly, nursing their thoughts, James occasionally reaching across the table to give Reigneth's hand an encouraging squeeze. An hour later they heard the sound of the truck on the gravel drive.

"Matt's back," James got to his feet.

Surprisingly, Matt was accompanied by both Jessie and Aaron. Grace stood up as soon as Jessie entered the kitchen. She had told James it was none of his business, but Jessie was a different matter:

she had the right to know exactly who it was her daughter was marrying. "I'm sorry, Jessie, sorry no one told you until now. I should have done, I know, it's just that… " her voice trailed away. This was so hard. "What must you think of me?" she whispered.

Jessie shrugged, "It was a long time ago, Grace, and what you and Matt got up to in your youth means nothing to me. The only one I'm concerned for is your boy. He's a sensitive soul." She went over to Reigneth and placed a kiss on top of her head. "Do you see where he is, love?"

Grace thought that a strange question to ask, but decided to ignore it, especially as Reigneth had begun to cry again. "No, I cannot see him anywhere," she gasped between sobs.

"You cannot see your girlie boy because he's not in any danger," James said, a soft smile on his face.

"That's right," Aaron said, coming forward to give Reigneth a hug. "Don't worry; he'll come back to you. You know he will. You've seen the two of you together often enough haven't you?"

Watching them, Grace was bemused. Whatever were they talking about? She looked again at Reigneth. There was something odd about the girl, she had always thought so. Grace got up from the table, she had to do something; couldn't just sit here. She proceeded to put the kettle back on for more tea. Thank God both Charlotte and Henry were staying with friends this weekend. She supposed they would have to be told. Her heart sank at the thought. Then another thought occurred to her. "Do you suppose he might have gone back to university early, Matt?" she asked, thinking as she looked at Matthew's face that he seemed in the last few hours to have aged about ten years. His face was grey and lined with worry.

He shrugged. "Maybe; more likely gone out onto the moor – but Rannoch's in his stable and I wouldn't know where to begin looking." He glanced hopefully at Reigneth, but she shook her head.

"Shouldn't we report him missing?" Grace asked.

"Not yet. He's a big boy now," James chipped in, "and he's only been gone a couple of hours. You're all overreacting: he's probably just walking somewhere trying to cool his head – he'll be hugely embarrassed if you send out a search party. Would you like me and Aaron to go and see to the horses for you, Grace?"

"Oh yes, thank you, James," she said gratefully. After they had gone, she looked up at Matt and Jessie. She caught the look that passed between them and surprised herself by saying, "Why don't you two and Reigneth go into the sitting room, you'll be more comfortable in there. I'll bring tea through in a moment."

Relieved to have the kitchen – her domain – to herself for a while, Grace bent over the back of a chair and shoved a tea towel into her face to stifle her sobs. It was nothing to do with the way Matt and Jessie were with each other, none of that seemed to matter anymore. All her thoughts and anxieties were centred on Johnny. *Pull yourself together,'* she told herself sternly. She could not let go; she would be in pieces. Stifling her emotions, she put the kettle onto boil and set a tray with cups, milk jug and sugar bowl, happy to be busy, hoping the activity would stem her flow of tears.

The afternoon passed slowly, the levels of anxiety rising with each passing hour. Grace phoned the university, but nobody had seen Johnny. Matt took Rannoch and went out onto the moor, but as it began to get dark he returned, shaking his head disconsolately. Reigneth repeatedly phoned Johnny's mobile; it remained switched off. Jessie kept in touch with Liz just in case there was any news at Home Humber, while James and Aaron went back to Higher Wedicombe to see to the stock for Matt. When it got to nine o'clock, after several more cups of tea and rounds of sandwiches, Grace announced that she would phone the police.

"No, Grace, wait," said Reigneth. "I do not know where Johnny is, but I do know he is in no danger. I do not think he is lost. Please hold on just a bit longer." She looked across at her mother, "Tell her Ma."

"Tell me what?" Grace asked, her skin prickling with apprehension.

Jessie shrugged, "I am surprised you have never noticed that Reigneth is special. She has the gift of sight. It is not something we tell people and I ask you to keep it to yourself. Not because we are ashamed of it; far from it – but because it has the potential to make my daughter's life – and therefore your son's – a misery."

Grace gasped, "You are telling me she is a... *seer*?"

"Among other things, yes," Jessie nodded, putting a comforting arm around her daughter. "If she tells you to wait, then I would urge that you do."

Eyes wide, Grace stared at Jessie, feeling doubtful about this revelation, yet strangely comforted. She had thought the girl was odd; had not suspected Reigneth was as special as her mother claimed. Now it all made sense. Grace looked across at Matthew, her eyebrow raised. When he nodded, she added, "Very well; one more hour, and then I think we must phone the police and report our son missing."

At ten o'clock, the landline ringing in the hall startled them all. Grace sprang up to answer it. "Johnny, at last!" she gasped into the phone.

"No, not Johnny, Mrs Wilmott; it's John Marsh, the landlord at the Drover's Arms in Widecombe. I've got your lad here. He's been here since this afternoon and I'm afraid he's the worse for wear. I thought I'd better call you."

"Oh dear, is he very drunk?" She knew the answer. It would never for a moment have occurred to her that Johnny would seek comfort in alcohol. He simply wasn't a drinker. Not normally.

"Well he hasn't had *that* much, but he did seem a bit upset about something when he got here and he's had a few. I don't think he can make it home without some assistance."

"Thanks for letting me know, John. He never could hold his drink. I'll come and fetch him straight away," Grace said weakly. Her knees wobbling with relief, she slammed down the phone and saw that everyone was gathered around her. "He's in the Drover's Arms – drunk," she added, unnecessarily.

"You all stay here, I'll go fetch him," Matthew said, making his way to the door and shrugging into his jacket.

"I'm not being funny, Matt," said James, "but do you think it would be best if Aaron and I went? Only... well, you know... he might be a bit upset with you."

It occurred to Grace that James was being strangely protective towards Johnny. She had not realised they had become friends. She looked at Matthew, who hesitated then nodded distractedly.

"Reigneth, you coming?" James said as he was leaving. Aaron was already out of the door and on his way to the truck.

"Do you think I ought to, he was so angry with me?" Reigneth frowned, "What do you think, James?"

"Get in the truck, of course you should come with us, idiot, none of this is your doing."

"Yes, love, you go," said Jessie, holding out Reigneth's coat.

* * *

211

Reigneth did not agree with James; in part, this *was* her doing. She should have told Johnny what she knew; she could have let him down gently. All day she had been regretting the choice she had made. She had known Johnny was hurting, but also that he was not *physically* hurt. That he had gone to the pub surprised her; she would have expected him to take off somewhere to get some space; had imagined he would be out on the moor. Even that had not concerned her – he knew it so well and would have come to no harm. Her concern had all been for his state of mind, and though relieved he had been found, it still was.

Arriving at the Drover's Arms, James and Aaron lifted a silent Johnny from the bar to the truck while Reigneth held the doors for them. She wrinkled her nose in distaste as a waft of stale air, shouts and muffled laughter came from the pub. Obviously very drunk, Johnny never made a sound.

"He's a lot quieter than you when he's drunk anyway, James," Aaron quipped.

"That's what worries me," James remarked.

At the sight of Johnny's white face and the dark circles round his eyes, Reigneth was unable to stem her tears. She wept silently and nobody spoke as they drove back.

Parking the truck, James lifted Johnny out and carried him upstairs, Grace leading the way.

"He's still out cold," she told Reigneth as she came back downstairs. "James is putting him to bed – he hasn't uttered a word. He'll be like a bear with a sore head tomorrow, but when he surfaces, I'll give you a call. I can only thank you all for your help and apologise again for having caused all this. Matt, I'm sure James won't mind giving you a lift back to Higher Wedicombe."

Reigneth could not believe her ears: it was like they were all being dismissed. She stood hands on hips, scowling, "I'm not leaving, I don't care what you say, and I'll never keep anything from him again, no matter whose secret it is," she announced. "I'm staying with him, Grace, whether you like it or not!"

Ignoring the flabbergasted expression on Grace's face and the sudden frown on Jessie's, Reigneth ran upstairs.

"You're OK, he's decent," James smiled, meeting her in the doorway of Johnny's room.

She flung her cousin a look of gratitude, dashed into the

bedroom and settled herself on Johnny's bed, cradling him in her arms.

Jessie had followed her upstairs and Reigneth waited for the tirade, but it never came. Her mother opened her mouth as if to protest, took one look at her daughter's face and obviously thought better of it.

"Well, I can see your mind is made up, Reigneth, so I will say goodnight," she turned away, almost colliding with Grace, who had brought a spare pair of Charlotte's pyjamas for Reigneth. Without saying any more, Jessie retreated downstairs, but Reigneth knew there would be a reckoning tomorrow. It could not be helped. Much as she loved her ma, right now Johnny was her chief concern.

"Thank you, Grace," Reigneth gave Johnny's mother a shy smile. "I'm sorry, I didn't mean to be rude, but I love your son so very much and I am partly to blame for what happened. I cannot leave him. When he wakes he will need me." She saw the flicker of pain that crossed Grace's face and added gently, "He is going to need you too."

"I do hope so," Grace smiled wanly. "He is a lucky boy to have you in his life, Reigneth. In fact, I think perhaps we all are. Goodnight then, my dear. I hope you get some sleep." With one last look at her son, she turned away.

Reigneth listened to her departing footsteps on the stairs and heard the murmur of voices in the hall. A few moments later, she heard the truck driving away. She lay back and looked up at the ceiling. *So this is my first night with Johnny,* she thought, *and he doesn't even know I am here*!

Chapter 25

The Way Forward

Johnny was so drunk and traumatised that he did not stir until the early hours of the morning, when he silently began to weep. Earlier, in that in-between stage of waking and sleeping, he was dimly aware that it was night time and that he was not alone; that someone was holding him and stroking his hair and that, impossibly, it was his beloved. But since that could not be, he realised he must be dreaming and drifted back into a fitful sleep.

Waking fully, sometime later, he knew it had not been a dream: Reigneth really *was* in bed with him. His head and heart both hammering he lay motionless in her arms trying to piece together what had happened. He acknowledged that this earth-shattering, life-changing discovery about his parentage was not what hurt the most. Even more hurtful was that Reigneth had known and had kept it from him. Everything else he could deal with. This fact only served to highlight for Johnny the intensity of his love for her.

She slept soundly now, her arm around him, cradling him, protecting him; his cheek resting against her breast. He smiled slightly. He had no idea how Reigneth had managed this, but he was sure Jessie was going to be hopping mad. He raised his head a little to see her better. The movement brought a wave of dizziness and nausea. He swallowed it down and gazed at her. She was so lovely, her hair fanned out over the pillow, her lips pursed together. Dreamily she opened her eyes and smiled at him. He tucked his arm around her waist and with a spark of wry humour was painfully aware that her mother had nothing to worry about: he could no more make love to Reigneth now than he could fly to the moon. With that thought, he drifted back to sleep.

Some hours later, he was aware that it was morning and that Reigneth was awake, her steady rhythmic breathing comforting to him. He could hear his mother clattering about downstairs in the kitchen.

Reigneth smiled gently, "Are you ready to get up?" she asked, easing herself out of bed. She looked beautiful even when wearing a pair of Charlotte's garishly patterned pyjamas. He grinned, and winced.

She grinned back, "You look dreadful by the way."

"I feel dreadful, don't ever leave me will you, Reigneth?"

"Don't be ridiculous."

"I'm sorry I was so angry with you, none of it was your fault. I kind of understand why you didn't tell me, but it was all such a shock and I suppose I blamed you a little. Forgive me?"

"Of course I forgive you and I'll never keep anything from you again," she looked contrite. "And by the way, so long as there are to be no more secrets between us, I had better tell you that you and I will have a baby brother by this time next year."

His mouth fell open; dumbfounded would not have covered what he felt. "Wow! Do Matt and Jessie know?"

"No; it doesn't do to tell Ma too much," she smiled.

"Reigneth, how do you keep it all in? Your head must be a very uncomfortable place at times."

She smiled, "It's better when you're with me; you tone things down a bit."

"Will you marry me, Reigneth? Will you be my wife just as soon as possible?"

"I thought you'd never ask." She leaned over to kiss him, murmured, "Sorry if this kills the moment, but your breath reeks of stale beer!" They both laughed and hugged one another.

"You didn't give me an answer you know," said Johnny.

"Do I really need to say it? I've known you and I were meant to be together since I was a *bitti chai*, but if you need to hear the words then yes, I love you with all my heart and soul and I will marry you just as soon as it can be arranged, please."

They exchanged contented smiles then Reigneth grabbed up her clothes and tiptoed to the door. "Which way is the bathroom?"

Over the next day or two, the knowledge that Matt was his father began to sink in, but Johnny was not yet ready to talk about it with either of his parents and managed to avoid them both. He had loved Harry, who had been a wonderful father and shown him just as much love and affection as he did the twins; Johnny felt sure he could not have known. It was hard to imagine Matt and his mother as a couple, it just did not seem to work, but apparently that is what they had been. Matt and Jessie, however, seemed to fit like two pieces of a jigsaw puzzle.

Johnny thought of all the times he and Matt had done things together, how easy their relationship had been and, of course, how alike they were. Not just in looks – although he had never recognised that until he saw the photographs – but in so many of their ways. As he slowly accepted the earth-shattering revelation, he was stricken with guilt about Reigneth. That he had been so horrid to her even for a moment was bad enough, but when James told him of the incident with Jed Cummings, Johnny felt even guiltier. His fury with Jed was matched by his fury with himself: if he had not gone storming off in a blind, selfish rage, he would have been there to protect her. As it was, he knew he was going to have to speak to Matt, but he did not yet feel able to confront either of his parents, not until he had got his own feelings sorted out. His way of dealing with it was to carry on as though nothing had happened, avoiding any kind of confrontation. He had always been the same: he hated unpleasantness of any kind, perhaps because he had so rarely experienced it. Johnny knew he had led a charmed life, he had been aware that his mother adored him from the moment he was born and he knew that whatever happened, that would never change.

He had many questions to which he needed answers, but he just could not bring himself to ask them yet. He wondered how his mother had ended up marrying Harry. Had she known she was carrying Matt's child? He knew his birth had been exactly nine months after her wedding because Harry had often joked about it, so he must have been conceived just before. No, she could not have known: he did not believe she had it in her to be so deceitful. She could not possibly have known she was pregnant on her wedding day, nor whose child she carried, not until he was born and she had seen his resemblance to Matt. Had she a choice in who she married or had she been coerced by her father? Grandfather Gill had died when Johnny was a child, but he remembered being frightened of him and neither his mother nor Granny Gill ever spoke of him. Maybe that was the answer.

So, had his mother loved Matt? Or Harry? Both of them? Neither of them? Johnny puzzled about this for a long time. Thinking back over his childhood he could remember no unpleasantness between Harry and his mother, but neither had there been much obvious affection – at least, not on his mother's part. But what was Matt's side of the story? While Johnny was unsure about his mother and was bitterly resentful that she had never told him the truth, he was fairly certain, from the way Matt behaved around her, that he had loved Grace. Johnny suspected this was why he had become a recluse, living in such a shambolic state and letting both himself and Higher Wedicombe go. He tried to imagine how he would feel if Reigneth upped and married someone else and could well believe he would react in the same way. The mere idea was unbearable. The more he thought about that, the more sympathy he had for Matt and the more he was inclined to forgive him for concealing the truth.

Keeping to himself at Higher Wedicombe, Matt had mixed emotions about the whole incident: he was glad that his lad knew the truth at last. Pretending had always been hard for him, but the way in which Johnny had found out distressed him and he blamed himself. He mused that people never reacted in the way he expected them to. Jessie, he knew, had been shocked by the news and had insisted on a period of time for reflection for both him and Grace, and, of course, for herself. He could not blame her. He knew it was not that he had fathered Johnny which concerned her, but that he had kept the knowledge to himself. At the very least, he should have told Jessie as soon as he saw that Johnny's and Reigneth's relationship was becoming serious, and certainly when he had asked Jessie to marry him. That he had not done so was because he had been terrified of losing her. It was perhaps an irrational fear, but that made it no less real, and the longer he had left it the harder it had become, so he had let things slide.

Now, after a couple of days of not seeing her, he was distraught. He could not bear to be away from her. He missed her terribly. By the late afternoon on the third day he could stand it no longer and decided to drive down to Home Humber and beg her to talk with him. Just as he was about to get in the Land Rover, Grace drove into the yard.

She wound down the window, "Matt, are you going out?" she called, bringing the vehicle to a halt.

He paused, his hand on the car door, "I was just going over to Jessie's. Can it wait, Grace? I need to get this business with Johnny sorted out."

"Well that's why I'm here, Matthew." She got out of her car and walked over to him. "Look, I'll come straight to the point. Now that our secret is out... er, well... I was wondering if perhaps we ought to give things a go? You and me, I mean," she flushed and looked down at the ground.

Matt's mouth fell open and for a moment he stared at her in amazement then collected himself and shook his head, "No, Grace, I don't and neither do you, not really, do you? It's too late for us; our time is in the past. It wouldn't work, not now. I mean, thanks for the offer and everything, but let's just agree to be the best of friends, eh?" He gave her a friendly smile and was relieved when she nodded. "Has Johnny said anything?" he asked.

"No, he's been avoiding me."

"Ah well, give it time. Thanks for coming over, Grace. I appreciate why you did, but... "

"OK, Matt, I can see you want to go." Grace got back into her car, "See you sometime then," she smiled and with a quick wave, was gone.

Driving away from Higher Wedicombe Grace felt an enormous sense of relief. Her suggestion had been genuine and she had been thinking of Johnny when she made it, but she needed order in her life and knew she could never have achieved that with Matt. She would always be fond of him and was pleased they had reached an understanding.

Negotiating the ruts in the track away from the farm, Grace sighed. She just wished Johnny would talk to her so she knew what was going on in his head. Her nerves were frayed and she needed a hug from her darling boy, but he was reserved, holding everything inside. She knew she must wait for him to come to her. There was no pushing Johnny, she gave a rueful smile. He was just like his father:

he did things in his own way, in his own time. He was a generous, kind-hearted boy, though. Things would come right eventually, especially with Reigneth at his side.

There had been things about Reigneth she had not understood until Jessie had said what she had about her daughter's capabilities. Grace was not sure if she believed it was possible for anyone to foresee the future. But it made no difference to how she felt about Reigneth. She liked the girl, there was something about her loving nature that drew you in, you just could not resist her.

Arriving home to a dark, empty house, Grace felt very lonely. Henry and Charlotte were over at Home Humber so often these days. She had still not plucked up the courage to tell them about Johnny. They had doted on Harry. Would they reject her too?

As she put her key in the lock she heard the phone. Thrusting open the door she lunged for the receiver just before the answer phone clicked in. Out of breath from rushing, she panted, "Hello?"

"I haven't made you rush have I, Grace? It's Izzy."

"Izzy! It's so good to hear from you; what are you up to?" Grace was amazed at just how good it was; she had always liked Izzy.

"I thought I'd catch up with Johnny, I've missed him this week, is he better? When is he coming back to uni?"

Grace was puzzled, but caught on quickly; Johnny had obviously told her he was unwell to explain his absence. "Yes, yes he's better, he'll be back soon. Isn't it time you visited us again?" Grace genuinely had missed this whacky girl.

"Next holiday I'll be there; you just try and keep me away," Izzy laughed. "Tell him I rang will you? Tell him to ring me and that I think he's been a bit mardy!"

"OK, I will, you take care." Grace smiled as she put down the receiver. Perhaps things were not so bad after all.

Chapter 26

Aftermath

Thursday evenings were always full of anticipation for Reigneth. Mondays to Thursdays were sheer hell away from Johnny, but on Fridays he had no lectures and would take the train back from university to be at her side when she returned from college. She spent each week longing for Friday, and each week she wondered how it was possible to be so excited over something that had become commonplace. Even speaking to him on the phone made her heart flutter.

At last it was Thursday again. Reigneth went to bed that night in a fever of excitement, filled with thoughts of tomorrow. In the middle of the night she came half awake with an inexplicable feeling of dark foreboding. After a few restless minutes, she drifted back to sleep and was plunged into a dream.

Night time: the room dimly lit by the rays of a street lamp shining through the kitchen window. The woman was small, petite, the type of woman men liked to protect and care for. She was pretty, but her face was contorted and anguished, her hands raised to protect her head as a huge fist came crushing down on her. The force of the blow ricocheted her head backwards, bursting open her lower lip. She did not cry out, this was not a first for her. Perhaps if she made no noise there would be no satisfaction for him in his physical victory over her. She struggled to keep upright, knowing from experience that once she was down the kicking frenzy would begin. Clarity and focus were becoming difficult. This was the third blow to her head; the previous two had been delivered in the bedroom.

A fourth blow thumped down, this time landing on her left

ear. Her consciousness was hovering on the brink. He would have to stop soon: he would not risk too many visible injuries, but his rage was not abating. Her internal injuries from his vicious sexual assault were not new to her and she knew the bruising would eventually subside, so long as she had some respite for a little while. Hopefully, he would be contrite enough to give her the breathing space she needed. He usually was – afterwards.

A fifth blow caught her under the chin, flipping her head backward and she was almost gone. Her knees buckled, she clutched desperately to the side of the kitchen unit. Almost in slow motion she sank to the ground. His huge bulk loomed over her. Drawing back his right leg, he kicked at her viciously, aiming for her stomach, but the blow landed in her neck, crushing her windpipe. Gurgling, bubbling sounds came from her mouth. Then silence.

Awake! Awake!

Reigneth sat bolt upright, her pyjamas a soggy mess clinging to her body. Sweat covered her from head to toe. She trembled with the aftermath of the dream. The worst dream she had ever had. She could still see the broken and pummelled form of the woman crushed against the wall; the huge man rigid with rage. She did not know the woman, nothing about her was familiar. She did not recognise the man either; she had not seen his face only the brutish size of him.

Reigneth knew the woman was dead. She began to shake uncontrollably, her body jerking in spasms at the horror she had witnessed. She knew sleep would not return to her. She knew that night after night she would see this murder until eventually it happened.

Not wanting to disturb the whole household, a shower was out of the question. Reigneth quickly stripped her bed. Her sheet and quilt cover were damp and unpleasant. In the bathroom she washed herself down and changed her night clothes, hoping these mundane and tedious tasks would do something to calm her racing heart. She went downstairs to make herself a drink, curled up on the settee with Jukel and eventually fell into a restless sleep.

She woke the following morning to see her mother staring anxiously down at her. Jukel was snarling; it was what had woken her. Reigneth came fully awake. "Juk, be quiet!" she pulled her hands through his coat.

Glancing warily at the dog, Jessie proceeded cautiously, "What is it, Reigneth? I only have to look at your face to know something is wrong... " Jukel snarled again, standing four square in front of his mistress, his lip curling back to show his teeth.

"Down!" Reigneth ordered and shook his ruff, "Quiet, I said! Sorry Ma, I don't know what's got into him."

"He's only protecting you, love. He knows you are distressed about something. Are you going to tell me what it is? You look dreadful, why are you up so early?"

"I've been here a while; had a dream, a bad one," Reigneth choked on a sob.

"Oh, love, I should have known. I'll go and get you a nice hot cup of tea and then you can tell me all about it." With a perplexed look at Jukel, Jessie hurried away.

Normal sounds of the household getting up did not seem to register with Reigneth, she felt dazed and was so distraught she did not know what to do. She had dreamt of a murder as vividly as if she had been the unknown victim. She wanted to tell all the family, to beg them to help her, but what could they do? The man and the woman were strangers. They could have been anywhere. Reigneth decided to wait for clarity, she had no other choice, which meant she would endure these dreams nightly. *What happens if I recognise one of them?* she thought. There were no answers.

Reigneth did not go to college; her mother rang in to say she was sick. Exhausted, she stayed on the sofa, Jukel lying beside it threatening anyone who came too near to keep their distance. The day dragged on and despite her family being aware that she had dreamt something terrible, they did not pester her, they knew to be patient. She reassured them it was not to do with their family and all they could do was wait. They all knew she was having a tough day and that she would likely have to endure an even tougher night.

"Are you going to try to eat something, Reigneth, you've had nothing all day?" Jessie asked when it got to tea time.

"Sorry, Ma. Couldn't... just couldn't... feel sick."

Even Johnny's arrival did nothing to lift Reigneth's mood. He at least was able to sit next to her on the sofa: the only person Jukel allowed near without a warning growl. Johnny was desperately concerned about her and it took all her strength to reassure him, but other than telling him that her dream had been a bad one and

222

that she knew she would have to endure it again, she resisted putting into words what she had seen.

Reigneth's bedtime regime was protracted that evening, trying to delay the time when she would have to go to bed. The family sat with her in the sitting room, talking quietly amongst themselves, but bedtime could not be put off forever.

Anxiously, Johnny kissed Reigneth's brow. Glancing up at Jessie, he said, "I think it would be best if I... "

"Stay with her, yes, I know," Jessie finished his sentence. "It seems to help her. I'll look you out a pair of pyjamas."

"Er... is that OK? I mean, you don't mind... ?"

Jessie smiled at him. "I minded the first time, but since then you've set a date for a summer wedding and while Reigneth is not yet 17, in truth she is older and wiser than all of us put together and you are her chosen partner for life. So no, Johnny, I don't mind and I trust you to look after her."

Reigneth gave them both a wan smile, more glad than she could say that Johnny was to stay with her. His presence seemed to calm her racing heart. She was amazed her mother had consented to him sharing her bed. Since Matt had come into Jessie's life, she seemed so much more relaxed about everything.

A slight smile tweaked at the corners of Reigneth's mouth when, a little while later, Johnny came into her room wearing a pair of Aaron's pyjamas, which were adequate, if a bit small. She watched him settling himself in for a long night, leaving the bedside light on the better to aid her without startling her. *I must look dreadful,* she thought, as he took her carefully in his arms and soothed her to sleep.

In the early hours of the morning the dream came again, exactly the same as before, only this time she was not an onlooker, she was the victim.

Twisting and turning in order to protect her body from the sustained and vicious attack. Everything was intensified, the pattern of his shirt, the type of boots he wore. The noises made as his fist connected with her head. The agony. The sickening gurgling as his last death-delivering kick crushed her windpipe. She could not breathe. Her body shook with the tremors reverberating through it; she looked towards the assailant's face and...

* * *

Writhing and whimpering like a child, Reigneth felt something cold touch her arm; the effect was dramatic. Instantly she leapt up, crouching at the end of the bed like a terrified animal, her gaze darting to where she had felt someone touch her. In that second she resembled something not quite human, unaware where she was, hardly recognising Johnny's face. With the realisation that she had still to identify the murderer, she emitted a high-pitched keening sound. Wildness hung about her as her eyes flicked from side to side directing her gaze around the room.

The bedroom door pushed open and Reigneth slowly became aware that James, Jessie and Aaron were standing in the half light from the landing and that Johnny was kneeling on the bed, frozen lest he startle her again, his eyes wide with horror. As Reigneth came to her senses, he edged towards her. She noticed his movements were slow and precise, as if she was a wild bird he was afraid would start into flight. She was bathed in sweat and shaking uncontrollably. Johnny stretched out his arms to hold her.

"I can't see who it is. I cannot see yet," she mumbled against his chest, and then she was weeping as though she would never stop, loud hacking sobs racking her body.

Once calmer, Reigneth was aware the dream had intensified, and from experience she knew it would continue to do so each time it repeated. Perhaps another night would give her the identity of the murderer. She had seen the face of the woman, who was a stranger to her.

What if they were both strangers?

If Reigneth had been allowed to carry on dreaming she would have seen his face; everything was leading towards this. If only she had not been woken, but she could not blame Johnny, he did not know any better; she should have warned him.

Exhausted from the intensity of the dream, Reigneth prayed that it could be resolved quickly. As this 'gift' of hers was growing and intensifying she realised that she could not cope with the physical demands on her body. For the first time she became aware of her vulnerability, seeing a future for herself that might not be a happy one – not unless something happened to change this. Staring around at the people she loved, Reigneth knew they would do anything for her, but they were powerless in this instance to help her and she felt desolate.

Jessie took care of the practicalities, helping her to the

224

bathroom while Johnny and James changed her sweat-soaked bed linen. Aaron crouched silently in the corner, his face pale, his brows drawn together in a frown. In his customary place at the bottom of the stairs, Jukel whimpered.

It was almost dawn before Reigneth and Johnny were back in bed. He held her gently in his arms, neither slept. Johnny did not ask her about the dream and Reigneth was grateful for that: thankful for his sensitivity. He seemed to know without being told that she could not bring herself to speak of it. She knew she had to endure it again and again, the thought of it made her tremble.

The following day passed slowly, Johnny and Jukel never leaving her side. Reigneth ate nothing. She was afraid. Afraid for the woman she had seen beaten and bruised; afraid for herself, for if this was what her life was to be like, physically she could not cope and if that was so, how could she condemn Johnny to a life with her? She was being selfish and for the first time it occurred to her that she should let him go. As much as the thought appalled her, she resolved that unless this had a happy outcome she would leave him. She loved him too much to subject him to years of endless suffering. She hoped beyond all things that the situation could be resolved for the abused woman and for herself, but most of all for Johnny; her love knew no bounds.

Saturday drew to a close. Richard and Liz had gone early to bed, leaving Jessie and the boys in the sitting room. They were having a bedtime drink beside the dying embers of the fire. Reigneth had gone for a bath, Jukel stretched out across the bathroom door.

"I have never seen her as bad as this, Jessie," James commented, bringing his hand up in irritation to rub at his face.

"Don't get yourself so wound up," Jessie said, eyeing the nervous twitch ticking at his cheek, a sure sign he was agitated.

Johnny sat at the table, head bowed, hands covering his face. "I just feel so helpless. I was no use to her at all. I don't think I should have woken her when she started whimpering. I shouldn't have touched her."

Jessie laid a hand on his shoulder and gave it a little shake, "It was only natural, Johnny, you weren't to know. Don't blame yourself."

"I can remember when she was like it once before, around the time when Granny Mary died," Aaron said to Jessie. "I was staying with you and Uncle Joe and sleeping in Reigneth's room. She scared me half to death with that same banshee howl and I ran in to you crying."

"Yes, I remember that," Jessie gave him a gentle smile, "it was when she dreamed of Granny Mary's passing."

"She's so weak, Jessie," Johnny looked up, his distress evident, "and she's not eaten a thing. I don't know what to do for the best."

The conversation ended when Reigneth came back into the room, large black smudges beneath her eyes. Wavering slightly she grasped the back of the sofa to steady herself.

Her heart swelling with love for them, Reigneth looked at their anxious faces, aware that they were delaying the moment of bedtime for her sake. She attempted to joke about it, her lips curving in a half-hearted smile. "Well, I suppose there's no putting it off any longer. Let's see what the rollercoaster is like tonight, shall we?"

Johnny leapt up from the sofa and went to her side, putting his arm around her. "I'm not going to touch you or wake you tonight, Reigneth, no matter what, but I'll be there right beside you, do you hear me, my darling?" He kissed her softly on the lips. "It will be all right, somehow I know it will."

Reigneth nodded, reassured by his angelic smile. They all trooped up to bed and Jukel took up his station at the bottom of the stairs.

Returning from the bathroom, Johnny propped himself up with pillows and prepared for a long night. Reigneth could smell the toothpaste on his breath as he leaned over to kiss her, treating her as though she were a piece of fragile glass. There was no passion in his kiss, just warmth and comfort and for that she was grateful. She heard murmured voices outside her door: James and Aaron were camped out on the landing.

"Don't you think this is all a bit excessive, camping on the landing?" she said.

"They feel better the nearer they are to you, it comforts them," Johnny reassured her.

"It must do – I've never known James come upstairs to bed before," she smiled. She settled herself down to sleep, taking a sidelong glance at her girlie boy: *He is so beautiful,* she thought just before she drifted off to sleep.

This time she was the onlooker again. The first assault had already taken place in the bedroom and they were now in the small kitchen. The man rained blows down on the defenceless woman just as before, but this time the angle on the scene was slightly skewed and Reigneth could see both of them in profile. She noticed the man's large hands and long gangly arms, swinging like an ape's. His face in profile was repulsive to her. She recognised the large angular jaw and over-full lips wet with saliva. She recognised the sneer of his mouth as he looked at his terrified wife. Reigneth had never met her, but now at least she knew who it was and her heart went out to her.

As she watched, he brought up his fist to deliver the blow that would catch the defenceless woman under the chin and smash the teeth of her bottom jaw resoundingly into those of her upper. Reigneth drew in her breath and waited for the noise as the two connected. It did not come. The only noise she heard was her own voice growling like an animal.

The blow landed not on the abused woman's chin, but on Joe Gray's forearm!

Reigneth gasped: suddenly, her dad was there! He was standing between Jed Cummings and his wife, guarding Alison Cummings's fragile body. A warm feeling seem to flow through her. She knew then that Alison was not to die; her dad would stop it. Relief washed over her body like a cool refreshing breeze. Oh Dad, she thought, I love you so much.

And then everything went black.

It was obvious to Johnny that the dream had ended and that Reigneth had fainted. Just as before, at some time in the night she had begun to twitch and writhe, her hands grasping at the bed linen like claws. She had been muttering and whimpering, begging someone or something to stop. He made out the anguished words, *"Stop it! Leave her alone!"* Grasping at the bed clothes, Reigneth, her back arched, had emitted a loud feral growl. She had sounded like an animal. She was angry, that much was clear. Johnny was convinced that in her dream she was trying to protect someone. To see his beloved in such desperate straits had distressed him immeasurably and it had taken all his will power not to intervene.

"Is she all right?" James asked as both he and Aaron pushed open the bedroom door.

"It sounded a bit dodgy there for a minute," Aaron muttered, anxiously peering at his cousin.

"I think the dream is over, but she's fainted," Johnny said quietly. "She's OK. Look at her face."

Reigneth's lips were lifted in a soft smile and she looked utterly at peace. Cradling her, he whispered, "Can you hear me, Darling? I've got you, you're safe now," he rocked her gently, relieved at last to have her in his arms. Moments later, Jessie came in with a bowl of water and warm flannel and washed Reigneth's face.

She came round slowly and smiled at them, her gaze lingering on each face in turn, almost as if she was drinking in their love and gaining strength from it. To Johnny, it seemed that all the anxiety of the previous day had suddenly evaporated.

"It's going to be alright," she said. "Dad's dealing with it. He will help me."

Johnny felt a wave of fresh anxiety for her; she must have forgotten her dad was dead. "Reigneth, my darling," he said softly, "your dad passed away, he cannot help you, but we are all here. You are safe now."

Reigneth looked up at him, but did not seem to see him. He could feel her shivering. She was becoming chilled, her sweat beginning to dry on her body. He held her tightly in his arms, rubbing her back to warm her. Glancing over her head at the others he saw James and Aaron exchange knowing looks.

"She'll be all right now then, if Joe's there," said Jessie with a sad smile.

Dumbfounded, Johnny gazed at them, his eyebrow raised in query, the hairs on his skin prickling. "Eh? You mean... he... er, Reigneth... ?"

The three of them nodded. "Yes," whispered Jessie, "her da comes to his *bitti chai* when she needs him."

Chapter 27

Confrontation

The following day, Reigneth slept late and woke feeling considerably better. She was not as perturbed as she had been the previous day; somehow she knew her dad would deal with Jed Cummings. She did not know exactly how, but her tortured mind could not deal with the specifics.

Reigneth was aware that all her family were staying near to her and in fact she became slightly agitated if they were apart. Wherever she was, Jukel was close by, a low rumbling growl coming from him if anyone tried to get between them. She touched him constantly for reassurance and would not allow him to be taken away from her.

The week dragged by, someone always staying with her so she was never alone. Johnny had not returned to university, he could not be persuaded to leave her while things were unresolved. Not wanting them to worry any further, she had told no one the specifics of what she had seen, merely reassuring them that everything would work out well and that nothing in her dream would affect them or their loved ones. It did not return again that week and Reigneth, feeling more relaxed and knowing her mother was worrying about her, made an effort to eat properly, although she had no appetite.

Jessie had never known her daughter to be this upset for such a prolonged time and was relieved when she seemed to be getting stronger. Reigneth was still somewhat preoccupied and distant, as though she was waiting for something to happen, and Jessie, afraid for what that might be, made sure someone was always within call. Most often it was Johnny, but sometimes James or Aaron too.

Matthew was a frequent visitor and they had talked a lot about his past. She had come to understand why he had never revealed the truth about Johnny and had forgiven him. It was hard not to; she loved him. Jessie knew she would never love another man in the way she had loved Joe, but the fact that it was not the same with Matthew did not make it less in her eyes – just different. He had told her of Grace's offer and she had questioned him, wanting to be absolutely sure that he had no lingering feelings for his former love. She had also urged him to talk about things with his son, but for the time being, Johnny was far too anxious about Reigneth. Never leaving her side for any longer than he had to, he had made it obvious that he did not want to discuss it, with Matt or anyone else, at least not yet.

Once her relationship with Matt was back on a firm footing, Jessie had again turned her attention to Higher Wedicombe and, with her sister's help, by the end of the week had worked miracles. There was still quite a bit to do, in that it needed decorating and refurbishing, but now it was at least cobweb, grime and dust free. The boys had been over to help lift the heavy furniture so she could clean behind it and at last she was satisfied that the place was more or less habitable.

They had all been helping at Higher Wedicombe that afternoon. Jessie had taken with her a beef casserole she had prepared earlier, ready to reheat on Matt's range, and Matt had found a bottle of wine to go with it. The occasion developed into an impromptu house warming and everyone was tucking in appreciatively, except, Jessie noticed, for Reigneth. She was pushing the food around on her plate, but she was fooling no one.

"What's the matter, *chai*, don't you like it?" Jessie asked.

"Yes, it's lovely, Ma."

"What's the matter then? Don't keep it to yourself, love."

Reigneth gave a weak smile and put down her knife and fork. "It's Jed Cummings. He is on his way here to see us."

Everyone glanced at each other, eyebrows raised, except Matthew, who frowned and shook his head. "I don't think so, Reigneth. I told him in no uncertain terms that he was no longer welcome here and he was lucky I didn't have the police on him," Matt smiled reassuringly at Jessie and Reigneth.

"Even so, he's coming and he's hopping mad and scared," Reigneth insisted.

"Don't be daft, Sweetheart. Even if it's true, he'll never get to hurt you," Johnny comforted her.

"You're *trashed*, Reigneth," James gave a roguish grin. "With me and Aaron here, that rotten thief wouldn't dare to show his face."

"I'm not *trashed*, I'm just warning you."

Jessie put down her knife and fork, her appetite suddenly gone. With a lump in her throat and tears beginning to well in her eyes, she stared at Reigneth and whispered, "He's here, isn't he? I can feel him."

"Yes, Ma, he's here," Reigneth said.

James and Aaron stopped eating. Johnny and Matthew looked at one another, their eyes mirroring their puzzlement.

As the tears began to trickle slowly down Jessie's face, Matt thrust back his chair and came at once to her side, sliding his arm around her shoulders and hugging her. "Jessie, love, whatever's the matter," his voice was full of tenderness. "Jed isn't here, what are you talking about? There's nothing to be afraid of."

"Not Jed, Matt, Joe. I can feel Joe here."

"He is, Mam," said Reigneth, "he doesn't want me to have to face Jed alone. It was Jed in my dream you see."

Jess was aware of the sudden tension in Matt's arm. She saw that Johnny was looking all around the room, searching everyone's faces and that James's tick had started twitching at the corner of his mouth. Feeling comforted by Joe's shadowy presence, Jessie smiled through her tears. They probably all thought she was mad. All except Reigneth, of course, who was nodding and smiling at her.

"You all right, James?" Johnny asked.

"Yes, fine. I'm just a bit chilly and the hair on the back of my neck is standing to attention. Uncle Joe never had this effect on me when he was alive. I was never 'trashed' of him then and I'll not be now he's 'mullered'."

Reigneth smiled at James, "He loves you, James, he says you are the guardian in this world, and he in the next."

"OK, so now you're freaking me out," Johnny said, addressing no one in particular. 'Trashed' means frightened, yes? And 'mullered'?

"Dead," Aaron said, rolling his eyes.

"Well I have to admit it is a bit cold in here suddenly," Matt said, moving to stoke the fire. Smiling reassuringly at Johnny, he squeezed Jessie's shoulder and went back to his place at the table.

"Something's different about you, Reigneth. Something more is going on here. What else do you see?" James asked.

"I've changed quite a lot since we've been in Devon. I don't always have to touch people now to see things, James. All my senses are heightened and acute: my sense of smell, sight, touch, taste and hearing – all of them. Sometimes, when people are just talking normally, it sounds like they are shouting; it upsets me a bit. At other times there's a peculiar scent about some people and I can almost taste them on the very tip of my tongue. It's really odd. I can sense Jed Cummings is evil: he is a bully to his wife and children and he has depraved, salacious habits that make his wife's life a living hell." Tears started to Reigneth's eyes and she shuddered, "It's like I sometimes *feel* her pain."

She looked across at Johnny and sent him a warm, loving smile, "But all these sensations tone down a bit when I'm with Johnny, he gives me some respite from it all; makes me feel stronger."

Jessie nodded; she had increasingly sensed this in her daughter. "I knew things had changed with you, love, but I didn't know to what extent. Is everything clearer now?"

"Oh yes, much clearer Ma and getting stronger all the time."

Before Reigneth had a chance to explain further there was a loud persistent banging on the back door, which was then flung open. Jed Cummings's huge figure towered in the doorway. He was a huge man, bigger even than James, with large, fleshy, unattractive features and a misshapen nose that had once been broken.

Matthew leapt to his feet, his face red with anger, "Well Jed, spit it out seeing as you've thought fit to burst into my home uninvited."

James got up to stand beside Matthew, towering over him. He bunched his fists, said, "Oh look, Reigneth, it's the man who thinks we stink. What would you like me to do to him?"

Jessie stayed in her chair, as did Aaron. Johnny rushed to stand by Reigneth, sheltering her with his body. He was narrowly beaten to it by Jukel. The dog stood four square in front of her, snarling. Reigneth reached down and held onto his collar.

Jed Cummings took a step backwards. Jessie saw his look of hesitation as he stared first at the dog and then at James's fists. Like all bullies he was a coward.

"It's her… " Jed pointed a trembling finger at Reigneth.

Ever since his confrontation with Reigneth, Jed had not slept well. During the past week his anxiety had increased. He felt as though he was being watched. Every evening there had been a tapping sound, like finger tips on his bedroom window. His wife could not hear anything yet every night it became louder, more persistent. Drawing back the curtains each night he had been unable to see anything, but he had begun to hear whispering. Annoyingly, he could not hear what the voice was saying, but it would not be silent either. Again, his miserable wife insisted she heard nothing. All this had started since his run in with that Gypsy bitch at Higher Wedicombe, damn her.

Now, standing in front of them all, he felt stupid. What was he going to say? That she had cursed him? He was not going to be that much of a fool, but then again, what else could he say since it was what he firmly believed? He licked his lips, stood there with his mouth hanging open.

"It's her," he said again, "that little Gypsy b… " Jed's voice trailed away as, with a glance at that great hulk, James, who looked as though he would happily floor him, he thought better of saying 'bitch' and finished, "lass." He shuddered, added, "She's put a curse on me. That's what she's done. And I wanted it lifted, right?"

"Oh, this is going to be good," James sneered, his eyes wet and his shoulders shaking.

Jed squirmed, feeling more of a fool than ever. It was obvious James was laughing at him, struggling to hold it in. He felt his anger rising. "And keep that damned dog off me," he shouted as Jukel strained against the collar, lips curled back, slavering.

"A curse? You surely don't believe such things do you, Jed?" asked Matthew.

"I thought I didn't, I was sure I didn't, but weird things have been happening at our house ever since she threatened to set the dog on me," Jed responded. "Vicious brute ought to be put down."

"Let me get this right," said Matthew, his mouth twitching. "Are you here to complain about the dog or a curse?"

It was too much for James, who spluttered into laughter.

"And," Matthew continued, "do I take it you mean ever since the time you entered my house and attempted to steal from me?"

For the first time, Jed realised he should have thought twice about coming here. Clearly, Matthew was not going to let drop the business of the money. His next sentence confirmed it.

"You ought to think yourself lucky I didn't have the police on you. I've a good mind to call them now, though, Jed. What do you mean by coming here and insulting my daughter like this? How dare you!"

"Your d-d-daughter?" Jed stuttered. "You don't have a daughter that I know of."

"Ah, but I do, Jed Cummings, I do now. That little Gypsy lass's mother and I are about to be married."

Jed's eyes swivelled back to Reigneth, his mouth gaping like a landed fish.

Reigneth hated his mouth, it was the feature about him she hated most – soft, fleshy and always moist. It made her shudder, especially when she thought of his frail, subservient wife.

"Whatever," Jed said, recovering his surprise and glaring down at her, "I want it stopped right now."

"I have done nothing to you, Jed," she said. "I have not cursed you; it is merely your own guilty conscience." Forcing herself to meet his angry stare, she added, "I think you had better be on your way, and perhaps you should think what you do in the future. Most especially, be kinder to your *wife*!"

Reigneth saw her barb had hit home: a knowing look spread over Jed's face. "Don't you threaten me, you dirty little gypo," he blustered, fear flickering behind his eyes.

Johnny and James sprang forward.

"NO!" Reigneth shouted, "don't touch him. Now get out, Jed, or I really will set the dog on you." She felt rage rising up in her, the power of it almost overwhelming. She loosened her hold on Jukel, who sprang forward so that her arm was at full stretch. Johnny leaned across to help her hang on to the dog's collar.

Jed took one look and flounced out of the door, slamming it behind him, whereupon every door in the building began to bang back and forth on its hinges, the echoes reverberating throughout the house. The noise was deafening. The temperature in the room dropped until it resembled the inside of a refrigerator and everyone's breath came out like gusts of steam. A sudden crash brought their attention to the side table where a heavy, cut crystal vase exploded into hundreds of fragments, spilling water over the table and onto the floor, along with the flowers that Jessie had arranged in it earlier that day.

Reigneth's body was vibrating uncontrollably, the force of her temper intense. She had experienced it before, but never as strongly as this. It took her some moments to regain control of her emotions. She did not feel unwell, she felt strangely excited: powerful. To Reigneth this was a revelation. The one thing she hated about her gift was how weak it made her feel, yet now that weakness had seemed almost to evaporate. She stood, fists clenched into tight balls, her body pulsating from the power passing through her. It was neither anger nor fury; it was energy: an energy she knew at some point she would be able to control, but just yet the control was lacking. Her body felt alive with it and she knew she was the one who was generating it. Breathing deeply, she worked on calming her emotions until eventually the power began to subside and she was able to master whatever it was. Frowning in concentration, Reigneth was dimly aware that her family were watching her as if mesmerised and that Jukel was whining at her feet, a wary look in his eyes as if he did not know who she was. Absent-mindedly she buried her fingers into his fur. Everything seemed distant to her as if she was not physically there. The exhilaration she had felt moments before began to fade and all the doors in the house, which had been wafting back and forth as though with a life of their own, gradually stilled.

And then Johnny lightly touched her cheek and pressed his lips softly to hers. Breaking through her concentration, his kiss brought her back into the moment from wherever it was she had been.

"Your face is just too beautiful to wear a frown," he teased, his voice soft and reassuring. Her gaze locked onto his and they smiled at one another as if nothing else in the world existed.

Watching them and seeing her daughter's face come back to the Reigneth they all recognised, Jessie realised that Johnny had not been surprised by what had happened. It was almost as if he knew of the power Reigneth could exert. Jessie was torn apart with conflicting emotions. Like an electric shock, she had felt the supernatural force radiating from Reigneth and it frightened her. She thought the force had been created due to Joe's presence; that somehow her daughter had taken on Joe's temper. The intensity of it made her fear for Reigneth. It was too much.

"You have to ask your dad to leave us in peace, Reigneth: to give us *both* some peace. You have James and Jukel, and you have Johnny. They are protection enough." Jessie could not believe she was asking Joe to go; to let them fend for themselves.

"It's hard for him to leave us, Ma, especially when he hears others being unkind and sees them mistreating us. I need Da as never before," Reigneth sat back down at the dinner table and resumed absent mindedly pushing her food around the plate. Only Johnny joined her, slipping his arm around her waist.

Jessie exchanged a worried glance with Matt and moved over to stand by the range. The room was not as cold as it had been, but she still felt chilled to the bone. James and Aaron, talking together in low voices, were leaning against the wall and looking at Reigneth as at a stranger, James rubbing at his face.

"It doesn't surprise me, Aaron," James was saying. "Think how Uncle Joe was when anyone riled him. And I always knew Reigneth had a temper on her, just like her da. Do you remember that time when we were little kids and that lad... er, Thomas Small, I think his name was – was bullying you?"

"Yeah, rotten devil made my life a misery until he got sick: never had no more trouble from him after that, though, why?"

"That's what I'm remembering. He got sick after Reigneth lost her temper that day when she saw him deck you. He had pains in his stomach all through the night after that. The doc thought it was his appendix, but it wasn't and they couldn't work out what was wrong with him, remember? He was off school for days. Did you think it a coincidence? If Reigneth and Uncle Joe are both after Jed Cummings, I almost pity him!"

Jessie had heard enough. "Reigneth, you've got to stop this now," she begged. "Don't let your dad do anything to Jed, you know his temper. Joe will finish him."

"Calm down, Jess," Matt said. "You talk as if Joe is still alive; it's not possible that he's here. There is no such thing as ghosts or an afterlife," Matt said with conviction.

Ignoring Matt, James added his plea to Jessie's, "You know you'd not wish to hurt anyone, Reigneth, even a moron like that, not *really* hurt anyone."

Reigneth looked up at them, her eyes glittering venomously; her expression uncharacteristically hard. "Even if I did, James, I really don't have any say in it," she shrugged, "but Dad will just have a bit of fun, I daresay."

"I've never seen you so angry, what's got into you?" Jessie could hardly speak she was so distressed. "It's like your father's possessed you!"

"You're wrong, Ma. It's nothing to do with Dad, it's all me. Jed's a terrible man. You don't realise, none of you do," Reigneth was calmer now.

"Is this about the dream, Reigneth? What are you sensing from him? Tell me," Jessie pleaded.

"Ma, like I said I don't always have to touch people now, he is so bad I can read him across the room. He beats his wife all the time – almost to death – and he does other things to her that he shouldn't. The man is evil; inhuman. One day he'll kill her."

Jessie knew she had no choice but to accept what Reigneth said, so she tried another tack. "How many times have you felt your dad with you?"

"Not often; only when I'm worried or upset. Mainly he's happy that Juk is always with me; he likes Johnny and he knows James will protect me, but when I get scared he comes to me. As soon as I knew Jed was on his way here, I knew Da would be with me. He hates him as much as I do."

"Well I'd hate to cross *you*, Honey, that's for sure," James laughed. The smile disappearing as suddenly as it came. "And what's the thing with the doors? Scary or what!"

"Doors? Whatever are you talking about, James?"

He glanced at Jessie and shrugged helplessly. Clearly Reigneth had no idea what had happened around her when Jed had barged out.

Jed was still running, stumbling down the farm track to where he had left the car. He slammed it into gear, furious that the chit of a girl had dared to speak to him like she had. He'd get the stinking Gypsy scum by herself one night, see if he wouldn't. Then she'd pay for it!

Driving along the top road to his home, his mind wandered as he thought of the pleasure he would derive from getting the girl on her own one dark evening. They could not watch her all the time. He would bide his time, he would make her pay.

Suddenly, a shadow crossed the road in front of him. He trod down hard on the brakes, stalling the car. Getting out to inspect what he had hit, he could see nothing. Returning to the car, he found it would not start. After several goes, his irritation and anger increasing by the minute, Jed swore: this was all he needed. It was about four miles to his home by road. He was neither confident nor knowledgeable enough to go across country. Getting out of the car, he searched in the boot and found his torch. He heard something scuttling about in the bushes nearby and shone the beam. A huge black dog stood there staring at him, its yellow eyes glowing in the torchlight, a steady growl rumbling in its chest. Jed knew it was about to pounce. His heartbeat cranked up a notch. If he could just get back in the car it could not get to him. He drew back his arm to throw the torch, hoping to confuse it.

The dog pounced.

Jed dropped the torch spun on his heels and began to run, his breath rattling painfully in his chest. Expecting to feel the slavering jaws tearing into him at any moment he ran until he could go no further then turned, panting, to face it.

There was nothing there. Amazingly he seemed to have outrun it. His legs trembling, Jed bent over to get his breath back, the intensity of his relief making him retch.

As suddenly as it had disappeared, the dog was there again. With a cry, Jed backed off, the dog followed, driving him away from the road. Stumbling in the long grass, Jed began to realise it was not going to attack him. It could have done that several times over: it was as if its aim was to shepherd him onto the moor. Jed panicked, hesitated. The dog leapt.

Jed toppled backwards falling headlong into the mire. Thigh deep he was wedged, both legs in. He knew well enough not to struggle. If he stayed still he might not sink further. The stench from the rotting debris was disgusting. He looked around him for something to grab hold of. Once again, the hound from hell had disappeared.

Unaware of how long he remained there, Jed heard someone coming, treading steadily through the moorland grasses.

"Hey there," Jed cried. "Help me!"

A man appeared in the moonlight, slowly sauntered over to where Jed was wedged, now waist deep in soft, oozing mud.

"Hey, man, am I glad to see you!" Jed called. "Could you give me a pull out of this stuff; don't step any further, lie flat on the grass and just lean over."

"Sure thing," the man said, squatting on his haunches and lighting a cigarette. "You seem to be in a bit of a pickle," he drew in a lungful of smoke and blew it out in Jed's direction.

Jed frowned, he did not know the chap and his accent was not local. "Stop mucking about. Help me," he said, then as an afterthought, added, "please."

The man gave him a sly smile. "Well now, you are well and truly wedged," he stated.

As he spoke, something glinted on the man's face. Jed peered more closely and saw something twinkling in his mouth, reflecting the moonlight. Gold teeth! *Unusual,*' thought Jed. Who the hell was this guy out here on the moor at night? He felt a prickle of apprehension.

"Well, are you going to help me out or not?" Jed snapped, his irritation getting the better of him. "Don't step any further forward, lie down and try to reach my hand, you need to spread your weight."

"Is that so? Well I would, but I have just one problem, I don't think you want *my* assistance, you don't like my sort," the man advised.

"Your sort? What the hell do you mean? I'd have any sort help me out of this!" A worm of fear uncurled in Jed's gut. He started shivering uncontrollably, chilled to the marrow.

"A dirty gypo, I think was what you said."

With this the man flicked his cigarette end at Jed and walked slowly away.

Jed saw the butt burning brightly next to him. He cried out in fear as he felt his body slip deeper into the mud. The Gypsy with the gold teeth was gone.

All evening both Jessie and Reigneth were restless. Jessie had busied herself clearing away the food and washing up, helped by Aaron and Matt. They moved into the tiny living room, which seemed overfull with everyone there, but with a log burner, it was cosy and warm. Reigneth sat in the window seat, her toes still buried in Jukel's fur,

Johnny squeezed up beside her, his arm around her waist.

"I expect we ought to be making tracks home, you lot," James stood, making ready for their departure. "Thanks for the evening, Matt, it was… " The telephone ringing cut across whatever he had been going to say.

Matt went into the hall to answer it. "Hello? Oh, hello Alison, yes he was here earlier, but he left some little time ago now."

The others all looked at each other, listening to the one-sided conversation. 'Alison?' James mouthed at Reigneth. She nodded, mouthed back 'Cummings.'

"Don't worry," Matt was saying, "I'll take a drive and see if he's broken down." He rang off and came back through to the living room.

"Jed Cummings never returned home," Matt said, looking cautiously at Reigneth, a query in his eyes.

"I can't see anything, Matt, perhaps I don't want to and it's not an exact science," Reigneth said casually.

Matt shrugged, "I think perhaps, as much as I dislike saying it, we had better take a drive. He will have taken the top road home most likely."

"We'll come too," James stretched his big frame and nudged Aaron to stir himself.

"Shall Juk and I come too?" asked Reigneth, without enthusiasm.

"No, better not; you and Jessie stay here in the warm – you'll just freak him out," Matt replied.

They had not driven far when they saw Jed's car, headlights on, door open.

"This doesn't look good," Matt said, pulling up behind Jed's vehicle. "Grab a torch, Jono, there's one in the back."

He began to shout Jed's name. They all heard a faint voice calling.

Slowly, picking their way across the moorland, they eventually found Jed. He was up to his shoulders in mud, his arms raised above his head. He was barely conscious and mumbling to himself.

"I'll do it," said James. "It's not a task I relish mind," he remarked, getting down to lie full length on the wet, marshy ground, "I can't bear to touch the moron." He stretched out his strong, muscular arms, reaching his hands out to Jed. Johnny and

Matt each hung on to one of James's legs and pulled, while Aaron held the torch and murmured encouragement.

Eventually, with a great sucking noise, Jed was pulled free. He stank: dead and rotting vegetation and black slime clung to him. He was babbling still, one hand clenched into a fist. "I told you it was her cursing me, this is her doing. A Gypsy left me here to drown in the mire. I have proof here in my hand: his cigarette butt. I'll prosecute him for this, I can identify him too; he had gold teeth. Jed continued babbling, ranting on and on about a hound from hell and the Gypsy leaving him for dead. It was obvious the man was much affected by his experience.

Matt exchanged glances with James. "I think he needs a doctor, I'll call emergency services," he said, reaching for his mobile.

Jed was becoming more and more incoherent and difficult to physically control. Hysteria soon followed and by the time the paramedics arrived with a stretcher, he was in need of sedation. Once the ambulance had gone, blue light flashing and siren blaring as it sped off down the moorland road, Matt drove them home.

Reigneth, still sitting on the window seat, saw the lights coming into the yard. "They're back," she said to Jessie.

"I'll put the kettle on." Jessie got up from her chair beside the fire and wandered into the kitchen.

Later, telling the tale over a cup of tea, Matt said, "To be honest, I rather fear for the man's sanity. He said a guy with gold teeth, who smoked, left him for dead! Poor chap's completely lost it," Matt shook his head.

Casting anxious glances at Reigneth, Johnny went to warm himself by the log burner. Looking back at her, he saw that with a wistful smile she was lifting her hand to press it against the window pane. There was nothing outside that he could see.

On the other side of the pane, Joe's hand exactly mirrored hers. He mouthed, 'I love you,' and was gone. Reigneth watched him disappear, anger welling up inside her. She could not keep quiet any longer.

"Before you say anything else, Matt, my Dad had gold teeth and smoked and he *was* on the moor with Jed tonight. He would not have left him for dead though, he's not a murderer. Jed Cummings is a liar. He may not regain his sanity, but on the up side, Alison Cummings will not lose her life. And before you ask, her exit from his violence was to be on the mortuary slab. That is what I dreamt. A dream so horrifying that I hope you never have to witness anything like it in your life. I don't want Dad to leave us in peace, Ma. I need him for the things I cannot achieve without help. I am sure there will be other things like this."

Reigneth was tired and angry; not usually prone to hysterical outbursts, she was unable to control her tears. Face all wet, annoyed with herself for being weak again after she had felt so strong earlier, she wondered why she could not always feel that way. "I want to go home to bed; I've had enough for one evening," she announced, sliding off the window seat. "Come on, Juk," she clicked her fingers and the dog followed her obediently into the hall.

At last understanding what the dreams had been about, the others all seemed lost for words. Reigneth shrugged on her coat and called, "Well, are we off? Ready when you are." It broke the spell and there was immediate activity as everyone grabbed a coat, said goodnight to Matt and, still fitting arms into sleeves, filed out into the yard. All except Jessie, who lingered for a private moment with Matt before hurrying to catch them up.

On reaching Home Humber, Reigneth headed straight for her room, she slowly mounted the stairs, each leg feeling heavy and difficult to move, she felt so very weary. At that moment she had great sympathy with Granny Mary. "Was it like this for you too?" she whispered.

She heard Johnny say to her mother, "I'm going up to her, Jessie." Then, as if he was expecting trouble, he added, "She needs me."

"I know she does," came Jessie's reply, I had imagined that you would."

Some moments later, Johnny tapped on Reigneth's door, lifting the latch without waiting for her response. By then she was in her pyjamas and perched stiffly on the edge of her bed, her fists balled tightly in her lap, her whole frame rigid with anxiety and anger.

"Come on, let's get you into bed, you're exhausted. You know, Reigneth, I think I am beginning to grasp that our roles are to support one another in all ways," he said gently, placing a kiss on her cheek. "I cannot even begin to imagine what it is like being in your head!"

Reigneth gazed at him, nodded and managed a smile, but her mind was on her mother, wondering what she was thinking and feeling.

Downstairs, Jessie, lost in thought, was remembering her mother-in-law, Mary Gray, in her last days. Mary had been anxious to tell her what would come in the future and now Jessie was glad that she had, for it helped her to understand what was going on. Mary had said that she had seen their family flourishing and that one was to come who would be the heart of it; that Reigneth was their prophet and that her powers would grow and magnify, aided by her environment. "The Heart and the Prophet; the Guardian and the Chronicler," Mary had repeated over and over, but at the time, Jessie had not the faintest idea what the old lady was rambling on about. Now, though, she had begun to understand. Johnny, who, through his goodness and talents would keep Reigneth grounded, happy and sane, was the Heart. Mary had told her to watch for the man with the angelic face of a child. Had she only said he would be a *Gauja*, Jessie would have recognised him straight away; it had simply never occurred to her that he would not be one of their own kind. Aaron could only be the Chronicler. Mary had always said he would never let them forget who and what they were and would promote their culture and people. James, then, with his strength and honesty, was the Guardian. Mary had known how important the four of them would be to one another. They had all underestimated her, except, perhaps, her son.

Jessie stood by the Aga listening. The house was quiet now, the only sound, from Jukel's soft snores at the foot of the stairs.

"Oh, Joe, my darling love, I didn't mean to hurt you," she whispered, but your mam was right; I think it is time to leave things to the young ones now. You need to rest in peace, my love and so do I."

Even as she spoke, Jessie knew he was not there. Sadly, she switched out the lights and made her way to bed.

Chapter 28

Atching Tan (Stopping Place)

Reigneth was amazed to learn, a few days after the incident with Jed Cummings, that his wife had visited Higher Wedicombe to thank Matt for rescuing her husband. It mystified Reigneth that Alison could still find it in her heart to have feelings for Jed, and she had to remind herself that, of course, the murder had been foreseen only in her dream: nobody knew of what might have happened had Joe not intervened. Alison may have been brutally abused in the past, but now, thankfully, she would be safe.

When Reigneth bumped into Alison in Chagford a fortnight later, she was pleased to see the woman looked well and happy. All the bruises had faded and the constant troubled frown was gone. Reigneth introduced herself – it seemed strange to do that; having seen Jed's wife so often in her dreams she felt as if she knew her, but they had never actually met and until she mentioned her connection with Matt, Alison had no idea who she was.

"So how are you?" asked Reigneth.

"Very well, thank you." A smile hovered around Alison's mouth, "The girls and I are moving away – going to live with my parents."

"Oh? Well I'm sure you and the children will be very happy."

"Yes, I think we will," Alison smiled and was about to walk on by when she hesitated and turned back, "It's odd, but I feel like I've known you for ages."

Reigneth laughed, "I probably remind you of someone else."

"Yes," Alison nodded, "that must be it," and with another smile, she walked away.

* * *

The fortnight Jed had been in hospital had given Alison the confidence to leave him for good, especially since it did not seem he would be following her anywhere. Jed had spent a lot of that time sedated and indeed, when she visited the hospital he had often been asleep or so drowsy he was not aware of her. When awake, his hand clutched desperately at something in his fist and he babbled on about it being a Gypsy's cigarette butt; proof that someone had been on the moor with him that night and left him for dead. He could see it quite clearly, he told everyone, holding out his hand, surely they could too? The nurses, doctors, Alison and everyone he showed it to, saw only a tiny piece of wood nestling in his palm. Whimpering, he told them that the Gypsy who had thrown it at him stood at the end of his bed at night grinning and flashing his gold teeth at him.

It was decided, after some consultation with Alison, that her husband should be moved to a psychiatric hospital for an indefinite period.

When Matt brought her this news, Jessie grimaced: Joe protected his own, didn't he? So he would not harm a hair on anyone's head, would he? Jessie said nothing to Matt, but she knew better. She knew her man; she knew he would wreak vengeance on anyone who hurt his *bitti chai*.

No one doubted the extent of Reigneth's powers after that momentous evening at Matt's place. Talking it through with Johnny a few days later, Jessie was not surprised when he told her he now understood why Reigneth had been so afraid in Wistman's Wood. It was clear to him that she saw and heard things that others did not. She must have thought she was in danger of being corrupted by the evil she felt in the wood. "It's the only time I've ever seen her truly afraid," said Johnny. "I wish I had understood at the time what she was going through."

Jessie let him talk, glad he had gained so much insight into Reigneth's gift. It would stand him in good stead in the future, of that she was sure.

After the incident with Jed, James took over as Matt's stockman. A job he was happy to accept, he was good with the animals, strong and hard working. Matt remarked to Jessie that he considered himself lucky James had agreed to it. She was glad about it too:

Reigneth was so much happier having her cousins around her. Remembering what Mary had said, it came as no surprise to Jessie that both Aaron and James had elected to remain in Devon.

James soon settled into a routine, although he had never had a 9 to 5 job and had always been his own boss. He had finally acknowledged that he could not be far from Reigneth. It was his role in life to look after her and so wherever Reigneth was to be, he would be there too. Even so, the transition to living permanently in Devon was hard for him. Like Jessie, he found the narrow lanes and high banks claustrophobic and stifling. Matt and Johnny had taken him riding up onto the moor and this helped to ease things somewhat. Having conceded that his love for Reigneth was in no way sexual, it was simply that he needed to be with her, James was no longer tormented by jealousy. Seeing her and Johnny together, he knew they were exactly right for one another, two pieces of the same puzzle. In fact, he had grown quite fond of the lad. Johnny was like that: you just could not help liking the quirky little devil!

However, James had point blank refused to move to Higher Wedicombe. He was determined he would not be climbing up any stairs to his bed. All his early life he had lived in a trailer; then briefly at Granny Mary's bungalow. Living in a house had been a big culture shock for him. Stairs? It was never going to happen! The Pritchards had completed restoring the single-story annexe at Home Humber, so he had taken up residence there and it suited him fine.

His feelings for Charlotte confused him: he cared for her, but restless as he was, he could not consider being committed to her – or anyone else for that matter. James knew that his life was to be inextricably intertwined with Reigneth's and nothing could change that. How many women would put up with that he wondered? Added to which, Charlotte was a *Gauja*. Could she adapt to his way of life? He had not thought for one minute that he was prejudiced in any way; that was Jessie's prerogative. Or so he had always thought. You could have knocked him down with a feather when she had got so close to Matt. What with her, Reigneth and Aunty Liz, marrying *Gaujas* must run in the family, he thought with a wry smile.

James had been looking for an opportunity to talk to Reigneth on her own, but these days it was as if she and Johnny were joined at the hip. That morning, feeling low, he completed his chores then sat on the dry-stone wall enclosing the farmyard and mulled things over. His thoughts rambled on: who would be his other half; the other piece to *his* puzzle? She would have to be tolerant, that was for sure; someone who would accept his relationship with Reigneth; someone who loved Reigneth as he did or at least loved her partner. As he contemplated this, James realised this train of thought was leading him back to Lotti, where it was always meant to lead him. He had found her and it did not matter whether she was *Gauja* or Romany, she was meant for him. Reigneth must have known this all along. Thinking of Charlotte brought warm sensations to James: her big, wide blue eyes, her cheery disposition and enthusiasm for everything. Yes, he could love her – did love her.

Hearing the click of the farmhouse door he turned to see Reigneth skipping along the uneven yard. She knew when he was low even when the feelings were only just beginning to creep up on him. She came towards him and hunched up on the wall next to him, linking her arm through his.

"Tell me what to do, Reigneth. I am so confused: I don't see my way forward and things don't seem to be getting any easier. That little girl and I are as different as a canary and a hawk," James sighed.

Reigneth laughed, "Poor James, so tormented. I take it you're the canary?" she teased.

James turned his mouth down, "I'm very confused, don't joke with me, Honey."

"What are you asking me, James? Do I see a Gypsy lass for you on the horizon in Devon? No, I don't, but the choice is yours, always yours. You don't *have* to stay here."

James shrugged, "Of course I do. You already know I'm in it for good or ill, don't you."

"Yes, I do, but don't ask me to explain as I am quite unable to as yet, it's something to do with what we are, but things are becoming so much clearer. We can never be apart, I know that as sure as I know anything and further than that I'm not going to worry and neither should you. We are together for a reason; that reason is just not clear yet."

They were silent for a while. It was a warm, sunny day for so early in the year. With a critical eye James looked across at the ponies gathered around the split bale of hay he had put out for them in the home paddock. If this weather continued they were in for an early spring, which would save on the hay.

Reigneth spoke again, breaking into his thoughts. "I don't think you should underestimate Charlotte, though. She's astute and has a good brain. Johnny says she is more like Harry in that way. She's not as immature as you think and I certainly wouldn't liken her to a chirpy yellow canary, James. Just because she's a *Gauja* is not reason enough not to be with her if you love her. Let your heart guide you and don't worry about things so. If you do choose Charlotte, I see a happy life of contentment and love for you both."

"What else do you see, Reigneth?"

"I see a lot of travelling for us all."

James grinned and his mood began to lift. "I'd like that," he commented.

"I see a lot of problems finding single-storey accommodation," Reigneth said, her expression dead pan.

"Eh?" James was puzzled for a moment and then realised she was teasing him. A slow smile spread across his face. He felt so much calmer after speaking to Reigneth.

They saw Johnny and Charlotte walking up the yard towards them. Leaping off the wall, James lifted Reigneth down and hand in hand they went to meet them.

"So is this *rawnie* meant for me?" James asked, peering down at Reigneth.

"Always has been, James, always has been," Reigneth smiled, tilting her head to peer up at him.

"Smart little witch," he said, a broad smile on his face.

Chapter 29

A Thirty-Year Message

There was still much to do at Higher Wedicombe before Jessie's and Matthew's wedding, not only because Reigneth was to live there with them, but Aaron too. It meant they must get a room ready for him. Jessie smiled at the thought: she knew Aaron was happy for perhaps the first time in his life. He had put on a little weight and he seemed altogether more confident. That he was content was obvious: he sang, he whistled. He had always doted on Jessie. It was mutual; Aaron was like a son to her.

At about this time it dawned on Jessie that the man she was about to marry was a procrastinator. She hated to see idle hands and after the last debacle was determined that Matt should do his own clearing up. They carried on where Johnny and Reigneth had left off, turning out paperwork and memorabilia that had lain untouched for years.

"Do you mind if I look at some of your old photos, Matt? I should like to see you as a boy," Jessie said as they heaved a drawer full of papers out onto the floor.

"Of course I don't mind, you never need to ask. Scruffy looking tike I was too, I can tell you."

Jessie smiled to herself: some things never change, she thought fondly.

After gathering up the photos still scattered on the floor where Reigneth had dropped them, and being amazed at just how alike Matt and Johnny were as children, Jessie lifted out a flat cardboard box and began to look through it. Yet more photos, only these were even older, mostly faded, some sepia tinted. Old photos always made Jessie feel sad: so many earnest faces of people long dead looked out at her; a single moment captured for all time. How transient people's lives were. How silly it was to let things fester when life was so short. What seemed so important was, in the scheme of things, no more significant or substantial than a snowflake melting in the sun. Nothing really mattered except loving one's family and living as good a life as one could, while one could.

"You must get things sorted out between you and Johnny, Matt," she said suddenly.

"I will, I will. I'm waiting for the right moment."

"Well don't wait too long, love."

Among the photos she came across a brown envelope that was still sealed, it was addressed to Matthew. "Matt, there's a letter here you've never even opened!" Jessie shook her head incredulously.

Matt looked at the envelope, "I've never seen this before. How did it get in with Gran's old photos? I think that's my mother's writing!"

Ripping open the envelope, Matt took out two pieces of notepaper. Four photographs fell out with them. Two were of a dark-haired young man, very similar in looks to Matt and Johnny. The other two were of the same person, but he was with a girl, Matt's mother, both smiling at the camera.

Matthew picked up the letter that had sat waiting for him for nearly thirty years and read it in silence. When he had finished, he passed it wordlessly to Jessie then, his face wet with tears, he studied the four photos.

Curious, Jessie read the letter:

My dearest Matthew
At last I write to tell you some of the things you should have been told long ago. It has always been so painful for me to talk of your father, who I loved with all my heart. I find myself with time on my hands following a spell indoors with pleurisy and pneumonia. I always had a sickly disposition quite unlike you and your father, who was always as fit as a fiddle.

His name was Nathaniel Buckland and we met when his family came in the summer to help my father around the farm. They always stayed during June and July. I was 12 when he first started visiting and we became inseparable.

Each year our friendship would be renewed, although as he got older he was expected to work alongside his father, so our time together was limited.

Nathaniel was tall and muscular, very dark-haired and dark-skinned. He had a fabulously wicked sense of humour.

When I was 16 and he 17, he asked me to marry him and travel with them on the road. I knew I loved him even then, but was terrified of the thought of leaving home and especially frightened of living the life of a Gypsy. I said I'd marry him when I was older, but asked him to stay with me at Higher Wedicombe and make a life here.

He declined, saying he'd marry me the very next day, but live in a house? Not likely. He felt he could not be happy if he was unable to move about. He needed the fresh air and the wind in his hair; he said it was his life's blood.

The year I was 17 they came again and as always Nat and I were together, both knowing that this arrangement could not continue, it was too painful for us to be so often apart. The following February he returned to the farm saying he could not be away from me. He left two weeks later, telling me to book the wedding for June when he'd return and he'd stay and work for my father, anything was better than being without me.

One month later, his parents returned to tell us he had been killed in an accident on a farm. He had sustained head injuries and had died three days afterwards. His parents said he had asked them to contact me and tell me he loved me.

I did not realise for some time that I was carrying you. The grief of losing Nat was so great I gave neither care nor thought to what was going on around me. Of course, I had no way of contacting Nathaniel's parents and they never came back. I think maybe they knew the memories would be too sad for them, seeing me and knowing how happy their son had been at Higher Wedicombe. I never saw or heard from them again.

You are and have always been the best part of my life. I never married. I could not forget your father, why would I when he was perfect for me?

Be a good boy for your grandparents, my son, they love

251

*you dearly. The photos enclosed are the only ones I have of
your father.*

*I once received a postcard from him, he did not write
much as schooling had not always been available to him, but
I end this letter as he signed off to me, perhaps one day you
may discover what it means, it must have been something
lovely for him to use it.*

Choomias, my lovely boy.

"What does it mean, Jessie, *choomias?*" Matt asked when she
had finished reading.

Jessie smiled, "Kisses, Matt, it means kisses." Her heart ached
for him: for thirty years this letter had lain unopened. Matt was
not so much of a *Gauja* after all: his father had been Romany!
Well, thought Jessie, his mother had not known how to find the
Bucklands, but she certainly did. One thing a Gypsy could do was
find her own kind. She smiled: her wedding list had just doubled in
size, not so much a small affair after all!

The very next day, Jessie began a mission to track down Matt's
Buckland relatives. Maybe with some luck Nathaniel Buckland's
parents were still alive and would be overjoyed to realise they had
a grandson and a great-grandson. Jessie fervently hoped so. She
observed that the letter had knocked the stuffing out of Matt and
she knew that thoughts of his poor mother were never very far from
his mind.

Matthew needed to keep busy and his tendency to procrastinate
became a thing of the past. Determined to turn over a new leaf,
with renewed vigour he set about making Higher Wedicombe Farm
fit for its new mistress. He was also determined to talk to Johnny
as soon as the opportunity presented itself. Never again would he
waste time and not tell those he loved how he felt.

The opportunity came quite soon. For some time he and Johnny
had been looking out for a horse for Reigneth, intending it as gift
for her birthday at the end of August. The mare she customarily
rode was Matt's best brood mare, a pretty pony, but much too quiet
for Reigneth's undoubted skills. Johnny had told Matt he wanted
something more like Rannoch for her. They had expected it to take
them a while to find the right animal, but as it turned out, one of

Grace's breeder friends had a Highland colt for sale. It was closely related to all his mares, so could not be used for stud and was to be sold on, he'd said. The colt had a kind and genuine nature, but was unbroken. Not seeing that as a problem and delighted to be able to help, Grace arranged for Matt and Johnny to go and look at the animal together.

Matt could not help wondering if she had done it deliberately. If so, he mused, it was unusually astute for Grace. He arrived to collect Johnny, feeling slightly ill at ease: they would be in the car for most of the day and if this went badly it would be a traumatic day for both of them. Grace was waiting with Johnny in the yard as he drove in.

"I've decided that you should take the Range Rover, it's far more comfortable than your old Land Rover," Grace greeted him, leaving very little room for discussion as she handed the keys to Johnny.

Both stared at her, but said nothing.

"I've packed you some sandwiches and a flask," she added, putting a full carrier bag on the back seat.

"Thanks, Mum. See you later then," Johnny gave her a peck on the cheek.

As he turned away to get into the car, Grace winked at Matt and mouthed, 'Good luck!' He was astounded.

At first the atmosphere was strained and quiet, but Matt was determined that since he had a captive audience and things needed to be resolved he simply had to make the effort. Nervous tension made his stomach tighten as he looked at Johnny's profile, cleared his throat and began with, "I'm glad I've got you to myself; we need to talk."

Johnny grunted, watched the road and said nothing.

After a few more miles and beginning to think this journey would remain silent for the duration, Matt was trying desperately to think of another opening, when at last Johnny spoke.

"I don't understand any of it. When I looked at the photos of you, you were so... so... " his voice trailed away.

"Perhaps it would be easier if I just tell you how it was, would that help?"

"Yes, I think it would."

"OK then." Matt paused briefly, wondering where to start.

Clearing his throat again, he decided to begin with their school days. "Grace and I were always together when we were little. We did everything as a pair. She was my best friend all through school and she was always there for me. When my mum died, and again later, when my grandparents passed away, she comforted me and we grew very close. Your grandparents, the Gills, well they didn't like me much. Not only was my family quite poor, but I was too wild for them, too uncontrolled. I wasn't like I am now. I was a handful to say the least and old man Gill, well he always brought out the very worst in me. Grace hated that side of my nature. She only felt happy when I was on my best behaviour."

"The Gills always treated her like she was a princess and of course, when Harry came along – him being so perfect and his father rolling in money – well, from the outset they wanted her to marry him. I know now that they only wanted the best for their daughter, but at the time I found it very hard to take. Harry was... well, you more than anyone know what Harry was, always so polite, so well mannered. I think Grace thought I'd never settle down. At times I knew I frightened her. Hell, lad, at times I frightened myself! I was so angry a lot of the time, angry that my family had died and I felt so alone. The bloody farm seemed to swamp me. I was only young, so much responsibility, but I loved your mother. I mean really *loved* her. She was the sun, the moon and the stars to me... "

Matt swallowed. Reviving these old memories was bringing him out in a cold sweat. Johnny had said nothing, his gaze still fixed firmly on the road. Matt continued with his story. "Well anyway, Harry arrived and made a beeline for your mother and I believe he truly loved her. She never was unfaithful to him after they were married and she didn't know she was having you when she married him. When she fell pregnant straight away she knew there was a remote possibility that you could be mine – we were together the day before her wedding, you see. It was wrong of me, I know, but I knew she was undecided and I was desperate; would have done anything to persuade her to run away with me and I guess all that fraught emotion ran away with us both! But you should talk to your mother about this you know. Hear her version of events."

"Would I hear the truth?"

A cynical smile hovered on Matt's lips, "I suppose we both deserve that. Has she told the twins?"

"Yes."

"How have they taken it?"

"Shocked, just as I was. They couldn't believe it at first. I think we all feel a bit cheated really. And we feel cheated for Harry's sake too, although I think he never knew?"

"No, he never knew – or at least, he was never told – I do not know if he guessed. Our paths rarely crossed so he never got a good look at me." Matt paused, said in a rush, "You may not want to hear this, lad, but I love you; always have from the moment I first saw you and knew I had a son."

"And when was that?"

"Not until you were about eight. Your mother hadn't told me about you, but I bumped into you one day and the resemblance between us was so marked. It was like looking in a mirror. I knew then – or at least, I knew it was a possibility."

"I think I remember that. I ran into you outside the shop and I thought you seemed really kind."

"Yes, well that's when I thought you might be mine. I would see you from a distance occasionally and each time I did I became more convinced. After that I kept out of the way, afraid of what I would say, what I would do. Above all, I did not want to do anything to cause a problem in your life. I knew you were happy; I used to catch glimpses of you on the moor. I badly wanted to give you something; something special from me that you would treasure even if you didn't know who I was."

"Rannoch."

"Yes, Rannoch: he was the best I'd ever bred," Matt sighed. "It was the first time I'd seen Grace in years. After that, she sent me photos of you growing up. It was all I had of you and I was grateful. She worships you, Johnny. Don't shut her out. Be angry with me if you need someone to vent your feelings on, but not her."

"Did she love you?"

"Yes, I think so, at first, but I think she loved Harry too, and she had a lot of pressure from old man Gill – he had a bit of a temper and he was hard on her, you know? Used to take his strap to her when he'd had too much to drink," Matt swallowed, "I know it's wrong to speak ill of the dead, but God, I hated him for that." He was silent for a moment, then added, "Marrying Harry was the easiest option for her, but I don't think she would have done it if she had not been fond of him – and he was a very good father to you."

"Yes, he was. Do you still love her?"

"I think I will always love her, but not as I love Jessie. Your mother and I were never really suited. We would most likely have made each other miserable in time. Jessie, though, she was meant for me. As it turns out we're more ideal for one another than we at first realised. Did you hear about your grandfather, Nathaniel Buckland?"

"Yes, Reigneth told me. Amazing really – that accounts for how dark in colouring we both are I suppose."

"I suppose."

They were both silent for a while. Matt was torn: on the one hand he was relieved to have told his son everything there was to tell, but on the other, he was afraid he had driven him away. He turned to look at Johnny's angelic profile, saw the frown creasing his brow. "Are we OK, Johnny, will we be OK?" Suddenly he needed his son's reassurance, as if their roles had reversed.

Briefly, Johnny took his gaze from the road and gave Matt a wry smile, "Yes, of course we will. Do you think Reigneth would rest if things were strained between us? Ultimately I think we shall all do exactly as she wishes." They both smiled at that.

"And besides," Johnny added, "the way I feel about Reigneth has helped me to understand how it must have been for you. I wish you could have told me the truth, Matt, or at least encouraged my mother to do so, but I don't blame you for what happened and I'm grateful for your honesty now. You must understand that for me Harry will always be my father, but I have often thought of you as my big brother and I guess that won't change."

"Big brother, eh?" Matt smiled. "So long as you can forgive me, big brother's OK with me."

"I forgive you," Johnny grinned. "And just to set your mind at rest, I don't blame my mother either. It can't have been easy for her. I will talk to her, tell her how I feel."

Matt nodded. He felt all wrung out and by the look on his son's face, so did Johnny. He cast around for a change of subject, "Well what's this animal called then?"

"'Torin', he's the same colour as Rannoch. We probably should have brought the trailer."

"No. Don't want to seem too keen. We need to negotiate.

They're asking enough money. Fancy a sandwich?"

Chapter 30

A Buckland Invasion

The wedding day dawned and the weather looked promising. The forecast was for sunny spells with no rain. Matt was hoping it would remain dry as some of Jessie's relatives had come in trailers. They had parked them on his top field and he did not want them to get bogged down. Some of the family intended to stay on after the wedding for a holiday, always anxious to spend time together savouring one another's company as these times were rare.

As Matt stood at the front of the church waiting for his bride, he was amazed at how full it was. Hadn't Jessie said she was keeping it small? Her relatives had obviously overflowed onto his side of the church and there was standing room only at the back. He felt uncomfortable in his new suit and was glad of the reassuring presence of Johnny at his side. The vows were what he was looking forward to more than anything else. He could not wait to be Jessie's husband.

Various members of her extended family were definitely giving him the once over, particularly a frail looking elderly couple sitting in the front row on his side of the church. They never took their gaze off him and Johnny, which made Matt feel a little uncomfortable. Not for the first time it seemed to him that old people were sometimes rather rude, as though the rules of common courtesy no longer applied to them, staring like they were.

Funny the things he noticed. Perhaps it was because he felt so calm that he was able to take in every detail around him. The little church was filled with flowers: on the end of each pew, at the altar and round the doorway. His lad looked like an angel standing next to him and although he knew Johnny had combed his hair, it still managed to look gloriously untidy. Not for the first time he gave thanks for the wonderful turn his life had taken, no one person deserved to be as happy as he was right now.

The bridal march began and he turned to see Jessie, resplendent in a cream, calf-length dress, which showed off her skin tones to perfection. Her hair was pinned up, not in her usual style, but placed in soft curls on her head, which had the effect of softening her whole face. She looked stunningly beautiful and Matt's breath caught in his throat as she walked slowly towards him, her hand resting lightly on her brother-in-law's arm. Richard looked as proud as Punch as he led her down the aisle, and the bridesmaids, Reigneth and Charlotte, in the aubergine-coloured creations that complemented the bride's cream, looked absolutely lovely.

The ceremony went without a hitch and soon the bells were pealing in celebration. Matt thought of the time long ago when the sound of wedding bells had made him cry like a baby. He felt like crying again now, but this time with happiness.

The wedding reception was to be at Home Humber, but with so many guests, Richard had laid on a marquee for good measure.

Taking their places to welcome everyone, the happy couple began shaking hands and thanking people for coming. Matt was astounded at the number of Jessie's relatives: every single one of them must have come. When he saw the elderly couple approaching, he said out of the corner of his mouth, "Who are these two? They have been staring at me as if I was from Mars!"

Jessie laughed, "A little surprise for you, my husband. Wait and see."

Matt was completely taken aback when the old lady came right up to him, stood on tiptoe and took his face in her hands. She stared up at him for a moment then, with a nod and a smile, she kissed him.

"Hello, grandson, I'm Mary Buckland. Your da was my beloved son, Nathaniel, and this old fella here," she gestured at the elderly man beside her, "is your grandfather. You are so like your father, Matthew, I would have known you anywhere." She flung her arms around him and they hugged. Next, he clasped the hand of his grandfather. The old man did not say much, but Matt could see the pride and delight in his rheumy eyes.

Matt was speechless and the tears welled. He needed no telling who had organised this. He turned to Jessie, "Thank you, wife," he said, thrilling to the sound of those words.

Jessie just smiled at him, "These are all *your* relatives Matt, every one of them." She chuckled, "No one can find a Gypsy like another Gypsy."

Matt was overwhelmed: barely a year ago, he was a lonely, embittered recluse, old before his time and with no one to call his own. Now he had a wife at his side, a son he no longer had to hide, a beautiful daughter and a huge family. *I must have done something right!* he thought.

All the Romanies he had ever met had in one way or another been larger than life. The Bucklands were no exception and they all wanted to hug him and welcome him into the fold. He could not imagine being happier than he was at this moment. He saw Grace, smiling sweetly at him from the crowd of well wishers, she seemed genuinely happy for him and in that moment he knew with absolute certainty that in spite of everything, he would not have had it any other way. He turned to smile at Reigneth, who stood beside him in the protective circle of Johnny's arm. She returned his smile and as if she had read his thoughts, said softly, "Everything has happened as it was meant to, Matt."

The introductions were still not complete and Mary Buckland, having hugged Johnny and wept, for he was the image of her Nat at that age, now stood before Reigneth, who was to become her great-granddaughter. Mary smiled through her tears, although she felt ill at ease. There was something about this girl that was odd. Looking into her eyes, suddenly she knew without being told that Reigneth had the gift of *dukkering*. Mary was afraid. At her age one of the few things on her horizon was death and she preferred the Grim Reaper to come uninvited rather than as an expected guest. She did not need some chit of a girl to tell her when that might be.

Reigneth did not hesitate: she stepped forward and hugged the old lady, "I have so missed my Granny Mary," she whispered in her ear, "And now I have another one. I am so happy to meet you and I know we will have *lots* of time to get to know one another."

Understanding the hidden message, Mary took Reigneth immediately to her heart: how could she not? Beauty ran through this girl's core like letters in a stick of rock. "Thank you, child," she said, "I am happy to meet you too." She directed a beaming smile at both Reigneth and Johnny, her eyes once more brimming with joyful tears.

Johnny smiled back at his great-grandmother, but he was perplexed. He had noticed of late that Reigneth was becoming much more tactile with everyone. He wished for the hundredth time that he could know what was going on in that complex head of hers. "Does she know what you can do, Reigneth?" he asked, looking after Mary as she shepherded his great-grandfather away.

"Yes, I think she does or at least she feels it, senses I'm a bit different. Like most old people she feels death close and is frightened. I think I was able to reassure her a little. I don't even have to touch folk now: I can read them just from being near. I just avoid the ones I know are going to be hard. With family, touching makes the visions clearer.

"Is it easier to live with?" Johnny's concern for her was paramount.

"Much, much better, especially with you beside me; I love you," she whispered.

He squeezed her waist and kissed her gently, "I love you too, my darling. Our turn next, I can't wait."

Later, when the introductions were done, the cake cut and the speeches over, the tables were pushed back to make a space for dancing. Johnny's friends from university had once again come down to provide the music and, of course, Izzy was included in that number.

The wedding party was in full swing and Reigneth, James and Aaron had disappeared. Johnny, trying to avoid drinking too much alcohol, sat clutching a glass of apple juice, next to Matt and Jessie. Smiling at them he thought what easy company they were, their happiness encompassing everyone. He knew that Reigneth and her cousins were preparing some entertainment and waited eagerly to see what they were up to.

The three of them entered the marquee. Reigneth had changed into the dress she wore at her birthday party, she had let down her hair and carried Joe's accordion. All three wore tap shoes. Johnny smiled in anticipation.

"It has long been a tradition in Romany families to step dance,"

Jessie explained. "When they were on the road there was always room for a bit of wood to dance on. Joe's family, the Grays, were particularly musical and their instruments, mainly accordions, squeeze boxes, fiddles and zithers, were all easily transportable."

Johnny nodded, bending his head towards Jessie so he could hear her above the noise. "I guess that's a major concern when space is at a premium."

"Oh yes," Jessie smiled, "and items purely for pleasure were a luxury, but over the years the Grays earned money as entertainers, so the instruments provided an income. Hush now, they are about to begin."

Johnny sat back nursing his drink, his gaze fixed on the stunning girl who would soon become his wife.

Once on the stage, James's infectious grin spread as he introduced them. "To anyone who doesn't already know us, I'm James Boswell and this natty pair are Reigneth and Aaron Gray. We're going to do a bit of stepping; we'll set you off, then come up as you wish. For those of you who don't want to come up here, there's a 'shy board' over in the corner there." Throughout the marquee there was a buzz of comment and titters of laughter. "OK, then," said James, "we will begin."

Reigneth started playing the *Bluebell Polka* and it was James up first to dance. His footwork was excellent and he was surprisingly light-footed for a big man. Watching him, Johnny remembered how he had felt so jealous when James had danced with Reigneth before. It was strange to think of that now they were the best of friends. After a while, James took over on the accordion.

"What'll it be Reigneth?"

"*Buffalo Girls*," both Reigneth and Aaron piped up together.

They began dancing and were perfectly synchronised, but Aaron was absolutely amazing: he danced with panache, his arms undertaking little flourishes and he seemed to swagger as he moved. Johnny was entranced: they were an impressive pair. He looked around the room until his gaze found his sister. He grinned at her: she was looking up at James like he was some sort of god.

Ever since he had got up onto the stage, Charlotte had not been able to tear her gaze away from James. Not for the first time did she notice how handsome he was. So tall and powerful. His black hair was slightly curly and his brown – almost black – eyes, which seemed enormous, distracted her so much she always found it difficult to concentrate when talking to him. His skin was as dark as Jessie's, the colour deepened and enriched by the Devon air. He sported two tattoos, one on the inside of his left forearm, and a Celtic band on his right upper arm. She had never found tattoos appealing before, but as with all things to do with James, this only added to his allure. With his pierced ear, he reminded her of a pirate; a very large, very kind, very sweet and protective pirate.

Feeling someone's gaze on her, Charlotte turned her head and caught Johnny grinning at her. He looked so happy. It was strange to think that he was her *half*-brother. It had been a shock to learn about Matt and their mother, but it didn't change the way she felt about any of them: they were her family and she loved them. It might have been different if her father had been unhappy, but he had never seemed so and she was fairly certain he had never known Johnny was not his son.

After Johnny's day out with Matt, he had filled in all the details for her and Henry so they both understood how it had come about. Henry had been quite blasé about the whole thing, "It happens... " he had said with a shrug. Charlotte knew that her mother and Johnny had since had a heart to heart and things between them seemed just as they always had done. It had never bothered her that Johnny was so obviously their mother's favourite, he was her firstborn after all – and anyway, she and Henry had each other; she had always felt closer to her twin than to anyone else, but Johnny was her big brother and that made him special. She grinned back at him and gave him a little wave, then turned her gaze once more to James.

The evening wore on and Johnny, as ever people-watching, spotted his mother with James on the other side of the room. She was smiling up at him and the big amiable guy was laughing and joking with her. For the first time that Johnny could remember in a long while, his mother looked completely relaxed. Jessie had referred to James as 'the Guardian' and he now understood what she had meant. Reigneth's cousin had a natural, easy way with him. Certainly, the day Jed Cummings had come to the house, James had been anything but affable, but that was in protection of his own.

263

Johnny understood them all so much better now: how they loved and protected one another, how loyalty was high on their agenda. He smiled to himself: he ought to – he was a quarter Romany after all!

Then he noticed something else, he saw for the first time the softening of James's eyes and his warm easy smile as he gazed at Charlotte. Needless to say, the smile was reciprocated in full measure. What a turn up for the books! Reigneth had not said anything, but of course she must know. Charlotte would be lucky to have James. Funny how things turned out: if they married, he and James would be brothers! If anyone had told him that a year ago he would have thought they were deranged. He wished his mother could find some happiness; she looked so lonely, so small. But he knew she was not as fragile as she seemed. He was glad they had talked. She looked in his direction and he gave her a beaming smile.

Johnny cast about the room and saw that Grandma Buckland was still watching him and Matt, as she had been all day. He wandered over to her, "You having a good time, Mrs Buckland?" he asked, genuinely interested.

"You had better call me Gran, young fella. I'm having a wonderful time. You and your dad are a sight for sore eyes. Don't mind me staring, it's like my lad is alive again. The resemblance is uncanny; it could be Nat here with us. You and your dad are Bucklands in all but name and it gladdens my heart. Your grandfather would say the same, but he's gone to find his bed. It's been too many years since we had so much excitement," she smiled. "And I see your dad is getting restless to have his bride to himself!"

Johnny laughed, "Well we won't let them go just yet. I want to see Matt trying to step."

The old lady giggled, tears of laughter moistening her eyes as she patted Johnny's hand, "That will be something to see. Mind you, I notice he hasn't touched a drop all evening, you might be surprised. His dad was a wonderful dancer."

The revelry continued until the early hours and both Jessie and Matt were exhausted when they eventually managed to sneak out of the festivities and drive home to Higher Wedicombe. Someone had decorated the Land Rover, but thankfully, there were no tin cans to wake the neighbourhood.

Jessie lowered herself into the unfamiliar bed and was suddenly overcome with the enormity of what she had done. She had never thought there would be anyone for her but Joe and here she was married to someone else. She was Mrs Holbrook instead of Mrs Gray; she had a *Gauja's* name. Even knowing Matt was half Romany was no comfort just now. She loved him, of course she did, through and through, but it was only now, lying here in Matt's bed, that it came to her she was being unfaithful to Joe. No one but he had ever made love to her. Appalled by the thought, she was unable to hold back her tears and wept for her dead lover, deep, racking sobs that seared her throat.

Matt held her in his arms cradling her like a child. "Oh Jessie don't cry so, everything will work out well, I love you, Sweetheart," he whispered.

He knew why she was crying and in a way he understood. Until they had met, they had both loved only once and both so completely. He could never have imagined making love to anyone but Grace. He could not help comparing his reality with what he had once thought his future held: Grace was small, slight and almost too fragile. The woman beside him now was strong and lithe and yet fragile in a different way. He realised that Jessie's need of him would always outstrip that of Grace, who, despite her fragile appearance, was tough and unyielding. Jessie was gentle and loving, wise and caring. With her he would always come first, while Grace had given the impression that her own needs were paramount. But he had loved her anyway. He did not know much about Jessie's relationship with Joe, but he knew she had loved him heart and soul – so of course this was going to be difficult for her at first.

Murmuring gentle words, Matt stroked Jessie's hair and held her close, making no demands on her, just letting her weep. He was going to make her happy: as happy as he had been from the moment she had agreed to become his wife. If he was sure of one thing, he was sure of that.

The crying ceased as the light of a new dawn filtered through the window and Jessie fell into an exhausted sleep. Looking down at her tearstained face, Matt smiled ruefully. This had been their wedding night. But there would be many other nights; he did not mind giving this one night over to Joe.

Chapter 31

The Guardian

A couple of weeks after the wedding, Grace sauntered into her kitchen on the tail end of a discussion taking place round her huge kitchen table. It seemed that Johnny and his friends from the band were faced with a dilemma: their drummer, Matthew Johnstone, had taken up his sticks and walked. They were all in the doldrums about it: Izzy was incensed as were the others, all except Johnny who was being philosophical.

"We will just have to resign ourselves. If the music we're playing doesn't appeal to him then we can't expect him to stay," he said, with a shrug.

"That's all very well, Johnny, but what are we going to do? We need someone and quickly, we've got a gig coming up," Izzy moaned. There was a chorus of agreement.

Grace sidled past the table making for the kettle. Having just finished mucking out she was conscious that she brought with her the smell of ponies and manure. She wiped her hands on her trendy overalls, said cheerily, "Anyone for a cup of tea?"

"How come you can smell like a stable yet still manage to look so trim and smart, Grace?" Izzy complained, which brought a laugh.

"No tea thanks, Mum, we were just leaving," said Johnny. "We're off to Home Humber," he smiled. "Jessie, Matt, Reigneth and Aaron are staying back at Liz's place while the builders install a new kitchen at Higher Wedicombe and we are invited to lunch," he explained, giving her a wave as they all got up and trooped out of the door.

Grace tightened her jaw, her mouth set in a hard line, "You can always stay here for lunch some days you know," she retorted as her daughter passed through the kitchen and hurried after them.

"Sorry, Mum, they're having a band discussion and anyway, it's Jessie's baking day," Charlotte chirped dashing out.

"Traitoress daughter deserting me for cake," Grace quipped. She knew they'd be back later, but she could not help but feel a little jealous – after all, she wasn't perfect – not like Jessie! Grace never baked so there was little more for her to say, but the house seemed suddenly very quiet with them all gone.

She was just filling the kettle when Johnny reappeared at the door, "Pull your overalls off and come with us, Mum, one more won't make much difference to Jessie."

Grace needed no more persuading. Her overalls cast aside and hands washed, she shrugged on a clean jacket and got into the Land Rover beside Johnny. Some of the others piled in the back and the rest went in a car belonging to one of the other lads. Grace found she was actually enjoying herself: somehow, being with a crowd of noisy teenagers lifted her spirits. She hoped Johnny was right and that Jessie would not mind having an uninvited guest.

At Home Humber, Jessie knocked the freshly cooked loaf out of the bread tin and placed it steaming on a board in the centre of the table. She knew she deserved her reputation as a fabulous cook and was happy that a crowd of youngsters was coming to decimate her morning's labours. She loved to have them all around her, and Liz and Richard didn't seem to mind a houseful of teenagers, though Richard, affable as ever, had taken himself off to his studio, "For a bit of peace and quiet," he had mumbled. Jessie did not want peace and quiet: for her it was like being back in Lincolnshire with all the young uns about. Only Matt and James were missing and they would no doubt amble along later once they had seen to the stock at Higher Wedicombe. Jessie was happy, happier than she had a right to be, happier than she had been in months.

The crowd of noisy teens bustled into the kitchen commenting on the appetising smells of homemade stew and bread that hit them. Jessie, however, was prepared for them. She stood guard at the kitchen sink and shooed them away as they hovered waiting to wash their hands. The *Gaujas* amongst them had managed on a number of occasions to defile the pot washing bowl by washing their hands in it, resulting in several trips to the hardware store to purchase yet another new one. It was not going to happen again. As Liz directed them all to the downstairs bathroom, Jessie relaxed. Only then did she notice Grace standing hesitantly just inside the door.

"Hello Grace, how nice to see you." Surprised, Jessie welcomed her, feeling a little nervous and hoping it did not show. Grace as usual looked so smart, making Jessie feel self-conscious. She was sure there must be flour in her hair and knew her face was hot and flushed from cooking.

"I hope you don't mind me coming uninvited, Jessie, if I'm intruding... " Grace's voice trailed away.

"No, no not at all, you're very welcome, Grace. One more won't make a difference. Have a seat and make yourself comfortable," Jessie smiled, wishing Matt were here. Liz was no help: she was still frogmarching teenagers to the bathroom. Making herself busy, Jessie began to serve lunch, happy to have something to occupy her hands.

Soon the babble of conversation was filling the room obviating the need for her to think of something to say to Grace. *By, they're a noisy lot,* she thought, smiling, as she tried to keep up with what they were saying.

Izzy was grumbling as usual, but this time it seemed with just cause: the band's drummer had left them in the lurch evidently.

"James is a drummer you know," Jessie commented, "he's been in a couple of bands." They all stared at her. Izzy's face lit up, she liked James. Charlotte blushed at the mention of his name. Johnny looked amazed.

"Blimey, isn't it enough that he's living here and now you're saying I've got to put up with him in the band as well?" he commented in mock dismay.

Reigneth giggled, "Actually, I think he has more energy than technique, Ma."

"At this stage we don't care; any port in a storm! Get him here, Reigneth, if you can," Izzy pleaded.

"If she *can*? It's keeping him away that's the problem," Johnny said, stuffing into his mouth a piece of bread so large he had no room to chew it.

Jessie could not believe the appetite the boy had on him. She had no problem with that, but it was perhaps fortunate that Grace, now deep in conversation with Liz, had not noticed her son's lapse in table manners.

"Shall I ring him then?" Reigneth asked.

Johnny could not answer. He shrugged his shoulders, pointed at his mouth and rolled his eyes, which looked as if they were about to pop out of his head.

"You are such a child," said Reigneth, smiling as she pulled out her mobile. "Hush everyone, I can't hear," she shouted. They all quietened and listened to the one-sided conversation. It seemed James was already on his way.

Clearly ecstatic to be asked, he arrived within half an hour. "I knew it was the right thing to move down here," he grinned at Johnny. "Miss me, J?"

Johnny scowled; his response muffled, his mouth still full, this time with second helpings.

Lunch was a protracted affair as everyone waited while James and Matt polished off what was left.

"Good thing we arrived when we did, Matt, that little bugger has hollow legs," James smirked and looked at Johnny, who scowled in return. This banter between the two of them had become something of the norm for them and Jessie suspected they enjoyed playing to the gallery.

Having finished his lunch and two cups of tea, Johnny stood. "Let's see what you've got then, Boswell."

When the youngsters had all trooped out, Matt pushed his chair back and stretched, directing a satisfied smile at Jessie and Liz. "It was good of Richard to let them set up their equipment in his barn; it's great for their practice sessions. What with that and your cooking, Jess, Home Humber's becoming a hive of industry."

Liz gasped and put her hand to her mouth, "Richard!" she exclaimed. "I forgot to save him some stew."

"I didn't," Jessie smiled, "there's a plate for him in the oven and there's some bread in the bin. I made two loaves."

"Oh, Jess, you're a life saver. I'll take him a tray."

"May I come too?" Grace asked; her offer to help with the washing up having been firmly turned down by Jessie. "I'd love to see inside Richard's studio."

"Yes, of course, follow me," said Liz, "he will love showing you round."

When they had gone, Jessie started gathering up the dishes; if the empty plates were anything to go by, her reputation was deserved. Matt came up behind her and wrapped his arms around her waist. "It's no wonder I love you," he said, kissing her on the nape of her neck.

She bent her head forward, enjoying the sensation of his lips on her skin, goose bumps rising on her arms. "Aren't you going to join the young 'uns?" she asked.

"I'd rather stay with you," he murmured. "Jono won't miss me with all his mates around him."

Johnny led the way into the barn, whereupon James peeled off his shirt to reveal a vest type T-shirt underneath and muscles that were unbelievable.

"Charlotte, you're gawping," Johnny teased. He enjoyed making her blush. "Is the shirt removal really necessary, Boswell?"

"I get hot," James said, wielding the sticks, "it takes a lot of energy." He winked at Charlotte, whose face went an even deeper shade of red. Seating himself comfortably at the drums he made one or two adjustments then began to play.

They were all surprised at his ability. It was true, as Reigneth had said, it was more energy than technique, but even so he had great potential. And more besides: he brought fury and passion to his drumming.

"That will do for us, James," said Izzy when he paused after a spectacular drum roll and everyone clapped appreciatively. "What do you think of when you're drumming?" she asked, "You had a peculiar expression on your face."

James laughed, "I imagine I'm beating Johnny's head for *choring* my girl," he beamed a smile at Reigneth and pulled a face at Johnny, who shook his fist then cracked out laughing.

Watching the interplay between James and Johnny, Reigneth smiled to herself: not just a drummer but a great friendship had been discovered today. It was the beginnings of roots for James and would ease the restlessness that had been plaguing him. She knew that with his addition to the band, over time they would change from being a group of friends just playing together to become a professional band working and collaborating at a whole new level.

Reigneth was excited by the thought.

They practised for the remainder of the day and the difference in the music was astounding. It was as though James acted as a catalyst: the passion of his drumming fuelled Johnny's drive further, and for them both, love was the inspiration.

As Izzy later commented, over hot chocolate at supper time, "All we need now is a name. What are we going to call ourselves?" After several minutes, one or two rude comments and a lot of unsuitable suggestions, nobody had come up with anything constructive. Nothing seemed to fit. Reigneth was not worried about it: she knew an apt name would reveal itself to her eventually.

Chapter 32

Premonition

Reigneth woke to the early morning sound of bird song. For once, her first thought was not that she was one more day nearer to her wedding. Her mind was too full of the strange dream she had just had, which though confusing, was not frightening. Sitting up in bed she hunched the duvet around her and tried to fathom out its significance. The dream had been clear and strong and very colourful; different to others in the past. She knew she had been waiting for this dream for a very long time for it was of their future, of that she was sure: their future beyond her grandmother's prophecy.

Wide awake now, Reigneth knew she would not get back to sleep. She felt invigorated having slept deeply; in fact she felt healthy and energetic most of the time now. It was still early and although well into June, the dawn air was quite chilly. Pulling on her dressing gown she stuffed her feet inside her slippers and made her way down the granite staircase – the only thing about Higher Wedicombe that she did not like – stopping at the bottom to make a fuss of Jukel and let him out into the garden.

The kettle seemed to take an age to boil. Reigneth wrapped her arms around her chest hugging her body to warm herself. Whilst she waited she shuffled into the tiny lounge. Small red sparks in the bottom of the wood burner indicated that it was not quite out. Adding more logs and opening the vent in the bottom, she tried to breathe more life into the embers. Within ten minutes it was beginning to spark. Reigneth let Jukel in, made herself a mug of drinking chocolate then sat beside the fire, sipping the hot, sweet drink appreciatively. She could hear someone padding along the landing and knew who it was.

Every day, Reigneth's senses were becoming increasingly heightened and everything seemed magnified. She felt as if she could almost count the hairs on Jukel's back. From quite some distance away, she knew the sound of James's long loping stride out in the yard. Closer at hand, she identified the swishing of her mother's dress as she busied herself about the house, and Aaron's light, almost hesitant footsteps as he made his way along the landing and came gingerly down the staircase.

He came into the lounge rubbing his eyes, his dark mop of hair sticking out in every direction. He smiled when he saw her but he looked puzzled. "What are you doing up so early? Couldn't you sleep?" He frowned, a slight anxiety in his voice, "You didn't dream, did you?"

"Yes, yes I did, but it was a good dream." She nodded her head emphatically, reinforcing the fact to herself: "Yes – surprisingly good."

Aaron relaxed, "Hmm; let me hear it then."

"Shall I get you a drink first?"

"No, just tell me... don't stall."

"Actually it was really odd, I don't know where we were but it was a sort of grassy clearing. I was outside myself, as often happens in my dreams. I could see Johnny and me standing there together. We looked so much alike, Aaron. It was like we were the same person. We were hand in hand and looked strong... incredibly strong. No fear in our faces and our eyes, they were dark and so penetrating," she stopped briefly to clarify things in her own mind.

"Go on then... what are you waiting for?" Aaron urged.

"Just gathering my thoughts; be patient! James stood on my left and you were on Johnny's right. You both looked the same, well not looked the *same*. You looked like you, if you know what I mean, but... "

"OK, Reigneth," Aaron cut in, "I understand, we were ourselves, but we looked strong like you and with weird eyes." He perched on the edge of his seat all attention now.

"Yes, that's it exactly – and we just stood together. Then, taking in the wider scene I saw that all around us and around the clearing there were tall, very tall trees. It must have been winter as there weren't any leaves on them. Through the trees people started walking slowly towards us. There were men, women and children and they all had the same pale, unhappy faces with dark hollows around their eyes."

"I thought you said this wasn't a bad dream! It sounds pretty bad to me.... a very bad dream." Aaron fidgeted in his seat, frowning."

"You're repeating yourself, Aaron."

"That's because you're scaring me. Do you not think it's scary? I need some reassurance here that it's not going to end badly."

"Calm down, Aaron, it's not scary, be reassured. It's our future."

"You gotta be joking!"

"Nope, bear with me," she smiled at him over the rim of her mug. "Now where was I?"

"Pale people with hollow eyes," Aaron shivered.

"Oh yes, well, they all looked unhappy and they had one thing in common: they were all dead."

"Eh?" Aaron's mouth hung open and his face paled as he stared at Reigneth. "OK, so how can this be good? No wonder they looked unhappy! Being dead is not good, no matter how you look at it. Being dead is really, really bad."

She smiled at his expression, "Don't worry, I told you, there's nothing to worry about. You keep taking me off track. Yes, they were all dead and in the front were three girls who all looked the same, like they were the same person. Actually, they looked a bit like Charlotte at first glance, but when I looked closer they were different in subtle ways. One was angry and the other two, well they held out their hands to us; they needed us. They wanted to be found."

"Were they lost?" Aaron frowned in concentration.

"I don't know. I couldn't see anymore really."

"Oh, well that's just great! So when the punch line comes you pull the 'I can't see anymore' stunt and that's supposed to reassure me? So how's this gonna affect us? What is your interpretation?"

"I think we're going to find them and that brings me to another thing: I've thought of a name for the band."

"Have you noticed how you dart about from one thing to another? We're talking about a bunch of dead people one minute and then you start talking about the band. This is the most bizarre conversation I've ever had with you!"

"Sorry. Do you want a drink now? I'm going to make another." As she tripped off to the kitchen, Reigneth was aware of Aaron staring after her, muttering to himself that he didn't much fancy finding a bunch of lost zombies.

A few minutes later he had a mug of hot chocolate in one hand and a digestive biscuit in the other. He curled up his legs on the small sofa next to the fire, which was now starting to give out some heat. "OK, so carry on," he said, chewing his biscuit.

"There's not much else to say really, other than that we are going to help find them. Oh, and the band: I thought 'The Lost Souls'.

"That's a good name," Aaron nodded, "a *really* good name."

"Yeah, I thought so."

"OK, so how are we going to find these dead people?" Aaron stared at her, his expression a mixture of fear and intrigue.

"Well, actually I think they will find us," she paused in concentration. "Yes, I'm sure they will find us."

"Don't tell me dead people are coming to the house, Reigneth, 'cause I don't think that's such a good idea."

"Stop worrying about details, Aaron. All I know is that it's not scary and there is no need to worry."

Aaron was not convinced, "So when is all this gonna start then, you know, the cadavers knocking on the door?"

"Not yet; not until after the prophecy is complete. We will all be different then and before you ask, I don't know in what way, I just know we will be changed."

They both sat drinking their hot chocolate staring at one another. "Please can I not be the one who has to tell the others," Aaron said, grimacing.

"Hmm – I think it best not to say anything to James or Mam just yet. Let's wait awhile. They'll only start worrying."

"Are you crazy? James will kill us if we keep this from him. Oh, and by the way, how are we going to help dead people without anyone knowing about it? Your secret has to be kept regardless of who we help or what we do."

"We don't need to worry about that – and don't ask why 'cause I really don't know. Aaron – *relax*. I truly am not worried."

Chapter 33

Engagement

It was almost the end of term and Johnny and the band were booked to play at the Engine Shed, a club and students' union bar attached to the university. For the first time they were billed as The Lost Souls, all having enthusiastically adopted Reigneth's suggestion. Only Aaron and Johnny were aware of its significance. Keeping her promise never to keep another secret from Johnny, Reigneth had told him how the name had come to her.

Naturally, Reigneth wanted to see the band play at what was their first official public performance and begged Jessie to let her go. In fact, nobody wanted to be left behind and so all seven of them set off from Higher Wedicombe: James, since he was to play; Matt, Jessie, Reigneth, Henry, Charlotte, Aaron and, of course, Jukel.

Looking around at them all as they piled into the car, Matt could hardly believe how his life had changed. Some time ago he had conceded that with his growing family, the Land Rover was not up to the job anymore and had decided to replace it. Without telling Jessie, he had looked out for a bigger, more comfortable vehicle: he did not want her to be making do. After much thought, he had selected a new Land Rover Discovery – well, not new, he wasn't prepared to go quite that mad – beating the dealer down as much as possible. After years of scrimping and saving it was hard to break the habit of a lifetime, but in fact, Matt had quite a lot of money stashed away. He intended to keep it that way: money equalled security to Matt and ever since he had been left to fend for himself at the tender age of eighteen he had needed to feel secure.

Jessie was different to him in that respect. Money meant very little to her. He envied her that; her security had always been her family. "Now don't go getting yourself in debt for a new vehicle, Matt, we can go in James's truck and Johnny's Land Rover," Jessie had urged caution, worried for him as soon as she got wind of his plans. "You've already spent so much on the house."

"I'm not getting myself in debt, love, we can afford it; we're not paupers. I'm not having my beautiful wife putting up with things and making do."

"You are a lovely man, Matthew Holbrook," she had smiled. She had smiled even more when he drove the seven-seater Discovery into the yard the following day.

The trip was duly planned: the young ones were to stay overnight with Johnny, who occupied a house separated into three flats. The other band members lived in two of them while Johnny shared the third with Izzy: an arrangement that had suited them well since moving out of halls two years before. James, Reigneth, Charlotte and Aaron were to squeeze in with Johnny and Izzy, who had begged and borrowed camp beds and sleeping bags for them all. Matt had booked himself and Jessie into a hotel and was looking forward to having his wife to himself for a change. Jessie, however, was not entirely happy with the idea, "Matt, I don't think we should leave them to their own resources," she chuntered anxiously.

"Jessie, they are teenagers! Relax the reins a bit, my darling, they're a sensible lot. Nothing will happen to them with James there," Matt reassured her.

He knew well enough that young people needed time to themselves. It had surprised him how closely Reigneth was supervised and he had often wondered why she had not bucked against it more than she had. He had expressed his amazement on the occasions when Jessie had permitted Johnny and Reigneth to spend the night together. The circumstances were unusual and she trusted them, Jessie had told him, adding tartly that Reigneth was a good Romany girl and would remain a virgin until she was married. Matt had raised his eyebrows at that, imagining how impossibly hard it must be for his son: he was a fit and healthy young fella and was obviously besotted with Reigneth.

They arrived at the flat, dropped the youngsters off and arranged to meet up later at 'Esprit', an Italian restaurant Johnny had chosen. This gave Matt and Jessie time for a little sightseeing and it seemed that Johnny had an excursion of his own planned too, for it was evident when they arrived that he was keyed up and eager to whisk Reigneth away.

"See you later, then," Matt said, after Johnny had admired the Discovery.

"Yes, see you," the young ones chorused, waving as Matt and Jessie drove away.

As soon as they had gone, James, Charlotte, Henry and Aaron clattered inside, laughing up at Izzy, who was leaning out the window making silly faces at them. Reigneth turned to follow, but Johnny forestalled her. He had been in a fever of excitement all day waiting for this moment. He grabbed Reigneth's hand, "Come on then, Sweetheart, I want to show you something."

Reigneth shook him off, "Hang on, Johnny, I need to go to the loo and have a drink before we go anywhere," she protested half-heartedly.

He smiled, knowing she found it hard to deny him anything. "Hurry up then. We don't have long if we're to get back in time, you're later than I was expecting," he complained.

"Well don't blame me. I wasn't driving!" She gave him a quizzical look before hurrying indoors. Moments later they were all crammed in the galley kitchen and Reigneth was glugging down a glass of milk, leaving a thin film on her top lip. Johnny grinned devilishly, kissed her and licked it off at the same time.

"Yuk, Johnny, gross," Izzy laughed.

"Nothing to do with Reigneth could possibly be gross," said Johnny. "Are you ready now, Darling?"

"What's the hurry?" James glowered, winding his arms around Charlotte who, not liking to be left out of anything, scowled at her brother.

"Yeah, where are you two off to, Johnny?"

"Never you mind," Johnny grinned, tapping the side of his nose and winking at James. "We'll see you later." He dragged Reigneth away, shouting back for someone to feed Jukel, who stood with his tail tucked between his legs because his mistress was leaving him behind.

Johnny hurried Reigneth along a maze of interesting little streets to 'Usher's', the tiny tucked away jeweller's where he had bought Reigneth's pendant and bracelet the year before. Thomas

Usher, the elderly proprietor who had established the business thirty years ago, could be relied upon to stock unusual quality pieces, both new and antique. When passing the shop a couple of days ago, Johnny had wandered in to look at engagement rings and seen one that he really liked. It was outrageously expensive, but Johnny did not care. Nothing was too good for Reigneth. He had arranged for Thomas to keep it back for him along with a selection of other rings, promising he would be back with his girlfriend in a couple of days and asking him to remove the price tag of any that she wanted to look at.

As he and Reigneth, breathless and laughing, entered the shop, Thomas Usher looked up with a warm, friendly smile. The two female assistants stopped what they were doing and gazed at Johnny adoringly. He grinned at them. He had flirted with them both in a harmless, bantering way when he came to look at the rings: he was used to the way women looked at him, never sure if they wanted to mother him or kiss him, which always made him laugh.

"Hello, Mr Usher," he said, "this is my fiancée, Reigneth Gray." Johnny led her forward with a feeling of such pride that he thought he would burst with it.

"I'm very pleased to meet you at last," said Thomas, extending his hand, "and may I say that Mr Wilmott was correct. The pendant does exactly match the colour of your eyes; it looks very well on you."

Johnny smiled. He could see the old man was spellbound by Reigneth's beauty. He was conscious too that the assistants were gazing at her in awe. She was so very lovely, her face flushed with excitement, her poise and grace belying her young age. Johnny could still hardly bring himself to believe that this gorgeous creature had agreed to be his wife and had to keep pinching himself just to be sure he was not dreaming.

Reigneth fingered the pendant, which along with the bracelet Johnny had given her for Christmas, she wore for much of the time. "Thank you," she said, her face lighting up with a smile, "I love it."

"I believe your young man wanted you to look at this," Thomas smiled at Johnny, leaned under the counter and brought out the ring. Reigneth gasped, looked at it then at Johnny, then at Thomas and then back at the ring. "It's exquisite," she breathed.

It lay nestled on a small cushion of black velvet: five diamonds,

279

the largest stone in the centre flanked on either side by four smaller ones, graduated in size and held in a fine, intricately worked setting of yellow gold.

Though pleased by Reigneth's reaction, Johnny was anxious not to force his choice on her: "Well I thought so, but you don't have to have this one, Sweetheart. It is your ring and you must have the last say. If you want something different, perhaps coloured stones, then Mr Usher will show you some more. Whatever you want, you shall have." Johnny picked up the ring, smiled broadly at Reigneth and reached for her left hand, intending to slide the ring onto her finger, certain that it would be a perfect fit.

"Please can I just hold it first Johnny?"

"Of course," he said, placing the ring in her palm. She held it tightly and closed her eyes.

Johnny understood. The ring was obviously old – Thomas Usher had dated it to around the early 1900's – and Reigneth would want to reassure herself that no bad luck or unhappiness attached to it. He glanced up at Thomas, who was staring at Reigneth, clearly perplexed that she had closed her eyes instead of examining the ring.

A slow smile spread over Reigneth's face. Opening her eyes, she handed the ring back to Johnny, "It's perfect," she said, holding out her left hand to him.

He slid the ring onto her finger and as he had known it would, it fitted as though it had been made for her. He gazed into her eyes and was suddenly overcome with emotion. Swallowing, he looked away in an effort to collect his thoughts, afraid that he would disgrace himself and weep like a baby from sheer happiness. He was aware that Thomas Usher and both his attendants were similarly affected, all looking dewy eyed. Clearing his throat he said croakily, "It's a perfect fit, Reigneth, do you like it?"

"Yes, my beloved, it's beautiful." She looked down at her finger, admiring it for a moment and then she pulled it off and replaced it on the black cushion. "I love you so very much, Johnny. Please don't be offended, but as beautiful as it is, I do not need such an expensive ring to cement our commitment."

Ignoring their audience, Johnny stopped her mouth with a kiss. He picked up the ring and slid it back on her finger. "I know you don't and neither do I, but I want you to have it. Please, my love, wear it for me. I'm so happy, Reigneth."

She smiled up at him, nodding wordlessly; tears spilling from her eyes and tracking her cheeks.

Thomas Usher removed a large white handkerchief from his waistcoat pocket and blew his nose, "Er... " he cleared his throat, "have you named the day yet, Mr Wilmott?"

"12th of August," they replied simultaneously and laughed.

Reigneth had been quite adamant on the date of the wedding even though it was a Friday. She had mentioned something to do with stars and that the date needed to be precise. It made no sense to Johnny, but he would marry her any day of the week – tomorrow if she chose.

"Well, may I offer you my congratulations and sincere wishes for your future happiness," Thomas Usher said.

"Thank you," Johnny checked his watch and added with a smile, "we must go – and we'll take the ring." He handed over his credit card and with a nod of understanding, Thomas Usher dealt discreetly with the payment.

As they stepped out of the jewellers, Reigneth stretched out her hand admiring her engagement ring. "Lovely isn't it," she sighed.

"Absolutely beautiful," Johnny murmured looking not at the ring but at Reigneth.

She giggled, "I meant the ring."

"That too," he smiled.

Reigneth shook her head, "You constantly surprise me. I had no idea you intended to bring me here or buy me an engagement ring today. Why didn't I see it? How are you able to do that? I don't understand how you can block your thoughts from me the way you do; nobody else can."

Johnny laughed, "Search me. I don't do it intentionally. By the way, did you know August 12th is the beginning of the grouse shooting season?" he bantered.

"Oh well, if I'm stopping you shooting grouse we could always rearrange the wedding," she teased then frowned, "though actually, we may have to wait another year."

"What!" Johnny clowned dismay. "Please tell me you're joking." Sidestepping a passer-by and pulling Reigneth out of the way he said, "Seriously though, what's special about the 12th of August? It's a Friday too – don't tell me it's the star thingy again."

He stopped walking, drew Reigneth towards him and traced the outline of her cheek with his fingertips.

"But it's true. Algol will be eclipsing that night and it's important," she said seriously.

"Ah, so it's not the wedding ceremony itself that's important?" he teased.

Reigneth flushed, "Of course it is, but we have to be united under Algol, Johnny. Granny Mary told me so when I was tiny and I have always known it."

He shook his head in disbelief, "You are so superstitious, Reigneth. By 'united' I suppose you mean we'll make love?"

Reigneth glanced down at the pavement her ears pink with embarrassment. Amused, Johnny hugged her to him, "And what happens then," he murmured in her ear.

"Then the prophecy is complete."

"And?"

"And then we shall be as one, there will be many changes in us both," she replied.

"Changes – what sort of changes? Our feelings for one another will never change will they?" Johnny felt slightly ill at ease. He wanted nothing more than to spend the rest of his life with Reigneth.

"No, that will never change. We are to spend the rest of our very long lives together, but we will become more alike. I will become stronger and not as susceptible to evil."

Johnny nodded, but he did not really understand. He took her hand and they resumed walking. He had never felt Reigneth was susceptible to anything. She seemed incredibly strong, never had coughs or colds and her mother had told him she'd had none of the normal childhood ailments. He wasn't exactly sure what she meant by 'evil', until he remembered Wistman's Wood, and how ill she had been after dreaming about Jed Cummings. But he was much too buoyed up to give it serious thought today, so he put it out of his mind. All that mattered was that they loved each other and were going to be together for the rest of their lives. He did not care what date they got married – he had only been joking about grouse; it was not in his nature to kill anything – so long as Reigneth was happy was all he cared about. He broke into a run and grinned at her, "Come on, Reigneth, I'll race you."

* * *

Reigneth grinned back and set off after him, ensuring he stayed just ahead of her, although she was just as fleet-footed as he. Returning back to the flat, their spirits high, they found a note pinned to the door to say the others had already left and that Jukel had been fed and walked.

"Bags I shower first," Reigneth said breathlessly, quickly laying out her clothes and rushing to the bathroom. Ducking into the shower she realised she had forgotten to fasten her hair out of the way and there was no time to wash it. Pulling her towel around her she ran to her room to get a band for her hair and dashed back to the bathroom. Johnny had obviously thought she had been in and out of the shower and walked in ready for his.

Reigneth hesitated in the doorway; Johnny stood there in just his jeans. She eyed his muscular chest then looked up into his face. He was staring at her and she flushed, aware that she was barely covered by the skimpy towel. Within seconds they were in each other's arms. Their kisses were demanding: uncaring what time it was or where they were supposed to be. Reigneth's arms reached up around his neck, her fingers twisting into his hair, the towel dropping carelessly to the floor. Johnny's kisses became more urgent, the feel of his skin against hers was wonderful; the smell of him intoxicating. Her breathing quickened, rasping in her throat as he showered kisses down her neck to the soft indentation near her collar bone, the intense sensations making her gasp and shiver. Dimly, in the far reaches of her consciousness, Reigneth became aware that they were not alone. She froze.

A stifled cough came from the open doorway. "Bet you're pleased I'm not Jessie, eh?" Izzy drawled, a comical edge to her voice.

Mortified, Reigneth drew her breath in sharply over her teeth, aware that Johnny was hiding her nakedness protectively against him and looking daggers at Izzy over her shoulder.

"Don't you think you ought to be getting ready? It's six-thirty you know; nice bum by the way," Izzy chuckled as she carried on past the bathroom on her way to the room she was sharing with Reigneth.

Johnny bent to retrieve the towel from the floor, working his way up her body, placing light kisses on her calf, her thigh, her shoulder and finally on her face while enfolding her in the towel.

With both hands on her shoulders, he held her away from him and smiled into her eyes. "Soon, my love, soon," he breathed.

Reigneth by now was quite unable to breathe at all and felt in danger of fainting, much to Johnny's obvious amusement. "Never thought I'd have that effect on anyone – remember to breathe, Sweetheart," he grinned at her with apparent calm, but his eyes were wild with excitement and his hands were shaking.

Trying to regain her composure, Reigneth blushed, stepped back and grasping the towel with one hand, pushed him reluctantly outside the door, closed it then scuttled into the shower. Some ten minutes later, her thoughts so disjointed she was quite unable to focus on anything, Reigneth dashed into the bedroom.

Izzy laughed at her, "Come on, hurry up, we'll be so late. I'll help you get dressed."

Until five minutes ago, no one had ever seen Reigneth without her clothes, not since she was a child. She was a very private person, but in truth she felt sort of muddled just now and rather than be embarrassed, she was grateful for Izzy's help.

"You know, I think you and I had better go on a shopping trip before the wedding; to get some clothes for the honeymoon and some new lingerie for you," Izzy wailed as she spied Reigneth's plain if serviceable underwear.

"It's alright for you. I have to have bras that actually do something in the way of support," Reigneth said grudgingly, only too well aware that she had yet to find the money to buy new clothes. Her underwear left a lot to be desired, but money was scarce. It had never seemed to matter before.

"You should be so lucky! Wish I had your boobs, I'm as flat as the proverbial pancake," Izzy's grin spread right across her face. "I thought we might try some makeup too." Suddenly, she caught sight of Reigneth's hand. "Oh my God! Your ring! Let me look. Wow, that's exquisite. Johnny has surpassed himself," Izzy gushed.

Reigneth held it up for her to see then suffered Izzy's ministrations as she wielded the makeup. A little eye shadow, mascara and lipstick later, even Reigneth had to admit it made a difference, enhancing the planes of her face and bringing out the violet colour of her eyes. She had never worn makeup before and wasn't entirely sure she liked it.

Izzy deftly brushed through Reigneth's hair a wistful look on her face. "Everything about you is so lovely. No wonder Johnny loves you so, you really are breathtaking. Funny thing is, I don't fancy you at all!"

Reigneth laughed and clasped Izzy's hand lightly, "You know what they say: beauty is only skin deep," she quipped. "Seriously, it is as much of a curse as it is a blessing." Making a decision in that moment, Reigneth added, "And anyway, you will find someone soon, someone to love," she smiled sweetly and holding on to Izzy's hand, looked into her eyes. "That girl you were seeing last year, the blonde girl in the coffee shop? She wasn't right for you. Don't be afraid of what you're feeling, Izzy. I know you are confused at present, but it's OK to love a boy. Everything will work out for you in the end. You'll be happy. We're your family now," she finished.

It went against all Reigneth's instincts to do this and she wondered why she had and if she would have cause to regret it, but she had grown fond of the girl and could not bear to see her unhappy.

Izzy looked at her with awe in her eyes, "How do you know about that? I mean, I didn't tell anyone about Linda – not even Johnny. And how do you know I have feelings for a boy?"

"I'm a Gypsy and it's in your tea leaves," Reigneth chuckled, a wicked glint in her eye.

Izzy's mouth was hanging open in a quite unattractive way as Johnny entered the room. "What's up Iz? Has Reigneth whacked you with the hair brush for being so bossy?"

"She's just said she can read tea leaves," Izzy gasped.

Johnny cracked out laughing: "Tea leaves? I hope you didn't take her seriously. You look like a rabbit caught in the headlights. What has she told you?"

"How long have you known about this, Johnny?" Izzy ignored the question.

"Known what? That Reigneth has a special gift? Since last year, amazing isn't she." He reached out and tenderly stroked Reigneth's cheek, "You look lovely, Sweetheart." Suddenly he was serious as he looked back at Izzy, "You cannot say anything Iz, not to anyone; no one at all. Do you understand? Only the family knows. I am not sure why she chose to tell you." He looked quizzically at Reigneth, who smiled.

"I trust her and besides, she *is* family, Johnny, and is going to be even more so."

"Really?" Johnny turned again to Izzy, his eyebrows lifted in surprise. "Well, whatever, like I said, you must not tell anyone at all, OK?"

"I wasn't going to. I'm just stunned, is all – and that's putting it mildly."

They were slightly late getting to the restaurant and the family greeted them with as much affection as if they had been away for months rather than hours. Once the excuses were made and the ring admired, things really took off and the champagne flowed.

"Only one glass for you young man, engaged or not, we don't want you falling off the stage," Matt made light of trying to limit Johnny's alcohol intake.

"That's probably the only way we'll get some applause," James quipped. "Of course, some of us can drink more than others," he grinned at Johnny and winked at Reigneth. Charlotte giggled, tucked securely under his right arm.

Jessie looked at her watch, "What time are you supposed to be on stage?" she asked.

"In ten minutes!" James and Johnny chorused, pushing back their chairs.

"You go on," said Matt, "I'll settle the bill. We'll be right behind you."

Chapter 34

The Lost Souls

The Engine Shed was packed out and the atmosphere lively. There was a coffee bar at one end of the room and a stage at the other, with a few tables and chairs around the sides, but for most of the audience it was standing room only as The Lost Souls took to the stage. Swallowing hard, Johnny tried to calm his racing heart, his stomach churning. Forcing a smile, he winked at Izzy and they began to tune their instruments. Johnny, of course, was the lead singer and played lead guitar, there was their usual bass guitarist and an additional keyboard player. Included in the eclectic mix were a saxophone and flute, and with James on the drums and Izzy playing either the violin or keyboards, their music – a sort of alternative rock with a touch of folk – was difficult to label. The kids in the audience began to cheer in anticipation.

Johnny noticed that Jessie and Matt had secured a table on the side lines and looked like a couple of fish out of water. Matt had his hands over his ears, which made Johnny laugh. Searching the crowd for Reigneth, as soon as he spotted her his nerves dropped away and a sense of calm washed over him. Everyone else around her faded into insignificance and for a few seconds it was as though he and Reigneth were the only people in the room. Thrown by the intensity of his feelings, Johnny stood motionless, drinking in the sight of her. It took a drum roll from James to bring him back to the moment. Turning, he saw James and Izzy watching him, both were smiling. He nodded to the rest of the band, grinned and mouthed, "Ready?"

"You bet," Izzy yelled over the noise of the audience, who

cheered even louder as Johnny struck the first chord and began to sing. He was on fire; the music electrifying and the kids were working themselves into a frenzy, the Engine Shed throbbing and pulsing with sound. Johnny, playing to the crowd found, much to his surprise, that he was dancing as he sang. He had never felt so free before and was enjoying every minute of it, his eyes focused solely on Reigneth.

On and on the band played, each number outstripping the last and the kids whipping themselves to fever pitch, stamping, clapping and cheering. Johnny kept his gaze on Reigneth feeling that he could do anything with her there: it was as if he had never really lived before he had met her. She was his world and without her he was nothing. Her presence was essential to his very being and he was continually amazed that she felt the same.

Taking a breather while James thumped out a mind-blowing solo, he saw that Reigneth, who was standing with Charlotte and Henry, was hemmed in on all sides by noisy teenagers. He worried for an instant that she was uncomfortable with their proximity and was reassured when she sought his gaze and laughed up at him. He relaxed: seemingly she was having a good time and being a normal teenager for once, like all the others dancing and stamping to the drumbeat. He wished only that she was up here beside him: that would be perfect. Her voice was equal to Izzy's or any of the other band members and she knew all the songs. If only she could be persuaded to perform with him, but she was adamant. Perhaps with time he could change her mind. He smiled wistfully at her and as he began once more to play, he saw Aaron pushing through the crowd to her side and wondered idly where he had been.

"God, it's loud!" Aaron shouted into Reigneth's ear then stood back to grin at her.

She nodded, "Aren't they great!" she yelled back. "Where've you been?" she asked absently, not taking her gaze off Johnny, her face lit up with pride.

"Me? Nowhere," he protested. Following her gaze, Aaron had to admit that even to his eyes, Johnny looked good. Like Reigneth, he wore black and his hair, which he had grown to his shoulders, floated back from his tanned face as he strode with leonine grace about the stage.

Aaron had missed the first half of the performance and had hoped no one would notice that he had mysteriously disappeared. Trust Reigneth! The gig was going tremendously well: looking around, it made him smile to see that even Matt was unable to keep still, his fingers tapping out the beat on the table. He was smiling at Jessie, a look of such tenderness in his eyes that Aaron's breath caught in his throat. Matt was a lovely man; so right for Jessie. Aaron knew instinctively that Uncle Joe would have liked him.

Beside Aaron, Henry was shouting something in Charlotte's ear and pointing into the crowd. The twins both burst out laughing and Aaron, looking to see what was so funny, spotted the band's erstwhile drummer, Matthew Johnstone. He was glowering up at James and judging by his expression was none too pleased to have been usurped in the band, which, to add insult to injury, was proving so popular. 'Serves him right,' Aaron thought, he was the one who had let them down after all.

Turning back to the stage, he observed that Reigneth and Johnny only had eyes for each other and that Charlotte was staring in open-mouthed adoration at James. Watching the expression on her face, Aaron almost laughed out loud. He wondered if Jessie knew what was in the wind – probably, not much got past Auntie Jessie. Ah well, at least she and Matt would be spared the expense of yet another wedding. The bride's family traditionally paid and Grace Wilmott was the kind of woman who would be in her element organising her daughter's big day. What a turn up for the books, though: James falling for a *Gauja*! Who would have thought it? Aaron wondered if that was why his cousin had seemed more settled of late, or was it because he had become so much a part of the band? Probably both: certainly James seemed to be enjoying himself. Being in The Lost Souls was providing a much needed release for his pent up frustrations and his fury and passion seemed to energise their music. It pleased Aaron immensely that James had brought a Romany influence to their sound. The effect was a foot-stamping rhythm that demanded audience participation.

The kids were ecstatic now and Johnny on stage was magnificent, playing to the crowd like a true showman. Aaron had never seen him look so confident, nor had the band ever sounded so good. He wondered if it was Reigneth's presence in the audience that had freed up Johnny's inhibitions. He watched her for a moment, observing the glances she exchanged with Johnny: it was as though an electric current zinged between them. Only, of course, being Reigneth, she felt Aaron's gaze on her and turned to look at him.

She bent towards him and shouted, "Isn't he fantastic?"

"Yes, I've never heard him sing or play like it," and truthfully he hadn't. "What have you done to him, Reigneth?" he grinned.

Reigneth laughed, "Never you mind!"

"You should be up on stage with him. You know that's where he wants you to be. It's you who inspires him to compose all this lovely stuff, you know."

"I just *couldn't*," she said with a frown, "I'm nowhere near good enough."

"That's not true," Aaron shouted, but with a shrug she had turned away and was now swaying to the beat and waving both hands in the air like all the rest. He grinned to himself. He knew how much Johnny wanted her to join the band: not only did she have a great voice, but she was a reasonable musician too. It was only her inherent shyness that prevented her from succumbing to Johnny's wish – that and her anxiety about being observed – and given that normally she could refuse him nothing it was a measure of how much of an obstacle the idea of singing in public was for her.

But not for much longer: Aaron had a plan. He knew he was being manipulative, but if he played the waiting game as Johnny intended, she might never get up on stage and Aaron wanted her to as much as Johnny did, although for different reasons.

While Aaron had inherited musicality and had a wonderful voice, he had never learned to play an instrument with any great skill. His father had always discouraged it. Recently, however, he had taught himself to play the harmonica and according to James, was quite good, but Aaron had no aspirations to be in the band. He saw for himself a different role: he wanted to promote The Lost Souls and be their manager. He had no doubt in his mind that they were going to be successful and in Aaron's opinion no one epitomised the Romany culture more than James and Reigneth – Johnny too, to a lesser extent, now they knew of his heritage. Aaron felt, had always felt, that the way to educate people and stop prejudice towards Romanies was through the younger generation and what better way than through music? Granny Mary had left him the task of ensuring that the Romany heritage and culture was not forgotten and he intended to carry it out to the best of his ability.

Aaron smiled to himself with satisfaction: it had cost him £200 to bribe the lead singer of the next band, Enigma, to delay his appearance along with his two backup vocalists. It was money well spent. Enigma only ever did cover versions and Aaron had made it his business to find out what numbers they were to perform. By dint of seemingly casual questioning over the last few days – mostly of Izzy, who had seemed happy when he had sought her out – Aaron knew that Johnny was not familiar with these numbers. He also knew that James and Reigneth were and that in fact some of them were James's favourites. Aaron knew Reigneth well enough – perhaps better than anyone else with the exception of Johnny – to know that she would never let James down. He had not prompted anyone about what was about to happen, knowing that Johnny would never be able to keep it from Reigneth, and Aaron did not want her forewarned. This had to be done on impulse, giving her no time to think about it.

The Lost Souls had just finished their last encore and were taking a bow when the expected phone call came. Aaron saw Johnny reaching for his mobile, blocking one ear with his finger. Saw him shake his head and hold the call while he bent to say something to Izzy. They both look across at James and then Johnny nodded and spoke into the phone. Aaron knew the content of the call: one of Enigma's band members was telling Johnny that three of them had been delayed and asking if he could stand in for them until they could get there. As Aaron had hoped, without apparently giving it a second thought, Johnny had volunteered James. Now he watched the drama play out on stage. Saw Johnny speak to James and, as Aaron had known he would, James was protesting, refusing point blank to get up and sing in front of so many people – unless, of course, Reigneth was right up there beside him.

Aaron smiled, satisfied: it was all happening as he had hoped and he had to admit to himself that he was a genius. He watched James leave the stage and make his way towards Reigneth and knew that once James got her on stage and they sang the first number, she would be OK. That would be the beginning. He felt good about this. The only slight flaw in his plan was that he had to find some way of paying back the £200 he had borrowed from Matt, but he would worry about that later.

He had known Reigneth would never let James down. He saw their heads bent together, James waving his arms about, pointing to Johnny who was watching them both from the stage. It was impossible to hear what they were saying as the audience were stamping, applauding and calling for more. He saw Reigneth flush, smile at James and then at Johnny and then give a reluctant nod, dragging a little behind as James took her by the hand and led her up onto the stage.

Aaron felt just a little guilty: he knew it was hard for her, after all she'd had a lifetime of hiding herself away. It had made her reticent about doing anything that put her in the limelight. This could be classified as very much in the limelight. All he wanted was to have them do a couple of numbers. That would be enough to overcome her anxiety and it would never be a problem for her again. Quickly, he dashed up to the stage and handed James his harmonica, knowing it would be needed for some of the numbers. James looked darkly at him, suspicion flaring in his eyes, but Aaron just shrugged and grinned, hurrying off the stage as the diminished Enigma band came on, to a roar of approval from the audience.

Back on the floor with Henry and Charlotte, Aaron watched as his underhand method was vindicated: both James and Reigneth were slowly beginning to relax and enjoy themselves, with James singing and Reigneth doing backing vocals with Izzy. Johnny, his gaze fixed on the young woman he loved, stood strumming in the background and looked positively ecstatic.

Reigneth loved music; it was in her soul. She was soon dancing to the familiar songs as if she had forgotten the audience was there. James was clearly taking delight in her obvious pleasure, his large frame swaying in time to the beat. Part of Reigneth's charm was that she was singularly unaware of just how attractive she was; she was equally ignorant of her sexual appeal. It extended not only to Reigneth: James too was physically compelling. The crowd at the front of the stage was packed solid with young men and women, all mesmerised by this young couple, both of whom were so alike with their dark, Romany looks, their voices soaring together in magical harmony.

The second song was just as wonderful. James held out his hand to take Reigneth's, but instead of taking it she held out her palm and twined her fingers within his. To Aaron, watching from the audience, this summed up their relationship: their destinies intertwined; inseparable forever.

Although very late, the Enigma's lead singer and vocalists eventually arrived and much to the chagrin of the audience, James, Reigneth and Izzy relinquished their spots. Aaron smiled with satisfaction – mission accomplished.

Making his way to where Jessie and Matt were sitting, Aaron felt decidedly smug. He looked up to see Jessie eyeing him suspiciously.

"Your doing, I take it?"

"I don't know what you mean," he said, winking at Matt.

Jessie noted the wink and smiled lovingly at Aaron. She was relieved that he was living with them. She had never been able to understand how Eli seemed not to appreciate his son, always comparing him unfavourably to James. There could not be two boys more different: they were chalk and cheese and both were special. Jessie loved them equally, James so strong and loyal and Aaron quick-witted and intelligent. Aaron, she knew, had a gift of his own no less startling in some ways than Reigneth's. He had a brilliant memory, whether it was for something he was told or something he had read, he forgot nothing. Exams he found effortless, despite having missed schooling during the summer months when Eli decided he'd had enough of being cooped up on the site and took his family off on the road.

She chuckled to herself turning to Matt as Aaron moved away to stand with Charlotte and Henry. "He really is a cheeky little monkey. Never misses an opportunity, that one. I suppose you knew what he was planning?"

Matt grinned at her and tapped the side of his nose.

Chapter 35

Celebrations

The rollercoaster of preparations for Reigneth's wedding was well underway. She gritted her teeth, smiled sweetly and tried to look enthusiastic. It was and never would be about what *she* wanted. Were that the case it would be the smallest wedding in history. As it was, the family, all of them, were in full flood. So far they had got up to no fewer than six bridesmaids and the dresses they preferred looked like something out of Disneyland. Reigneth was beginning to despair.

"Alright, alright, we'll do this your way, Ma, but I definitely get to veto the dresses and bouquets," she at last piped up. "All this lace and bright colours for the bridesmaids is not what I want, and what's more I intend getting my dress in Exeter."

Liz and Jessie looked at her with horrified expressions as if she had uttered obscenities. Most Romany girls they knew purchased their gowns from a specialist bridal shop in Liverpool, no expense spared, but here was Reigneth favouring a local dressmaker. They were both appalled. "Oh, this is going to be such a shabby do," Liz muttered, exchanging dismayed glances with Jessie.

"Say what you like," Reigneth retorted, "I do *not* want to look like a meringue and I don't want any lace. I mean it, Ma, and I don't want huge bouquets either, and only white flowers," she huffed.

"This just gets worse! Reigneth your family will expect a big occasion, you are very special to them," Jessie coaxed.

"Ma, all my life I've tried to hide what I am, it has made me a bit shy about having a fuss made. I really do want to marry Johnny in church, but please don't make me dress how everyone else wants. I concede on everything else. Please, just let me choose the dresses for me and the bridesmaids myself," Reigneth pleaded, relieved when after a few more minutes of wrangling they at last agreed a compromise.

Reigneth had more worries than just the ceremony on her mind: the money she had available to her was a pittance. She dared not ask her mother for more: the wedding was already costing a fortune, but her scant wardrobe badly needed replenishing. Something Izzy had said had hit home: her underwear was sadly lacking and whether she liked to think about it or not, it was something Johnny would witness for himself all too soon. The thought made her squirm with embarrassment.

Even more worrying for Reigneth were Johnny's plans for their honeymoon destination. He was trying to keep it a secret from her. Was he mad? That it was somewhere sunny with a beach and palm trees she could definitely see, but as she had never travelled abroad she was unable to recognise anything, so had no idea where it might be. Wherever it was, the thought of going so far away terrified her. Johnny had insisted that she apply for a passport, had done all the paperwork for her and paid for it himself – thankfully. However, the more Reigneth thought about it the more agitated she became. She did not want to be away from her family. What if she where to dream while abroad without their support? And without Jukel! It did not bear thinking about. Her experiences with Jed Cummings had left her feeling very vulnerable. She had been shocked by how much the dreams had affected her physically and dreaded something similar happening again.

The whole business of the honeymoon was becoming ever more of a trial for Reigneth and as she grew increasingly agitated, even the wedding plans took a back seat. She knew she needed to speak to Johnny about how she felt. She had to stop his thoughts running to grandiose plans for somewhere warm and relaxing. Reigneth knew she would never be able to relax in this situation. Wherever Johnny chose to take her, she needed James and Jukel to be there too, which ruled out going abroad. Of course, if James went with them then so would Charlotte and, leading on from there, Reigneth could not see Aaron – or Izzy for that matter – being left out of anything. The thought brought a wry smile to her lips: honeymoons were meant to be for the happy couple, not six people plus a dog! It was never going to happen. The best plan was to give up on having a honeymoon altogether – why did they need one anyway?

With these thoughts going round and round and keeping her awake at night, Reigneth began to feel guiltier with each day that passed. Nothing for Johnny was as it should be: he was already giving up so much for her. Screwing herself up to talk to him about it, her aim was to get him by himself – preferably when he was not armed with a stack of holiday brochures for exotic places with sunny climates!

Their next ride together provided a perfect opportunity and by a stroke of good fortune, as they were walking the horses along the track leading up to the moor, Johnny brought the matter up himself.

"I get the feeling you've been reluctant to talk about it, Reigneth, but now I've got you to myself, what are your thoughts on the honeymoon? Your passport has come through so we could go just about anywhere you wish."

Aware that Johnny was watching her closely, Reigneth tried and failed to keep her face blank. Anticipating that he might be angry with her – after all Johnny deserved a holiday too – her mouth went suddenly dry and she bit her lip, not sure what to say. She could not bear the thought of disappointing him, nor did she want to cast a shadow over this lovely sunny day. Not for the first time she felt their relationship was placing too many restrictions on him and it worried her.

She gave him a nervous smile, "I was going to talk to you about it, so I'm glad you brought it up. The thing is, Johnny, I don't really want to go that far away. I'm just a little anxious about being among strangers and far from home, you know? I'm sorry if… "

"No need to be sorry, Darling," he cut across her. "I understand, really I do." He nudged Rannoch up beside Reigneth's borrowed mount – the sweet-natured but rather too placid mare that seemed reluctant to move any faster than a walk. "Come on, let's head over to those rocks then have a breather and talk some more," Johnny pointed to the rocky outcrop on the skyline and urged Rannoch into a canter, Jukel, tongue lolling, running ahead of him. Still biting her lip, Reigneth followed.

Seeing Reigneth was falling behind, Johnny brought Rannoch to a stop and waited for her. Not long now and she would have her own stallion, he grinned to himself. Having succeeded in negotiating a satisfactory price for Torin, Matt would not fetch the colt back until a few days before Reigneth's birthday, just weeks away now. Until then it was a closely guarded secret, but Johnny could not wait to see Reigneth's face. It would be some time before the colt was ready to be ridden, of course, but at least she would have that to look forward to and with Matt's help would be able to break him herself.

As she caught him up, Johnny fell in beside her and seeing her tense, anxious expression he smiled to reassure her that he was not annoyed with her. Far from it – if anything he felt a sense of relief. He was not at all surprised she did not want to go far from home and had been wondering for some time if he should shelve his plans to whisk her off to some exotic location. He had been thinking of Goa, but it had often crossed his mind how frail and ill she had been following the dreams about Jed. He mulled this over while they ambled along. Spending those nights with Reigneth while she had been dreaming had been a frightening and enlightening experience for him. Of course he knew there would be a next time: this was to be the pattern of their life together. He did not shirk his responsibilities. Next time he knew not to wake her, not to touch her; not to tax her physically. Such mental strain had a huge effect on her physical well being. One of the main reasons he had wanted her on stage with him was so that she was not in a crowd of people experiencing sensations from all of them. All he ever wanted was to protect her and keep her from harm, and judging by the strained look on her face when he had asked about the honeymoon, he was clearly not succeeding. Causing her grief was the last thing he wanted and so, hastily, he adjusted the plans in his head.

As they reached the rocks, Johnny dismounted and grinned up at Reigneth. "You don't need to say anything more about the honeymoon, my darling. I hear what you are not saying. Leave it with me, just don't worry about it. Let's just look at our criteria: you need James and Juk to be with us don't you."

Wordlessly, with an apologetic shrug, Reigneth nodded.

"Could you leave Juk for just a couple of nights do you think, if you weren't too far away?"

"How far is too far?" Reigneth looked anxious.

"Perhaps a few miles – say ten at the most."

"Yes, that would be OK." Reigneth turned her mouth down, "I'm so sorry, Johnny, really I am, it's just that... "

"Stop looking so guilty," Johnny laughed. "There really is no need, I promise. Anyone else besides James?" he asked, the smile still flickering on his lips.

"I don't have the right to expect this of you," Reigneth said. "I feel as if I am condemning you to a restricted half-life. How selfish is that?"

A pained expression crossed her face and somehow Johnny knew where her train of thought was leading her. "Don't even think it, Reigneth," he said, exasperated.

"You don't know what I was thinking."

"Yes I do; you were thinking I would be better off without you. That's utter rubbish. I didn't exist before I met you. I need you just as you need me. We are one; neither of us is complete without the other. Leave it to me, the honeymoon will be wonderful, just don't *worry*. All you have to do is trust me, OK?"

He got back onto Rannoch and they continued on their ride. Reigneth seemed to have relaxed and was chattering about James and Charlotte. Johnny grinned to himself and let her talk, ideas about the honeymoon already springing into his head.

Within two days he had things pulled together and with the others sworn to secrecy, Gidleigh Park Hotel, only five miles from Chagford, was booked for three nights. Of course, he knew where Reigneth really wished to go: she needed to go home, the home she had known as a child; she needed all her family to meet him. They would go to Lincolnshire. He smiled, imagining the expression on her face when she found out. It would be a wonderful surprise – if he could only keep it from her.

He set about putting his plans into place: their party was to include Izzy, Aaron, James, Charlotte, and of course Jukel. Johnny chuckled to himself, *Perhaps it would be best to hire a minibus. Some honeymoon!'* Only Henry would be missing as he had plans to take off travelling with one of his school friends after the wedding.

Preparations complete, a feeling of relief spread through Johnny. It was the right decision. Holidays further afield would have to wait until Reigneth was better able to cope with her premonitions. Somehow he knew that time would come.

Filled with an enormous sense of gratitude that Johnny was being so understanding, Reigneth stopped worrying about the honeymoon, and clothes came once more to the fore. She need not have worried, for once again, Izzy came to her rescue. They were lingering over a cup of tea at Higher Wedicombe when, with a conspiratorial wink at Reigneth, she announced, "I think you need to take us shopping this weekend, Johnny. There are things Reigneth needs before the wedding."

"She cannot possibly need anything else," he responded absently, not looking up from his newspaper. "We seem to have been shopping constantly."

Izzy was not to be put off. "She needs a going away outfit and some underwear."

At the mention of underwear, Johnny lowered the newspaper, a broad smile on his face.

"Yes, I thought that would make you perk up, pervert!" Izzy scolded.

Frowning at her, Reigneth blushed and looked down at her feet.

"I cannot tell you how excited that makes me, Iz," Johnny teased.

"Way too much information thanks," Izzy curled her lip in mock disgust.

Reigneth pushed back her chair, her face red. She knew Johnny was only teasing, but it made her feel uncomfortable. She moved away from the table and busied herself loading the new dishwasher, which Matt had insisted on providing for Jessie now the house was so often full of teenagers.

At Izzy's insistence, Johnny agreed to tag along and bankroll the shopping trip. Out of some warped sense of humour, he suggested they drag James and Aaron along too. Of course, if James went then so would Charlotte. Izzy took control of organising everyone and soon they were assembled and ready for their trip to Exeter.

Once in the city, Charlotte and Izzy excitedly discussed which shops they wished to go to for Reigneth's trousseau. Smiling in disbelief, Johnny, having ensured he had plenty of cash on him for the occasion, peeled off a thick wad of notes and handed it to Reigneth. "Look, we'll only hinder you. Why don't you girls go off and do your own thing and we'll meet you back here in, say," he checked his watch, "an hour?"

"An *hour*," Izzy screeched, "make that three!"

Shaking her head, Reigneth pushed the wad of notes back at

Johnny, visibly upset by his generosity. "I can't take all that," she whispered.

"In less than two weeks, my darling, you will be Reigneth Wilmott," Johnny said with mock severity, "and what is mine will be yours." He smiled, leaned in to whisper in her ear, "Choose something pretty. I'll be allowed to see it by then."

Reigneth blushed, grasped the cash and stuffed it into her pocket, too embarrassed to utter a word.

"We'll see you later then. Have fun. Ring us when you're ready." Johnny grinned at James and Aaron, "Come on you two, there's a good music shop in Fore Street."

Reigneth looked wistfully after him, but Charlotte and Izzy grabbed an arm each and joyously whisked her away for some serious retail therapy.

For a while the boys ambled along in companionable silence, but very soon James's long stride was outstripping the other two and Johnny held Aaron back. He had been looking for an opportunity to speak to him ever since the gig in the Engine Shed.

"Come on then, let's have it; how much?"

"What do you mean how much?" Aaron tried to bluff his way out of it.

"Now come on, Aaron, how stupid do you think I am? How much did you have to pay Enigma's vocalists to be late?"

"OK, so you're not stupid. Two hundred quid and – worth every penny I'd say," Aaron said defensively. "I borrowed it from Matt," he added sheepishly.

Johnny peeled the cash from the diminished wad of notes in his pocket and handed it to Aaron with a smile. "*Well* worth it, I'd say. You're a genius. Give this to Matt, and here's another fifty for thinking of it!"

A wide grin passed over Aaron's face. "Glad you're on the same wavelength. Thanks, Johnny, you're an OK guy."

Once inside Larson's music shop, James made his way to investigate the drum kits, and Johnny the guitars. They could not resist trying the equipment out and very soon a crowd of teenagers had filled the shop.

The girls had finally finished shopping and were weighed down with bags. Hot and considerably bothered, Reigneth was relieved when it was all over. She had been mortified by Izzy and Charlotte walking in and out of the changing room whilst she was in the middle of trying underwear on. "You know, you are both so bossy," she had protested.

"Stop being a prude, it's easier for us to keep passing you things, it saves time. Just relax, we've seen it all before and we know far better than you what suits you," said Izzy.

"Perk up, Reigneth, I've never known a girl who hated shopping," Charlotte teased. "It's going to be so cool having you as a sister," she hugged Reigneth then hesitated and turned crestfallen to Izzy. "Hey, sorry Izzy, I mean… it's cool having a friend like you too… " her voice trailed away.

Izzy laughed, "It's OK, Charlotte. My feelings aren't hurt so long as I get a hug too! I'm not your normal run-of-the-mill girl, you know. I'd much rather be with the lads most times, but I have to say I've enjoyed today," she smiled warmly at both the girls.

Shopping completed, a telephone call ascertained the boys' whereabouts. Packages in hand, they approached Larson's to find a crowd of youngsters standing around the shop doorway, pushing to get in and craning their heads to see who was responsible for the amazing sounds coming from within.

"Honestly! They're doing an impromptu gig. You can't take them anywhere," Charlotte grumbled, but with a big smile on her face. Pushing through the jostling crowd, Izzy looked determined to join in the spontaneous performance, if only she could get through.

Feeling suddenly dizzy, Reigneth turned away intending to head back to the car, but James had spotted her over the heads of the crowd. Bringing the performance to a halt, much to the disappointment of the assembled audience, he pushed his way out of the shop and with a frown of concern, reached out for her.

"You OK, Honey?"

"I'm fine, just weary is all – and way too many people. I need to get away somewhere quieter."

"Sure?" He eyed her intently.

"Sure, stop worrying." She smiled up at him, "Hey – that sounded good, James."

"Yeah, it's a great drum kit, much better than anything I've played before." He turned his mouth down, "Way out of my pocket, though. Let's go find something to eat. We can go through the Close, it'll be quiet enough there and there's a good cafe in the Cathedral." He beckoned to Aaron then turned to Charlotte and seizing her packages in one enormous hand, put his arm around her waist.

Reigneth stood to one side waiting for Johnny as the crowd of teenagers dispersed. Looking through the shop window, she saw he was speaking earnestly to the proprietor, Jeff Larson. It seemed that Johnny was flashing the cash again – it was James's birthday in three weeks and it looked like he was going to get a drum kit. Smiling to herself, Reigneth was touched by Johnny's generosity.

He came out of the shop, a satisfied grin on his face. "Hello darling, did you get everything you wanted?" Not waiting for her answer, he picked up the packages and grabbing her hand set off after the others.

Chapter 36

Young Joe

The last fitting for Reigneth's, Jessie's and Izzy's dresses was booked for two weeks before the wedding. The family, including the four remaining bridesmaids, would arrive during the week and Reigneth and James were to take them for their last fitting. Ryalla and BB were usually quite well behaved, but the same could not be said for the twins Ellen and Eleanor. They were a lively pair to say the least.

Jessie felt a knot of excitement in her stomach when she thought of seeing her family. They would come in two and three trailers at a time, arriving without fuss as quietly as snow falls in the night. They would leave the same way, the ash left by their fires the only telltale signs that they had ever been. Matt had been as good as his word and got piped water and electricity to the top field, the best drained and most accessible bit of land Higher Wedicombe had to offer.

Everything seemed to be running smoothly and now all she had to think about was getting this dress to zip up. Another tug and yes... oh, no! That had done it. The zip had broken. Jessie came out of the fitting room a puzzled frown on her face. She had never put on an inch in her life except when she had been having Reigneth.

And that is when it hit her.

She cast her mind back to her last period and could not remember when it was. The possibility of becoming a mother all over again had simply never occurred to her. She and Joe had long hoped for a brother or sister for Reigneth. It would have been a joy for both of them, but it had never happened and eventually, so filled with love for their *bitti chai* that she had begun to doubt she had enough love left for another child, Jessie had decided it was probably just as well and stopped thinking about it. And yet here she was, only newly married and... it was unbelievable!

Going back into the dressing room she sat on the small stool in the corner and that is where Reigneth and Izzy found her, zip broken, mouth agape.

"Hi, Mam, you OK?" Reigneth cheerily asked her.

"As a matter of fact I think I need a bigger dress," Jessie said absently, her mind racing.

Reigneth began to laugh and hugged her mother.

"Oh, Reigneth, why didn't you tell me?" Jessie asked, perplexed.

"I didn't want to worry you with so much else going on. There is only so much you can cope with, Ma," Reigneth kissed the top of her mother's head.

"Then perhaps you'd like to tell me when the baby is due and whether it's a boy or a girl," Jessie said more tartly than she had intended, eyeing her amazing daughter. Pregnant! Whatever would Matt say? She needed time to think about this.

Reigneth, understanding, gave her mother a gentle smile. "Do you really want to know, Ma? No surprises? Perhaps you'd better think on it."

"Yeah!" Izzy screamed excited at the news. "Does Johnny know? He'll be ecstatic."

With a small shake of her head Reigneth frowned at Izzy signalling her to keep quiet. Jessie would be furious if she thought her daughter had told Johnny and not her. Luckily, her mother was too bound up in her own thoughts to fully take in what Izzy had said.

"Shall we take you home, Ma, perhaps you had better talk to Matt?" Reigneth suggested. "See if he wants to know what you are expecting before I tell you, eh?"

"Oh, Reigneth," Izzy said, "is it true? And can you really tell if it's a boy or a girl?"

"Hush, Izzy, of course she can," Jessie said, easing herself up from the stool and still looking utterly bemused. "Please, nobody say anything to anyone until I've had an opportunity to talk to Matt."

"Of course we won't, Ma – will we, *Izzy*," she looked ferociously at her friend.

"My lips are sealed," said Izzy with a grin.

After explaining the problem to the dressmaker and requesting a quick fix to the dress in time for the wedding, the girls set off to the car park where Johnny was waiting in the Discovery.

The journey home was strained, with Jessie gazing unfocused out of the window and Izzy being uncharacteristically quiet.

"What's up?" Johnny whispered to Reigneth.

"Tell you later," she whispered back.

Returning to High Wedicombe, Johnny went straight off to help Matt, who was with James and Aaron, busy repairing the top field fence. Jessie wandered through to the sitting room and plopped herself down on the sofa next to the wood burner. Reigneth, having made a fuss of an ecstatic Jukel, joined her there.

"I'll put the kettle on then shall I?" Izzy enquired from the doorway. No one replied. Without waiting for an answer she made herself scarce.

Tears filled Jessie's eyes, "I can't do this, Reigneth. I could never love another child as I do you."

"You don't have to love it the same," Reigneth was careful to say 'it' rather than 'him'. "You'll love it differently: we'll all love it, but love it you will, Ma." Reigneth sighed, exasperated, "Ma, I can't keep calling the baby 'it'," she smiled gently, coaxing her mother.

Jessie jerked her head up quickly. "Boy or girl?" was all she said.

"It's a little boy, Ma, he'll be born in March and he'll be perfect: a bit of Johnny and a bit of me. Don't worry, everything will be all right, better than all right – and Matt will be like a dog with two tails," she smiled.

By the time Matt came indoors an hour later, Jessie had rallied and was sitting with Reigneth and Izzy sipping a mug of hot, sweet tea.

In a very short time Matt had become used to his creature comforts and always looked forward to his dinner, but this evening there were no tantalising cooking smells to indicate that food was anywhere on the horizon. Both Jessie and Reigneth seemed very subdued when he walked into the sitting room, unlike Izzy who looked – to coin one of James's phrases – 'fit to bust a gut'. All in all things looked a bit dodgy as far as Matt could see.

Reading the atmosphere immediately, but unable to read their expressions, he sat in his favourite chair by the wood burner and braced himself for whatever was to come.

"Well, let's have it then; what's up?" A gentle smile hovered on his lips as he looked at Jessie: she was either very pleased or very anxious about something – he could not decide which.

Jessie cleared her throat, swallowed, opened her mouth to say something then closed it again. After a moment, she tried once more, "I don't know how to tell you this, Matt… " her voice trailed away.

"What? Tell me what, Jess? Whatever's wrong?"

Reigneth stood up her face breaking into a broad smile of excitement. "Oh, for goodness sake, Ma spit it out! You're worrying the poor man."

Mystified, Matt looked from one to the other of them then got up from his chair and squashed himself down next to Jessie on the small sofa, at which point Izzy jumped up and said, "My cue to make more tea." She winked at Reigneth, "I'll leave you to it. I'll peel some spuds for dinner while I'm about it, shall I?"

"Thank you, Izzy, that would be helpful," Jessie nodded. Moments later, Izzy could be heard clattering about in the kitchen talking to the boys.

"Come on, love, what is it that Reigneth wants you to spit out?" Matt asked exasperated.

Jessie shifted her position to be closer to him and in almost a whisper, uttered, "We're going to have a baby, Matt. I'm pregnant." Her lips quivered as she spoke and her eyes were wet and glistening.

Matt's stared in disbelief, his jaw dropped, he was incredulous. He could find no words. Tipping his face down into his weather beaten hands, he remained like this for such a long time as to have them all worried. Slowly, bringing up his head, unable to focus, embarrassed by the tears that clouded his vision, he wiped his eyes.

Jessie looked at him, her face similarly awash with tears, "I'm sorry, Matt… " she faltered. "I'd hoped you would… I mean, I didn't wish to upset you."

"*Upset* me?" He took her hand in his own and kissed it, whispering, "Are you *sure*?"

Jessie nodded, but Reigneth, with an expression that could only be described as smug, arched her eyebrows and peered down at him intently, "Will the sun rise in the morning, Matthew?"

He smiled through his tears: he loved Reigneth; he loved how she was beginning to be able to treat her gift with humour. He knew this was because of Johnny: the boy eased her burden and she really was becoming quite a card.

"Oh Jess, I'm not upset," he reassured. "I cannot begin to find the words to tell you how happy this news makes me." Tenderly he placed his hand on her stomach with an expression of such wonderment that both Jessie and Reigneth laughed out loud.

"Not that it matters, but is it a boy or a girl?" he asked. Unaware that Izzy knew of Reigneth's gift, he spoke in barely more than a whisper lest she overheard, though judging by the sounds of laughter coming from the kitchen that was unlikely.

Jessie smiled, "Reigneth says a little boy, about mid-March and he'll be beautiful, Matt; perfect."

Again, Matt was silent for a long time as he tried to absorb this wonderful news. It was something he had hardly dared to hope for.

"Are you *really* pleased, Matt?" Jessie asked hesitantly. "You wouldn't just say that for my sake would you?"

"'Pleased' doesn't even begin to cover it, Jess; I'm overjoyed, but what about you?"

"Do you need to ask?"

He looked into her eyes, smiled and shook his head. Wordless, he went off into a world of his own, thinking of how to say something important, but so choked with emotion he was having problems being coherent.

Eventually he spoke. "I think we should call him 'Joe', what do you think Jessie?" His arms were around her and they were both silently weeping. On the edge of his awareness he knew that Reigneth had tiptoed away.

Reigneth, who could see young Joe's future as clearly as she saw her own, went through to the kitchen to give Matt and Jessie some time alone. Sitting around the table, Johnny, James, Aaron and Izzy looked up at her expectantly.

"You've told them," Johnny grinned.

Reigneth nodded and Izzy clapped her hands.

"So how's about telling us?" James and Aaron chorused.

"Reigneth and I are going to have a new baby brother," Johnny announced proudly.

There was a momentary stunned silence then James guffawed. "That's great news. I can't wait to see Auntie Liz's reaction! So then, what's for dinner? I suppose those two will be in cloud cuckoo land and want waiting on."

"Actually, I ought to be getting home," Johnny pushed his chair back.

"Oh no, Johnny, please don't go," Reigneth pleaded.

"Yes," said Aaron, "stay for dinner."

"Who's cooking?" asked Johnny.

"I am," James replied, "and it's not something you'll want to miss."

Aaron groaned, his expression of mock dismay making everyone laugh.

James smiled at Reigneth and seizing the frying pan waved it at Aaron.

Reigneth guffawed "Well this is something I have to see: a Romany man cooking!"

"I can cook I'll have you know, but as you obviously doubt my capabilities I'll hand the job over to you." He plonked the frying pan into Reigneth's hands and added, "And I'll have two sugars in my tea, thank you. Is that chauvinist enough for you?" He smiled and gave her a big wink, which made them all laugh the louder.

Clutching the frying pan, Reigneth looked around at them all and her heart filling with love. *You great big, adorable, lovable fool,'* she thought, smiling at her favourite cousin before transferring her gaze to her beloved Johnny, who sat at her side.

Chapter 37

Reality

Higher Wedicombe had never had so many pretty girls within its walls. Reigneth and her bridesmaids practically filled the kitchen, drinking a glass of wine and chatting excitedly about the big day tomorrow. Even Jukel had decided enough was enough and retired to his beanbag beside the Aga, one eye open, his gaze fixed firmly on his mistress.

"You really should all try to get an early night," Jessie tried to make herself heard. The noise was unbelievable, most of it coming from Izzy who was shrieking with laughter.

Reigneth smiled, humouring her mother as Jessie went to lock the back door before going to bed. "Don't lock it yet, Mam, James is on his way."

Suddenly aware that Charlotte had heard her, Reigneth gave a weak smile, fished around in her pocket for her mobile and waggled it at Charlotte, who laughed.

"Just for a minute there I thought you were psychic," she giggled.

Reigneth, who had not used her mobile since texting Johnny earlier, gave a hollow laugh.

Soon afterwards James made an entrance, a big embarrassed grin on his face as he looked around at the bridesmaids, until his gaze settled on Charlotte. "I just wanted to have a chat with Reigneth," he muttered almost inaudibly.

Reigneth, already out of her chair, guided him into the lounge leaving the babbling girls behind them. Charlotte watched them go, a huge question in her eyes. He smiled back at her and mouthed, 'Back in a minute,' then the door closed and he and Reigneth were alone.

"You were expecting me," James accused, looking slightly overwhelmed by the fact that he had turned up uninvited.

"What do you think?" Reigneth smiled, "And I know what you want to talk to me about." She grinned, rolled her eyes and added, "Again."

"I had to come," he said apologetically. "I know we've talked about it before, but I *have* to know that you have absolutely no doubts. That you know this is the right thing."

Reigneth watched him struggling for the right words as he perched on the arm of the sofa, his gaze directed at the floor. "Tomorrow it will be too late… " he shrugged awkwardly.

Sitting next to him on the sofa, she took his large hands in hers and waited until he looked at her. "Oh, James, how can I convince you? I cannot live without him. I don't know how to explain it other than to say that he completes me. It's not just that I want to be with him, I *have* to be with him. He's as essential to me as the air I breathe. He is my life."

She looked up at her big cousin, who was only trying to protect her, and gazed into his eyes, her expression intense as she attempted to set his mind at rest. "I've always know it was him, since I was small," she smiled. "Remember years ago when I first told you about my 'girlie boy' and how cross you were? I've waited all my life for him to come along. You and I have never lied to each other, James. You can stop worrying about me: I have absolutely no doubts at all."

Gazing down at his hands, hers still clasped around them, James nodded. "You know that I love you – that I have always loved you. It's not the same as what I feel for Charlotte. I can't really put into words how I feel, Reigneth, but it's like you and I are bound together by some invisible force that I know nothing can destroy. Quite simply, I know – have always known – that we are meant to be together. How do I explain that to Charlotte? Who in their right mind would take me on knowing that I have this inexplicable longing to be constantly with my female cousin?" He laughed, but his eyes looked pained.

"Then tell her about me. It will strengthen your relationship, not break it; trust me."

"I cannot tell her, I will not, I vowed never to tell a soul," he frowned, his expression tortured.

They were silent for a while. Beside them a log shifted in the wood burner sending up a flash of sparks. The noisy chattering from the kitchen had sunk to a background murmur.

"I hope she will understand why I came to see you and not her. I don't want to hurt her feelings – I really do care for her, Reigneth."

"Then it's high time you told her that you love her, James."

"I know and I will, but she needs to understand that the future must include you too, how do I explain that?"

"Like I said, tell her about me! If you don't, I will," Reigneth said, more sharply than she intended, but she was somewhat exasperated. She had given him leave to tell Charlotte, knowing it would strengthen the bond between them, but he would never break his vow, not even with the woman he was to marry, so it would be up to her. She sighed, hoping he could grasp what she was about say.

"Once Johnny and I are married, James, Granny Mary's prophecy comes to pass: the four of us – you, Aaron, Johnny and me – united as we're meant to be. This is what is *meant* to happen. It is why you feel as you do."

He frowned, "So then, what is that supposed to achieve other than that Gran was right all along? Why is this so important?"

"James, we are meant to do something special with our lives, already there's a difference in me. I'm stronger, much stronger! You have no idea. Each of us makes the others stronger – together we are invincible. I think we are meant to use our gifts to help others."

His frown deepened, "How do we do that when we can never reveal what you can do, Reigneth?"

"I don't know. In the same way I know all three of you will change, but not how. It's infuriating, but we must be patient. It will be revealed to us in time."

At last the tension left James's face and he laughed, "Well, if I'm going to change I hope I develop more brain cells."

"Now that *would* be an improvement!" Reigneth teased, giggling as James rolled his eyes. "Come on," she said, "let's get back to the others, and don't worry, I'll speak to Charlotte."

He held out his hand and pulled Reigneth to her feet, giving her a quick hug. "Thank you, Honey," he murmured.

Reassured, James led the way back to the kitchen. He knew his cousin had loved her girlie boy even before she had met him, a fact that never ceased to amaze him, but he was beginning to appreciate the depth of that love and to realise that it was entirely mutual. Johnny was an odd little fella that was for sure: he had a way of 'spacing out' which was disconcerting – James always assumed it was when he was mulling over bits of music and composing in his mind. Although they ribbed each other unmercifully, not only had he become very fond of Johnny, he had grown to respect him too. Their relationship had developed into one of close rapport and constant teasing that always made James laugh.

He felt a wave of relief as he absorbed the implications of what Reigneth had said, yet still he found himself seeking reassurance. "We'll always be together though – right?" he asked, turning back, his hand on the kitchen door.

She beamed at him, "Always, James, always – until we are very old and decrepit."

He laughed, "Not sure I like the sound of that."

Pushing open the door, James's expression softened when he saw Charlotte. Yes, he thought, he could work through this if she would be patient with him. Noting that right now she looked a bit miffed, he walked over to her and smiled into her anxious eyes. "It's OK, Honey, I just needed to sort out some family stuff with Reigneth." He took her hand in his and brought it to his lips. "Really, it was only an excuse so I could get to see you," he murmured, surprised to find that it was not quite a lie – he always was pleased to see her.

Relieved to see the anxiety fading from her eyes to be replaced by her usual happy sparkle, James stayed to share a glass of wine with the girls, instructing them before he left not to get too drunk and be late to bed.

Chapter 38

The Big Day

Matt smiled fondly at his wife as he watched her bustling around the kitchen: Higher Wedicombe had not had a bride within its walls for more years than anyone could remember and then, within the space of a few months, along came two. Never in his wildest dreams could he have imagined such a thing. Jessie had everything organised with military precision. She, Liz and James's mother, Constance Boswell, had spent the day before decorating the marquee and then the church. Jessie had sighed with satisfaction at the effect they had achieved.

Their parish church, St. Michael's the Archangel, was festooned with flowers, beginning at the arch of the doorway in a huge bower of blossoms that cascaded each side of the door and over it. The pews had flowers on the end of each one and enormous arrangements adorned each side of the altar and the font. The combined scent of them all was glorious.

"Well, I may have been unable to have my say on the dresses, but the flowers – well that's another matter!" she had remarked to Matt when she arrived home tired but happy. She had been disappointed at first when Reigneth had insisted on all the flowers being white, but now had to concede that it looked magnificent.

This morning she was insisting they all had a good breakfast and the table was piled with covered dishes of sausages, scrambled eggs and crispy bacon.

"An army marches on its stomach," said Matt, grinning at Jessie's puzzled expression as she paused from cutting slices of toast and waved the bread knife at him.

"That's hardly an apt comparison, Matt."

313

"Oh, I don't know. I think they should be afraid... very afraid," he laughed, coaxing a smile out of her.

"Oh very funny... " she said, with more than a hint of sarcasm, but she could not keep a straight face. "May I remind you that Johnny is a willing participant, not a sacrifice?"

"Only joking, Jess. You've not laid a place for yourself I see?"

She grimaced at him, "No, couldn't stomach it. Little Joe is making me feel a bit queasy again."

All concern, Matt removed the knife from her hand, "At least have a cuppa, love, I'll make the toast. I think I can hear movement upstairs, the infantry are on their way," he grinned.

The girls emerged and grazed their breakfast rather than sitting down to tuck in. Izzy, the last to show her face, looked decidedly peaky. They had all been very late to bed and Izzy, who had drunk more wine than the others, was clearly feeling the worse for wear.

"Fancy you girls drinking too much the night before the wedding!" Jessie tutted, "Can't say I didn't warn you."

"Not me, I'm perky," Reigneth bit into a sausage and smiled at the same time.

"Just black coffee and paracetamol for me, please," Izzy sat at the breakfast table and covered her head with her hands.

"I'll go and check the stock, Jess," Matt beat a hasty retreat just as Ryalla and the twins, Ellen and Eleanor, came babbling into the kitchen. All three girls were to be bridesmaids in addition to Izzy, Charlotte, and James's sister, BB. The younger ones had been made to go to bed early and were full of energy. Once plied with food and a sugar rush kicking in, it was not long before they were running around the house screaming and generally getting into mischief.

Izzy groaned, "Jessie, can't you make those kids be quiet, the little demons are doing my head in."

"It's your own fault," Jessie handed her two headache pills and a glass of water. "Where's Reigneth gone?"

"Upstairs to get her hair done."

"Are you going to be alright, Izzy?" Jessie frowned at her in concern. "You've got to have your hair done yet. I don't want you to be poorly and not enjoy the wedding."

"Just keep those little monsters away from me," Izzy moaned. "I'll be OK once the pills kick in."

"Next!" Charlotte shouted from upstairs. "Izzy, get yourself up here." Moments later, looking lovely, her pale blonde hair interwoven with flowers, Charlotte leaned round the door, "Pamela's ready for you now."

Pamela Gray had travelled down with other family members. She always did their hair on any special occasions. Her mother, Sadie, was there too, helping the girls to dress. The atmosphere upstairs was calm and serene, unlike the mayhem from the little monkeys rampaging downstairs. Squeals and thudding footsteps sounded from the sitting room and Jessie rolled her eyes. "Off you go, Izzy, I'll bring you all up a cup of tea," she said.

Dishwasher loaded and tea brewed, Jessie was just about to take a tray upstairs when she heard Reigneth coming through into the kitchen, her voice light and full of excitement. "Best make more coffee for Izzy, Ma, she looks dreadful."

Jessie turned towards her daughter, but for a moment could not utter a word. The front of Reigneth's hair had been scraped back from her face and fastened in soft curls that cascaded down her back, falling onto the rest of her lengthy tresses. Her hair was perhaps Reigneth's most stunning feature. As black as pitch it hung almost to her waist, thick tresses that glistened and shone, the soft curls bouncing and swaying with her every movement.

"Oh Reigneth, you look so lovely. Our Pamela's excelled herself this time."

"Hasn't she just." Reigneth smiled. "Shall I steer the little ones in the direction of the bathroom? If they arrive at the church clean and tidy it'll be a miracle."

"Thanks, love, but Matt will be back in a minute. He can look after them; you've got better things to do."

"Oh Ma, poor Matt, that's mean. It was your idea to have the twins as bridesmaids," Reigneth grinned.

"Must need my head testing," Jessie laughed. Moments later she heard Matt kicking off his boots in the back porch and went through to break the bad news. He was still grumbling good-naturedly as she hurried upstairs.

Aunt Sadie and Jessie made quick work of dressing Charlotte and stood back admiring their handiwork. Izzy, still moaning constantly, was going to be a bit trickier.

"We told you not to drink so much, you goose," chided Charlotte, a wicked smile on her lips. "Drink lots of water, it'll be more help than coffee; you're dehydrated."

Ryalla stood with BB, expectant smiles on their faces as they eyed their dresses, though Ryalla looked a little tense and pale. "You all right, Honey?" Jessie asked kindly.

"Yes thank you, Aunt Jess, it's just that I'm afraid I might trip over and spoil everything."

"Don't worry, you'll be fine," said Jessie, fastening the tiny seed pearl buttons down the back of Ryalla's dress.

With the girls dressed the upstairs seemed suddenly very crowded. "I thought you said you didn't want the dresses to be too full," Jessie shouted through to Reigneth.

"I said I didn't want them to look like meringues," Reigneth shouted back from her bedroom. "Instead they look like water lilies, very pale pink water lilies." As she finished speaking, Reigneth emerged from her bedroom, dressed and ready for the biggest event of her life.

There was a sudden silence as everyone stood, mouths agape, staring. Jessie's eyes filled with tears, "Oh Reigneth, you look so beautiful."

Smiling at her mother, Reigneth surveyed the girls and with a sigh of satisfaction she nodded. "Girls you all look so lovely; where are the twins?"

"Never you mind," said Sadie, "I'll deal with those little monkeys. Just you keep those dresses clean or it will be pond weed instead of water lilies."

Reigneth suddenly got a fit of the giggles as she watched Izzy trying to negotiate her dress through the doorway and out onto the landing.

"Well thank God for that!" she exclaimed when she succeeded. "This thing has got a mind of its own. I'm only used to wearing jeans," she grimaced at Reigneth in mock horror, "this could end very badly!"

"You'll be fine," Reigneth reassured.

Standing on the landing, Ryalla was staring at herself in the full-length mirror.

"You OK, Ryalla?" Izzy asked. "You don't look too happy."

"Feel a bit sick, Iz," Ryalla frowned.

"It's nerves that's all. I feel sick too. Stick with me, we'll be OK."

Comforted, a thin smile appeared on the child's face. "My dress

316

is pretty isn't it? I like the embroidery round the neck and the bow on the back."

"You look lovely, Ryalla," Izzy reassured her. "Come on, let's go down."

Smiling at one another they made their way downstairs.

Stealing a last look at herself in the landing mirror, Reigneth admired her dress. It was exactly as she had imagined, the soft sheen of the white silk glistened as she swayed and twirled. The bodice was tightly fitting, though not revealing, its scoop off the shoulder neckline richly embroidered. The same embroidery echoed around the hem.

Reigneth was brought back to the moment hearing her mother's voice as she bustled about trying to get everyone in order. Matt had gladly relinquished the twins and she could hear Sadie attempting to keep them under control while getting them dressed, and dress herself at the same time. "You need any help Sadie?" she called.

"Never mind me, I'll manage," Sadie replied, huffing and puffing and red in the face with the effort as she came slowly down the stairs, holding back the twins behind her.

"Come on Reigneth, veil next." Jessie adjusted the veil, pinning it in place with a small tiara of white flowers. The gossamer thin fabric, embroidered lightly around the outside edge, hung full length to the floor. Jessie cast a critical eye over her daughter, smiled and said, "Ready?"

"Oh yes, definitely, more than ready," Reigneth hugged her.

"Careful! Mind the veil," Jessie cautioned, readjusting the folds.

Matt, having had a quick wash and shave, had changed and looked splendid if a little uncomfortable in yet another new suit, purchased for the occasion. He marshalled the bridesmaids into an orderly line and proceeded to hand out the bouquets. These were small and consisted of white flowers with small-leaved variegated foliage trailing down. They looked very natural, almost as if they had grown in that state. For the twins someone had come up with the wonderful idea of pomanders: lethal weapons in Ellen's and Eleanor's hands!

Sadie, having negotiated the stairs, now stood at the end of the line, a twin in each hand, her hat askew and hair a little untidy.

'Our Pamela', who had no intention whatsoever of touching the twins any more than she had to, stood beside her. She eyed the little girls with distaste. Pamela always favoured leopard skin, her dress looked as though it had been painted on and her black patent, six-inch stiletto heels finished off her outfit. Jessie, whose dusky pink dress matched the colour of the bridesmaids' outfits, eyed her a little dubiously then turned her attention to Sadie as she struggled with the twins.

"Oh these kids are a handful. I don't know how Sylvia manages them," Sadie said, trying to hang on to the squirming children, her hat now threatening to slip down over one ear.

Matt laughed at the sight of her, but the reluctant offer of help he felt duty bound to utter was forestalled by the sound of vehicles pulling up in the yard. Instead he smiled, announcing, "That'll be James. Time we were leaving."

The wedding cars had been parked as close to the front door as could be managed and James walked into the tiny sitting room, which now seemed full of pink silk and squawking children. Ryalla looked pale; Izzy looked hung over and Charlotte looked absolutely lovely.

"You lot ready then?" A huge smile creased his face at the sight of Sadie and the twins. Catching sight of Matt, who was just about to give them their pomanders, a guffaw erupted from James that he could not contain. "Whose idea was that? You gotta be joking!"

The little girls prodded and poked one another, "Geroff will you," screeched Ellen just as her twin brought up her fist.

"Enough!" James bellowed. The twins were both so surprised they stood stock still and gaped up at him. Looking shamefaced as James spoke angrily in Romany telling them they were disgracing their family, they were instantly quiet.

"You just need the knack," James beamed at Matt. He heard the sound of someone making their way gingerly down the staircase. It could only be Reigneth. Preparing himself for the sight of her, knowing she would knock him for six, James looked up and was not disappointed. His eyes filled with tears: she had never looked more beautiful. "Aw Reigneth, you look so lovely, my darling." His voice was gruff with emotion as he held out his arm for her. "I can't believe I agreed to give you away to that girlie boy!"

318

She smiled at him and placing her hand lightly on his arm, whispered, "Thank you James. I love you too."

At the church the ushers, James's father and Aaron, looking very smart in their morning suits, a white rose pinned to their buttonholes, joked happily with one another and the guests, guiding them to their respective pews.

Similarly adorned, Henry and Johnny had taken their seats at the front of the church, but Johnny found it impossible to relax and could not take his gaze away from the church door.

"Calm down Johnny, she'll be here in a minute," even Henry's unruffled temperament, so much like his sister's, did not succeed in calming the groom.

"I just need to see her. I'll be OK as soon as I see her," Johnny insisted, clenching and unclenching his hands.

And then she was there, standing with James in the doorway. With the sunlight cascading into the church casting a hazy light at her back, she looked like an angel. Johnny's heart missed a beat and a slow steady smile spread over his face. She was so beautiful he could hardly breathe.

Henry tugged at his sleeve, "Turn round, we're ready to start."

Johnny could not turn, could not take his eyes from her as she began walking down the aisle.

As Reigneth started her journey towards her soul mate, he flashed her his most disarming, crooked smile and it seemed to her that everyone on the periphery of her vision just faded away, leaving only Johnny in focus. Her heart beating wildly, she kept her gaze on him and him alone. It did not matter to her who was *Gauja* or who was Romany. All she knew was that this was what was meant to be.

This was her destiny.

Coming Soon

The Lost Souls

JANE GRAY

Follow Johnny and Reigneth's love story as they are plunged
deeper and deeper into a supernatural world...

Find out more at www.janegray.webs.com

Lightning Source UK Ltd.
Milton Keynes UK

178695UK00002B/29/P

9 781906 236731